Praise for Deidra Duncan's *Love Sick*

"Compulsively readable, *Love Sick* is equal parts sexy and angsty. Deidra Duncan nailed all my favorite aspects from medical dramas."

—Julie Soto, *USA TODAY* bestselling author

"Amid a realistic portrayal of the highs and lows of medical resident life, enemies-to-lovers tension and nonstop banter fill this resonant and romantic debut. Heartfelt and smart, *Love Sick* is just what the doctor ordered."

—Emily Wibberley and Austin Siegemund-Broka, authors of *The Breakup Tour*

"Bursting with laughter, the joy of found family, and spicy will-they-or-won't-they tension, Duncan's debut about the struggles of OB-GYN residency is the perfect book for *Grey's Anatomy* fans who wish they could start the Meredith-and-McDreamy journey all over again. Readers who love workplace romance, enemies-to-lovers banter, and STEMinist heroines will have a ball."

—Ashley Winstead, author of *The Boyfriend Candidate*

For the OG group therapy crew.

And to everyone who is wondering whether that character is you.
It probably is.

Love Sick

DEIDRA DUNCAN

CANARY STREET PRESS

**CANARY
STREET
PRESS™**

Recycling programs
for this product may
not exist in your area.

ISBN-13: 978-1-335-50752-5

Love Sick

Canary Street Press
22 Adelaide St. West, 41st Floor
Toronto, Ontario M5H 4E3, Canada
CanaryStPress.com

Printed in U.S.A.

Acknowledgments

Y'all. I can't even believe we've made it here. *Love Sick* started out as therapy for me. Rage therapy, yes, but therapy all the same. As I exited residency and made my way into the much kinder world of private practice, I started thinking back on my experiences in training, and I sort of went... What the *actual* fuck?

Did that really happen?

Yes. Yes, it did.

While the specific experiences of Grace & Co. are complete fiction, they are grounded in fact. Reality, unfortunately, was much worse.

Needless to say, the book was my way of working through it all, and then I added a love story because, um, duh. I want to thank you, the readers, for giving it a chance, and I hope you enjoy their story as much as I enjoyed writing it. Without you, this book would never have come to pass, and Julian and Grace would only exist in my head. It's because of you that I get to leave the world of medicine for a bit and enter a place where things always end in a Happily Ever After. I am forever grateful.

A million thanks go to Tess Callero, who picked this story out of the 4.2 billion email queries in her inbox. None of this would have happened if not for you, and I will never be able to express how thankful I am that you are my agent. Also, can we just tacitly agree that your tact filter over all my emails is now a necessary part of my life?

To Cat Clyne, who saw the gem of this manuscript before its edges were polished and turned it into a sparkly non-blood diamond. I'm so happy to have you as my editor, and thankful I found someone who believes in me like you do.

Lila Selle, thank you for creating such a wonderful cover to showcase this book. Grace's smirk could not be more perfect. A big thanks to Dana Francoeur for your thorough copyedits. Perhaps one day I will understand how to properly use em dashes. To the whole gang at Canary Street Press, I cannot express how honored I feel to have you all on my side.

My heartfelt thanks go to Andrea and Kelly with The Future of Agency, who helped expand the reach of this book to far greater lengths than I ever could. And to Hannah, who assisted me with my social media presence and helped me see that such platforms can be used for things other than consummate evil. (I still feel they're mostly evil, though.)

Thanks to Shivani Doraiswami for helping me navigate the world of Hollywood. I still don't understand 90 percent of the terms used in those contracts, so thank you for being my dictionary. You are priceless.

Mad respect to my original betas from Critique Circle—Stacesween, Debbyw, Bjensenjr, Mommabaird, Sammiller, Jaron, Endeavor, Dabbler. You helped transform this story from a manuscript into a novel. It wouldn't be half as good if not for you all. Thank you so much for sticking with me.

A large portion of this book was inspired by true events, so I feel thanks are due to my real-life inspo:

Sarah Grace White, for initiating group therapy, and also being—quite literally—the best and most supportive friend I could ever hope for. If they had a Tinder for BFFs, I would swipe right on you forever.

My residency class, Ashlin Paz, Gloria Perez, Luanne Solis, Micah Wright (and honorary member Christa Littrell), for surviving the trenches with me.

Dr. William Po, for dealing with the above residency class with grace (I'm sorry I yelled at you that one time).

Dr. Corey Babb, for being the devil on my shoulder who convinced me to become an ob-gyn.

OSU Medical Center, for serving food so gross, it inspired an entire theme in this novel (I'm still bitter about the "employee" gifts, by the way).

St. Francis Hospital, for the PTSD. May your ASCOMs lie in everlasting torment somewhere in hell.

Mi Cocina, for inventing the Mambo Taxi.

Taylor Swift, for your red lips and novel-inspiring songs.

Thank you to the RNs at Cape Coral Hospital, who are utter gems (dare I say, sapphires?) and an absolute credit to their field. You all make this job a hundred percent better. Ignore the stereotypical bitchy nurses in this novel. They are just plot devices. And please forgive me in advance when I'm inevitably grumpy in the middle of the night. It's not you. It's me.

A huge thanks to my partners at Premier Women's Care, especially Samaris Corona, Shannon O'Hara and Aparna Eligeti. If I have to take call, I'm glad it's with you. Let's get a drink next time Blaise is on.

To Ashlin and Rachael, you two truly are my biggest fans. You have read everything I've ever written, even the trash first drafts, and you always manage to make me feel like I'm not a total failure. Seriously, I don't think I would have pursued any of this so hard if it weren't for you cheerleading me from the background. Rachael, I'm sorry about the confusing throuple in that one book. I promise I won't make you read the sequels. And Ashlin, I apologize that Lucas and Sofía didn't beat this novel to print. If that book ever sees the light of day, it will be entirely because of you.

Another planet-sized hunk of thanks goes to my sister, Ali. You have been here from the very beginning, reading and rereading and then reading again, even though doom scrolling has destroyed your attention span. You are the rock I run to when I feel wobbly, and I can't imagine my life without you (so don't die, okay?). I'm still annoyed that you live so far away.

Thank you to my family, especially my in-laws, Donnie and Linda. Your love and support in all our endeavors have made this infinitely easier. Thank you for loving my kids so much. They are incredibly lucky to have you as their grandparents.

And I saved the best for last. None of this would have been possible without my husband, Olen. You have been my coconspirator, my strategist, my shoulder to cry on, my realistic sounding board. Beyond that, your love and constancy have built a secure home for us and our two tornadoes (and that stinky beagle, too), and there is no place I would rather be than by your side. I love you, and I can't wait to see what the future has in store for us.

Dictionary

ASCOM /azˈkäm/ *n.* **1** an internal hospital phone **2** the noise you hear in your nightmares **3** the thing you wish on your worst enemy

attending /əˈtendˌiNG/ *n.* **1** a physician who has completed residency and is responsible for training residents **2** a person who doesn't want to work, but always thinks you are not working hard enough

chief /CHēf/ *n.* **1** a resident in their last year of training **2** a bitter and detached human who lacks all emotion

hospitalist /ˈhäˌspidlˈist/ *n.* **1** a physician who specializes in treating hospitalized patients **2** a hater of residents **3** a person who is impossible to please

intern /ˈinˌtərn/ *n.* **1** a first-year resident **2** an overworked, overwhelmed idiot **3** a fifth-year medical student

L&D /el (ə)n dē/ *n.* **1** labor and delivery **2** where babies deliver **3** the spiciest unit of the hospital

pimping /ˈpimpˌiNG/ *v.* **1** when upper levels ask increasingly more difficult questions to specifically make you look like an idiot **2** the best way to remind residents they're at the bottom of the hierarchy

program director /ˈprōˌgram diˈrektər/ *n.* **1** the attending in charge of a residency program **2** a man with an endless supply of chocolate

resident /ˈrez(ə)dənt/ *n.* **1** a physician in training **2** a person who works eight million hours per week **3** a peasant

Julian

JUNE, YEAR 1

What torture-loving freaks burn bonfires for pleasure in the muggy heat of a Texas June? We don't do this back home—and I'm from Florida, the land of the crazies. The conversations around me hum as I stare into the flames. My thumb rubs a slow trail along the neck of my beer bottle.

I take a swig and frown.

Warm IPA.

Yum.

"Yo, Santini." Maxwell DeBakey offers me a cold bottle. "You need a refill?"

I pour out the dregs of mine and take the new one. "Thanks."

Maxwell settles next to me, the firelight flashing gold over his dark sweaty skin. "No problem."

"Why are we having a bonfire in June?"

He shoots me a smile. "BrOB-GYN tradition."

A flicker of amusement stills the bottle halfway to my mouth. "BrOB-GYN?"

He chuckles and shrugs one massive shoulder. "Male residents stick together. Otherwise, the women would eat us alive."

Hmm. Would they, though? Would they really?

My lips press together to keep the instinctual sarcasm tucked neatly inside. Probably unwise to make waves before I've even started, but I can't quite stop the sardonic grin at the irony clattering through my head—*beware the assembly of females, for they will destroy the world!*

I take another swig, and cold hops bubble down my throat. Maxwell starts his fourth year—his *chief* year—in a few days, whereas I start at the bottom. The lowly intern. My first year of residency, and one of only five admitted to the small Texas University OB-GYN program at TUMC.

I'm still not sure how I scraped by with a spot here. It's a good program, and I wasn't a shoo-in. Not only did my scores leave something to be desired, but the initials after my name aren't the revered MD.

Julian Santini, DO.

Doctor of Osteopathy. The redheaded stepchild of the medicine world, thought to have chosen osteopathy because we couldn't get into the more traditional allopathic schools.

I'm the only DO in the program. One of three in the entire hospital.

Back in March, thirty-five hundred doctors vied for fifteen hundred OB-GYN spots across the country, and somehow, I got one. Was it my interview? My letters of recommendation? Blind luck? Regardless, the stark awareness that I don't deserve this means I need to tread carefully.

I have a lot to prove and very little faith that I can do it.

"You ready for next week, man?" Maxwell asks. "Labor and delivery is hopping. July first comin' fast."

My gaze strays to the fire. "I think so. Who decided to punish the runt of the litter by putting me on L&D first?"

I can't help but wonder if they're testing me. All service lines—labor and delivery, surgery, specialty rotations, etc.—are assigned by month, constantly rotating, and for some reason, *I'm* the first intern to cover the L&D floor. It's not only the most arduous rotation, but also the one with the longest hours. Trial by fire.

Maxwell snorts. "Runt of the litter? Doubt it. Besides, *I'm* your senior. That ain't punishment, bro. We'll have fun."

The ungodly heat rolling off the flames distorts my view of the men on the other side, all chatting with beers in hand. To my left, one resident regales two others about a surgical case from earlier that week. To my right, Maxwell settles deeper into his chair.

The house and backyard belong to Asher Foley, a soon-to-be third-year, and clearly a bachelor. I suspect he was in a fraternity at some point. The entire property is tricked out—fancy deck he claims to have built himself, gaming room with surround sound, full bar that takes up half his kitchen, and a cookie jar of condoms on top of his fridge.

Subtle.

The statement piece of his living room is a poster with elaborate and colorful cursive letters that reads I'm Not a Gynecologist, I'm a Vagician. Beneath the phrase is a rainbow watercolor cartoon of a hand pulling a uterus from a top hat. When I pointed at it, eyebrow raised, Asher insisted it was his Secret Santa present last year. Maxwell gave his head a subtle shake, then accused him of buying it on Etsy.

I had no words.

Of the twenty resident physicians in the program, only six are male. Four of the male attending physicians—our bosses—have also showed for the tradition tonight. I arrived not knowing the women were routinely excluded. Maxwell says they have their own traditions, but I'm doubtful.

I imagine what my sisters would say about this vaguely misogynistic ritual.

It's disgusting, Julian. How could you participate in such behavior?

I'll have to explain I was tricked into it when I talk to them later. Hopefully they'll understand.

Being the brother of four older sisters is as annoying as it is amusing. Their lessons from my childhood have stuck in my brain, shaped me. One of their favorites: men who exclude women from work gatherings are likely chauvinists and probably have small dicks.

They're often dramatic, but rarely wrong.

About the chauvinist part, at least. As for the other portion of that hypothesis… I try not to think about it.

"It's not just a rumor," someone says behind me.

Maxwell and I turn as Dr. Levine and Dr. Kulczycki, two of our attendings, approach from the house with fresh drinks.

"What's not a rumor?" Maxwell asks.

"About the intern." Dr. K waves a hand. "You know, the girl."

Maxwell's eyes widen. "Oh. That." He turns toward the fire. "How do you know?"

Dr. Levine, his lean cheeks rosy from either heat or alcohol, gives me a bland smile. Firelight dances in his blue eyes, and his close-cropped gray hair doesn't hide the sheen of sweat over his balding forehead. "Chen basically confirmed it."

Dr. Chen, our program director? My curiosity piques, and I glance between Levine and K.

Dr. K snorts, scratching a hand through his dark hair, glasses falling to the end of his sweaty hooked nose. "Chen said he was looking into it. He didn't confirm anything."

Levine rolls his eyes. "We all knew it was true two days ago."

"What's true?" I ask.

Everyone turns toward us, quieting.

Maxwell swigs his beer. "We heard a few days ago that one of the interns got her spot by sleeping with someone in GME."

What?

The Graduate Medical Education office serves as the liaison

between the medical center and the accreditation council. In essence, they're our governing board.

A twinge of cold tightens the muscles in my body as the past eight years flash through my mind—every pricey tutoring session and lost night of sleep, every illegal tablet of Adderall I bought off my friends because I didn't have the time to get formally diagnosed with ADHD, every girlfriend who complained I studied too much and left me for someone else.

I'm not naturally studious. Getting to this point wasn't easy for me. I mean, it isn't easy for anyone, but there were bleak days over the past few years when I wasn't sure I'd make it. When a few missed points on a board exam meant the difference between achieving my dream or walking away with no degree and a mountain of student debt. If some girl got her spot by dishonest means…

I tighten my hand on my sweating beer bottle.

Another of my sisters' favorite sayings: unethical people are trash.

"I'm still trying to figure out which one it is," says one of the two male second-years, Liam Heaney.

My fellow intern Kai catches my attention, mouthing, *Did you know about this?*

I shake my head. Kai Campisi is thin and taller than my six foot one, with sandy hair that's perfectly slicked to one side. Even the one-million-percent humidity hasn't managed to dislodge whatever product holds it in place. I met him two hours ago, but I've since learned he's dry, straightforward, and gay. That last I only know because when he shook my hand he said, "You're cute. Gay or straight?"

"Um. Straight."

He dropped my hand and handed me a beer. "Too bad."

We've been chatting on and off ever since.

Asher, the man of the house, breaks into laughter. "You're kidding, right? Come on, Liam. You've seen their names. Of the three girls on that list, who is the most likely to fuck her way to the top? Raven Washington, the married woman with a toddler; Alesha Lipton, who had higher scores than any of us; or Sapphire Rose, the girl whose name could be plastered on a Las Vegas cabaret marquee."

An inward wince follows that description. The same thought ran through my mind when the names of my co-interns made it to my inbox. I shoved it into the far reaches of my brain where the things I'm ashamed of live, like the time I ripped up my sister's fancy art project because she told me my new haircut looked like thirteen-year-old Justin Bieber.

But really, what type of parents name their daughter Sapphire Rose and expect her to be taken seriously?

If this stripper-intern truly screwed someone for her spot, I might lose my goddamn mind.

Except...what if it isn't true?

What if it wasn't even her?

There's always more to the story.

"You're serious?" I glance at Dr. Levine. "She slept with someone to get in?"

Levine shrugs. "Told to us by a credible source."

How credible?

A few days ago, Alesha Lipton invited me to a group chat with the other interns, and we've talked for days. The Sapphire in that group barely contributes, so I have no frame of reference, nothing that tells me to believe one way or another.

Despite the injustice boiling in my blood, I tell myself to hold out judgment. Wait for facts. Even though my attending basically confirmed it.

Ugh.

Does it matter in the end? No. This doesn't concern me. It's not my business.

Head down. Stay the course. Four years and you're done.

Grace

My hands shake as I reach for the steering wheel. The GPS waits patiently for me to start my route, but the spiraling butterflies in my stomach have me pawing at the door handle. I'm going to throw up.

The door opens, and I lean into the humid night air. A deep breath clears the nausea. Another calms the flutters.

It's just a party.

The residency mixer is supposed to be fun, a way to mingle and party with my soon-to-be work family. I'll spend more time with these strangers in the next few years than my real family in California.

This is how you achieve the goal, Grace. This is what you've always wanted.

The dream of myself in that white coat—smart and successful and respected—has fueled my type A little heart since before I could remember. Being a doctor is all I've ever wanted. It's the ultimate symbol that I've done something worthwhile, that no matter what anyone says, I'm someone to be taken seriously.

The thoughts don't ease the crushing social anxiety that wraps around my chest like a corset.

What if they don't like me?

I pull out my phone.

> **Me:** I'm nervous

> **Mama:** You'll be fine, honey. Deep breaths.

I should've taken a beta-blocker. Instead, I've armed myself with the scarlet Louboutin heels I bought myself for graduation, and NARS Inappropriate Red lipstick. My long wavy hair has been styled into soft curls that fall down my back. My dress is, of course, red.

Anything but blue.

Sapphire.

With a slow breath, I back out of my parking spot and head to Dr. Chen's house, where the residency mixer will take place. In the group text with my fellow interns, we speculated whether there'd be hazing, but Alesha Lipton talked to one of the second-years. Apparently, the welcome party consists of booze, camaraderie, and a lot of talk about vaginas—a staple in any conversation with gynecologists.

I have yet to meet my co-interns in person, but our group message leads me to believe we'll get along well.

Pulling up to the corner lot, I grip my stomach while it re-awakens with flutters. The street curb is clogged with parked cars, but I squeeze my Camry into a spot between a driveway and a blue SUV.

The house itself is a cozy cottage style, with lights glowing from every window. Mature trees dot the yard, and a quaint chimney rises to one side. A Japanese maple grows beside the stairs leading to the front door. I allow my hand to brush the crimson leaves as I pass.

My knock is likely drowned out by the chatter inside, and no one answers. With one last nerve-clearing breath, I let myself in. The room is packed. I force a smile at the first person I see—a handsome brown-haired man with a large grin, wearing a pink T-shirt. A cartoon uterus with buff arms is splashed over his chest. Beneath the uterus is the word *Broterus*.

I blink at it, a tiny laugh catching in my throat.

The man chuckles. "It's breathtaking, I know." He holds out a hand. "I'm Asher. One of the third-years."

"Hi. Grace. I'm Grace."

He glances behind me as I shut the door, like he expects someone else. "You with anyone?"

"Nope. Just me."

His gaze roams my face. "You're one of the interns, then? Grace?"

I smile. "Grace Rose."

His eyes light up. "Ah. You don't use your given name?"

"Not if I can help it."

Laughing, he jerks his head toward the kitchen. "Let me get you a drink. What'll it be?"

"Oh. Um. Wine, please?"

"Red or white?"

I wave a hand at my dress. "Red, obviously."

He disappears into the crowd with a good-humored, "Obviously."

The combined kitchen-living area is thriving with bodies. The faux-brick floors lend a Tuscan vibe to the space, and the custom finishes—from the marble countertops to the built in entertainment center—speak of wealth.

I lock eyes with a few people, smiling at each, but no one is eager to adopt me into their conversation. Wandering farther into the room, I examine the wood planks on the vaulted ceilings when my chest bumps into someone's elbow.

A small splash of liquid on my ankle makes me wince. Not my shoes...

My gaze falls on the drink I knocked, a half-empty plastic cup, grasped in the most attractive hand I've ever seen.

Tanned, thin, long-fingered.

Elegant.

What a stupid thing to be attracted to.

As I take in the body attached to that hand, my skin flares with an odd, unexpected heat. He's tall. Dark-haired. Dark-eyed. His jawline is like whetted glass.

He grins, little dimples appearing in his cheeks, kind crinkles around his eyes. "Hey."

A portion of my anxiety unwinds. "Hi. Sorry." I glance at my leg. "I'm wearing your drink."

His dark stare locks on my ankle, then slides up my leg in a way I can *feel*, like his stupidly attractive hands are on my skin.

Whoa. Is it hot in here?

"Not a problem," he says. "Though I think I ruined your shoes."

I groan, staring at the sad stain in the silk bow at my ankle. "I loved these shoes."

He winces. "I could spill some on the other shoe. Make it match?"

"Oh, you'd be good enough to do that for me?"

"Anything for you, er—" He lifts his eyebrows, clearly hoping for a name.

"Oh, I'm Grace."

He holds his hand out, smiling. "Julian. Ruiner of shoes. Just please don't tell my sister. If she finds out I killed a pair of heels like that, she'll disown me."

I give him a little laugh. "Your secret's safe with me. So, wait. Are you Julian Santini?"

His smile falters, and his warm hand falls away from mine. "You've heard of me?"

I give him my full grin. "Of course. I've memorized all my co-intern's names. You're Julian Santini. The email said you went to LECOM?"

"The Bradenton campus." Those dark brows knit together. "You're one of the interns? You said your name was Grace?"

An awkward giggle bubbles in my chest, and heat rises in my cheeks. "Oh. I go by my middle name. My parents are hippies. They named me Sapphire."

The smile drops off his face. His entire demeanor changes as he straightens. "*You're* Sapphire Rose?"

"Er... Yes." I take a step back.

A disbelieving laugh precedes a sharp, almost cold appraisal of my face. "Of course you are."

My head jerks at his sardonic tone. "Of course—what?"

"Nothing. It's nothing. Nice dress, by the way. Matches the shoes. Sorry about that." He lifts his near-empty cup and re-treats. "I have to refill—"

The crowd swallows him before he finishes.

Shocked, I glance around, meeting the eyes of a few strangers who smile politely before returning to their own conversations.

He...he left? Why?

The knot of anxiety in my chest tightens, then tugs on my tear ducts. I paste on a smile and make my way through the kitchen, passing by Asher with my drink. I lift a finger to keep him from following as I slip into the connected dining room and outside to the empty patio.

A firepit roars beside a table full of ingredients for s'mores. I bypass it all and step around the side of the house, letting the warm brick dig into my back.

Two tears spill, and I swipe at them, breathing through the bleak sense of loneliness and affront. What *was* that?

Around the corner, the door opens, and the voices of a few party guests drift toward me. I shrink farther into the shadows at the side of the house.

"Dr. Levine is lit tonight," says a female voice.

A deep contemplative voice answers. "It's taken me three years to decide, but I'm positive he and his wife are swingers."

A few chuckles follow.

"She propositioned me at a party once," says another male.

"Shut up," Deep Voice says, the eye roll apparent in his tone.

"What happened to the red dress, Santini? Thought I might have an opening, then she talks to you and disappears."

"That was Sapphire Rose. She introduced herself, and I left to get a drink. I don't know where she went after."

Another tear falls when I squeeze my eyes shut. He'd *dismissed* me. Surely he understands that's not polite behavior?

Ugh. Why am I crying about it? Parties are too stressful.

"I know who she was," says the first voice. "I was getting her a drink, cockblocker."

Oh. It's Asher.

"The rumor doesn't bother you?" Deep Voice asks.

What? What rumor?

"Um. Did you see her? I'd give her a spot too if she'd put that mouth around my di—"

"Shut *up*, Asher," Deep Voice says. "My wife is here."

Wait, what the—

"I don't mind," comes the amused female voice. "Could she even find your dick, Asher? Like one of those stir straws, right? Girl would probably need a magnifying glass."

A chorus of laughter breaks out, and a smile touches my lips. I'm glad I didn't accept a drink from that douche.

"Yeah, yeah, Cat." Asher's voice is tinged with amusement. "You're hilarious."

Her feminine laughter drifts away. "Let me get you a refill, string bean."

The door opens and closes.

Deep Voice sighs. "You're such an asshole, Asher."

"I know. But hey, if *Dr. Rose* fucks to get ahead, I can show her all the fast lanes. She'll have the easiest intern year ever."

My mind spins in a million directions. *Fucks to get ahead.* Why do they think that about me?

I glance at my red dress. My red heels. Maybe—

No. It's not about tonight, or the way I look. These are pre-conceived notions.

Except, I don't have sex to get ahead in life. I don't have sex at all—not for the past two years. The last time had ended catastrophically—

It's like fucking an ice queen.

Yeah. No thanks to repeating that. The switch on my libido is flipped to a permanent OFF.

Well, it was off until that demonically tempting hand flaunted itself in my face not ten minutes ago. Who knew hands could be so alluring?

But then he just walked away...

Oh, my god. He knew about this rumor, didn't he?

My fingernails dig into my palms. The knot in my chest has my skin prickling, but my rising temper and the reminder of my last boyfriend has turned the butterflies to daggers. I step into the light, setting a hand on my cocked hip.

Julian's dark gaze glints my way, catching on my face. He elbows Asher, who turns toward me, grin fading. Two other men stand with them. Other residents.

"What was that now?" I ask.

None of them speak. The fire crackles between us. Heat and smoke permeate the air with burned cedar.

"Who told you I screw people to get ahead in life?" I ask.

"Um—" Asher rubs his neck and glances at the other men.

Does he think they'll have some magical lifeline for him? *Nuh-uhh, buddy. You're screwed.* "I think you misheard—"

I shake my head. A tear falls. "No, I think I heard quite clearly."

None of them answer.

"It's not true," I say, swiping the tear away.

Julian turns away. The sharp edge of his jaw throws shadows over his throat. The others exchange glances, clearly perturbed by the irate female in their presence.

I stomp toward them, my heels clacking on the travertine pavers. "What exactly did you hear?"

Asher adopts an expression like someone asked him to inform his girlfriend he has an STD—one he didn't get from her. "I don't—know?"

The tallest of the four meets my eyes. I recognize him from his Instagram. Kai Campisi, fellow intern. "They said you got your spot by less than upstanding means."

He's an intern—hasn't even started—and he already heard this about me?

My heart thuds as blood drains from my head, making me woozy. Four vaguely human figures waver in the heat above the fire, and the world fractures into starbursts as tears collect.

Years of similar incidents flicker through my mind. High schools boys snickering about giving them a striptease. College friends flippantly hinting I'd never need student loans. A bouncer at a club, upon checking my license, wondering whether I was the Sapphire Rose from PornHub.

Then med school. Oh, med school. And *Matt*.

"I didn't screw my way into this program." I cringe at the waver in my voice, but I want these words spoken, even if they don't believe them. "I have no idea who said that about me, or why, but I worked hard to be here. My GPA was perfect and my test scores were solid. I did everything I was supposed to do, and I earned my spot fairly. *Even if my name is Sapphire Rose.*"

Kai tilts his head, studying me with a small smile. "Get 'em, girl," he murmurs.

Asher's face pales. "Whoa. Chill out."

"Chill out?" I stomp my foot. "Seriously?"

The man I assume is Deep Voice stares at the ground, buff arms crossed.

Julian stills, the firelight glittering in his eyes like the flames of hell. Mouth tight, bottom lip pulled between his teeth, he taps his finger against the refilled plastic cup in his hand. I fantasize briefly about yanking it from his grasp, sloshing it in his face. Red wine would drip over that cut jaw and soak into his gray button-down. Ruin *his* clothes.

Would serve him right, since this is clearly why he walked away. He was kind and smiley, flirtatious even, then he heard my stripper name and made a snap judgment based on unfounded rumors.

What a dick.

I throw him a fiery glare. "I did nothing to you. You know *nothing* about me, and you judged me based on a rumor? Jerk move." Heart pounding, I turn on my heel and clack away, traveling around the back of the house so I won't have to face the partygoers inside. My ruined heels puncture the lawn as I hurry for my car, tears flowing freely. Why didn't I think to wear waterproof mascara?

I'm in the street beside my car when my name stops me cold. A glance over my shoulder shows Julian trotting toward me.

"Sapphire—"

"It's Grace." I swipe at my tears.

"Right. Shit." He throws his plastic cup to the ground, spilling the liquid inside, and offers me the remaining cocktail napkin. "Look, I'm sorr—"

"Who was I meant to have screwed?" I stare at his peace offering without taking it.

He stops short, three steps away. "What?"

"What bigwig was I meant to have screwed to get this spot?"

He runs a hand through his hair, ruffling the strands that lay over his forehead. "I don't know. That doesn't matter—"

"It does matter, actually. Funny that you didn't judge the fictional man in this scenario. Only the woman."

His dark eyes go wide. Incredulous. "That's not—how would you know who and what I was judging?"

"Because you walked away from me mid-sentence. Felt pretty judgy."

"That isn't what I—that's not—ugh." He drags a hand over his face.

Yeah. This guy already played his cards, and I have the winning hand. "Men like you are the reason women can never get ahead."

He cocks his head, voice hardened. "Men like me?"

"Misogynists. Men who accuse women of things they didn't do. Men who assume because I'm pretty and wearing a red dress and have a porn star's name that I'd spread my legs for anyone, especially if it came with benefits. You just called me a whore."

"Did those words leave my mouth? I said *nothing* to you. I don't want to be involved in scandals, so I excused myself. I'm sorry that hurt your feel—"

"They say there are two types of men who become gynecologists, Julian. Men who love women, and men who hate them."

In the dark, his crooked smile is fiendish. "And you think I'm the latter? Based on a single conversation and a misunderstanding?"

"First impressions don't take long."

The laugh that rumbles in his chest is low and angry, and he halves the distance between us. "I could say the same about you. You just threw a temper tantrum in front of a bunch of strangers instead of addressing us like a rational human. You essentially stomped your foot and walked away."

"I—"

"I'm sorry I considered for a second it might be true. I really am. I was told it was a fact by our *attending*, someone I won't trust in the future, okay?"

My mouth falls open. My *attendings* were saying this about me?

His voice softens. "For what it's worth, I believe you. You may think I hate women, but I don't. I don't even know you, and I hate seeing you cry over something like this." He takes my wrist and presses the napkin into my hand.

Maybe it's unfair, but all of my hatred for this situation lands squarely on him. I rip my hand away. "You're a jerk."

He lets out a bitter laugh and turns to leave, swiping his cup from the ground. "Nice. Thanks. Okay."

"And now you're just going to walk away?"

He spins. "What do you want me to do? How else would you like me to fix it? I didn't start the rumor. I didn't spread the rumor. All I did was walk away from you, and no one else bothered to come out here trying to make you feel better."

"Screw you."

"Screw *you*." He throws an irritated arm into the air, waving toward my car. "Weren't you leaving?"

I shoot him the deadliest glare I can manage. "You stopped me."

"Well, nothing's stopping you now."

I growl and stomp over to my Camry, the automatic door unlocking at my touch. "Better get out of the road. I'd hate for you to get run over."

Julian

JUNE, YEAR 1

The morning after the residency mixer, my sister's forehead scrunches into wrinkles on my phone screen. "What the fuck, Julian?"

"She called me a misogynist, Tori."

Her brown eyes blaze. "You accused her of something awful."

I love all my sisters, but I'm closest to Victoria, who's only eighteen months older than me. I don't love the way she's looking at me, though. "I didn't start the rumor."

"You threw it in her face." She props her phone up in her bathroom and grabs a paintbrush. No, a makeup brush. Same difference.

"I did not! I walked away. And I tried to apologize. She

wouldn't let me. I felt bad for her and tried to help, but she was mad and took it out on me."

Tori pauses in her efforts, throwing shade my way. "I say this with all the love in the world, but you're a dick."

I *am* a dick. I'd dismissed her outright, but she insulted me and wouldn't even hear my apology, so she's kind of a dick, too.

I shouldn't have been so distracted by that dress, but for fuck's sake, that dress was bewitching, and she had the shoes and devil-red lips to match. The woman is fucking gorgeous and for thirty seconds, my very straight male brain was befuddled. Sue me.

It's why I couldn't stop the flash of irritation when I learned her name. I'm human. I make mistakes. Then I reminded myself not to get involved. Be polite. Move on. Except…it's not exactly polite to abandon someone in the middle of a conversation.

Why did I have to throw out that sarcastic apology?

Nice dress, by the way. Matches the shoes. Sorry about that.

I am so cringe. I got riled up. Said something dumb, and now I'm annoyed with myself. Annoyed with her. Annoyed with it all.

She *cried*.

I rub my temples. Stupid headache. "Yeah, I'm a dick. I don't know how I can feel this bad and still be mad at her."

Tori smears something on her skin. "What that guy said about her is gross."

"Yep. Why do you think I chased after her?"

Something clatters into Tori's sink and she turns toward me. "What does she look like?"

Like a human.

Red lips. White skin. Black hair.

Not enchanting.

Not at all.

"Like those little spiders that live at the top of our lanai."

Tori snorts. "That pretty, huh?"

"A hot version."

Okay, so her skin is more tan than white, and her hair is more brown than black, and she has the kind of face that makes a person want to keep looking, but she's just as irritating as those spiders with the red spikes.

Men like you.

I scowl. "I'm not a misogynist."

"You were standing with them. You walked away as soon as you knew who she was. Can you blame her for thinking it?"

"God." I glare at Tori as she takes some black weapon to her eyelashes. "Whose side are you on?"

"Hers."

JULY, YEAR 1

Day one. We call the summer spike in deaths at teaching hospitals *The July Effect*. The medical errors of bumbling new interns are so numerous, many are overlooked. Despite layers of oversight, interns lack experience, and mistakes are frequent.

As an intern, I find these facts a tad nauseating.

I am determined to not fuck this up.

My sisters' encouraging first-day texts have the opposite of their intended effect. I'm reminded that I'm still a kid. A twenty-eight-year-old fifth-year medical student with some fancy letters after my name.

But not the good letters.

Six a.m. shift change, aka sign out, with the night resident—a bleary-eyed second-year named Whitney Couvelaire—goes smoothly enough. I complete rounds with few issues. At this lower acuity hospital, labor and delivery isn't slammed, but Maxwell and I are the only physicians on the floor. Seven post-partum patients are tucked in. Three laboring patients and a busy OB triage unit take most of our time.

Between patients, we sit in the doctor's dictation area. It's a tiny computer room meant for charting, but it's become a storage closet for educational dioramas, discarded instruments, suture and a bony pelvis replica with a doll named Darla used to teach the cardinal movements of labor. Darla wears blue overalls with a pink flowered shirt and has a teardrop tattoo. She's lived a rough life.

Papers are taped and pinned to every surface. Medical algorithms, resident schedules, anatomic diagrams, all of it plastered with cartoon dicks, memes and handwritten, well-timed notations of *that's what she said.*

"Look at this." Maxwell points at his computer screen. "Bed two got the TUMC special."

I glance at the monitor, open to the patient's lab results lit up like a Las Vegas casino.

"Christ. Is there any STD she *doesn't* have?"

"Syphilis." Maxwell scrolls. "Oh, and HIV. I'm gonna let you tell her about her new hep C diagnosis. Good practice for you."

"Thanks." My voice is dry, but I scribble another line on my to-do list.

"This is why we don't mess with dirty dicks, ladies," Maxwell murmurs as he flips to another patient's chart. "Doubt that asshole in the room with her will bother to get treated."

He proceeds to ask me a series of questions. How do you treat chlamydia in pregnancy? Does she need a test of cure? When? What about trichomonas?

Medical pimping at its finest. At least Maxwell's pimping style is nice. He shows me how to find the answer when I don't have it, instead of chastising me and telling me my patients will die. My attendings definitely won't be this civil.

My pager beeps and I frown at the digits *x5373*.

Leaning over, Maxwell groans out a sigh. "That's the ER's number. Welcome to your first ER consult. See what they want."

I make the call, jotting notes, but my pen stills at a lilting feminine voice behind me. The sound creeps along my spine, and my skin pricks like it's waking up after a long time without adequate circulation.

I sense a threat.

She's behind me. I'm not sure how I know it's her, but it's definitely her. Tingles raise the hair on my nape.

When I hang up, Maxwell lifts his eyebrows, throwing a give-it-to-me sign.

I slide him my notes. "They have a consult for pelvic pain. I told them to get an ultrasound."

Maxwell smiles and wags a finger at me. "Good man."

My sigh of relief is subtle but calming. Even the smallest orders take on life-altering significance now that I'm the one in charge. Each go-ahead for Tylenol or TUMS has to filter through my safeguards. My easily distracted brain is already exhausted.

Maxwell returns his attention to our visitor and I turn toward her.

Grace Rose, standing in the dictation room doorway, wears powder-blue surgical scrubs, two pagers clipped at her waist and a rainbow of pens in her breast pocket. The giant mass of curls from two nights ago is contained in a messy knot, wisps escaping around her face. Without the red lipstick, a single freckle on her upper lip stares at me. Weird place for a freckle. Distracting.

I sigh and look away. "What are you doing here?"

"I had a second, so I escaped." She turns to Maxwell. "Thought I'd come meet the senior on L&D."

Aw, you didn't want to see me too, Grace? I'm so sad. Even my inner voice is rolling its eyes.

Maxwell shakes her hand. "Sorry about the other night. I don't believe any of it, just so you know."

I throw him a raised eyebrow. That wasn't exactly the impression I got...

Grace smiles. "That's okay. And thanks."

Oh, so she'll accept *his* apology.

Nice, Grace. Guess we won't be best friends.

Releasing her hand, Maxwell leans back in his chair. "What are you on this month?"

"General surgery." Tight lines appear beside her mouth. "Four hours in, and it's already draining my life force."

"You don't like surgery?" Maxwell asks.

"I don't like surgeons." She crosses her arms. "Or, I don't like *these* surgeons."

"Of course you don't," I mutter.

Maxwell chuckles. "We all deal with a bit of hazing."

She scoffs and unclips a pager. "They gave me the penis pager."

Maxwell pulls a breath through his teeth. "Sucks."

I glance between them. "What's a penis pager?"

"Urology," they answer together, and Maxwell says, "A lot of old men who can't pee."

Grace throws a perturbed glance toward the ceiling. "Because that's why I went into OB-GYN. To look at old penises all day."

Maxwell laughs. I bite the inside of my lip. My pride won't allow me to find her charming or funny. She's a hypercritical shrew. End of story.

"My last consult had two propellers tattooed on his ass cheeks and was only too proud to tell me that he got them—" she deepens her voice "—*so I can go deeper.*"

Pride thwarted, I turn to my computer to hide my damning grin. Little Miss Priss has a sense of humor. Who knew?

"I think his junk not working is cosmic justice," she says.

I don't want to give her the satisfaction, but a snicker escapes anyway.

Her sparkling glare settles on me. "You think it's funny?"

"It's only funny that you're suffering." I shoot her a sarcastic smile. "Karma."

"You'll get your turn, Julian. Just wait."

"It's day one, girl," Maxwell says. "Get used to being the scut monkey."

Chastened, she bites her lip, hiding the freckle.

"I know." She stares hard at me, narrowing her eyes in accusation. "Some people are just rude."

Is that it, Grace? You think I'm rude? "Like us misogynists?" I ask, tone desert dry.

She opens her mouth to reply, but Maxwell interrupts her. "They're general surgeons. They foist their misery upon others. It's only a month. You can do it."

"Dr. Rose!"

Grace spins in the doorway, nearly colliding with another resident, a man an inch shorter than her. Without smiling, the stranger takes a pointed step back.

Grace's cheeks flood with color. "I'm—I'm sorry."

The man I presume is her senior resident this month looks her up and down. "You're not supposed to be on L&D. It's time for lunch."

Her mouth opens twice before anything comes out. "It's nine-forty."

"Eat when you can. Sleep when you can..." His head tilts, expectant.

"Um." She glances at me and Maxwell, eyes wide and panicked.

I know the phrase he means—a popular one amongst surgeons—but I lift an eyebrow, refusing to help this sanctimonious woman. A bloom of pleasure spikes my blood as she chokes and stutters.

The surgery resident's voice slows like he's speaking to a toddler. "Don't fuck with the pancreas."

A muscle in her cheek twitches. "How was I supposed to know that, Dr. Halliwell? I'm a gynecologist. Why would I be near the pancreas?"

Dour Surgeon sneers. "I forget you guys aren't real surgeons."

I resist the urge to snort. What a douche.

Maxwell mutters, "Okay, Halliwell," under his breath.

Grace's knuckles whiten around the penis pager. "This coming from a man whose attending kicked him out of the OR this morning?"

Whoa. That won't serve her well—even though the guy deserved it.

Halliwell's eyebrows shoot up and his jaw hardens. "He didn't kick me out—"

Maxwell stands, towering over the resident. "Take it easy on her, Halliwell, and stop being a prick."

A faint smile appears on Halliwell's humorless face. "I heard you guys let a DO in your program. Must have been really hard up."

Ripples of heat spread from my face downward. My ID badge is flipped backward, so he can't know that I'm the DO, but the reminder of never being good enough simmers in my bones. Like a virus replicating, it has insinuated into my very DNA.

Average student. Mediocre test-taker. Inattentive boyfriend. Too skinny. Too quiet. And now... DO.

I chose osteopathy. I wanted this.

Sometimes I wish I never had.

Fuck off, dickwad.

This is what I hate about medicine. The elitism. The hierarchy. The animosity between specialties. The malignancy.

This unfriendly surgery resident is everything that's wrong with medicine and the tiniest shred of compassion rips through my distaste for Grace's attitude. The poor girl has to be his slave for an entire month.

Maxwell shakes his head and reseats himself, not dignifying the asshole with an answer.

Halliwell smirks and motions for Grace to follow. "Come along, Doctor."

She obeys but turns to mouth *Thank you* at Maxwell. She doesn't spare me another glance.

"He's got a raging case of short-man syndrome." Maxwell spins in his seat, glancing at the fetal heart tracings. "But even if she didn't sleep with someone to get in, that girl's attitude is going to get her in trouble."

I shrug. If it does, she'll deserve it.

Maxwell jerks upright. "Shit!"

Startled, I turn to the monitor. Room eleven's fetal heart rate has dropped to the sixties—far below the norm. Adrenaline rushes through my system as I fan through the empty textbook in my mind, trying to remember everything I'm supposed to do.

Maxwell rises and claps me on the shoulder. "The baby's in distress. What are you going to do, Dr. Santini?"

Go assess the patient.

I hurry to room eleven. The patient moans as I enter, Maxwell following. Two nurses beat us there and have already placed oxygen. They roll the patient to her side. The patient's husband stands beside the bed, whispering encouragement.

What's her name?

Maxwell approaches the bedside. "Kaylee, how are you feeling?"

She moans again. "Hurts."

Maxwell turns to me. "How would you like to proceed, Dr. Santini?"

I glance at the heart tones again. Still non-reassuring. My sweaty hands clench. Why can't I think?

"Why don't you check her cervix," Maxwell says.

I nod and take a breath, donning gloves with nervous fingers. The slow beep, beep, beep of that baby's heart is a noose around my neck. The rate is half my own.

I'm inexperienced and my cervical check is amateur. I'm fishing for anything that might be a cervix. Sweat gathers at my neck and temples. Kaylee screams as another contraction hits.

Beep. Beep. Beep.

Aha! My fingers slide into a ring about the diameter of a tennis ball. "Six centimeters."

My gloved hand comes away with large clots of blood. Bright red saturates the bed beneath Kaylee. My stomach drops.

Maxwell raises his brows. "What do you want to do, Doctor?"

I don't know.

I'm terrified.

Unpracticed and unprepared, I stare at the heart tracing—a flat line at sixty beats per minute.

"Kaylee, your baby's in distress." Maxwell approaches her bedside. "You haven't dilated far enough to push and your bleeding has me worried something's wrong."

Fear clouds her eyes, and she wipes blond hair from her sweaty face. "Okay."

"What does that mean? Is the baby okay?" her husband asks.

"It means we need to move toward delivery now. We'll have to do a C-section. We're going to call Dr. K."

The husband visibly relaxes at the mention of our attending. Maxwell consents Kaylee for a Cesarean while the nurses prep. I stand useless off to the side, absorbing what I can.

Outside the room, Maxwell cocks his head. "What do you do next?"

"Call the attending."

My report to Dr. Kulczycki is a stuttered mess, and he pimps the shit out of me over the phone while we hurry to the OR, and just like I thought, he's not nearly so nice about it. He meets us there and continues to ask questions, digging deeper into my knowledge until I no longer know any answers.

He must think me competent enough because when we scrub in, he shoves me into the primary surgeon's spot and hands me a scalpel. "Sink or swim, Dr. Santini."

I've never primaried a C-section. I've observed dozens, memorized the steps, thrown a few sutures in the closure, but I've never cut my way down to a baby.

She has no epidural. No time for spinal anesthesia. The anesthesiologist has her asleep and intubated too quickly for me to run through the procedure again in my head.

Fuck, fuck, fuck.

He gives the go-ahead. With tingling fingers, I set the scalpel to her skin.

Splash and crash. That's what we call it. Splash of Betadine and a crash C-section, reserved for true emergencies. I have the baby delivered within two minutes—not the fifteen seconds a seasoned attending might have done, but well within time to save his life. My senior and attending correct every wrong move before I can make it and the entire surgery takes far longer than a normal Cesarean, but mom and baby live through it.

And so do I. Sweaty, shaking and possibly in some sort of shock, but I'm alive.

Back in the dictation room, Maxwell is teaching me to put in post-op orders when Dr. K enters. "So, intern, did you make the right decision, taking her to section?"

I'm at a loss. Is that a trick question? The baby was in distress. "Uh—"

Dr. K settles into a chair, hands over his midsection. His surgeon's cap covers his curly black hair and his glasses reflect the multiple computer screens around us. "Review the case with me. Did you make the right decision?"

"The baby was in distress."

He nods. "And?"

"And mom was bleeding."

A wide smile spreads over his face. "But, Dr. Santini, bleeding is normal in labor."

I scratch my jaw. "This was a lot of bleeding, though."

"Ah." His smile eases. "So what was her diagnosis?"

"She—she had a placental abruption."

Dr. K's eyes glint behind his glasses. "And what's the treatment for an acute abruption?"

"Delivery."

"Then tell me. Did you make the right decision, Doctor?"

"Yes."

"Good answer." Dr. K stands and walks away, throwing a last-second "Good job" my way before he disappears around the corner.

The adrenaline rush transitions into a surge of endorphins and I grin at the computer. "That was awesome."

"Yeah." Maxwell's deep laugh resonates in his chest. "Nothing like a good crash section to get the blood flowing. Welcome to OB."

Finally. The reason I chose this. All the late nights and years away from my family and massive amounts of debt will be worth it if I can learn to do this job well, to protect those who've received the shit end of the stick when it comes to health care.

Like my mom, who almost died when I was fifteen because her doctor didn't listen, or my oldest sister, whose first pregnancy nearly killed her when a pulmonary embolism went undiagnosed.

I can do better for them.

I will save lives and today is the beginning.

The Red Hot Chili Peppers play in the background and ESPN is on mute while I stare at the massive textbook on my coffee table three days later. My one-bedroom apartment is furnished with hand-me-down items I obtained from Facebook Marketplace, but the large Samsung TV and Bose sound system I bought new—because, *obviously*. Not that they get much use with the twelve—usually thirteen—hour days I work.

I'm supposed to study.

I know this.

Everyone knows this.

Doctors study. That's what we do. We're the nerds who abandoned our social lives in college to become awkward med students and rack up hundreds of thousands of dollars in student debt.

After eight years of forcing myself to read the same information over and over again and still not retaining it the way other students do, I'm running on fumes.

Fumes with four more years to go.

Williams Obstetrics is more than a thousand pages of information I'm supposed to know and it doesn't encompass even one-half of my specialty.

I take a swig of IPA and briefly wonder why I didn't become an accountant.

You wanted this, remember?

The spine cracks when it opens for the first time, the smell of paper and ink wafting over me. I shudder at the fragrance, one that takes me back to long nights in a lonely study cubicle above my med school library.

I'm three paragraphs into the chapter on maternal physiology when a growl ripples in my chest and I hop off the couch. Pacing in my living room, I whip out my phone, Googling whether the book has an audio version—no—and if there's an app—also no.

My fellow interns don't share my distaste for textbooks and lectures and studying in general. Not that I'm surprised. Again, doctors are nerds.

Me: Did everyone but me read these assigned chapters?

Sapphire: probably

Me: Do you speak for the group now?

Kai: I read them

Raven: Me too. Twice.

Alesha: I did too, juju. sorryyyyy

Sapphire: Told you

I scowl at the screen. Even in texts she's annoying. Her prim tone filters through the screen into my amygdala, firing all the neurons dedicated to anger. I switch to Maxwell.

Me: Do I really need to read this stuff?

Maxwell: They assign the same shit every year. You read it this year, you won't have to next year.

Maxwell: Or maybe you will. You got a thick head.

Me: good hands though

Maxwell: surgery aint everything, bro

Me: Chance to cut is a chance to cure

Maxwell sends a gif of Derek Shepherd from *Grey's Anatomy* doing his surgeon thing, and I laugh, but the smile fades fast as the behemoth on my coffee table beckons. A sip of IPA and a narrow-eyed gaze don't stop its silent taunts. I finish my beer, play *Wordle* and three levels of *Candy Crush*, text my sister, and manage six more paragraphs of the chapter.

Only four million to go.

Fuck this.

I'm going to bed.

Grace

JULY, YEAR 1

Our educational series, called didactics, is a five-hour protected period on Thursday mornings. We give each other lectures over various topics, learn practical skills, receive wisdom from our attendings, and go over high-risk obstetrical cases and gynecologic surgery. The definition of *didactic* is "in the manner of a teacher, particularly so as to treat someone in a patronizing way." Most accurately, it's a five-hour pimping marathon, and as interns, all the questions fall to us first.

Luckily, I study a lot, so I'm not nervous about that part.

Meeting new people, however...

Since I fled the residency mixer before I met anyone, I'm walking into this blind. A ball of tingles and flutters expands in my stomach as I climb the stairs to our clinic space on the second floor of the medical offices. Perhaps the Starbucks venti blonde latte in my hand isn't the best choice for my anxiety, but it's good for my soul.

The conference room is messy like the rest of the resident areas. Broken dioramas and instruments clutter the tables, as well as flyers and candy from pharmaceutical reps. Our malfunctioning laparoscopic simulator stands in the corner, gathering dust. One wall is cluttered with resident posters from previous conferences, and the wall of windows across from it overlooks a Best Western. The projector screen glows with a classic Windows desktop—green fields and blue skies.

A million. That's how many chairs are in this room. Chairs around the table. Chairs lined at the room's periphery. Chairs stacked by the door. All are empty except for two at the center of the table.

Two women interrupt their conversation with shy smiles.

"Hi," one says, pushing purple hair behind her ear.

"Hey." I settle next to the other—a woman with dark skin, black hair and large dark eyes. "I'm Grace."

"I'm Alesha Lipton," says the first.

"Raven Washington," says the other.

Fellow interns! The ball of flutters in my stomach eases. "Oh my gosh. I wanted to meet you guys the other night, but I had to leave the mixer early. You don't look like your pictures!" I face Raven. "I heard you've got a son, yes?"

"Yes." She smiles and shows me a picture of a small boy on her phone. "Monte."

"So cute!" I lift my gaze to Alesha. "And I heard *you're* a genius."

She snorts. "Hardly." Her chair rolls closer, squeezing the three of us together. "I was wondering where you were the other night. Thought it was weird you'd miss it."

"I wasn't feeling well."

Do they know about the rumor?

Raven nods. "Pre-intern jitters?"

"Something like that." I sip my latte and my soul squees in happiness. Yeah, definitely a good choice.

Alesha unpacks her computer and notebook before her brown eyes flick to mine. Those are some enviable eyelashes. What mascara does she use? "Well, you missed out on a wild night," she says. "Our attendings drink like fish. I beat Dr. Chen at beer pong."

I snort. "You're kidding!"

"Nope. Me and Julian. Have you met him yet?"

Managing to hold my smile despite gritted teeth, I shake my head. "No. Well, I mean, for a second I did. At the hospital."

So Julian was busy ingratiating himself to our attendings while I cried over false accusations. Awesome. Guess he couldn't have felt *too* bad for me. Any lingering guilt at my rudeness toward him disappears. I *knew* my dislike of him was on point.

Until this moment, I couldn't decide if I was more embarrassed that I chose him to blow up on at the residency mixer or irritated that he called me out on it. Now I know. I'm grade A irritated.

Regardless, if our antagonism at the hospital earlier this week is any indication, he's pretty peeved at me, too. We've established ourselves as adversaries. Joy.

Alesha whistles. "Boy's got game."

"I lost in the first round." Raven leans toward me and laughs. "And I even played with water."

A couple of older residents enter the room.

Alesha glances at them, then lowers her voice. "Let's go on an intern date this week, okay?"

Raven and I nod.

A brunette resident sits next to me—I think she's a third-year—complaining about a recent patient encounter. "Arguing about the Tdap shot again." She adopts a whiny voice. "'I don't want to put anything in my body. Would you do it if you were pregnant?'" The resident sighs heavily and rubs her forehead. "Do I think this vaccine is safe? Yes. Have I gotten it myself? Also yes." She holds up a finger. "But my body is not a temple. I do questionable things with it. I put questionable things into it. Don't go by me, bitch!"

The resident settling beside her chuckles. "My body is basically a fast-food drive-thru and a twenty-four-hour liquor store rolled into one. With a heavy dose of caffeine."

Brunette throws her head back. "Get whooping cough, lady. I don't care. I'm too busy worrying about this girl in the room next to yours who's tweaked out on meth."

I can't stifle my laugh and both girls glance at us, wide-eyed.

"Oh. Hi. Interns." Brunette pastes on a smile. "Sorry. Don't listen to me. I promise I'm not always this salty. I'm Mila."

I shake her hand. "Grace."

She makes no indication that my identity means anything, but her friend's gaze sharpens on me and she waves. "I'm Ling."

Raven and Alesha also introduce themselves as the room fills. I duck beneath the table to grab my computer from my bag. When I pop my head up, Julian is settling in the chair across from me. Cataclysmically dark eyes meet mine as I sit to my full height.

My hackles rise.

His hand is curled around a travel coffee mug, one long finger tapping. "Good morning, Sapphire."

Every muscle in my body goes rigid, and I struggle to keep the glare from surfacing. His stupid mouth lifts on one side— a knowing smirk hidden behind a sip of coffee. He plays the part of a polite colleague while burying tiny thorns under my skin on the sly.

All right. Throw down your gauntlet, Julian. I'm ready.

I toss out my prettiest fake smile. "I go by Grace, remember?"

The starless void of his eyes sparks once, then goes dark. "Right. I keep forgetting."

"It must be so hard to remember, what with all the gossiping you've been doing."

His eyes narrow, mouth tensing.

Alesha glances between us, skeptical brows scrunched. "I thought you said—you guys definitely seem like you've met."

I blink. "Oh, um—"

"Good morning, Alesha. Raven." Julian gives them a smile that actually touches his eyes.

Alesha leans across the table toward him. "Ready for round two this weekend?"

He chuckles. "Only if you bring your A game."

What the hell is this? He's nice to everyone else!

"Okay, let's get started." Dr. Ryan, our youngest attending, takes a seat at the head of table and sorts through some papers. "We'll start with the process of normal labor..."

Settling in to take notes, I open a blank document and start typing. After his lecture, Dr. Ryan turns to the interns, pelting us with questions. It's not a free-for-all. He addresses each of us in turn, prodding deeper into our knowledge until the answers become mysteries.

Alesha handles herself best, managing to cite the physiologic changes of the cardiovascular system in pregnancy with an impressive and almost scary level of accuracy. We stare at her, wide-eyed.

She lifts her shoulder like it ain't no thing. "I have a good memory."

To my utter delight, Julian stumbles over his answers after I shine with mine.

Ha! Justice!

When the onslaught is over, we lock eyes, and I raise one eyebrow, unable to contain the smirk.

He cocks his head, unsmiling. "You proud of yourself over there?"

People rise for bathroom breaks and coffee refills, but Julian and I stay glued to our chairs, locked in a staring contest.

"I am." I give him an innocent smile. "Are you?"

"What is *that*?" He points at my mouth. "You think that smile's fooling anyone?"

"Whatever could you mean?" I feign a confused look. "I'm merely smiling at my coworker."

A dark rumble that can hardly be called laughter emerges from his throat, connecting directly to receptors in my skin. Pinpricks wake, almost painful in their recognition of him, like my autonomic nervous system understands something I don't.

Danger! Run away!

His finger taps against his coffee mug, gaze burning into mine. "You're gonna be a problem, aren't you?"

"Don't think you can handle it?"

His face subtly resculpts itself, forming a challenging smile detectable only in his eyes. "I think you've underestimated me." He pauses to sip his coffee. "*Sapphire.*"

Sunday night, Alesha invites me to Mi Cocina, a popular Mexican restaurant with the best drinks on the planet. I slide into the circle booth beside her. She's dressed in a multicolored flowy dress, very Boho chic. My shorts and racerback are out of place next to her.

"This is a huge booth for just the two of us," I say.

She snorts. "Oh, no. I invited all the interns. I'm dubbing this our first Group Therapy session. Probably the first of many."

Raven slides in beside Alesha, eyes ringed dark. "So tired, but need chips and guac."

"How was your first twenty-four?" I reach for a tortilla chip.

"Awesome. Exhausting." She perks up. "But I did my first C-section!"

My pulse flutters. "Really? Tell me about it."

"Nuh-uh." Sitting between us, Alesha waves her fingers

in front of our chests. "You can explain that later. I need to know what's going on with you and Julian before him and Kai get here. I told them to meet us in—" she checks her phone "—fifteen minutes."

I feign a laugh. "Wh-what do you mean?"

She levels a stare at me.

Um. So what do I do here? It's not exactly classy to throw shade at a new coworker. I don't want to be seen as a gossip. During my indecision, the server approaches to ask for our drink orders. Alesha and I order Mambo Taxis. Raven asks for water and a side of guacamole.

"Fourteen minutes," Alesha says, tapping pointedly on the polished table in front of me.

"Fine!" I scratch at a dent in the wood and take six of her valuable minutes to explain the apparent rumor as well as my first—and second—encounter with Julian Santini.

Our drinks arrive in the meantime, and Alesha takes a sip of hers before holding out a hand to stop me. "Wait a sec. They said *you* specifically got into the program by sleeping with someone? Or just *someone* got their spot, and they assumed it was you?"

"Does it matter?" I sip my drink. The limey-sangria goodness warms my spirits. "They all assume it's me, so—"

"Yeah. That sucks, girl. I'm sorry." Alesha rubs my shoulder.

Raven nods. "That's unfair, but it'll blow over. All rumors do."

I smile. "Thanks for not asking if it's true. It isn't, in case you were wondering."

"Of course it isn't," Alesha says. "That would never get through GME."

"I never doubted it," Raven says around a mouthful of chips and guac.

My smile widens. "Anyway, that's why I don't like Julian."

Both women stay silent, averting their stares to their plates.

I narrow my eyes at them. "What?"

Alesha swallows. "Well, you *did* call him a misogynist when he was only trying to help. I mean, you know how he got in, right?"

I shrug, ignoring the judgmental voice that whispers he must have done something mind-blowing for a DO to get in this program.

"He coauthored several papers on disparities in women's health care. One was published in a national journal."

My mouth falls open. Hang on. Am I going to have to repeal everything I assumed about this guy? Being wrong isn't really in my top-five favorite things.

"How do you know that?" I ask.

She shrugs. "Word gets around, you know?"

I cover my squirmy discomfiture with a snort. "Well, if he's not a misogynist, he's still a douche."

Alesha grins wide, then laughs. "This is going to be fun, huh?"

A minute later, the booth jostles.

Julian scoots in beside me. "You think you can tolerate my proximity? Or should I sit at another table?"

I meet his dark eyes. "If I said yes, would you move?"

"Eh. And let you win?"

My arms cross of their own volition. "I can deal with you, if you can deal with me."

He shoots a longing glance at the door, but sighs when Kai sits beside him, effectively trapping him beside me.

"I guess we're doing this," he says.

I scoot away from him. "Just don't touch me. You have knobby-looking elbows."

He raises an eyebrow. "Now who's judging based on appearance, Sapphire?"

Would it be rude to slap him? "It's Grace."

"Oh, yeah," he deadpans. "I forgot."

The three others at our table exchange looks, but Alesha laughs in silence. "Oh yeah. This is going to be a fun year."

AUGUST, YEAR 1

Butterflies smother me the night before my first day of L&D in August.

Julian has regaled us of the thrilling adventures he experienced last month and my jealousy has been...well, a little difficult to tolerate. The guy's a show-off, and I'm ready for my turn. His first shift started with a crash section and he *primaried* it.

Mine tomorrow begins with a scheduled one—nice and controlled. Perfect for me.

Alesha is starting on L&D at our other hospital, so we quiz each other over FaceTime on surgical steps and fetal heart tones.

I take a breath. "We're going to be fine."

"Yeah. For sure, girl. We got this." Alesha's screen goes blurry as she checks a text, then she laughs.

"What?"

"The dorky boy sent me a gif of one of those *Star Wars* dudes wishing me luck tomorrow."

My face contorts into a scowl despite my efforts to remain neutral. "Julian?"

Alesha's face pops into view. "He's actually really nice, Gracey-poo."

I tap into my messaging app. No new messages. He's a petty man, our Julian.

At 7:00 a.m., I slather on the surgical antiseptic and head into the OR, gowning after my attending and senior resident, Aislin Hegar. One step toward the OR table and my attending, Dr. Levine, directs me to the first assistant spot.

I pause. "Oh, I thought—"

Gowned and gloved and masked, blue eyes barely visible

behind a plastic shield, Dr. Levine raises an eyebrow. "You thought what?"

"Nothing, sir." I dutifully move to the opposite side of the table and stew in jealousy over each cut made by my senior.

Dr. Levine points out all the steps as Aislin makes them. It takes everything in me not to snap, "I know!"

Afterward, I put in orders and dictate the operative note of the surgery I didn't perform while fighting a nagging twitch of anxiety. Is this about the rumor? Is he punishing me?

Aislin, bubbly and bright, grins. "You'll be ready for the next one now."

"Yeah, definitely."

But I don't get to do the next one, either. Or the one after that.

Several days pass before I reach the conclusion that my attendings don't trust me. They hold my hand through every procedure, quick to take over if I make the slightest wrong move.

On Friday of my first week, I sit through a lecture from Dr. Chen about how Pitocin—the drug we use to induce labor, prevent postpartum hemorrhages and generally survive on L&D—is the most dangerous drug we use. He orders Aislin to teach me all the Pit protocols.

"Do they always hover this much?" I ask her when he leaves.

She nods. "It's only because it's your first week, and they can tell you're nervous. Don't worry about it. They'll ease up. Now, come here so I can show you the Pit doses."

During a rare slow moment, I pull out my phone, opening the group message with my fellow interns, dubbed Pit It or Quit It.

Me: I need my people. Anyone free tonight for a rant session?

Alesha: Yesssss Group Therapy!

Raven: Oh that sounds fun. I'm in.

Kai: Hellz ya. Mico? Mambo Taxis?

Me: !!!!

Several minutes pass before my phone buzzes again.

Alesha: Julian??? wru

Julian: Do I have to? ICU rotation is sucking the life from my soul. I need sleep.

Alesha: Yes. You have to.

Julian: Fine. But you aren't getting charming Julian.

Staring at my phone, I snort so loud that Aislin asks me if something is wrong.

In my world, Julian Santini doesn't have a charming side. He's so un-charming that my ovaries cross themselves from fear whenever he's close, despite his tingle-inducing stare and touchable jawline.

He's proof that vile things can wrap themselves in glitzy, distracting packages.

I've begrudgingly accepted him as part of my friend group, but he isn't my *friend*. He's an unavoidable evil that exists in the background of my life. Like elevator music.

I'd rather Julian didn't show at dinner tonight—especially if he's grumpy—but even if he does, no version of him can be worse than what I've already experienced.

At lunch, I sit with Aislin and one of her best friends—an internal med resident. She's the chief on ICU, so we're surrounded by residents from her department, most of whom I've never met.

I keep to myself as they chat, but a voice behind me makes my neck twitch. That elevator music grows a bit louder.

"It's really not a problem, Rebecca," Julian says. "I'm happy to help."

He and a blond girl approach our table, both in navy scrubs and white coats. His smile is friendly and bright.

She melts as she stares at him. "But they were so heavy. Seriously, Julian. Thank you."

"What'd he do?" Aislin mumbles around a mouthful of apple—the only edible option in the hospital cafeteria today.

"Oh, he helped me take all those copies of *Harrison's* to the clinic." Blondie beams at Julian. "All thirty of them."

Aislin laughs. "Aren't those books like fifteen pounds each?"

My blood slowly turns to battery acid, and I'm sure I'm shooting daggers his way. This is the worst part of hating him—everyone else loves him. To others, he's polite and pleasant. Hard worker. Never complains. Kind.

Almost makes me wish we didn't start on the wrong foot. *Almost.* Not quite, though. I've seen his dark side.

Aislin gives him a teasing punch on the arm. "Such a gentleman, Dr. Santini."

Julian's gaze touches on me, but skirts right past. "I try."

"Not that hard," I mutter with a snort.

He doesn't hear me. Or maybe he ignores me. Who cares?

When he leaves, Rebecca flutters. "Isn't he so nice?" She sighs, already half in love.

I swallow down the taste of vomit in my mouth to smile like I agree.

She perks up. "Do you have his number?"

A gleeful witch inside cackles as I give it to her, casually mentioning that he's really into texting all day to chitchat. And cat memes.

End of shift rolls around, and I shuffle to the call room to sign the patients out to the second-year resident, Lexie Zavanelli. Aislin gives me a "Good work today" before she leaves, and I take my time gathering my materials. Our call room is cluttered with books and surgical instruments, but it boasts a full-size bed previous residents stole from the neonatologist's call room when they closed the NICU a few years ago. Lexie curls up in it as I shove papers into my backpack.

"I hope I get some sleep tonight," she says.

"Nothing's active. The odds are in your favor."

"Yeah. I'm not looking forward to busy nights at Vincent."

Our training is divided between two hospitals. Lower acuity cases are here at Texas University Medical Center. High-risk cases go to St. Vincent, a regional trauma center on the other side of town, where Alesha's currently stationed.

I zip my backpack with fervor, giving an aggressive jiggle as it catches on papers inside.

Lexie sits up. "Something wrong?"

The desk's rolling chair swivels when I collapse into it. With the heels of my palms pressed into my eyes, sparks burst into my vision. "I feel like they aren't letting me do anything, and Julian had all these stories of all the amazing things he did last month. I'm just—I'm worried I've done something that makes them think they need to watch me. Like I'm unsafe."

"Well, you *are* unsafe." Lexie smiles. "Think about it. If they told you to run it all on your own, would you be able to do it? They're good doctors, and they're trying to make you one, too. Soak up everything and if they take the time to teach you something, savor it."

At her friendly gaze, a sliver of doubt breaks away and dissolves. "Thanks. That helps."

In the parking lot of the restaurant, I scrutinize my appearance and groan at the dried blood on my scrub pants from my deliveries earlier. If blood was a statement piece, I'd be so on brand this week. I haven't made it home with clean scrubs once.

At the hostess stand, the universe plays its usual tricks and I run into Julian, his navy ICU scrubs without a speck of bodily fluid anywhere.

Like he's handing out favors, he gives me the fake smile. I really hate that smile. His real smile is subtle. Refined. This fraudulent counterpart makes me roll my eyes. His dark hair is flawlessly messy, and I want to part it down the middle and stick a pair of Dwight Schrute glasses on him.

"Hello, Sapphire."

I take a cleansing breath. "You *know* it's Grace."

His brow creases, deceptive and false. "But Sapphire's your name, isn't it?"

"Not the name I go by." I glare at him.

"Hmm. I guess I forgot."

"Do you have dementia, Julian? Anterograde amnesia? Or is it just a lack of intelligence?"

His dark eyes meet mine, capturing me the way they always do, and a pulse wakes in my temples. He doesn't blink, and the various shades of brown in his irises wink in and out of existence. "It's that last one. Didn't you hear I was the DO pity hire?"

My attention drops to the badge at his chest, the one he's forgotten to remove.

Julian Santini, DO.

Few DOs make it into the residencies at TUMC. Vague speculations about him and the two DOs in other programs emerged in the beginning, but his universal likability—to everyone but me—outweighed any hearsay early on.

Lucky him.

It isn't that DOs are inherently worse. They're just... I don't want to say "less smart," but—

Maybe my biases are showing. I refused to even apply to osteopathic schools. Their reputation as inferior was enough to steer me away.

But in the end, Julian had the same training as me. The letters after his name don't really matter.

As I stare at those letters, he rips the badge off his chest, and his lightly stubbled jaw clenches. Hmm. *What happened to you today?*

Wait. Is that *empathy* blossoming in my chest? For Lucifer himself? No, no, no.

My fingers itch to shove him just to right the balance.

The hostess jerks me from that thought. "Er—two of you tonight?"

"No!" I step away from Julian. "There's five of us."

"Oh." The hostess points toward the patio. "I think the others might be out there."

We head that way, and I hold out my backpack. "You don't want to carry my books for me?"

He shakes his head. "You appear to be managing fine on your own."

"Oh, but I need a big strong man to help me…"

Snorting, he holds the door to the patio open for me. "You'd eat me alive if I tried." As I brush past him, he adds, "Like a black widow."

Nose in the air, I march toward our friends. "False. I am a beautiful and peaceful butterfly."

His flat disbelieving stare nearly yanks out a laugh when we reach the table, but I manage to hold it in.

"Sorry I'm late." Julian seats himself. "Sapphire made a scene at the hostess stand."

Outrage swells as I settle across from him. "I did not! You—" I take a cleansing breath. "You know what? Not today, Julian."

Alesha laughs. Kai gives me a side hug. I can barely pay attention to them.

Does Julian take *pleasure* in driving me mad?

The lift at the corner of his mouth does something weird to my insides. I'm choosing to interpret it as wrath. Or—offense? Whatever it is, it's very…warm.

He pulls out his phone and grimaces.

An evil grin spreads over my face. "Someone bothering you, Julian?"

His head jerks up, sudden understanding painted over his expression. "Did you give her my number?"

The giggle is too hard to suppress. I'm Ursula cackling at Ariel's stupidity. Bellatrix Lestrange celebrating Sirius Black's death.

He bristles. "You are—"

"A genius?"

He scowls. "The worst."

The others sit quiet, stares ping-ponging between us.

"Just block her number, if you hate it so much." I shrug.

His lips part, and he shakes his head. "That is unbelievably rude."

"Rude? Since when do you care about being rude? You—"

Alesha pats the table. "Now, children. Let's get along tonight. Eat some queso." She leans back in her chair to catch the server's attention, lifting her Mambo Taxi and holding up three fingers.

A genuine smile flashes on Julian's face. "Did you just buy me a drink?"

Why don't I ever get smiles like that?

Because he hates you.

Oh yeah...

I don't want his smiles, anyway.

"Who said I'm buying?" Alesha laughs at her own joke.

I turn to Raven and Kai, forcing myself to focus on something else. This stupid guy has hijacked my thoughts tonight, and I want them back. "What are you guys on again?" I ask.

"Clinic," says Raven.

"Ah." I gesture toward her slacks and blouse. "Explains the clothes."

"I'm suffering with internal medicine." Kai sucks down one

drink and starts on his next. "Do you have any idea how much I hate hyponatremia? Rounds took *five hours* today."

I groan.

"So, what did you need Group Therapy for?" Raven asks.

Before I can answer, the server sets a fresh Mambo Taxi before me, and I bounce in my seat. "Heaven!" I face Raven after taking a large gulp. "I'm sort of getting tired of the handholding. I want them to trust me."

"You strike me as a girl who likes a little handholding." Julian shoots a scathing glance my way.

Under the table where no one can see, I flip him off with both hands. "I wouldn't expect you to understand. Your month was awesome, and they let you do it all."

"Right. A misogynist like me could *never* understand."

My eyes narrow. "God, you're never going to let that go, are you? I only meant that it sounded like you got your hands dirty on day one, and they still haven't even let me hold a scalpel."

His scorching expression disappears. "Wait. They haven't let you primary?"

I shake my head.

Brow wrinkled, he takes a sip of his drink. "That's weird. I wonder why."

Kai breaks the tension by leaning toward the middle of the table. "Do you think that server over there is single?"

Julian turns his attention to the chips in the middle of the table, scooping a liberal amount of queso. "Don't bother. He's been staring at Sapphire since she sat down."

Kai slumps. "Of course."

"It's *Grace*," I say under my breath, but I sneak a peek at the man in question. Damn, he has nice eyes. And arms.

The idea of him blooms through my brain, and I take it to its logical conclusion. He'd want sex, and I'd clam up.

It's like fucking an ice queen.

The words haunt me. They probably wouldn't still hurt so

much if I hadn't been foolishly in love with Matt when he said them.

I jerk my gaze from the server. Not worth it.

"See something you like, Grace?" Alesha asks, wiggling her eyebrows.

Kai sighs. "I do."

I pat his arm. "You're free to take your shot. I'll be your wingwoman."

His stoic face breaks into a smile. "You're good people, Gracey."

The evening progresses without incident from there, and Julian stops antagonizing me. The dinner is exactly what I needed—to de-stress with my squad. Nothing has changed at work, but just knowing I have these people beside me in the trenches is enough to perk me up.

After food, I stretch. "Time to go?"

"Yeah." Alesha lets out a yawn. "Vincent is kicking my ass."

I'd almost forgotten Alesha was on L&D at the other hospital. "Do they let you primary over there?"

She drops her gaze, messing with her purse. "Um. Yeah. It's not a big deal, though."

My shoulders fall. *Yes, it is.*

Is it the rumors? How worried should I be about this?

Kai hangs back as we head toward the parking lot, making eyes at the server, who eyes him right back. Guess it wasn't me he was staring at...

Alesha kisses Kai's cheek as she passes. "If you screw that guy and it goes south, we will still be eating here on the reg. Just so you know."

He gives a distracted, "Yeah, okay," and goes in for the kill.

In the parking lot, Raven hugs me goodbye. "Cheer up, love. It'll all turn out fine."

I nod and slip into my car, cranking the volume. Singing is unadulterated stress relief, so I scroll through my phone and decide on my Epic Trailer Version playlist. I'm in the mood for some drama.

A mile down the road, I spy Julian's truck behind me in the rearview mirror. What's he doing? Is he…following me?

No. Surely not.

But I hop on the highway and exit with him still behind me. What is happening right now? When I turn into my apartment complex, and he follows, a confused tangle of emotions settles in my chest, part exasperation, part exhilaration.

His black monstrosity of a truck pulls in beside me.

Frazzled, I gather my things and slam my car door, stomping to the front of his truck. "Why are you following me?"

He shuts his door with more reasonable force. It beeps as it locks. "What are you talking about? I thought you were following me."

With a scoff, I point at his truck. "You were *behind* me, Julian."

"You sure?"

I grind my teeth. Audibly.

He flashes a smile at the ground and thumps his fist on his truck. "I wasn't following you. I live here."

"No. I live here."

He glances over the entirety of the property around us, his face in eerie shadows cast by the streetlight overhead. "It's an apartment complex. I think more than one person lives here."

He can't be serious. "You've lived here the whole time?" I ask.

He chews his gum, head cocked, scrutinizing me. "Yes, *Sapphire*. I've lived here for weeks."

I gasp. "Does that mean it's cursed?"

"I *definitely* cursed it."

"I should probably move." I spin and stride toward the stairs. But seriously. I can't live in the same complex as him. What the heck?

"Would make my life more pleasant," he mutters.

His footsteps follow me up the first flight, a not-unpleasant heat slipping down my spine as I imagine him inspecting my body.

"Did you know you have blood on your scrubs?" he asks.

I lurch to a stop at the landing, and he crashes into me. It knocks me forward into the handrail. He grabs it for balance, his other hand encircling my upper arm to steady me. For two full seconds, the length of his lean body presses against my back, and I learn the thin cotton of scrubs does nothing to hide the hardness of muscles or the heat of skin.

He isn't large or brawny. I expected him to be a little soft, far less intimidating than the angular strength now tattooed into my memory.

He wrenches away. "I'm sorry. Are you okay?"

I turn, flushed from head to toe. "Yeah. Sorry."

"It's fine." He clears his throat. "What floor are you?"

I point toward my apartment. "Second."

He nods for me to precede him up the stairs. I hesitate at the landing, but he continues. "I'm on the third. Goodnight, Sapphire."

He climbs the steps without hurry, at ease and straight-backed.

"It's Grace!" I call.

"Right." He doesn't look at me. "I'll remember next time."

Julian

NOVEMBER, YEAR 1

Hiding in a doctor's dictation area, I hold the phone tight to my ear. "Yes, Mom. My flight is on Tuesday."

"Julian, if you miss Thanksgiving, I swear—"

"I bought the ticket. I'll be home."

"It's bad enough you're missing Christmas. Who works on Christmas?"

I sigh. "Babies don't care about holidays, Mom."

Her tone chastises. "Your sisters have been looking forward to seeing you. They say you never text."

"I work ninety hours a week."

She snorts into the phone. "It takes seven seconds to send a text, son."

"Mom, I have to go. I'm supposed to be working."

"Don't you dare miss that flight, Julian!"

"Goodbye."

"Julian—"

I hang up and press my hand over my eyes, trying to find patience. Ever since Dad died when I was two, she's focused solely on her children. As the baby, my new distance chafes at her overbearing maternal instincts.

My sisters understand, but Mom doesn't recognize how hard I worked to get here—never mind that I chose this path because of her life-threatening hemorrhage when I was fifteen. We almost lost her. I'd never been so scared in my life.

Teenage Julian was kind of a mama's boy.

I frown. I'm still a mama's boy, aren't I?

God. I'll never escape it.

My gaze drops to my phone.

Me: Mom is guilt tripping me again.

Tori: You probably deserve it, BB

That fucking nickname. They started with *baby*. Then *bebe*. And now just *BB*.

Tori: Oh, she texted me about it.

She sends me a screenshot of her message chain with Mom, wherein my mother has serial-texted my crimes.

Ma: Julian hung up on me

Ma: I don't think he's coming for thanksgiving

Ma: I might as well sell his furniture

Ma: Victoria are you there?

Ma: Your brother has abandoned us

Ma: Will you bring eggs when you come later?

Ma: Do you think he has a girlfriend?

Tori: Yes, I'll bring eggs.

Ma: We should invite his girlfriend

Suppressing my groan, I shove my phone in my white coat pocket. My mother does the typical passive-aggressive thing when she thinks I've mistreated her. I get the silent treatment, which is somehow both a relief and a guilt-inducing nightmare.

I'll have to call her later.

My phone buzzes again and I ignore the text from Rebecca, the internal med resident Grace sicced on me a couple months ago. Rebecca is tenacious as hell and wearing me down. I'm going to end up on an unwanted date with her soon, all thanks to Grace Rose.

One day, I'll find some terrible form of payback for this.

Spying a small cactus with a spiky red flower propped in the window, I snap a quick picture and send it to Grace, captioned, "Found this. Made me think of you."

Prickly and red. Describes Grace Rose perfectly.

My senior resident, Sarabeth Steiner—a short, round, pleasant woman—pokes her head into the dictation room. "Hey, Santini, you done on the phone?"

"Yeah."

"Let's get lunch." She straightens her glasses and motions me to follow.

Together in the resident lounge, we grimace at the lunch offering.

"I hate fish Friday," she says.

I nod. "I'm making a sandwich."

The room isn't large, and round tables with mismatched chairs take up most of the space. At the deli station, I bump into Alesha.

"What's up, Santini?" A big grin shows off her straight teeth as she tucks a few blue strands behind her ear.

I nod toward them. "New hair?"

She shoots me a *look*. "As if I'd keep the same hair for long."

My laugh dies in my throat when a shiver chases all the way down my spine. How does my body know? It's like a sixth sense. A superpower.

I could have gotten super strength or precognition, but no. I got Grace Radar.

I turn as she rounds the corner, staring at a bottle in her hand. "Alesha, they only had chocolate. Is that—" She looks over, and our eyes lock.

Heat tugs deep in my chest.

I offer my bland smile. "Hello, Sapphire."

She's done something to her face. Darkened her eyelashes or something. It's...pretty. The harsh fluorescent lighting does nothing to dampen the effect. Those big hazel eyes—more green than brown today—blink three times before she says, "It's *Grace.*"

"Right." I tap my temple as the joyous imp who lives for her consternation dances inside. "I keep forgetting."

Her eyes narrow. "How's Rebecca?"

"I've been meaning to thank you," I say, teeth clenched. "She's great in bed."

"That's funny. She didn't say the same about you." She hands Alesha the bottle. "Hope chocolate is okay. I have to get back upstairs."

Alesha waves. "See ya, boo bear."

I track Grace's progress as she weaves through tables toward the door, her wavy hair spilling down the length of her back. The teasing whiff of that hair I'd gotten the night I bumped into her drifts through my mind. Effing toxic, she is. Her pheromones have imprinted on my subconscious.

Little does it know that attractive scent belongs to a harpy.

Once the door closes behind her, I face Alesha, who watches me through squinted eyes. A sly grin stretches her full lips. "You didn't really go out with that girl, did you?"

"No. That woman makes me want to claw my eyes out."

She grins. "Which one?"

"Take your pick."

"Poor Juju. He's so mistreated." She leans closer. "You know Grace is awesome, right? If you'd stop arguing—"

I jerk a hand up. "I don't argue. *She* argues."

"You provoke."

Right then, my phone buzzes. Grace has sent a picture of a festering abscess, captioned, "Found this. Made me think of you."

Ha. Clever girl.

Sarabeth meanders toward the deli station. "Was that Grace? What rotation is she on again?"

"ICU," Alesha says. "They're keeping her busy."

"Oh yeah. I heard." Sarabeth clicks the tongs as she decides on a meat.

Alesha and I exchange glances. She leans closer. "Heard what?"

Sarabeth shrugs. "That people have been hard on her. On account of how she got in and how she sleeps around."

Alesha's face hardens. "She doesn't sleep around."

"Oh," Sarabeth says, pausing.

"None of that's true," Alesha says. "It's all lies."

"That's unfortunate." Sarabeth throws some cheese on her sandwich. "But don't they say there's a grain of truth in every rumor?"

Woof. The frown on Alesha's face is legendary. "Well, *they* are idiots," she says.

I take my sandwich and follow Sarabeth to a table. "Is this why the attendings are hard on her?"

"Oh no. I think that's just because she's not very good."

Alesha bristles in the seat next to me. "What do you mean, she's not good? She's brilliant."

"Yeah, but it doesn't translate to practical knowledge," Sarabeth says around a mouthful of sandwich. "Knowing the answer in didactics doesn't do any good if you can't apply that answer to real life. She has a lot of work before she's ready for second year. They may hold her back."

Wait, what? I don't like Grace, but even I'm offended on her behalf. On behalf of interns everywhere. "That's not fair. She's not doing worse than any of us. We just started. We can't be perfect."

Sarabeth holds her palms out. "Hey, I've never worked with her. This is just what I've heard."

Alesha stabs at her food. "I can't believe they're being hard on her because of rumors that aren't true."

"Should we...do something?" I mutter in her direction, taking a bite of my turkey sandwich despite the sudden knot in my stomach.

Alesha shoves her plate away. "What are we supposed to do? I already tell people it isn't true whenever it comes up. Don't you?"

I nod, though the last time I did, the radiology resident who said it snorted and asked if I fucked her, too. If we hadn't been in a room full of attendings, I probably would have punched the guy.

I still might, if I get the chance.

"It'll die down eventually," Sarabeth says. "There's always rumors in the hospital."

"And then she said it was the best presentation on acute hypoxic respiratory failure she'd ever heard," Rebecca says with a coy smile. "Can you believe that? I barely know anything about it."

She takes a sip of her peach Bellini while I try to keep my

second-hand embarrassment off my face. Humble bragging makes my skin crawl. Can she not see the self-flattery she's oozing all over the breadsticks between us?

How did we wind up at this restaurant?

Oh right...

She asked until I ran out of excuses to say no.

The girl is persistent, I'll give her that.

I fidget with my napkin. It's become a damp twisted knot in my lap. "I'm sure you know more than you think."

She giggles. "I, like, *barely* understand it."

It's no secret that Rebecca is one of the brightest residents of her class. Is she playing dumb for my benefit? Because I'm the idiot DO who scarcely comprehends English, let alone respiratory failure.

Or maybe she thinks I'm one of those men who isn't attracted to women when they're smarter than me.

She's wrong on both accounts.

"I bet you understand it better than that guy." I point at a random man across the restaurant.

She laughs like it's the funniest joke in the world, drawing the attention of several people in this loud crowded room. "You're hilarious."

I'm not. I'm really, really not.

I gulp my Peroni and smear a finger through a puddle of water on the red-and-white-checkered tablecloth. Where the fuck is the pizza? It can't take this long to make a pizza. Dough, sauce, cheese, bake. Do they need help? I will help them.

"Anyway," she says in my silence, "Dr. Sharma asked me to give the lecture again to the med students. So weird."

"Yeah. Weird." It's not weird. This is what residents do. We teach med students.

"Should I tell her yes, do you think?"

"Uh." I blink a few times. "Do you...get a choice? Sharma's your program director, right?"

She gives a dismissive shrug, a move at odds with her smug smile. "I'm her favorite. She'll do whatever I want."

Weird flex, but okay. We're back to humble bragging, and I search for the server, taking a cleansing breath of garlic-scented air. *Please, God of Pizza, bless us soon.*

When my gaze lands on her again, she's staring at me. Her shiny blond hair lays in straight layers over bare shoulders, and her pale blue dress shows off her chest. Her brown eyes would be lovely if they weren't so penetrating.

She's pretty. Beautiful.

But so unattractive.

Why can't I be attracted?

She wants me to be. She's throwing signals at me like confetti.

"I—" My voice comes out croaky and I clear it. "I'd do it, if it were me."

"Yeah, I probably will." She takes another sip and leans on the table. The uncontrollable urge to appreciate the presented goods has my attention dipping...sinking...

Don't look!

It happens, anyway.

I'm a straight man.

I can't *not* look.

It's written in my DNA.

And yet—

Nothing. I got nothing. Why doesn't she do it for me?

"So do you have a cat?" she asks.

That's why.

"Uh—" My mind stutters. Why does she think I'm obsessed with cats? I suspect the answer has something to do with Grace Rose. "No. I don't, actually."

A pizza lands between us, giving me an excuse to not flounder under her stare for an extended period. She picks at her slice, giving me her entire life story while I nod and shove food in my mouth. The woman can talk.

And talk.

If she notices I haven't spoken in ten minutes, she doesn't let on, but it's better this way. She's happy. Look at her in the zone, summing up her family (one sister and parents still together), her friends (all doctors) and her life's goal ("I want to be a car-diologist. Romantic, right? Working with hearts?" *Chuckle, chuckle*) while I polish off half the pie.

She doesn't ask about me. I'm not sure what to think about that. Not sure if I care.

It's only when we're in my truck that she changes tack. "So what do you do for fun?"

I laugh. "What's fun? All I do is work."

"Oh come on." She playfully shoves my shoulder. "I'm sure there's something."

"I guess I have this Friendsgiving thing planned with my class this weekend. That should be fun."

She gasps, and I frantically search for whatever scared her, only to sigh when she says, "Oh, that sounds awesome! I'd love to come."

Uh.

Backpeddle!

"Oh, I think—it's just—an OB thing, you know? For the five of us, I mean."

Her shoulders sag.

Hold firm. Don't tell her you'll hang another time. Don't!

"I wish my class did stuff like that," she says.

"A little harder when there are thirteen of you."

She hums. "That's true."

I pull up to the curb by her house and slide out of my truck. She lets me open her door for her—something I always fret will be taken the wrong way.

Is it anti-feminist? I no longer know.

I half expect her to screech *"I can open my own door, Julian!"* but she only smiles and accepts my help to the ground.

On the porch, she unlocks and cracks the door before turning to me with a *look*.

Oh god...

"Do you—"

"Well, have a good night," I say in my brightest tone.

She searches my face. "I will. You—you, too."

She steps into me at the same time I raise an arm to shake her hand. My arm jerks back when my fingers connect with her stomach.

"No, it's fine," she says and enters my personal space.

This is so weird.

How do I tell her no without hurting her feelings?

She did nothing wrong. I'm simply an idiot.

She tips her face to kiss me. Four awkward seconds pass before my lips land on the corner of her mouth and my entire being cringes.

This isn't right.

She isn't right.

How I know this, I'm really not sure, but it's *visceral*.

I have no idea what I want, but the fact is incontrovertible—

I don't want this.

Later that night, I'm dozing on my couch with the game on mute when a frantic knock jolts me awake, splashing my hands with the beer I'd fallen asleep holding.

"Damn it."

The knock grows louder. "Julian!"

I pause on my way to the kitchen for a towel. *Grace?*

"Julian, I know you're in there. I see your truck in the parking lot."

I sigh. Definitely Grace. Could this night get worse? "Hold up, all right?"

Taking my time to wash and dry my hands, I bask in the impatience pouring in from the other side of the door. She's probably tapping her judgy little foot.

I swing the door open, letting in a gust of cold November air. "Yes?"

Her unholy amounts of hair are knotted at her crown, but escaped tendrils stick to her sweaty face. A smudge of white powder mars one cheek, and she's wearing a stained apron that says Kiss the Cook. My gaze darts at once to the freckle on her lip before landing on her eyes.

A frantic gleam sparkles there, and she looks…deranged. Her face lights up—the first happy smile she's ever directed at me. "Thank god. Do you have any sugar?"

"Um. No."

The smile melts, and her body wilts. "No? What do you use for your coffee?"

"I drink it black."

"God!" She stomps her foot as a snarl gathers in her throat. "Could you be any more of a Death Eater?"

I lean against the doorjamb. "I bet I could if I tried. You're more unpleasant than normal. Why do you need sugar?"

"For the cupcakes, Julian. Hello? Friendsgiving is tomorrow. You're supposed to bring something, too."

"I'm bringing beer."

The light returns to her expression. "Will you bring a good IPA?"

"I'm only bringing stouts. It's *Thanksgiving*." I say this last like she's an idiot for assuming anyone would want an IPA at such a sacred event, even though IPAs are the best and everybody knows it.

She glares and crosses her arms, squeezing her breasts together.

Ugh. Don't look, Julian. Why are you always looking?

That shirt-apron combo is low cut despite the forty-degree temperature. I bet her nipples are hard...

Stop!

What the hell is wrong with me?

"You're like an evil villain, Julian. Make sure you say 'hi' to Thanos for me at the next world-destruction planning sesh." She spins and heads toward the stairs, leaving me to stare at the flour powdering her ass.

"Oh, you'd definitely get blipped," I mutter under my breath, then groan because I know what I'm about to do.

Rubbing my face, I grab my keys. I need to pick up the beer, anyway. What's two extra minutes to grab sugar? At the grocery store, the temptation to buy only stouts pulls at my sense of justice, but I grab a case of my favorite IPA before heading to the register. I tell myself it's for me, but stuck deep in the contest of Who-Hates-Who-More?, I want to trip her up, do something nice to throw her off her game.

I set the bag of granulated sugar at her doorstep, snap a picture and walk away. Back in my apartment, I send it to her, captioned, "Found this. Made me think of you."

No one witnesses my diabolical smile as the tides shift in my favor.

Her reply is swift—a picture of a coffee cup shaped like Scar from *The Lion King.* "Found this. Made me think of you."

Alesha lives in a tiny bungalow about fifteen minutes from my apartment. In true Alesha fashion, she's styled it with colorful eclectic furniture and abstract art. In normal circumstances, the place reeks of patchouli, but as I step through the door, the scents of turkey and sage overpower it. Her two cats emerge from the darkness of the hallway to stare at me, eyes glowing.

Last to arrive, I make my way through the living room and enter a flurry of chaos. Alesha throws me a harried greeting as she bustles in the cramped kitchen, where every inch of granite has disappeared under dishes, spices and condiments. Raven and Kai are setting the dining table. Grace stands to the side, holding stacked Tupperware full of cupcakes.

I sneak around Alesha to set the beer in the fridge. "Can I help?"

She blows a blue strand of hair out of her face. "I don't even know."

Grace organizes the cupcakes on a small sideboard under a window.

I eye the perfectly swirled chocolate frosting. "I see you managed to find sugar."

She sticks her nose in the air. A secretive grin stretches those devil-red lips. "Yes, thanks to my neighbor upstairs. Have you met him? His name's Voldemort."

I chuckle despite myself. "No, but I recently ran into an evil witch all covered in flour who lives downstairs. Probably baking children into pies."

She chooses one of the cupcakes and swipes a finger through the icing, sucking it off with a pop. "Children, huh? Yum."

"Hey, Santini!"

I yank my gaze from Grace's mouth to find Alesha motioning for help with the turkey. The pan is unwieldy, but we get it settled on the stovetop.

"You made an actual turkey?"

She shoots me a smirk as she brandishes the carving knife. "It's Thanksgiving, Juju. Was I supposed to make fish?"

Raven wedges her head between us. "Oh, it smells heavenly. Can we eat now? I'm starving."

"Heard that," Kai calls from the dining room. "Let's eat before I have to be at the hospital. Shift starts in two hours, people. The vaginas won't heal themselves."

Grace meanders toward the table, nursing one of my IPAs. *I bought those for me*, I want to say. To see if she'll pout. If she'll argue. If she'll pour the beer down my throat until I'm drowning. What will it take to make her snap completely?

She gives me a subtle toast as she sits.

A festive centerpiece of fall-colored leaves and an excessive amount of glitter takes up most of the table, forcing us to set the side dishes at the periphery. The five of us squeeze into her four-person round table with barely enough room for our turkey-themed paper plates.

"Happy Friendsgiving!" Raven reaches for a dish.

Kai slaps her hand. "Heathen! We say what we're thankful for *before* we eat."

She wrings out her hand. "Jeez."

"I'm thankful I managed to get this food done before y'all got here." Alesha takes a swig of her beer, swiping a hand over her sweaty brow.

"And *I'm* thankful we managed to find a time when we're all off to celebrate," says Kai. "Even if I can't drink because I'm somehow the only one who works this weekend."

Raven taps her chin. "I'm just thankful to be here. Learning to be an OB. It's hard and sometimes I have to remind myself it's what I wanted, but it *is* what I wanted and I'm so lucky."

We all murmur our agreement, toasting each other.

Across from me, Grace sets her beer down and smiles, showing me her sparkling white teeth against those pretty red lips. Maybe her teeth are diamond-edged, the better to rip our throats out. Maybe her lipstick is blood from all the throat-ripping she does in her spare time.

Why am I always staring at her mouth? It's so annoying how pretty it is. It's even more annoying that she hates me for unfair reasons. I didn't do anything to her.

She takes a breath. "I'm thankful for you guys. Seriously, I don't know what I'd do without you as friends. I've—I've had a lot of trouble with social anxiety. You make it so much easier to deal with everything." Her hazel eyes sparkle from the candles in the room and when they finally land on me, a creeping foreboding wakes in my chest. She tilts her head, and her voice sharpens to a point. "Even *you*."

Oh, you lying little liar!

My pulse comes to life. "I'm thankful for Sapphire's continued hatred. Keeps my life interesting. At this point, I wouldn't know how to survive without it."

She scowls. "You'd probably die of ego overload, Golden Boy."

Her words brew a storm inside me that enlarges with each beat of my heart. "I'm golden? Why? Because I'm nice and people actually like me? Maybe you should try it sometime."

Color rises in her cheeks. "I *am* nice!"

I shrug. "Not to me."

Why is it so satisfying to get under her skin?

"God forbid someone on this planet doesn't like you, Julian."

"You guys!" Alesha waves hands at both of us. "Friendsgiving is not the time for this *thing* you do."

Grace's affront fairly sparks around her. "There's no *thing*. It's mutual loathing."

Kai gives a wide-eyed whistle, shifting his gaze to his plate. "Anyone else unsure whether they should be uncomfortable or turned on?"

Um. What the hell?

I'd say something to shut that down, but I refuse to look away from Grace, unwilling to let her win the staring contest. She mouths, *I don't like you*, at me. I don't react, glaring at the shimmer in that hazel without blinking. The lines between her eyebrows smooth out. Neither of us move.

Annoying habits aside, she is stunning. When her temper heats and she crawls out of her shell...

I have a knack for setting off that temper. Do I do it for the flush in her cheeks? The twist of her pert mouth? The way her breaths grow deep like I imagine they will when—

"Julian!" Alesha shoves a bowl of potatoes at me.

I clear my throat and take them, doing my best not to look at Grace for the remainder of the dinner. Eventually, Kai rises to leave for his shift, but Raven stops him. "Wait. We need to draw names."

Kai and I trade wary glances.

"Draw names for what?" I ask.

"Holiday exchange. Duh." Raven shakes her head like she thinks we're both stupid.

"Oh yeah. I forgot." Alesha stands to grab a sheet of paper, then tears it in five pieces. "Everyone write your name." She offers me the paper.

I hedge. "Do we have to?"

She sends me a stern Alesha-stare. "Yes."

Sighing, I obey. When she offers me the bowl of papers to choose from, I don't have to look to know whose name I've drawn. Radar is on high alert.

Her loopy handwriting looks nothing like my typical doctor-scrawl. Its elegance fits her like a surgeon's glove.

Grace.

Traveling to Florida in November is an unpleasant trial in patience with old people. The snowbirds have no sense of urgency, but at least I'm not going through Orlando International with the Disney crowd.

By the time I'm home, reclining under the sun-dappled shadows of palm trees dancing over my closed eyes, I'm ready for a beer and a nap. Instead, my gaze travels over the red, white, and black spiders that weave their webs at the top of our lanai, reminding me of Grace Rose, while five women pepper me with questions. I hold them off best I can, but my mother's pleas for me to move home cannot be ignored.

I rub my face and beg for patience. "Mom, I can't quit. I'll be done in a few years and I'll find a job here. I promise."

She fans herself, blond hair clipped up and tousled in the breeze, rocking in her outdoor recliner. "If you meet some girl and move farther away from me, I'll have a heart attack. Is that what you want, Julian?"

Tori sends me a knowing grin as she pulls a beer out of the outdoor fridge, tossing it to me.

I snap the tab open and hand it to Mom. "I'm not meeting anyone, okay? Stop panicking. You're being melodramatic."

"Yeah, Ma," says my oldest sister, Lauren. "Let BB live his life. He's a hotshot doctor now."

Lauren's two kids—my only niece and nephew—are swimming with her husband, Ben. They squeal as Ben launches them in the air, water sprinkling over us when they land. Lauren beams at them.

She married young, but my other three sisters are free spirits. Tori is a loner, a massage therapist with a side hustle of renting jet skis to tourists during Season. The twins, Bethany and Sabrina, are beach dive bartenders who are just as likely to bring a man or woman home to meet Mom as they are a new puppy.

Bethany shrieks and hops into the pool with the kids. When she pops up, she swims to the edge closest to me. "Don't you miss home, though?"

"I didn't match into any of the programs here, Beth. Remember?"

"I know. I just—I don't want you to fall in love with Texas. We'll never see you."

Fall in love with Texas? Has she met me?

Sabrina lounges on a chaise with her sunglasses hiding her eyes. "I've done the research. Florida has really high malpractice premiums. Don't let that scare you, BB."

"Christ." I massage my temple. "Why are we even talking about this?"

You love them, Julian. Remember that.

Tori drops onto the arm of my chair and throws her arms

around me. Her silky brown hair tickles my nose. "Because we wub you, and want to smother you to death."

"It's working." I swat her hair off my face.

She chuckles, then whispers in my ear, "I'll distract them, and you can escape for a nap, okay?"

My spirits lift. "Really?"

She nods. "You owe me, though."

I kiss the top of her hair and make like I have to use the restroom. When I fall onto my childhood bed with a sigh, my phone buzzes. A thrill of energy zaps through me at the name displayed on the screen.

I open the message to find a selfie of Grace in blue scrubs, rainbow pens in pocket, sitting in our dictation room. She holds a black coffee mug right beside her beautiful smiling face. Written across the mug in white letters are the words *DOs 'DO' it better.* Another text comes, a simple message that flushes warmth across every inch of my skin.

> **Sapphire:** Found this. Made me think of you.

I zoom in to her face and the little freckle on her lip, then to the rest of her, welling with pleasure when I find a splash of blood soaked into her scrub shirt. I circle it and send the picture back to her.

> **Me:** You have blood on your scrubs.

> **Sapphire:** I hope you die a slow death from palm tree poisoning.

I can't help the laughter that overcomes me. Turning into my pillow, I snicker like a child. It should be concerning how much I look forward to riling her up, but I can't find it in me to care. Grace Rose's irritation is the most satisfying part of my life right now.

Imagine how satisfying she'd be if—
I cut the thought off before it drifts into dangerous waters.
Beware.
There be monsters.

Grace

DECEMBER, YEAR 1

Mom's incandescent smile glimmers out from my phone screen. "I booked your ticket with points."

"Thanks, Mom. I can't wait to see you guys."

"Me too, angel baby. Thanksgiving wasn't the same without you. Can't wait for you to get here."

Dad's voice echoes through the speaker, though I can't see him. "Tell her Thanksgiving was weird without her!"

"I just did!" My mom sends a flustered look off-screen, snowman earrings bobbing, then returns to me. "Your father is doing a cleansing ritual. No technology. You understand."

Spinning in my rolling chair in the call room, I press my lips together to keep from laughing. Didn't know technology was so toxic to the system.

My parents are *always* doing some ritual or fast. They're staunch believers in essential oils, positive vibes and healing crystals. Each wear a sapphire because they believe it protects against negative energies and calms the mind.

They named me Sapphire for the same reason. Shortsighted on their part, unfortunately. When I grew breasts, the world's view of me evolved from a quirky little girl to a porn star. But if naming me after a gemstone is the worst thing they ever do to me, I'll count myself lucky. My parents are amazing.

"How are all the vaginas, baby girl?" Mom asks.

I laugh. "They're doing fine, Mama."

"That's good. I always say, when *she's* not happy, I'm not happy."

"And neither am I!" yells my dad.

My mouth drops open. "Oh my god. Gross!"

"Honey, you're a sex doctor. You need to get over the prudishness."

"Not with my parents, I don't!"

A text comes through from my senior this month. "Hang on, Mom."

Asher: Lunch?

Me: Sure. Meet you down there?

Asher: Sure thing, baby cakes.

I snort. Asher's a pretty good teacher. He isn't as much of a douche as I originally thought. His blatant flirting is a pervasive theme in any conversation. I'm not even sure he knows he's doing it. It's wired into his genetic code, or something. And he's not picky, either. He flirts with every female in his vicinity—including some patients—and somehow knows when it's welcome and when it's not, thereby skirting around a sexual harassment accusation.

I have *almost* forgiven him for his crude comments the day I met him.

"Hey, Mom, I have to go."

"All right, honey. Call me later."

My month with Asher has been more productive than my last month on L&D. He's charmed our bosses into letting me primary most surgeries now. When I'm allowed to do my job, that lifelong dream feels a bit more attainable—the one of the girl in the white coat who's commanded the respect of her peers. The competent woman, sure of herself and her place in the world. Surely, that will be me someday, right?

Doubts creep in that perhaps the title of "Doctor" doesn't come with a preloaded certificate of accomplishment. Maybe confidence isn't something that can be awarded to me with enough time and effort. Perhaps it comes from within.

I shake myself.

Regardless, Asher's insistence and pull with the attendings has been invaluable, but I still get bumped due to silly excuses.

It has to be the rumor. Or, *rumors*. The first one was bad enough, but it spawned a whole host of vague gossip that paints me as a harlot who uses sexual favors to get out of the hard parts of training. Apparently, our call room is my own personal red-light district.

It's crazy how information mutates in the hospital. Last week, I overheard a nurse being reprimanded for giving the wrong dose of medication to a patient. At the end of the day, everyone was whispering that she'd done it on purpose because she was selling the extra fentanyl on the sly. By next week, the gossip mill will put her in jail and the patient in the morgue.

Thanks to that single rumor in June, I started with a reputation in tatters, and due to idle speculation, it's only shredded further from there. Crawling out of this hole is impossible. If it weren't for the fact that I'm 92 percent positive it's negatively affecting my training, I'm not sure I'd even want to try to crawl out anymore.

In the resident lounge, Asher and I find a round table in the corner. He pimps me over hemorrhage protocols while chugging a protein shake and I pick at the unfortunate lunch offering—mystery meat. Yum.

After five minutes, he huffs a laugh. "Jesus. You know this shit better than I do."

I lace my fingers on the table. "I study a lot."

A grin warms his face. "I see that. You should get out more."

"That will never happen," Julian says, sliding into a seat next to Asher, apple and bowl of soup in hand. "Sapphire wouldn't know fun if it bit her in the ass."

I glare at him and his stupid scrubs and his perfect hair and the stubble on his cut jaw that reminds me of Robert Pattinson. Because *of course* my subconscious would compare this man to Edward Cullen—pretend boyfriend of my preteen self.

Julian wouldn't feed on animals. No. He'd go straight for the human carotid.

I lean my elbows on the table. "Ha. You're so funny. You know all about funny, don't you? Being best friends with the Joker and all."

His eyes flash, almost like they're lit from within. Hmm. Does he actually like this fighting thing we do? Every time I start something, he seems to just…come alive.

"Yeah," he says. "Him and the Riddler are taking me out for drinks later. It's a whole thing. Don't tell Batman."

Asher laughs. "What're you on this month, Santini?"

As usual, Julian's intense stare is locked on me. "Surgery." He tilts his head. "It's really not as bad as I was led to believe."

I scoff. Under my breath, I mutter, "That's because you're a man."

"Or maybe it's because I don't complain about everything."

I lean farther over the table and lower my voice. "You'd complain too if they spent the whole month using you as a sounding board for their hallowed thoughts on how terribly OB-GYNs are trained and anytime you tried to defend yourself, they were too distracted by your tits to listen."

Asher's snort is a distant intrusion into my standoff with my arch nemesis.

"Well. To be fair, my tits are very distracting," he says.

His eyes remain focused on mine, but his peripheral vision is tangible, and I have to fight the urge to cross my arms over my chest. Everything slows. Heat creeps up my neck, burns across my cheeks. His face hardly moves, but as he takes in my reaction, satisfaction gleams in that bare expression.

He won that one, and we both know it.

To my utter horror, Daniel Halliwell sits next to Julian, disgusting hospital slop on his plate. He nods in my direction. "Grace."

I strangle an awkward laugh. It comes out as a choke. "Hi."

Asher glances at me, then folds his hands behind his head. "Thought you were too good to sit with us peasants, Halliwell. Your people kick you out?"

Daniel looks around the room, empty of other residents. A few med students huddle together around one table. "You're the lesser of two evils."

Asher gives his head a small irritated shake. "I'm honored."

I sit straight and try for a smile. "Are you Julian's senior this month, Dr. Halliwell?"

Daniel scrutinizes Julian. "Yeah. He's actually got some talent. Gives me hope for your specialty, after all."

I curl my painted pink nails into my palms, but keep my smile frozen in place. He wouldn't know if I had talent because I was never allowed to hold a scalpel or suture.

Julian perks an eyebrow, sending a challenging expression and mouthing, *You want me to show him my tits?*

"That's good," I say faintly, numbing the desire to laugh.

Asher chuckles under his breath. "You're gonna die alone, Danny." He turns to me. "You done? Let's go check our laboring patients."

I nod and gather my trash while he throws his away.

"I'll meet you up there," he says. "Gotta pee."

Okay, then. "Thanks for the info," I mutter.

"Hey, Grace? Wait up."

Halfway to the door, I turn to find Daniel approaching.

"I wanted to ask you something," he says.

"Oh. Um. Yeah?"

My palms grow inexplicably sweaty. This man made my life a nightmare for a month. He treated me like a dumb Barbie. One day, his memory will be a trigger for PTSD.

Behind him, Julian sits at the table, scrolling through his phone.

Daniel must have forgotten he's there because he says, "I have a table reserved at that steakhouse, Primus, on Friday."

"Okay…"

"You want to come with me?"

My mouth falls open, and I try to ignore Julian in my peripheral vision as his gaze burns into me. It's almost painful, his stare. Like lasers drawing heat to the surface of my skin.

"I—um—like, a date?"

Daniel's *are-you-stupid* expression is familiar. "Yeah, Grace. Like a date."

My eyes disobey every strand of logic in my head, and I glance at Julian. He is *glowing*, the deadly smirk on his face so full of humor that every muscle in my body contracts, ready to flee. Is this karma for the Rebecca thing? I take it back, universe! I never meant any harm. Please don't punish me.

Pressing a hand to my cheek only hides half the blush. I take a staggered breath. "I'm not sure if—"

"Oh come on," Daniel says, smiling. *Smiling!* Like we're

friends. "I've heard about it all. You don't have to be coy. At least I'm offering to buy you dinner first."

Ice floods my veins. "What?"

His gray eyes narrow and he shoots me a skeptical expression. "Seriously?"

"I don't know what you're talking about, Daniel."

With a condescending twist of his lips, he says, "Wow. You've got the pseudo-innocent thing down, don't you, Grace?"

I stiffen. "I don't think dinner would be a good idea. I'm sorry."

Turning on my heel to flee, I shut my eyes against his muttered "Bitch" as I pass.

One last look at Julian goes unnoticed by him. Smirk gone, that dark predatory gaze is fixed on Daniel. I don't have the headspace to process that, so I ignore it completely.

Back in the dictation room, Asher is furious when I tell him why I'm teary-eyed.

I wipe away the moisture with the tissue he gives me. "Why do people think this about me, Asher?"

A contrite crease appears between his eyebrows. "I don't know. I don't know how it all got started, Grace."

"So people just assume I'll sleep with anyone?"

He winces. "There's been talk you've been around. I'm so sorry I ever believed it. Sorry I said that shit back in June."

"I don't...do that." I sniffle. "I never—"

"I know. I do set people straight when they say it in front of me." He lowers his voice to a mumble. "Not that it shuts anyone up."

"How do these rumors keep getting started?"

Shrugging, he clicks his mouse a few times. "It's just conjecture. When I was an intern, I spilled some of that acid we use to treat genital warts on a woman's butt cheek, and for almost a year, any time someone mentioned a resident fucking up, it was always, 'Was it Foley?'"

"Oh gosh," I say, laughter breaking through my tears. "Was she okay?"

He waves a hand. "She was fine. We joked that I gave her ass a chemical peel. But what I'm saying is that this is the same thing. If there's talk of a scandal, your name always gets thrown in the mix."

"I don't even date! I haven't in years."

His eyes widen a fraction. "Why not?"

I blink several times at the computer monitor in front of me, its blurred light fracturing into starbursts. My voice shrinks, and my shoulders slump. "I—the last time—he broke my heart."

No. He shattered my sanity.

The clammy sensation of his sweat from the last time we slept together still sometimes phantom-clings to my skin. I didn't come—I rarely did—but he did, and his breath fanned over my skin, an invisible stain, as he stared at me.

"I love you, Matt," I whispered, smiling at him.

"I can't do this anymore, Grace. It's like fucking an ice queen."

The worst part is that I begged him to stay. He'd promised me forever. Told me we'd get married. Made me sacrifice for him.

The things I did. The things I let him do. Just so he wouldn't leave.

I hated myself.

And he left, anyway.

Because I'm cold in bed.

Asher pulls me from my thoughts. "I proposed to a girl last year."

My head spins, and not even the tears can mask his sad smile. "What?"

"She laughed in my face and left me for a cardiologist. They're getting married this spring."

I touch his arm. He chuckles, covering our moment with good humor until we're both chortling.

"We're a couple of messes," I say.

He shakes himself. "Life is messy."

An hour later, my phone buzzes.

A picture from Julian lights up my screen. He holds someone else's badge reel in his disturbingly alluring hand. It reads Bitches Get Shit Done.

> **Julian:** Found this

> **Julian:** Made me think of you

> **Julian:** But if you ask me

> **Julian:** Daniel Halliwell is the bitch

A watery laugh hitches in my chest, and I go back to work. So he *does* have a light side, after all. Who'd have thought?

The next day, I enter the resident lounge and find Daniel sporting a black eye. I turn to Asher, asking what happened with a pointed raise of my eyebrows.

He shrugs and gestures toward Julian eating his lunch in the corner. "Here's what I heard—"

"Seriously, Asher? Rumors?"

He raises both hands. "Hey, do you want to know, or not? I got this from Maxwell, who got it from Julian, so it's reliable."

With a reluctant sigh, I motion him to continue, half hating myself that I'm entertaining any rumors at all.

He lowers his voice even though the room is busy and crowded. "Julian just happened to point out something Halliwell did wrong in front of his attending. Attending tells him to fix it, right? So Halliwell tried to make Julian do it, to which Julian said something along the lines of *clean up your own mess. I don't work for you.*"

I gasp.

"I know, right? Like, bro. Yeah, you do work for him. He's literally your senior resident. Anyway, Halliwell and him got into a screaming match in the gen surg call room, and that's when you came into the picture."

My spirits fall. Or lift. I'm not sure. "Me?"

"Julian said something like, *learn to treat my fellow interns with respect, or you won't get any respect from me.* Halliwell figured out what he meant, and I think he might have accused Julian of doing...something...with you. Julian gets in his face. Halliwell pushes him. Julian pushes him back. Julian said Halliwell tripped over the rollie chair and hit his face on the desk." Asher breaks into gleeful, vindictive laughter.

When Julian looks up, I blink at Daniel, then return to those depthless brown eyes. Julian doesn't smile, but a blatant satisfaction comes alive in his face and he winks before returning to his lunch.

Casual. Hot.

Damn vampire.

"He did *what?*" Alesha asks Saturday night as we snuggle into my couch for movie night.

I lift a shoulder. "I don't know for sure. No one *confirmed*. But there were strong hints that Julian Santini defended my honor."

Snowden is paused on my TV while Alesha and I nurse glasses of Cabernet, and Raven drinks her lime La Croix. A candle in the middle of my coffee table fills the entire apartment with the smell of fresh-baked sugar cookies.

Alesha shakes her head. "That boy is good people. I don't know why you don't like him."

I laugh. "At this point, it's habit. Also, his persistent urge to call me Sapphire just to annoy me is infuriating."

Stretched on the chaise portion of my sectional, Raven gives a knowing nod. Her black braids are loose around her shoulders. "We're family, aren't we? It's like your brother—it's okay for him to annoy you, but if someone else wants to mess with you, he gets protective."

I ignore the bitter taste that rises at Julian being regarded as my brother.

Alesha snorts. "Brother. Yeah, *that's* why he turned into a caveman."

Shrugging, Raven toasts the air. "To irritating men who take care of bad guys for us!"

The three of us giggle and talk turns to work as it usually does. Eventually, Raven and I pounce on Alesha about her relationship status.

She pours another glass of wine. "I don't date."

"Why not?" I thrust my glass toward her for a refill.

She eyes me. "Why don't *you*?"

My eye twitches. "I had a bad experience last time I tried."

"Care to elaborate?" She hands back my filled glass.

"Um. Well. The last guy I dated—"

Destroyed my trust in men?

Manipulated me into performing demeaning sexual favors?

Told me he loved me and wanted to marry me, all while screwing a dozen other women?

Gave me chlamydia?

"—wasn't very nice."

Alesha shoots me a skeptical stare. "Then why'd you date him?"

Because I didn't know any better.

Love's a lie. I don't know why anyone falls for it.

"It doesn't matter. Look, I don't even flirt with men and the rumors that I'm a slutty little skeeze still get spread all over the hospital. Can you imagine what people would say if I actually dated someone?"

Alesha's shoulders fall, and she drops her gaze to her glass.

"Maybe the rumors would go away if you dated someone. People would lose their ammunition."

I snort.

Raven cups my shoulder. "It's not fair."

Tears prickle in my eyes, but I smile and sip my wine. "It's fine. It isn't a big deal."

I disregard the voice rustling in my subconscious, insisting it *is* a big deal. *It's breaking you...*

Raven changes the subject. "Isaac and I are thinking of trying for another one."

"What?" Alesha bounces on the couch. "Baby Washington?"

Raven nods, her smile glowing. "Monte is almost three. I think I'm ready to start over."

I snuggle next to her. "You'll make the cutest preggo."

She laughs. "Let's finish this movie."

Dr. Chen's annual holiday party the Sunday before Christmas is apparently a booze fest disguised as a potluck, and I have never been more ready for a party. Six months of intern year are almost finished, which means I'm on the downhill slide into second year.

This is cause for massive celebration.

I slip into a Christmas dress—forest green with a red belt about my waist—and spritz my hair with gold glitter. Satisfied I've covered the dark circles beneath my eyes enough that I don't look like an OB resident, I slip on my new red heels and coat and step into the cold night.

On the sidewalk below, the thunk of steps above brings my gaze upward. Julian rounds the landing, clad in a black sweater covered by a black peacoat. A green scarf hangs around his neck and his dark hair is parted roguishly off to one side. A single rebellious lock falls across his forehead. When he sees me, he pauses on the steps and slips his hands in his coat pockets.

I meet his eyes. "Julian."

"Sapphire." A quiet smile refines his entire face. His lips hardly move, but his eyes come to life. This smile-without-smiling thing he does is disarming. I could never pull it off.

I resist it so hard, but my mouth disobeys and a grin breaks free. I look at the ground so he won't see it.

"You going to Chen's party?" he asks.

I glance at him through my eyelashes. "What gave it away?"

He descends the steps with meticulous care, his attention fastened on me. "The lipstick."

A small embarrassed laugh bubbles in my chest as my body goes hot and cold all at once. "Christmas red. You like?"

He reaches the ground and stops an arm span away, shaking his head. "Devil-red. Like your nails."

My nails are a shiny, sparkly red. They are *beautiful*, and he is the *worst*. I glare at him. "At least I'm not dressed like Draco Malfoy."

No-smile turns into a smirk. "Touché. Want a ride?"

My mouth falls open. "You—you'll—in your truck?"

His eyes laser-focus on my parted lips before he shoots a half smile at the sky. "Is there another type of ride you might want?"

Was that…innuendo? Treacherous heat dances along my skin.

"Broomstick, perhaps?" he adds.

"Ha, ha. I was going to Uber so I can drink."

"Well, I'm not drinking, and we live in the same place, so if you want to save money…"

I nod before I've actually decided. Or maybe my body just decided for me. "Yeah, okay. That'd be great. Thanks."

He jerks his head toward the parking lot. I follow him to his truck, canceling my Uber on the way. The passenger seat hovers at the level of my shoulders. My heels slip on the running board and I almost kill myself in a graceless maneuver onto the seat.

A silken sensation slips around every nerve as the door closes and I'm inundated by his scent. A tiny pulse stirs between my legs.

Welp. This is a mistake. I now have to face the undeniable

fact that the scent of Julian Santini does weird, erotic things to my body.

Is there anything more intimate than breathing someone into my lungs? Letting the essence of him saturate into my bloodstream and filter into every organ? What if my body grows receptors for him? Adapts to him? *Wants* him?

I cross my legs and ignore it, glancing at him as he pulls out of the parking lot. He's chewing gum. It makes the muscles in his jaw ripple.

He's not cute.

Look at that jawline, though.

He's rude.

But he knows how to smile without using his mouth.

That's not hot.

It absolutely is.

"Why are you staring at me?"

I snap my head forward, but fire scalds my skin. "I'm just trying to figure out why you're such a jerk."

"Takes one to know one, Sapphire."

"*Grace.*"

He flashes me a quick grin. "Oops."

I huff as we roll to a stoplight. "You're working Christmas?"

"Yes."

"Sucks for you."

He taps on his steering wheel with his thumb. "You'll get your turn. What are your plans?"

God, he smells good. I have to readjust the vent so the heat blows in my face in hopes of eradicating his godforsaken scent from my nose. "I'm going home. I fly out tomorrow."

"Where's home?"

"Danville, California."

He smiles. "A Californian. Should've known. And how does your family celebrate the holiday?"

I cross my arms. "With a tree and presents. What about you? Animal sacrifices?"

"No, that's Easter."

The light turns green, illuminating his face. Such a careful driver, he obeys every traffic law and allows other drivers passage before him. He has the patience of a frickin' saint, and my knee jiggles as he refuses to go faster than the speed limit. We aren't late, but the familiar agitation before a party gnaws at me.

Those dimples go full-scale adorable when he grins. "I think you forgot to put out some fires when you left hell. Your hair has embers in it."

"They're sparkles, Julian. They're pretty."

"Is there anything about you that doesn't sparkle? You're practically a *My Little Pony*."

I should take offense to that, but can't. *My Little Pony* was a staple for me as a kid. "I'd rather be that than Gollum."

He side-eyes me, eyebrow lifted. "You're kind of a dork, aren't you?"

A startled laugh climbs my throat. "What?"

"*The Lord of the Rings, Harry Potter, Avengers*. Just...dorky references. But it keeps me guessing. Will you call me Darth Vader or Prince Joffrey next? Maybe Feyd-Rautha?"

"You would be a Harkonnen," I mutter.

He chuckles.

I shrink in my seat. "Shut up. You understand the references, so clearly you're a dork, too."

He nods. "And unashamed of it. But I should warn you, I have a date with Maleficent later, so we're gonna have to leave this thing early."

Defying my wishes, a chuckle escapes.

"That reminds me." He checks his blind spot before changing lanes. "Did you know I had to go on a date with that girl you gave my number to? She wouldn't stop texting me. Hints didn't work. Finally caved and took her out a couple weeks ago."

My chuckle grows a distinct edge, and now I'm cackling despite a thin weave of poison speeding my pulse. The picture of him out with that blonde IM resident is an ugly one I don't want in my head. The cackle hides my discomfiture. "Are you madly in love now?"

"Yeah, we married yesterday. Didn't you hear?" He shakes his head. "She's so—her tenacity is... Just, *please*, Grace. Torture me any other way, but please don't give my number out to women."

My full attention locks on his face. Adrenaline floods my system. "You called me Grace."

He gives me a double take. "What? No, I didn't."

"Yes, you did. You called me Grace."

"I..." He scratches his temple and shifts in his seat. "Okay?"

"Did you confront Daniel Halliwell for me, Julian?"

He scowls. His grip tightens on the steering wheel. "Daniel Halliwell is an asshole."

"Julian?" My voice is soft.

"I would have done it for any of you girls. It doesn't mean anything."

I lean toward him when a muscle in his clenched jaw tics. "Then why are you being weird?"

"I'm—I'm not."

I'm still staring at his sharp profile when he pulls to a stop at the curb of Dr. Chen's millionaire cottage and looks at me. Glittering Christmas lights stipple his skin and sparkle in his eyes. I can't look away from him. That lock of hair is so attractive I want to cut it off. Because he's evil, and evil isn't appealing.

He's not evil. He's a knight in shining armor who tears into people for you.

Violence isn't attractive.

Tell that to your libido.

"We're here, she-devil." His voice has deepened.

I fold my hands in my lap. "I'm a perfect angel, Julian, and you know it."

"Hmm." He reaches for his door handle without looking away from me. "Angels don't wear that color lipstick."

He does the no-smiling smile and slips out of the truck. The door thunks shut.

Holy—

What just happened?

A supernova erupts in my chest, imploding my entire body. It doesn't feel like animosity, either. It's hotter. Blistering.

I fumble for my own door handle, but he opens it from the other side, offering his hand to help me down.

"Why do you have such a tall truck?" I try to keep my heel from slipping on the running board again.

"Because I'm a tall man."

That's for damn sure. Even in my heels, he towers over me.

I slide from my seat. His shoulder helps brace me as I land on the ground close enough that I can smell the cinnamon gum on his breath. Once I'm steady, we spring away from each other. He locks his truck and we head inside.

The kitchen is full of people filling plates. Christmas carols on the overhead speaker system can barely be heard above the chatter.

Maxwell, bedecked in an ugly Christmas sweater and reindeer antlers, cocks his head as we walk through the door. "Did you guys come together?"

"What?" I laugh and reflexively push Julian away from me. "No. What? Why would you think that?"

Maxwell eyes me, the space between his brows narrowing. "Because you walked in together?"

Julian laughs under his breath. "Chill out, Hermione." He shakes his head and turns to Maxwell. "I drove her. You ready?"

Maxwell nods. "You in?"

"Yeah." Julian joins him, lifting his chin toward me in good-bye. "Have a drink. Take the edge off."

I stare after him.

"Boo!"

I jump, almost screaming.

Kai roars in laughter. "Damn, girl. Play your cards closer to the chest."

"What?"

He stares after Julian, then shoots me a knowing look.

"Shut up!" I hiss. "Gross."

He throws an arm around me. "Let's get you some Christmas wine. Raven's covering L&D, but Alesha needs her sidekick."

He leads me to Alesha, deep in conversation with Lexie and Asher.

"I'm not kidding!" Lexie says while Alesha giggles.

Kai hands me a glass of wine. "What aren't we kidding about?"

"I got an ER consult today for a vaginal laceration. I asked her what happened. She said she was performing a Wiccan sex ceremony that involved a crystal dildo."

My mouth drops open. "Did it break?"

Lexie shrugs. "She said she got a little aggressive."

Grinning, Asher leans toward us. "Pretty sure Practice Bulletin sixty-nine discusses crystal dildo for orgasmic dysfunction in Wiccan populations. Do crystal dildos work? Synopsis: no."

"Depends what you use them for. Level A recommendation: sex magic." I shoot a wink at Asher, and he bumps my shoulder with his, laughing. His Christmas sweater says *Brodolf the Red-Nosed Gainzdeer*. I point at it. "Where did you even find that?"

"I never reveal secrets, Gracey-kins." His contagious smile drags me straight into our normal camaraderie. This month with him has been awesome, and I want to make sure he knows it. He may have said some crappy things in June, but he's more than made up for it.

We're friends, Asher and I. Good ones.

Our attendings grow rosy-cheeked as the party escalates. Which of them are on call? I hope it isn't Dr. Levine, who's slurring his words. He's drunk enough that he unabashedly bursts into our conversation, proclaims Lexie has *the best tits in the program* and stumbles away.

Kai's eyes grow wide. "Well, *that* was uncomfortable."

Lexie grimaces. "It's not the first time he's said that to me."

I'd tell her to file a complaint, but we all know it would go nowhere.

"Do you all remember Cora?" Lexie asks in a hushed voice.

Alesha leans closer. "The third-year who got kicked out last fall?"

I shoot her a look. How on earth does she know this?

She shrugs. "The stories get around, girl."

"Yeah," Lexie says. "I heard she was sleeping with Levine, and that's why she got fired."

Asher shakes his head. "Nah. I heard she was addicted to coke."

I roll my eyes. "I heard she was a space alien who came to earth to kill us all. You guys, rumors are so stupid."

Alesha straightens. "You're right. Why are all the rumors about women?"

"They're not," Lexie says with a small laugh. "I heard one of the second-year peds residents shirked his shift last week to karaoke Disney songs with one of his patients."

"That's not even scandalous!" I say. "It's just precious. Where's the rumor that he gave his attending a blow job for an extra day of vacation?"

Asher grips my shoulder, giving one reassuring squeeze. I pat his hand in silent thanks. Luckily, the conversation soon turns elsewhere.

I'm three glasses deep, slightly tipsy, and cracking up at Asher's jokes when a commotion stirs in another room. Alesha and

I trade curious glances and head toward a smaller room with a poker table in the middle. People crowd around as Julian and Dr. Chen face off, the only two left at a table set for seven.

I know nothing about poker, but Julian's pile of chips is far larger than Chen's. An intensity settles about the room.

"What's going on?" I whisper to Asher.

"Chen's annual BrOB-GYN poker game."

"You don't play, Asher?" Alesha elbows him.

"Sometimes. I was too busy trying to get out of the friend zone this year." He wiggles his eyebrows at me playfully.

I snort. "Whatever."

Chen and Julian take each other's measure. The round plays out with an exchange of cards and some tossing of chips. Hands revealed, groans and whoops fill the room.

Asher catcalls Julian.

"Did he win?" I ask.

Asher glances at me, eyebrows drawn together.

"Yeah, I know," I say. "I'm clueless."

He laughs. "Yeah, girl. He won."

With a smile, Chen stands and shakes Julian's hand, murmuring something near his ear. Julian showcases his crooked grin.

"This year's victor!" Chen raises Julian's hand.

Everyone claps and toasts. Alesha shrieks and jumps into Julian's arms. He gives her his real smile, crinkles and all.

"You think something is going on between them?" Asher nods toward my friends. "They seem really close."

I start to answer in the negative but pause. What if…

No, Alesha would tell me. She tells me everything. "I don't think so."

Right?

Surely not.

We wander back to the party and snack on brie and Grinch brownies. Asher and Aislin take turns trying to one-up the other on funniest patient encounters. Nearly in tears from laughter, I stiffen when electricity opens a current over my skin, raising all the hairs on my body.

He's behind me. He isn't touching me, but his presence is tangible. My heart trips in my chest.

Beside me, Asher grins, greeting Julian with a lift of his chin. "Hey, Santini. Nice game."

"Yeah, thanks." His voice is beside my ear, but he leans closer anyway and the tips of his fingers touch my elbow. His scent engulfs me. "You ready?"

Asher looks between us, the smile slipping off his face.

I turn my head to meet his dark eyes. "Already?"

"Some of us have to work in the morning, Sapphire."

"I could take you home later if you want to stay," Asher says.

I wave my hand and back away from the group. "It's fine. He lives in my building, so it isn't out of his way."

"I'm sure it's not," Asher says. The words are sharper than normal, but he's smiling.

Hmm. What's this now? I think the alcohol is messing with me. I move in for an embrace, which Asher returns at once. "Thanks for a good month," I say. "Merry Christmas."

"Safe flight tomorrow. Have fun with mommy and daddy."

I shoot him a sour face. After hugging Alesha and Kai good-bye, Julian and I head out.

In the darkness of his truck, I study the way the streetlights pass over his face, casting shadows in interesting places. "Congrats on the game."

He shrugs. "It's easy to beat a bunch of intoxicated people at poker."

I chuckle. "Is that why you didn't drink tonight?"

"Yep. Bragging rights." The no-smile flashes at me. "Next time, you can be the DD."

Something in the rear of my mind purrs at the words *next time.*

Back at our building, we walk side by side up the stairs. When I reach my landing, I turn to say good-night.

"What time is your flight tomorrow?" he asks.

"Early."

He scratches his neck, then examines our empty surroundings. "I have something for you. Do you have a minute?"

I'm stunned to silence for only three seconds before I say, "Sure."

"Let me go get it. I'll be down in a sec."

My apartment is clean, but I scan the living room for anything embarrassing just in case. My heels fly toward my bedroom with two swift kicks. I throw my coat over the entry rack.

His knock on my half-closed door startles me, flooding me with butterflies. I swing it open to find him holding a cardboard box with a red Christmas bow.

"I got your name for Secret Santa."

Sparkles bloom hot and fast in my chest, spreading to my mouth. A smile breaks loose. "You did?"

He nods, forlorn.

"Julian Santini, hater of all things Grace Rose was forced to find her a Christmas present?"

His lips press into a flat line.

"Whatever could be in there?" I slip closer to him. Cold December air mingles with his scent, icing it to something dark and exotic.

"You have to open it to find out," he says.

Close enough to take it, I hold out my arms. He shifts the box to my hands.

I stagger under its weight. "Holy—what is in here?"

He lifts one of the cardboard lids, and I peek in the package. Sugar.

Granulated sugar. Powdered sugar. Brown sugar. Cane sugar. Sanding sugar. Splenda. Sugar cubes.

My gaze shoots to his, "What the hell, Julian? What am I supposed to do with all this sugar?"

Merriment gleams on his face. His cheeks grow rosy. "I suggest using it to bake the children. Helps with the bitterness."

My disobedient mouth twitches into a smile. "Do you think this is funny?"

He nods as the laughter takes hold, then pinches the bridge of his nose. A fuzzy little ball of warmth expands in my stomach. That's such a cute laugh...

"I think—" he tugs on a lock of my hair "—it's hilarious. *Sapphire.*"

"You *know* it's Grace," I say, voice softer than I want it.

"Right." He brushes a hand over his mouth, hiding his self-congratulatory smile. "I keep forgetting."

"You are so difficult. Fine. Come in, and I'll get your present." I'd been planning to leave it on his doorstep tomorrow morning, but I need to even the scales.

His smile disappears. "Wait. You got my name, too?"

A cynical chuckle vibrates in my throat. "As the world works perpetually against me, I'd think that answer obvious. Come in, Julian. It's cold outside."

"Come in...to your apartment?"

I wave my hand about the place, from the carpeted floor to the popcorn ceiling. "Do you think I have Julian traps in here? I don't bite."

His expression blanks. He rocks on his feet at the threshold.

"Julian?" I tug on his coat lapel. "The heat."

After crossing over and shutting the door, he lingers in the entryway. His attention travels from my worn blue sectional to the art on my walls to my bookshelf. It isn't until he steps into the living room that the sensation of my space being disrupted, invaded and conquered sweeps over me.

I flush from head to toe. "Hang on. Let me get it."

Heart racing, I set the box of sugar on my dining table and

slip into my bedroom to grab his gift. The mirror snags my attention and I fix a few stray glittery hairs before stepping out.

He eyes the present like it might explode in his face. I kick myself that I didn't think of that. A frickin' glitter bomb! Pink glitter. Maybe with unicorns.

The witch hiding in my limbic system titters evilly, hoping she gets his name for Secret Santa next year.

He takes it in his hand. "Did you wrap this?"

"Of course I did. Why?"

"It's very…sparkly. It has ribbons. And a bow."

I throw my hands in the air. "Is it *too* pretty for you, Julian?"

His gaze leaves the gift, straying to me. "Yes."

I sweep an impatient gesture toward the box. "Then *unwrap* it."

Several seconds pass before he blinks and slides a finger under the edge of the paper. He pulls out the green and silver coffee mug I'd found on Etsy, complete with a snake as the handle.

A dark eyebrow arches. "Slytherin."

"Now everyone will know exactly what you are when you drink your coffee in didactics." I shoot him a satisfied smirk and clap him on the shoulder, but my focus zeroes in on the hard muscle beneath my hand, palpable despite his winter coat.

Squee!

He doesn't look built under the scrubs and black Henleys he wears, but the marble beneath my hand is lean and cut. My mind conjures potential images of him shirtless and every nerve ending in my body jolts energy to places I refuse to acknowledge.

The air thins as my hand lingers on his arm. My survival instincts flare red and scream at me to let go.

I don't.

If he was a lion and I was a zebra, I'm not sure I'd run.

His eyes go dark. Raptorial. Like he can smell the pheromones. My stupid hormones melt my willpower.

Look how sexy he is, they say. *No one with that jawline can be evil.*

He holds up his Slytherin cup, rattling me with a lopsided grin. "I guess they will."

I release his arm like he's electric. My lips part, uncertain what game he's playing.

He brushes the tip of his thumb over my bottom lip, down to my chin so he can pop my mouth closed. "Merry Christmas, she-devil."

Julian

Among a group of IM residents on the general medical floor, Dr. Sharma's unblinking eyes zero in on me. "Dr. Santini, please present your patient."

Internal medicine is kicking my ass. I can only thank the scheduling gods that my IM rotation is the shortest month of the year. My attending is practically a Mensa genius and her uncanny ability to quote directly from UpToDate, the most used point-of-care medical resource, makes my skin itch.

I am dangerously dehydrated. I haven't sweat this much since I was training for that marathon in college, and back then I had the time to drink fluids and eat meals not singularly composed of MSG. When was the last time I peed? Yesterday?

My patient is a fifty-year-old man with a GI bleed of unknown etiology and a recent heart attack necessitating stent placement. It's a tricky combination. I finish my lackluster pre-sentation outside his hospital room and trail off, hoping Dr. Sharma will take it easy on me.

"So you've replaced fluids and blood," she says. "Is he still bleeding?"

"Er—yes?"

"Yes or no, Dr. Santini?"

"Yeah. Yes. He's still bleeding."

She raises her eyebrows. "And what are you doing about that part?"

"I consulted GI. They're seeing him this morning." My palms dampen the papers in my hand, scrawled notes smudging to create some artistic study in fear and desperation.

Two blinks. That's what she gives me. How do I read that? Is she pissed? Disappointed? Regretting that she's staring at my stupid face instead of inventing some state-of-the-art medical technology like her brain is *supposed* to be doing?

"Is he still on his blood thinner?" she asks.

"Yes?"

"*Yes or no*, Dr. Santini?"

"Yes."

She pauses. The tense atmosphere smothers me, and every other resident looks away from the carnage. I can't blame them. Instead of the information that Dr. Sharma might want, my brain helpfully supplies me with the urge to turn and run. *We're crashing and burning!*

Dr. Sharma widens her eyes expectantly. "But he's bleeding. Do you see any problem with this?"

"So I'll—stop the blood thinner." I hate that it sounds like a question.

"He had a cardiac stent placed three days ago."

"Then I'll...not stop it."

"You have to pick one, Dr. Santini. Which option is least likely to result in your patient being dead in the morning?"

A tiny pang of irritation hovers at the edge of the adrenaline coursing through my blood, finally scattering my remaining thoughts. I don't know what to do, but I don't want to *say* I don't know what to do. This innate desire to get questions right when they have nothing to do with my specialty or anything I'll ever be doing in the future is a hard one to shake.

She gives me an exaggerated blink. "You'll have the correct answer by lunch. Right, Dr. Santini?"

"Yes," I croak out. Guess I'm not eating again today.

She moves to the IM intern, lifting the weight from my shoulders.

My only saving grace is the fact that Rebecca, the girl who never gives up, isn't on service this month. Doesn't stop her from texting me every day, offering "help." I thought I was clear when she tried to kiss me that we were better as friends, but to her, *friends* must mean dates and sex and eventual marriage with lots of babies.

She sent me a meme this morning of a cat in a white coat captioned, "You'll be fine. Just run a cat scan."

I might hate cats.

I'm looking forward to Group Therapy tonight.

The IM intern and I admit eight patients each before the night team arrives. That afternoon, I inform a patient's son his mother will need an MRI in the morning, and spend no less than forty-five minutes witnessing the guy's rant about the price of her hospital stay.

"I'll have to take out a second mortgage to pay for all the bullshit tests you want to run. You get some sort of kickback for all this? You're just scamming us for money, aren't you?"

I stare, speechless.

This is wild. A million things rush through my head.

The loss of my twenties.

The half million dollars in debt.

The obscene work hours.

The UTI probably forming in my bladder.

The exposure to communicable illnesses.

The constant threat of litigation.

And he thinks I'm scamming him for money?

Nah, bro. I scammed myself.

One day, some little boy will tell me he wants to be a doctor when he grows up, and I'll beg him to be an electrician instead.

That evening, I speed walk away from the hospital, then take refuge in The Strokes blaring through my truck speakers.

I arrive at Mico first and order a Mambo Taxi, rubbing my tired eyes while I wait. When I open them, my gaze locks on Grace at the hostess stand. She smiles at the woman before heading my way, settling into the chair across from me. Her blue Vincent scrubs are miraculously blood free, a rare accomplishment for her.

My drink arrives and the server who's been checking her out for months smiles. "Mambo for you too, Grace?"

She nods with a beautiful smile she's never thrown my way, all twinkling hazel eyes and flushed cheeks and bright teeth.

What would it take for me to earn that smile?

"He knows your name?" I ask when he leaves.

She fires a *duh* look at me. "He knows all our names. We're here all the time."

I lean my elbows on the table, cocking my head at her while she stiffens. "I will pay off your student loan debt if you can prove he knows my name."

Taken aback, she starts to say something when our phones ding. A text from Kai brings my screen to life.

She frowns. "Kai's not going to make it. He's stuck at the hospital."

I lay my phone face down on the table. "And then there were four."

"How's IM?" she asks.

"The seventh circle of hell. How's NICU?"

She grins. "A lot of drug babies I get to cuddle."

"I didn't know they let hellcats near the babies."

As planned, the grin falls off her face, replaced by those fiery narrowed eyes. "The babies love me, Julian."

I bet they do…with that ample chest to rest their heads.

"Did they tell you that?" I raise an eyebrow.

The enticing flush of color on her cheeks shouldn't turn me on. It's her angry face, not her I-want-to-do-you face, but I imagine this is the closest I'll get, and I haven't had sex in… God, when was the last time?

No wonder I'm hard up.

The server sets her drink down.

Grace turns to him with a dazzling smile. "Thank you, Eric." She points at me. "Do you know his name?"

The surfer-esque server glances at me like he's seeing me for the first time. "Er—James?"

Her face falls. "Oh."

I nod at him. "Yeah, that's it. James."

He retreats, and I spear her with an I-told-you-so look.

"At least he got the *J* right," she mutters.

I chuckle. "He picked the most white guy name he could and threw it out there."

Our phones ding again, this time from Raven telling us her babysitter called out and she won't make it.

"And then there were three." She sips her drink.

A burst of edgy energy has my fingers flying over the screen.

> **Me:** Alesha? You still coming?

The three little dots appear and disappear, and I set my phone down.

Grace takes a drink, smirking at me around her straw. "Scared to be alone with me, Santini?"

Yes. I snort. "No."

Riding close quarters with her in the dark of my truck in December had been an enlightening lesson entitled *Things You Can't Have But Want Anyway*. That was the last time I was alone with her, but a niggling voice in the back of my mind has been encouraging me to find excuses to do it again.

She's smart. Funny. Pretty. Smells like a Victoria's Secret Angel.

Suppressing a sigh, I remind myself I don't know what an Angel smells like.

Sex and flowers and magic and sex.

Shut up, stupid voice. She hates me. Unfair, but true. That should be enough to shut down whatever base urges my starved and sleep-deprived brain wants. *Should* is the operative word there.

Both our phones ding, and we dive for them. Alesha's reply makes my heart thud three uncomfortable times in my chest.

"What the fuck is a cat emergency?" Grace glares at her phone, then lifts her gaze to me.

I gasp. "Did you just say the f-word?"

She stares around the restaurant. Our friends have abandoned us and now we're stuck on what could accurately be deemed a *date*.

A possessive and predaceous monster inside me grins—not a promising sign. Despite my own sound logic, I lean toward her, wanting to know if she's brave enough to stay. "We doing this, then?"

The freckles across her ashen skin stand out stark. "I already have my drink, Julian. It's sacrilege to leave Mambo Taxi on the table."

"Then drink up, Sapphire. You're going to need it to deal with Lex Luther all evening."

A sly smile curves her lips. "How was your date with Maleficent by the way?"

"The dragon didn't do it for me." My nonchalant shrug has her laughing.

"Does that mean Khaleesi doesn't have a chance, either?"

I stir my drink. "You familiar with the Hot Crazy Matrix? The Mother of Dragons is way too high in the danger zone."

She snorts. "As if you'd have a chance."

"I don't know." My finger taps against the glass. "I can be pretty adorable when I want."

With a roll of her eyes, she says, "I will pay off *your* student loan debt if you can prove that's true."

"An impossible task. You hate me, so how could I prove it?"

Her stare drops to my hand for two seconds, then jerks to the side. She takes a large draw on her drink. "I don't *hate* you."

I bark out a single disbelieving laugh.

She shakes her head. "I just *want* to hate you. You make it impossible."

My pulse abruptly decides to sync to an EDM beat. "Oh yeah? How's that?"

"You're absurdly nice, even when you're heckling me. You buy me sugar and defend my honor and give me rides. And you do that—that thing." She waves her hand in my general direction.

My skin is on fire. "What thing?"

"With your mouth. You know, the *thing*. When you've said something funny or clever, or when you're getting under my skin. You do that smile without smiling."

I stare, at a loss. "Huh?"

"Ugh. Never mind."

The server returns and we both order our usual—Tacos Mi Tierra.

When he leaves, she tilts her head, studying me. The green in her eyes is brighter today. She's never allowed me close enough to examine all the colors, but the fading light from the windows ignites a hint of jade and emerald.

"So you think you're adorable?" Her nose scrunches. "I think I'd like to see Adorable Julian in action."

My sixth sense prickles, and I narrow my eyes. Where is this going? "His charms are reserved for children and women he has a chance with."

She laughs. "At least you're honest. So no girlfriend, then?"

"Why?" I raise one eyebrow. "You interested?"

A dorky little snort buzzes in her nose and she coughs to cover it. "You'd love that, wouldn't you? Mocking material for the rest of time."

"What about you, then?" I ask. "Where's your lucky man?"

"Ha!" She goes for a chip, breaking it into pieces over her plate instead of eating it. "Lucky? I'm sure you imagine any man stuck with me is cursed."

The idea of it strikes like lightning, being *stuck* with her...

Tasting that tempting mouth. Running fingers down her throat to her chest. Undressing her. Coaxing her down on a bed. Pressing those knees open while she whispers *please.*

That's not a curse.

It's a gift.

A benediction.

The man would be a lucky son of a bitch, and an acidic tang poisons my blood as he takes the shape of Asher in my head.

Shit. Is this—are these *fantasies*? Is this *jealousy*? About Grace Rose, the irritating girl who—despite what she says—loathes me? Dr. Sharma must have scrambled my brain today. It's the only explanation.

Her eyebrows knit together, fingers twisting her straw. Crap. Did she say something?

"It was a joke," she mutters.

The server sets another Mambo Taxi before her. She wiggles in her seat.

Surfer Bro's gaze dips to her chest. "Your food will be out soon."

Her smile glows as she looks at him, and the hibernating caveman in my brain stirs and grunts. This isn't good. I'm tempted to call it cruel, even, having a crush on Grace. The universe is punishing me for not knowing when to stop blood thinners. I'm sure of it.

"It's just a drink," I mutter.

"It's the best drink in the whole world."

"I know one that's better. I'll show you sometime."

She lifts an eyebrow, teeth clamped around the straw. "Oh, Julian. Don't make promises you can't keep."

The tone of her voice when she says my name is always the same, all prim and haughty, like she wants to lecture me.

And now I'm picturing her in a schoolgirl outfit, brandishing a piece of chalk.

"That!" She points at my mouth. "That's the no-smile."

Um.

No.

That's eye fucking.

And now I know I have a tell.

This is—is *horrifying* the right word? It's going to be a problem, is all I'm saying.

I force my face into a different expression, anything to hide the thoughts in my head. "That's just a regular smile."

"Your mouth doesn't move, Julian. It's all in your eyes."

Stop looking at me so closely! "Eyes can't smile, Grace."

She stiffens, eyes wide, gaze sharp.

I realize my mistake a beat too late. "Sapphire. I meant—"

"Nope." The beautiful smile dawns. "You said it. That's twice now, Julian. What's gotten into you?"

You. "I—nothing."

Her mouth. I can't stop staring at her mouth. I'm powerless in the face of that smile—pure happiness, innocent joy. Simply because I said her name. That's all it took? And here I thought baiting her was entertaining.

But this—this is so much better.

The woman is disturbingly sweet, and I'm beyond disarmed.

All my weapons lay on the table between us She's free to pick up any she chooses and destroy me.

Except she doesn't. She folds her hands and lifts her chin, still smiling bright. "I win today, Julian."

Shivery pricks wake beneath my skin as I push away a sense of inevitability. This tug-of-war between us is mutating into something else, isn't it? She won't only win today. She'll continue to win, over and over, taking pieces of me each time.

How much will I wind up losing to this woman?

A couple minutes later, our food arrives—a welcome distraction—and an hour after that, I'm standing in the parking lot with a spitfire who's had three Mambo Taxis and refuses to acknowledge she's too tipsy to drive.

She puts her hands on her hips. "Your truck is too tall for me, Julian."

"Then I'll lift you up."

She scoffs.

I hold my hand out. "Give me your key, Sapphire."

"It's in my bra."

My gaze drops at once to her breasts, sadly hidden behind loose blue cotton.

She snaps in my face. "Eyes up here, Santini."

"You can't mention your bra, then expect me not to look. I'm human."

She places a red-tipped finger over her lips in thought. "Hmm. And this whole time I thought you were one of the Nazgûl."

I give her a sarcastic laugh and grasp her shoulders, directing her to my truck. "Come along, dork."

She sighs. "How am I supposed to get to work in the morning?"

I open the door. "I'll drop you here before I go to the hospital."

She spins to face me. "The rumors, Julian. Remember? People already think I sleep around. I can't be seen doing the walk of shame!"

Ugh. I hate that those thoughts enter her head, that she has to alter her behavior based on misinformation. I want her smile back—the real one I can feel deep in my stomach—so I aim to lighten the moment with a joke. Except when I lean toward her, the scent of her hair draws me in and temptation beckons. My voice grows deeper instead of lighter. "The walk of shame only applies if you fuck me."

Why!

Why. Why. Why.

Her mouth goes slack. No snappy comeback. No signs of affront. Her eyes darken, and we freeze for three seconds before she clears her throat.

Stupid, Julian!

I take the opportunity to grasp her waist, lifting her into my truck.

By the time I'm settled in the driver's seat, her arms are crossed and she's glaring straight ahead, back in her prissy little box. My soft laugh is drowned out by the engine. The car connects to my phone, continuing my last playlist.

Her eyebrows scrunch together. "Is this Kanye?"

I side-eye her. "Let me guess. You're a Taylor Swift fan?"

Her lips purse. "Her voice is angelic, Julian."

"A savage woman who favors devil-red lipstick. Why am I not surprised?"

She mutters something under her breath and turns the volume up so we can't talk anymore. The devil in my head takes control of my thumb and it strays at once to the volume button on the steering wheel.

Don't do it, Julian. Let her win.

And yet—

Her eyes snap in my direction when the music volume descends to a normal level. Her indignation permeates the cab, and I laugh silently. A swelling sense of success grapples with my arguments that I don't really like her.

She's fun to rile. That's it.

It's fun because she gets all flustered and hot.

She hates me, right?

If she hated you, she'd be able to take her eyes off you.

I don't look, but her stare has fingers, grazing seductively down my face and throat. I'm half-hard wondering what she's thinking.

This is going to be a huge problem.

I call Alesha as soon as I step into my apartment, shaking off the Essence of Rose.

"What the fuck is a cat emergency?" I demand when she answers.

"Simba was acting funny. Then he started hacking everywhere."

I fall onto my couch. "You left me alone with her, Alesha."

"Oh, for fuck's sake. I can't anymore with you two. She's not a plague on this earth, Juju. Don't try to play like you don't like her." A loud meow punctuates her tirade.

"I tolerate her for the sake of world peace." I squeeze the bridge of my nose.

"Oh hell. Now she's calling me." Something clangs in the background. "If you've hurt her feelings with your weird hate-flirting thing you do, I'll punch you in the dick. You my boy, but she's my girl. Get your shit together."

Hate-flirting?

That's not what I'm doing.

…Is it?

She hangs up. I groan-sigh at the ceiling, then glance at the two texts waiting on my phone. The first is from Tori. Apparently, Mom is complaining I haven't called her in seven whole days. I ignore that one. The second is from Maxwell.

Maxwell: You working Saturday?

Me: Yeah, but only during the day.

Maxwell: BrOB-GYN meetup at Asher's

Me: I'll be there

We've switched from beer to whiskey at Asher's, and he's passing around his weed, which is a refreshing diversion. As I relax by the firepit and contemplate how much residency has driven me to escape reality with mind-altering substances, Maxwell plops beside me.

"I think I'm going to sign the contract."

More than a year ago, he was offered a position as a faculty attending when he graduates in June. He's the only one of the five seniors to be offered a position, despite their desperate need for more faculty. That he's the only male in the class likely had a lot to do with that. Maxwell DeBakey is a great doctor, but he isn't the best of his class. Sarabeth outshines him on every level, but to hear Dr. Levine talk about it, they never considered any of the women as viable candidates.

I don't get it.

"Residency wasn't enough torture for you?" I ask. "You need it to continue into your future, too?"

A laugh rumbles deep in his chest. The firelight flickers over the amber liquid filling the lowball in his hand as he raises it to his lips. "Residents do all the dirty work and I take home the big bucks. Doesn't sound like torture."

"You have to fix all their mistakes, though."

He side-eyes me. "Been fixing all your mistakes for the last eight months. What's new?"

I tilt my head in concession. Maxwell has been my go-to senior for panicked questions, last second uh-ohs, and shit-my-senior-is-going-to-kill-me-if-I-don't-fix-this-right-now moments. He's never complained and his patience never wanes. He'll be a great attending if he can keep it up.

"Then get ready to fix them for the next three years." I set down my empty glass. The world tilts to a sharp left. Fuck. I'm drunker than I thought, which means I need to slow down. Drunk Julian gives zero fucks about anything and says whatever he wants. I keep him contained as much as possible.

Maxwell rights me. "If you make it through the next three years."

I send him a sidelong glance and he holds his hand to his throat, pretending to choke.

"Ha. Ha." I roll my eyes.

"I'm just saying. There's more to being an OB-GYN than having decent surgical skills. Got to learn the medicine too, bro."

I search for Asher through the dark of the backyard, wishing for another toke. "It isn't easy to remember all that shit. I've never been good at studying."

"Sounds like it's time to find a tutor."

Grimacing, I shake my head.

"Four more months of hand-holding and you're on your own, Julian. You can't count on someone watching over your notes and orders, making sure you're not fucking everything up. Once you're a second-year, people stop looking so closely."

"I know."

"OB isn't a specialty where you can stop and read the algorithms before you act. Emergencies happen fast and you have to have the steps memorized or people die. Babies die."

"I *know*! Shit. You're not an attending yet. Stop lecturing me."

Maxwell lifts one giant shoulder. "Someone's gotta do it."

"Yo, Santini!"

I turn as Asher materializes beside me, offering me the vape pen. "Thanks."

"I gotta know. What's up with you and Rose?"

I cough on the exhale. "What?"

He cocks an eyebrow. "Come on, man. Driving her around. Going after Halliwell. You guys together?"

I hand him his pen. "Nah. She can't stand me."

Beside me, Maxwell snorts. My questioning look receives no answer.

"You sure?" Asher sits back. "'Cause I can't seem to get any traction with her."

It hasn't escaped my notice that Asher's been gunning for Grace, even if she's oblivious to it. He either has slow game or no game at all.

Or maybe she's not interested.

I like that last option best, if I'm honest.

She's too good for him. Too good for all of us. That shy smile, that pervasive intellect, that quiet kindness—she deserves someone great.

Oh god. What *is* this? Is she some kind of enchantress who's poisoned me in her favor?

Ignoring the inner turmoil, I shoot him a look. "You think maybe that has more to do with you than me? If I remember correctly, her first impression of you was overhearing you say you wanted her to suck you off."

He waves his hand, the movement smearing in my influenced vision. "Everyone knows I'm all talk." He shakes his head. "Whatever. If you say there's nothing, I believe you." Then he winks. "I'll find the key to turning her on eventually."

When I first met him, yeah, I thought he was a prick, but Asher has more to him than I originally thought. He knows how he comes across when he says shit like that, but it's completely at odds with how he behaves—the compassionate patient care, the ingrained sense of justice, the way he goes to bat for residents treated unfairly. He acts like he sleeps around, but drunkenly confided he hasn't been with anyone since his fiancée broke his heart a year ago. Asher's a decent guy, but in this moment, I hate him.

Not even the drugs and alcohol in my system can distract me. In slow motion, the image plays out, a horror movie in my mind. Grace smiles at Asher while unzipping his jeans, dropping slowly to her knees. Venomous heat erupts in my chest, and I squeeze my eyes shut, desperately searching for anything to make that image go away.

A snarling, primal animal wakes, immersing me in a deluge of jealousy I've never experienced, not even when my last girlfriend slept with my med school classmate.

My hands clench as I stare into the fire, fantasizing about throwing Asher into it.

Maxwell nudges my arm, leaning close to murmur, "Chill out, bro."

Yep. This is going to be a huge problem, and I don't even know what started it.

I lurch to my feet and head inside for an unneeded bathroom break. As I stand alone in the kitchen, the cookie jar of condoms on the fridge catches my attention and rapture dawns. Grace will know it's a joke, but I grin maniacally as I imagine her spine-snapped-straight, nose-in-the-air pseudo-affront when she opens the text. I take a picture of the jar and send it to her, followed by the typical caption.

> **Me:** Found this. Made me think of you.

> **Sapphire:** 😊 Don't you know anything about being slutty, Julian? My dirty affairs go bareback.

I stare at the word *bareback*, and a host of ungodly images flood my mind, each of them imprinting desires I don't want deep into the highest-functioning areas of my cerebral cortex, bypassing the more primitive locales.

Fuckity fuck, fuck, fuck.

This is a problem.

Grace

APRIL, YEAR 1

An hour-long PowerPoint barely scratches the surface of the issues encompassing female sexual dysfunction. Regardless, I furiously type into my Google Doc while third-year Mila Tischler lectures from the head of the conference table.

The slides on orgasmic dysfunction and hypoactive sexual desire remind me of my own sexual repression. The memories of what I did for Matt still make me want to vomit. I can't believe I did those things simply out of fear he'd leave if I didn't. Even when they hurt. When they made me cry.

A great cost, but a priceless lesson learned: love is a figment and believing in it will hurt you.

Why do I allow him so much power over me? Years later, and the whisper of *ice queen* still reverberates in my subconscious. It's illogical, and I want to heal. I want to move past it, but I just…can't. Instead, I drown out the voice with overindulgent color-coded notes.

Some insults simply cut too deep to heal. Some insults bleed forever.

As usual, Julian sits across from me, listening without taking notes. Nothing but the Slytherin mug sits before him. No notebook. No laptop. Not even a pen.

He's wearing glasses.

They are *not* hot.

Yes, huh. He's got Clark Kent vibes, girl.

Ugh. How is it fair that glasses make him cuter?

Where's my spare kryptonite?

Beside me, Kai leans in to whisper suggestive jokes in my ear *again*, distracting me as I stifle my giggles. It draws attention to both of us, but I'm not the only one with immature behavior. Several people snicker behind their hands at Persistent Genital Arousal Disorder, a phenomenon in which women experience physical arousal unrelieved by orgasms.

It isn't funny. It's not. But when Mila describes cases of women suffering dozens of unprovoked orgasms each day, everyone's maturity drops to the level of twelve-year-olds.

The last slide displays a picture of Michael Scott from *The Office* holding his World's Best Boss mug beside a quote bubble that reads, "Sex is like a good cup of coffee. It's all in how you make it, or how you take it."

"That's what she said," Asher quips from the back of the room.

I cover my face as laughter finally takes hold, and several others follow suit.

"Any questions?" Mila asks.

My hand shoots in the air.

"Of course," Julian mutters across the table, sipping his black-as-his-soul coffee.

I ignore him and ask her to clarify several points in the lecture, typing her answers as she gives them. People are accustomed to my questions at this point, but Julian still harasses me about it.

Four questions in, he lets out a loud sigh, widening his eyes at me behind black-rimmed wayfarers.

I glare at him. "What?"

"You realize the longer you ask questions, the longer we all have to be here."

"Forgive me for wanting to *learn* during this educational event."

The stares in the room bounce between us. Even the attendings settle in for our argument like it's a normal, expected part of their day.

He rolls his eyes. "Right. Because your questions aren't strategically designed to show off how much you already know."

That's not true! I stiffen in my seat. "My questions are designed to elucidate portions of the lecture I found difficult to understand, *Julian*."

He tilts his head. "Was it the desire, the arousal or the orgasm part that confused you, *Sapphire*?"

I glare at him. "What exactly did Palpatine promise you that you just *had* to join the dark side?"

The no-smile appears, dark eyes flaring as he stares at me. "Your silence." Then he points at the Michael Scott slide. "Along with endless cups of good coffee." He says it even-toned, eyebrow perked, and takes a single sip from his Slytherin mug.

Alesha bursts out laughing, as do several other residents and Dr. Levine.

Kai bends toward me, stage-whispering, "He won that one."

It takes every shred of self-control in me not to laugh, to smile, to stand up and run my hands through that perfect hair until he looks like I kept him busy in my bed for the last three days.

Kai's voice drops to a true whisper. "Look away, darling. You're staring. *Intensely.*"

Mila closes her PowerPoint, and the room rustles with people rising to take breaks, but Julian and I are still linked by our staring contest, and I'm transported back to several weeks ago when he leaned in close enough that his heat prickled all along my body.

The walk of shame only applies if you fuck me.

Why on earth did he say that? Why did he put that image in my head? Why won't it *leave* my head?

Goose bumps rise along my arms, and that black hole gaze finally pulls away from me when Maxwell taps his shoulder.

After the lectures conclude, I head to St. Vincent. My senior for L&D this month is my least favorite so far. Arista Herrera is a chief resident who has the worst case of senioritis I've ever witnessed. Utterly checked out, she lazes in our call room on TikTok while I run the floor by myself.

The OB hospitalists who serve as our oversight at Vincent are less than friendly. They range the gamut from cold and haughty (Dr. Narayan) to cold and hippie (Dr. Scarlett) to cold and sassy (Dr. Echols). Dr. Nguyen is the only pleasant one, but his retirement in a few months means he's reducing his shifts.

All four despise our faculty attendings for their lack of supervision, accusing them of abandoning us so the hospitalists are forced to do more work. The residents are stuck in the middle of the politics, ignored by our core faculty who care little for us and abused by the hospitalists who, by all appearances, loathe us.

Without my senior for guidance, the game I play balancing it all has become treacherous. I'm walking a tightrope, and it's only a matter of time before I fall. The ASCOM internal hospital phone snapped onto the waist of my pants barely stops ringing—nurses requesting med orders, informing me of triage patients, signing out on ED consults. I call Asher often since his schedule on GYN surgery is a little more free, and he's always willing to help me untangle the knots.

I stand at the nursing station where the screens display the fetal tracings from all twenty-five labor rooms on this floor. I'm most concerned about my patient in twelve, who has a raging case of meth-eclampsia. She's kind and thankful despite withdrawing from her drug of choice, but loopy from all the meds.

Judging by the heart tracing, the baby isn't too happy.

"Gosh, Dr. Rose," one of the nurses says in a falsely sweet voice. "You've lost weight."

That's because I'm so anxious, I can't eat, and I've gotten most of my calories lately from Starbucks and Mountain Dew, but thanks.

"Yeah." I glance at my scrubs, hanging loose from my body. Even my bras are a little too big.

"What's your secret?" she asks.

Um. Not having time to eat? Running around this hospital for thirteen hours each day? Generalized anxiety disorder? Take your pick.

I glance at her. She's about my age, and the badge clipped at her chest declares her name to be Ariel. She's thin as a thirty-gauge needle, so I can't imagine she's trying to lose weight. Some game is at play here, one I don't understand.

I paste on a smile. "No secret. Just…working a lot."

"Oh. Well, maybe not enough since you forgot to put in the induction orders on twenty-two."

"Oh shoot. Sorry."

Her sweet smile does nothing to hide the iciness in her eyes. "Maybe you could do it now instead of saying something snotty like you usually do."

My teeth grind. These women hate me. I've done nothing but work and try to be friendly, but I'm quiet and socially awkward, and I wear anxiety like an itchy body suit, so I think I come across as snobbish. Their cattiness is at a maximum. The night resident told me they complain about me behind my back. Maybe they believe the rumors, too.

I sit at the computer without saying anything and put in the standard induction orders—the ones she could have done herself in the same amount of time it took to berate me. When I glance at the tracings, twelve's heart rate has decided to take a nosedive into the eighties—not reassuring.

I meet the nurse in the room. What's this one's name? Krystal.

The patient is screaming, "Get it out of me! Get it out!"

Nine months into training, and I'm pretty immune to all this. The screaming. The heart rate decelerations. The bleeding that sometimes looks like someone turned on a faucet. I used to have a spike in my own heart rate, a flush of sweat under my arms. Now, I'm only hoping she's a good pusher so I'll have time to eat some peanut butter before the next disaster.

"Will you call Dr. K and Dr. Narayan?" I ask the nurse.

She nods.

The patient is nearly crowning, and the father of the baby shouts, "Oh shit! What's that?"

"That's your baby's head." I gown up, pulling a stool between the patient's legs.

Backup nurses flood the room, but Dr. Narayan is down in the attending lounge eating lunch, so I doubt she'll make it.

Two involuntary pushes, and the baby screams out her first breath. Distracted by the newborn on her chest, the patient doesn't react as I deliver the placenta and evaluate the laceration. This is my least favorite part of delivering babies—putting together the mashed hamburger meat left behind.

After numbing her, I go to work.

"Hey, Doc. Make sure to put in an extra stitch for me." The dad winks and laughs.

I look at him, blink twice and turn back to the laceration.

"No, but really," he says.

The sleep and food deprivation finally hits me when I meet his gaze and give a tight smile. "How small do you need it?"

The nurse assessing the baby snickers, and I return to my work while the dad flushes red.

Dr. Narayan makes it to the bedside when I'm a few stitches in and guides every throw. At the computer desk afterward, I'm flying through my notes and orders when she appears beside me.

"Dr. Rose, can you follow me?"

Startled, I save my work and trail after her, suppressing the sensation that I'm being called to the principal's office. Short black ponytail swinging, she opens the door to her office and ushers me inside. She doesn't offer a seat, so I don't take one. Instead, we stand beside the door.

She crosses her arms. "You need to stop butting into deliveries."

Taken aback, I gape while the familiar acidic corrosion of anxiety filters through my insides. "I was trying to help."

"It's my job to take care of patients. Your job is to help me. It's inappropriate for you to be delivering patients without an attending physician present."

"She would have delivered in the bed—"

"All of you residents do the same thing. You need to learn your place." Her sharp gaze bores into me. "Where is your senior?"

"Oh, I—"

"It doesn't matter. How about your attending? Isn't he supposed to be here when you have patients actively laboring on the floor?"

"She went from four centimeters to crowning. The nurse called him—"

"I'm tired of taking on liability for you all to work reckless and unchaperoned, and you need to be trained. It's their job to train you, don't you agree?"

I curl my lips inward, biting hard. It's my understanding that *she* is meant to be my chaperone while I'm working in this hospital, but I don't know all the closed-door arguments that've led to this level of bitterness.

It's like I'm a kid whose parents are divorcing, and each parent wants me to take their side when both of them are wrong. Meanwhile, I'm crying in the corner for someone to please buy me some cotton candy. After her tirade, which I'm sure was cathartic for her, but ruined my entire day, I whip out my phone and open the Pit It or Quit It message stream.

> **Me:** Narayan's in full Narayan mode today if you know what I mean

> **Alesha:** 🙄 So average day then?

> **Raven:** I'm sorry! Your day will get better.

> **Julian:** Or it will get worse, and you'll have to drown your sorrows in textbooks.

> **Kai:** 😄

> **Kai:** $100 says studying is her stress relief

> **Me:** At least I knew the answer when they asked us about pap smears earlier, Julian.

Julian sends a picture of him in surgery with Dr. Ryan, followed by a jewel emoji.

> **Julian:** Your hostility can't touch me, Sapphire. I took out a uterus today.

> **Me:** That's a diamond, not a sapphire.

Everyone else congratulates him, but I growl. Of course the attendings let him assist in a hysterectomy when he's supposed to be covering L&D. He's the golden child, so let's all shower him in gifts.

I open another message.

> **Me:** Thanks for taking the time to teach me repairs in December. I'm finally starting to feel good about them.
>
> **Asher:** You're a vagician!
>
> **Me:** Ha. Don't know about that. It could've been better.
>
> **Asher:** Practice makes perfect, sweetie-kins.

I chuckle and put my phone away, then settle down to chart. Beside me, the nurse is complaining that she had to work all three of her twelve-hour shifts in a row this week, and I quell the resentment that I'm on my nineteenth twelve-hour shift in a row.

If I complained, I'd be told I did it to myself.

You chose this.

Sometimes I can't remember why.

The image of my poised, respected future self has never felt further away.

Even my confidence in my repair is short-lived when Dr. Narayan calls a C-section on another patient and chastises me the entire operation for my poor surgical technique. The more she complains, the shakier my hands grow, until I'm unable to tie down a single suture without multiple attempts.

Afterward, she eyes me meaningfully. "You need work, Dr. Rose."

"Yes, Dr. Narayan."

"There's expired suture for practice in the resident lounge. I suggest you start there."

At shift change that evening, Arista barely listens as I sign out to the second-year covering nights, Ellyn Peterson.

I don't know Ellyn all that well, but she gives me an encouraging smile when Arista leaves without saying goodbye.

She folds the list I printed for her and sticks it in her pocket. "Vincent's tough. Just think of it as a strength-building exercise. Everyone treats residents like trash, especially female residents."

I manage a half-hearted laugh. "I'd like to give them a taste of their own medicine."

She lets out a resentful chuckle. "Wouldn't recommend it. You'll learn fairly quickly that when you treat people the way they treat you—" she eyes me closely "—they get real fucking offended."

Julian

July in Texas is death.

I grew up by the Gulf and have a fair understanding of heat. I'm convinced Texas is in a competition with the sun to see who can melt its population fastest, and they're both winning.

The shitty AC in my apartment isn't cutting it, so my only respite is the apartment pool. I throw on my trunks and head downstairs. Approximately one million people have the same idea as me. The pool is packed, but it's large. I pad toward the lounge chairs to throw down my towel and shirt when someone calls my name. My head turns, and I'm inundated by a heat beyond anything a Texas summer can do.

I trip over a lounge chair. "Whaa—"

Grace springs up from it. She wears a bright turquoise bikini with little white daisies all over it. It's more straps than material and tosses me no Hail Mary in the form of unsightly rashes or unexplained lumps.

Her body is *made* for sex. Now, I'm a gynecologist. Logic tells me that all bodies are made for sex—prolongation of the species and all that—but Grace's body is like someone poured an Ariana Grande song into an hourglass. She's rivaling the fantasy of Gal Gadot in my head.

And now I'm picturing Grace in full Wonder Woman regalia, and that's just—

"What?" She looks down at herself like she's done something wrong.

"You're—flowers."

"What?"

I wave vaguely at her suit without looking at it again. "You're swimming?"

She grins. "This is my only day off for the next three weeks, and I plan to spend it with a White Claw, melting under the sun until my skin blisters."

I swallow against the flames in my throat and stare at her hairline. "That's—good plan."

"Are you hurt?"

"What?"

She points at my foot. Ah. Yes. I stubbed my toe, didn't I?

Her eyes narrow, and I laugh. Don't know why. It just bursts out of me, uncontrollable.

I have never been this awkward. I am a total sleaze brought low by simple white daisies.

And fantastic breasts.

And delusions.

Throwing the towel on her chair, I mumble something about being hot before ripping off my shirt. I hop into the pool and stay submerged in the coolish water until the desire for her ebbs and my lungs beg for air. Breaking the surface, I've regained my composure.

My hands clasp the edge of the pool, and I sneak a peek at her.

She's sitting at the end of her lounge chair, head cocked, staring at me in question. "Did I just witness a heatstroke?"

It coaxes a smile from me. "Something like that."

Sweat has gathered on her brow and in her cleavage, but unlike me, she's luxuriating in it.

Her bare feet bring her closer, and she sits at the edge to dip her feet in the water beside me. "Is the great Julian Santini, Golden Boy, really made speechless by the sight of a woman in a bikini?"

My forehead falls to the backs of my hands where they grasp the pool edge. "I plead the fifth." I pause. "But like... Have you seen that bikini?"

She chuckles. "I'm starting to believe Adorable Julian does exist."

I pinch her toe beneath the water, and she screeches, jerking her foot away, but I grab both ankles.

She gives me a warning look. "Julian, don't."

The smirk on my face grows, and I tug. "What? Afraid you'll melt?"

She shrieks as I pull until she's at the edge, bracing her weight on my shoulders.

Her eyes widen. "No—"

Sinking beneath the surface, I snicker inwardly and she follows me underwater. The splash of her plunging below the surface reverberates, and bubbles float around my skin along with the brush of her legs as she kicks to the surface.

I come up for air again, already laughing.

She pushes my shoulder and wipes water out of her eyes. "This is cruel punishment for a crime I didn't commit."

"I'm sure if you dig deep, you'll find you deserved it."

She splashes me. "Is this what you wanted, Julian? You happy now?" She rolls her eyes before dropping her voice to a falsely seductive tone. "You got me all wet."

Sarcasm, but my dick still responds—a situation not improved by her hoisting herself out of the water, droplets streaming down her smooth skin, over the curves of her ass. She returns to her post at the edge of the pool, only now she's dripping wet.

I am an idiot.

She flicks water over me. "Well, Adorable Julian lasted all of thirty seconds. Now that that's out of your system, can I have normal Julian back?"

"Yes. I am back to functioning capacity."

She gives a satisfied nod. "I heard you're doing well on GYN."

I hoist myself out of the pool and sit next to her, feet dangling in the water. "Did you?"

"Chen said he was impressed."

Impressed for a DO, probably. I recently overheard some dickhead at the hospital joking that MD was the Coca-Cola and DO was the RC Cola of medicine. Off-brand doctors who couldn't afford the good letters.

So I shrug away the compliment, even though it might ease the quiet voice inside chanting I'm somehow deficient. I've always been good with my hands. Even as a student, I picked up on surgical techniques and anatomy quickly. It's never been hard, so it isn't all that impressive to me.

If only I knew how to study without being distracted by four hundred other things...

"Don't just shrug at me." Grace bumps her shoulder into mine.

"What do you want me to say? Yay, I *slay* at cutting people open and sewing them back together."

She scrunches her freckled nose. "That's a large portion of our job."

"Yeah, but I'm trash at the rest of it."

She looks out over the water where a group of kids play water tag, their exertions sprinkling us with droplets. "I'm good at the rest of it."

She *is* good. She always knows the answer in didactics. She completes her notes on time. Her instincts are on point. She'd never question when to stop blood thinners.

Grace Rose has the kind of intelligence that drips from every word she says. She can organize in ways my easily distracted mind can't even fathom.

So I nod. "I know."

"But no one cares because they still think I don't deserve to be here."

"That's not—"

"Yes, it is."

I press my lips together, forcing myself not to offer platitudes that won't help. Instead, I say, "Sometimes I wonder if they don't think I deserve to be here, either."

She pats my arm. "Because you're a DO?"

I nod-shrug because I don't want to say it out loud. Insecurities are a bitch.

"Well, at least you've got the surgery thing. I'm terrible at surgery. There's too much art to it. So I was thinking..."

Bracing my elbows on my knees, I trace her profile as she gazes over the water. "What were you thinking?"

"Maybe we could work together." She meets my eyes. "I could help you with the book stuff, and you could help me with the surgical stuff."

Blank. My mind goes blank. She wants *me* to teach her surgery?

"Why wouldn't you ask one of the attendings? Or the upper levels? I'm the same level as you."

She looks away, hiding her expression entirely. "Dr. K told me to wait until my GYN month. The uppers aren't really receptive. I could ask Asher, but he doesn't have the best surgical reputation." She shakes her head. "Never mind. I'll just ask him."

The idea of Asher in close proximity to her, intimate and alone, makes me want to vomit.

"I'm not an expert," I say. "I have a knack for it. That's all."

She sighs. "If you don't want to do it, just say so."

Another awkward laugh escapes me. "I want to do it. You're a genius. I'd be lucky to have your help. So...yeah, let's glow up our flaws. I just—I don't know if I'll help you as much as you'll help me."

She hides her proud smile by turning away, but I don't know why. She *should* be proud of her hard work and intelligence.

"Trust me." She grabs my hand and lifts it in the air. "With these, you can help me plenty."

Ugh.

So many double entendres there.

Without releasing me, she says, "You won't spare my feelings like Asher would. This will help us both."

Neither of us let go. Our connected hands fall to the concrete between us. She doesn't pull away.

Why isn't she pulling away?

Why don't I?

We're holding hands, half-naked. My brain short-circuits again.

This unrequited attraction to her is disastrous for my self-esteem, and now I'll spend *more* time in close proximity to her, constantly reminded of how—surgical skills notwithstanding—she's smarter and more competent than me and so fucking beautiful it makes my head hurt.

When did I develop this self-destructive streak? She's a wildfire, but I'm running straight toward her, knowing she'll destroy me.

We both stare down at our joined hands, and like a masochist, I slowly lace our fingers, one by one. She doesn't stop me.

Why doesn't she stop me?

Her tiny hand fits in mine like it belongs there.

She clears her throat, breaking the spell, then murmurs something about being hot. She slips into the water again, escaping my grasp.

Yep.

I'm doomed.

The only difference between intern year on June 30th and second year on July 1st is my medical license—and the fact that all my shifts are worked without a senior resident. I'm alone now, and my first twenty-four-hour shift by myself in the middle of July is a sleep-deprived marathon of reminders that I'm not ready to be by myself.

"The baby's in the sixties, Dr. Santini…"

"She's bleeding, Dr. Santini…"

"Methergine or Hemabate, Dr. Santini…"

"You forgot to put in orders, Dr. Santini…"

Maxwell is the only reason I'm able to survive the first part of the shift, but then he reminds me he's on vacation, and to leave him alone, so I switch to Pit It or Quit It.

Me: What is the dose of Methergine?

Sapphire 💎 : 0.2mg IM

Me: That's what I told them! They acted like I was an idiot.

Me: Morphine safe in 2nd tri yes?

Sapphire 💎 : Yes.

Me: Patient ate eleven Big Macs. Now vomiting profusely. Zofran?

Kai: wtf is happening.

Sapphire 💎 : Yes, zofran fine.

Me: Syphilis, pregnant and allergic to penicillin

Alesha: Sucks for her.

Sapphire 💎 **:** Consult infectious disease

Me: I need help!

Kai: You need an exorcist

Sapphire 💎 **:** Come to my apartment when you get home. I have a bunch of apps that will help you.

"I need help now!" I yell at my phone, startling the nurse beside me.

She gives me an unsure smile.

"Sorry." I rub my face. "Hectic day."

"Yeah, it's busy for a Saturday." She touches my shoulder. "Did you get sleep last night?"

I take a quick glance at her name tag. So many nurses work this floor, and I swear half of them are named Ashley. This one is Ariel. I search her face for one feature I might remember.

Blue eyes like the ocean. Ariel the mermaid.

"Not really." I blink, sleepy and slow.

I'm pretty sure I look like a more exhausted version of death, but she gives a thirsty smile, hand still on my shoulder. "Well, if I can help with anything, just let me know."

My eyebrows lift. Seriously? Am I being hit on right now?

"Here. I'll give you my number." She slides my unlocked phone from my weak grasp and brazenly proceeds to text herself, stealing my phone number.

"Thanks." I grab my phone with stiff fingers when she offers it. Sort of rude, just filching it like that. I would have given her my number willingly if she'd asked.

"No problem. You'll get better sleep tonight."

Yeah. Because I'll be in my own bed. Without an ASCOM.

In the last three hours of my shift, things slow and I sneak away to the call room to lay down. No sooner does my head hit the pillow than the ASCOM lets out a loud beep indicating its battery is low.

If I was a crying man, I'd cry. I really would.

Instead, I heave myself from the bed and return to the nursing desk to change the battery.

Later that night, I shower and eat, then head to Grace's apartment like she requested. Because I'm a good puppy who follows directions.

I'm pathetic.

She opens the door, a knockout in her red dress and devil-red lipstick, hair half up and curled.

"Oh." I blink at the vision before me. "Are you going out?"

"Yeah, remember? A bunch of us are going to that vodka bar. You said no because you had to work today."

I rub my eyes. "Right. I forgot."

A soft laugh precedes her hand grasping my wrist and dragging me inside. "Did you get any sleep?"

"Maybe like thirty minutes. I don't know."

She holds her hand out. "Give me your phone."

In Grace's hands, my phone feels safe. It's worlds different than seeing it in Ariel's. My entire life is on that device. I trust Grace not to snoop or send crude text messages to important people, which means I'm free to collapse onto her couch, eyes falling shut. Her whole apartment smells like her, but her furniture is a heady dose. I turn my face into the fabric, breathing deep.

She plops onto the sofa next to my head. "I'm going to download a bunch of apps, okay?"

"Mmm."

"This one helps with dosing and drug reactions. This one calculates DVT risk. This one tells you how to manage abnormal Paps. This one..."

She continues, but I drift, letting her dulcet voice be a lullaby. Stuck in the between world before sleep, I barely groan as fingers comb through my hair, gently scratching, lulling me further into the void. They slide my glasses off and I'm gone.

I wake to the smell of coffee, and blink at a ceiling that isn't mine.

"You are so lucky I'm nice and didn't draw a dick on your forehead last night."

Sitting up, I find Grace clean-faced, rumpled wavy hair flowing around her, wearing a loose T-shirt and pajama shorts, proffering a cup of black coffee.

She has never been more fuckable.

"I thought we could start our first lesson today, since your panicked lack of knowledge drove you to such extremes as to sleep in the enemy's lair last night."

"Technically, the lair would be your bedroom. I slept in the enemy's antechamber."

She laughs and settles next to me with her own much lighter cup of coffee, topped in whipped cream.

"How was the vodka bar?" I ask.

Blowing on her coffee, she smirks. "I didn't stay long since I had a sleeping dragon in my apartment."

I pull a face. "Did I ruin your night?"

"Nah. I got to flex the dress. That's all that matters."

I tip my head in concession. "That dress is a gift to mankind."

She stares at me, wide-eyed. "Was that a compliment?"

"It was a fact."

A smile breaks over her face, bright and buoyant, and my stomach doesn't fall. It disappears.

"I have to go." The words fall from my mouth.

Her smile fades to confusion.

I shake my head, trying to clear away this persistent impression that my entire life is syncing to her heartbeat. "I'll be right back." I set down my coffee and swipe my glasses from the table. "Brush my teeth. Get contacts."

"Oh." She settles deeper into the couch. "Don't take long. I've got plans for you."

I freeze. "Why does that sound like I might not survive it?"

She smiles into her coffee, evil and suggestive, and I leave before I do something stupid.

Like hit on her.

When did I become such a huge Grace Rose stan?

Forty-five minutes later, I'm glaring as she sits cross-legged on the couch beside me. "Homework?" I say. "Seriously?"

"Did you think I could mindfuck the information into your head, Julian? You have to work for it."

A wide grin grows on my face. "Hearing Miss Goody Two-shoes say *fuck* is always the highlight of my day."

She rolls her eyes. "I made it so easy. I *gave* you my flash-cards! You know how lucky you are right now? I don't share my flashcards with anyone."

"Such a greedy girl."

She smacks my shoulder. "Be serious."

"Fine!" I slump into the cushions of her couch. "I'll do your stupid flashcards."

What a waste of that satisfied smile. I can think of so many other things I could do to make her smile like that.

Ugh. Maybe studying with Grace is a bad idea. All I think about is sex.

I need to get laid.

Maybe she'll be into the idea of study-break stress relief.

"—then you won't forget." She finishes her speech with a nod of her head. *That's that.*

"What?"

She growls. "Are you listening?"

I offer a contrite expression, and she lifts her gaze to the ceiling, taking a deep breath.

Nah. She definitely won't be into casual sex, I doubt I could do casual sex with her. Well, if that's all she'd give me, I would, but that fantasy of her sleep-tousled and proffering morning coffee is irrevocable now. That's something I could wake up to every day for the rest of my life.

"Julian!"

I jolt.

She blinks at me. "Wow. How did you make it through med school?"

"A lot of Adderall and being okay with mediocre grades."

Her shoulders droop.

"Oh, and I slept with the dean."

For two seconds, she stares, owl-eyed. At my teasing wink, she descends into giggles, and I preen internally. It wakes a new craving inside me—the desire to make her laugh.

My phone buzzes.

Ariel (L&D): Hey Dr. Santini. You free tonight?

With an adorable and determined notch between her brows, Grace organizes papers into stacks to study. "Okay. We can work around your concentration issues. I'll get this in your head if it's the last thing I do. I promise."

She's so cute, this little bookworm. So sweet. Something inside warms and turns molten, asking me to stay by her side.

I leave Ariel on read.

Grace

SEPTEMBER, YEAR 2

Our outpatient clinic across the street from TUMC is run by the residents and overseen by our faculty attendings. Each resident is required one half day of clinic per week. For the first time since we started residency, Julian and I share the same time slot—Friday morning.

It's been nice—dare I say *fun?*—having him by my side. Turns out, his sarcasm is quite entertaining when it's not directed solely at annoying me.

I settle into my computer in the dictation room as morning sunlight streams through the windows behind me. Like the rest of the resident areas, the place is a mess, but I love it.

It's home.

My first appointment is a girl establishing prenatal care.

She's fourteen.

A lovely girl, if a little quiet, and quite diligent. She takes industrious notes on everything I say. The irony that those notes are scribbled in an outdated Lisa Frank notebook is not lost on me.

As I chart afterward, I sip my Starbucks and side-eye my clinic partner. "We still on for later?"

Julian continues to type. "One o'clock, right? Sim lab?"

I nod. In July, Julian and I spent our minimal spare time coaching each other, but all of August was lost since he was on nights and I was on days. Now that we're both on days again, we're back at it. I quiz him on medical diagnoses and treatment options, and he works with me on surgical techniques—the steps of procedures, suturing, practicing on models. He even set up a laparoscopic training box for us to use in his apartment.

He's getting better at the flashcards, though it seems to require immense effort for him to concentrate. I have to redirect his focus so many times each study session that a wild curiosity has risen, wondering what's happening in his head that's so distracting.

My improvement, on the other hand, has been slow but steady. He may not be the best student, but patient and thorough, he's a phenomenal teacher.

This week, the simulation lab opened after being closed for remodeling since the spring. The lab boasts a laparoscopic simulator, several training models and a DaVinci surgical robot console. He booked time for us to practice this afternoon.

"What about Group Therapy at Kai's?" I ask. "You coming to that, too?"

He slides a glance toward me. "Do I ever miss Group Therapy?"

"This drink you promised better be as good as you say it is if I'm missing out on a Mambo Taxi for it."

He gives his screen the no-smile.

"Darling!" a voice shouts behind me, and I turn to the door as Asher sweeps through. He beams. "And here I thought my day would be boring."

"Hey, Asher," I say. "What are you doing here?"

He pulls a chair between me and Julian. "Had to turn in some evals to Chen. And what are you fine people doing this morning?"

Julian points to his computer. "Obviously, we're working."

Asher sighs. "Oh, to be young again." He winks at me. "Actually, I don't miss second year at all. It's the worst. Did I ever tell you about the time I was given a punishment weekend shift because I was ten minutes late to a surgery a senior had claimed, then didn't show up to?"

My mouth drops open. "Seriously?"

"Yep. And the punishment shift I was assigned was *supposed* to be that senior's, so she slept in on the day of the surgery, *and* got the weekend free for her troubles."

Both Julian and I stare at him in horror.

"Yep. Second year sucks. But hey, it's already September, so only…nine months to go."

"Thanks for that reminder." Julian pushes away from the desk to see his next patient.

Asher and I chat a few more minutes before a chorus of oohs and aahs peal through the door. We exchange glances, and I slip outside the dictation room to investigate.

Asher bumps into me when I stop short at the sight before me. In the middle of a crowd of medical assistants, Julian cradles his patient's newborn baby girl. The new mom stands beside him, beaming, along with all the MAs. Julian's gaze is fastened on the sleeping baby. A soft smile plays at his mouth.

My insides scream in joy.

Wed him and bed him! Have his babies!

Whoa. It's intense, this sudden desire. I must be ovulating or something. Hormones are totally absurd.

This is *Julian*, I remind myself. Where is this even coming from?

"Isn't she beautiful, Dr. Santini?" the patient asks.

Julian nods.

Isn't he beautiful? Look at him. He's so pretty.

Um. No. False.

Then again...how rude would it be to remove the child from his arms so I can jump in them? His arms seem like a fabulous place to be right now.

Still smiling, he glances up and does a double take when he meets my eyes.

Father my children, please.

God, what is this? Attraction is a fickle, illogical thing. I have to forcibly remember that prettiness doesn't trump personality.

Though...is his personality really that bad?

Julian and I stare at each other a beat too long, only interrupted when one of the MAs asks to hold the baby. I blink away the nonsensical desire and the flutters in my stomach, then return to my computer.

My body is still humming though, which makes the remainder of our clinic time awkward as hell. I'm not even sure when Asher leaves, but I think I manage a goodbye.

Heading to the sim lab a couple hours later, I've put it behind me. Sort of. I've come up with a system in which I picture a frozen tundra every time thoughts of Julian arise.

He swipes his card to enter the lab and drags me inside. "You act like I'm taking you to hell."

"I've never liked video games, Julian."

He snorts. "You practically get off at the sight of flashcards, but dread playing with fake laparoscopic instruments. I'll never understand you."

I roll my eyes. "Yes. My mysteries are vast and deep."

"Then you'll like hell." He winks and my insides go all shivery. From the ice of the tundra, of course.

Located at the nearby medical school, the sim lab is all white tiles, white walls and white ceiling. Tables around the periphery are set up with surgical models. The robot console fills one corner and the LapSim another. A gurney with a simulation patient is pushed against one wall. The smell of fresh paint lingers in the air.

At the LapSim, Julian punches in his credentials and whizzes through the introductory information like he's done it a hundred times. The list of courses pops up and his previous scores display to the side.

My mouth drops open. I point at the total laparoscopic hysterectomy module. He has a perfect score.

What the—

"It took me forever to get that score," he says.

I stare at him, dumbfounded.

"It was a bet. Maxwell said I couldn't do it."

A grin spreads over my face. "What'd you win?"

The bridge of his nose turns a curious shade of red and he glances at the door. "You remember that first hyst I did by myself as an intern?"

I nod.

"It was supposed to be Maxwell's and he *got sick* at the last minute. I was conveniently the only one around to assist."

The back of my hand connects hard with his shoulder. "Julian! You're thieving surgeries?"

"It was gifted to me." He rubs his arm, as if my hand could do any damage to the marble there.

"Fine. Teach me your ways, Golden Boy."

He starts the basic training modules—the ones I'd started last winter and abandoned in total frustration. They aren't explicitly required, so I decided my time was better spent elsewhere.

Quitting definitely had nothing to do with the hit to my perfectionism, and the place was under refurbishment, anyway. Totally out of my control.

"It's all about depth perception." He opens a module on clip placement and grasps the instruments, long fingers sliding into the handles. My gaze snags on the movements. His tendons flex and his veins dilate as he works.

With his attention riveted to the screen, he's oblivious to my hand lust. What is it about his hands? Maybe it's simply that they're so capable. So skilled. I clearly have a competence kink.

They'd have that same proficiency on your body, Grace.

Frozen wasteland. Frozen wasteland. Frozen wasteland.

Don't kid yourself. You've been thinking this for months.

Look at him, smiling at the screen.

That jaw.

And he's so nice.

Ugh. He doesn't like me that way, does he? He hasn't given any hints. He doesn't flirt. Never makes a move. Do I even *want* him to like me that way?

"See?" he says. "Once you get the depth perception down, the rest is all hand-eye coordination."

He steps aside to let me grab the instruments, then stands behind me. I take three times as long to do what he did and make the simulated patient hemorrhage in the process.

"Okay." He tilts his head at all the fake blood spurting over the screen. "So you're as bad at this as I am at flashcards."

"I told you."

A smile touches his mouth while he bounces a couple times on his toes. "It's fine. We got this. Practice makes perfect. Do it again."

I do it three more times, and while I do improve with his suggestions, I still fail. Growling, I toss the instruments, but they're stuck in place so they go nowhere.

He laughs and clicks his tongue. "Patience, Sapphire."

"I really don't like being bad at things."

"No. You?" he says, sarcasm dripping from his voice. I glare and he chuckles, pointing at the screen. "Try it again." His hand touches my shoulder, firing electricity across my skin. "I promise you'll get it eventually."

I slog through the modules. He cheerleads the entire time. Sometimes, he places his hands over mine to demonstrate techniques he's learned, but it's lost on me as the brush of his skin and heat from his body steal all my attention.

Icy snow. Blasting winds. Cold, cold, cold.

But I'm on fire within.

When I finally pass a module, we high-five like I've saved a bus full of orphans. I'm not ready, but he pulls up the ectopic pregnancy module for fun and I make a fantastic accidental cut straight through the IP ligament. The patient bleeds out and Julian's chuckles become full-bodied laughter. His forehead drops to my shoulder.

Releasing the instruments, my hands fall to my sides, and I close my eyes to savor his proximity. "This is way harder than doing it in real life."

"Yeah. I've seen you operate. You're not this bad." The cinnamon on his breath seeps inside me. The heat of it fans over my back and around my neck, soaking through my scrubs.

His laughter fades and he takes a deep breath, lifting his forehead from my shoulder a few inches so his voice is a low murmur next to my ear. "Is it my turn to be tortured now?"

I nod and swallow against the sudden desert in my throat. "We could use one of the breakout rooms upstairs."

Small group sessions are common in medical training, and the med school has a ton of breakout rooms—perfect for one-on-one studying.

"All right." He heads toward the door.

We grab our bags and make our way to the elevator, then lean against the wall closer than we need to.

The breakout rooms are on the fourth floor, and the elevator is slow. Our hands rest mere inches from each other, but neither one of us closes the gap. I'm like a teenager in a movie theater, aching for him to hold my hand.

And the world is officially backward. I want Julian Santini to hold my hand.

Like he did by the pool. Remember that?

Pretty hands... Touching you...

Hmm. I'd almost forgotten about that. Maybe he does flirt a little bit.

A bucket of invisible sparks dumps over my head as the lustful creature inside takes control of my index finger and strains toward him. My knuckle barely grazes his, then retreats. My eyes go wide. Our heads turn toward each other. He raises an eyebrow.

"It was an accident." The words topple over each other as they exit my mouth.

The no-smile lights up his stupidly handsome face. "You wanna hold my hand, Rose?"

"What?" Heat spreads over my cheeks. "No! Of course not. Why would you—no."

The door opens, and I practically leap from the elevator.

Julian's mocking laughter follows me. "Come on. Hold my hand."

I glance back as I walk. His hand reaches toward me, inviting. A challenging glint dances in his dark eyes.

He *is* flirting. *Flirting.* With me. And I have the vapors. I have officially become Mrs. Bennet.

My poor nerves!

Scoffing, I race toward my favorite breakout room. We settle in chairs on opposite sides of the table.

Our eyes lock and for some inexplicable reason, my breathing deepens and my thoughts scatter across the table like candy from a tipped jar. If he's trying to throw me off balance today, he's certainly succeeding.

"All right." I try to smile. "You were supposed to study ovarian masses."

He pulls out his computer, a little notch between his eyebrows. "Yes. I did do that." He clears his throat. "Tried. I tried to do that."

I narrow my eyes and retrieve my own laptop. "Why don't you start with naming them?"

He taps his finger on the table. "So, you have your dysgerminomas."

I nod.

"And you have—your—germinomas."

I blink a few times. "That's...not right."

His shoulders fall.

"You didn't do your flashcards, did you?"

"I did..." His gaze travels to the windows behind me. "I did some of them."

Sighing, I turn on my computer, finally in my element. "Let's start at the beginning."

That night, I lift my lowball of iced silvery green liquid to eye level. "What's this drink called again?"

Julian's no-smile is in fine form this evening. He toasts me as he plops onto Kai's couch. "Unicorn Blood."

By the contents littering Kai's tiny kitchen countertop, the drink is part tequila, part St. Germain, part lime juice. A frilly curl of orange rind floating on top of mine has me curious about secret ingredients, though.

Standing beside me in the kitchen, Alesha stares at hers in wonder. "This slaps!"

Julian sips his own. "Told you."

Kai lives in a small apartment above a wealthy family's detached garage. His furniture is tasteful and comfortable, with cozy blankets thrown over the sofa backs and fancy lamps with multicolor LED smart bulbs glowing warm white. Alesha fought with him over the color, requesting turquoise for ambiance.

She received a sassy look as a response.

Raven sits beside Julian, lime La Croix in hand, and Kai perches on a bar stool at the open picture window connecting the kitchen to the attached space—part living room, part dining room.

Alesha leans over the counter to give Kai another pleading look. "Turquoise?" she asks for the third time.

Kai ignores her by skimming through his phone. I wander out of the kitchen, eyes still trained on my drink. I stop in the middle of the room.

"I didn't poison it, if that's what you're thinking," says an amused voice.

My gaze flicks to meet Julian's. "There's no way this is better than a Mambo Taxi."

Sparks light his eyes, and his lips curve into a slow smile. "How can you know you don't like it if you never taste it?"

Taste it.

Mind blank, frozen tundra miles away, I stare at his mouth. My heart simultaneously climbs into my throat and thunders against my ribs, and everyone else falls away from my consciousness.

My fantasies of him have multiplied throughout the day and I'm equally annoyed and intrigued by them.

It's a passing fancy. A curiosity. He's safe because nothing will ever come of it. There's none of the usual anxiety because it will never happen.

He couldn't possibly be interested in me, right?

So what would he do if I stepped closer? If I slid my legs on either side of him? I want to trap him against my body, all the softest parts of me pressed against the hardest parts of him.

What would his lips taste like?

Ice queen.

"Oh my god." Kai snaps.

I startle, upsetting the contents of my glass.

Kai rises to his feet, glaring at his phone. "Listen to this bullshit. 'Last Friday you received an email correspondence regarding an employee gift. I regret to inform you that residents are not included in this employee gift distribution. I apologize for any hurt feelings this may cause. That was never my intent. Best regards, Steven Langston.'"

Raven gasps and her eyes go puppy-dog large. "We don't get the gift? I wanted that Yeti."

Kai hurls his phone onto the counter. "Not only do I work four hundred hours a week. Not only do I have to park a mile away and shuttle because they don't have enough parking for employees. Not only am I yelled at when I get chicken strips in the cafeteria instead of choking down that free poison they call food. But now I don't even get the free tumbler I was promised as an employee of the hospital? IF I'M NOT AN EMPLOYEE, THEN I'M PARKING IN PATIENT PARKING."

My mouth drops open.

Um. What just happened?

A silence passes while he takes a huge gulp of Unicorn Blood, then thumps it on the counter.

Alesha moves to Kai's side and touches his shoulder. "You okay there, friend?"

"No, I'm not fucking okay. I have officially reached my Angry Era. I got bitched out by Dr. Ryan today for *mismanaging* a bleeding patient that I'd already run by Chen, who agreed with my plan. I then spent three hours pushing with a patient only to have the delivery taken by a fucking fourth year. Then I had to sit in on a transfusion committee meeting where they harangued me about how many blood products we use on L&D. LET THEM BLEED OUT. I DON'T FUCKING CARE."

"Whoa." Alesha guides him to a stool.

Kai isn't done. "I finished out my day by telling a med stu-

dent she needs to get off her phone and at least try to look interested. She assured me she was *so* interested, then whipped
out her computer and started typing furiously. Pause. More
furious typing. Like, bitch, I know you're just texting on your
computer. YOU'RE NOT SNEAKY."

Alesha hands him his Unicorn Blood and he takes another
gulp.

"Uh." Julian sits straight, lines marring his forehead. "These
are kind of strong."

Alesha shrugs. "He obviously needs it and he isn't driving."

Kai groans out a sigh and slumps. "Sorry. Bad day. Steven
Langston can go fuck himself with a wire toilet brush."

"It isn't his fault." Alesha hops onto the stool next to him.

Kai's death glare spears right through her. "I will strangle
you with my stethoscope."

"Oh, stop being dramatic." She waves her hand. "I thought
you were supposed to be the stoic one here."

Kai takes another huge drink, draining it. He reaches over
the bar for the mixer on the counter below and refills his glass.
"Don't worry. I'll be all bottled up again by tomorrow."

Raven rises to approach him, throwing her arms around
his shoulders. "Second year is really hard. I'm sorry you had
a bad day."

I set my drink on the sideboard to encircle my arms around
both Raven and Kai. Alesha is next, followed by Julian. The
five of us embrace each other in silence for several moments.

Raven clears her throat. "I have some good news. Isaac and
I are expecting our second next spring."

Alesha whoops and I jump, breaking the hug. We shift toward Raven, all of us converging on her. She giggles at the
hugs and congratulations.

When we separate once more, we all shift seats. Kai offers his
to Raven, who takes it. Alesha and Kai steal the couch, leaving
Julian and me the two remaining bar stools.

Alesha launches into a summary of her own day, but unlike Kai, she's elated. "The patient was fine, but the baby daddy, you guys. Oh my god. He was wearing two different shoes and had to leave when the patient was five centimeters because his brother—and I quote—*accidentally shot his dick off*. Then when he came back he forgot the patient's name because he has two women pregnant right now, and forgot which one was in labor."

"You're kidding." Julian stretches an arm across the bar and rests it behind me.

Alesha laughs so hard tears sparkle in her eyes. "I wish I was. When she finally started pushing, she screamed, *where is that fucker?* And it turns out he was out in the parking lot, smoking weed." Alesha wipes her eyes. "He missed the delivery."

Raven gives us the puppy-dog eyes again. "Aw! That poor woman."

Kai snorts. "I think the pregnancy is making you emotional."

"Um," she says with crossed arms. "Who was the one screaming about a mildly worded email earlier?"

Laughing, Kai tips his glass toward her. "Touché."

Julian retrieves my drink from the sideboard and hands it to me. "Just try it." He resumes his position. Behind me, his fingers tug on the ends of my hair.

Without breaking eye contact, I raise the glass to my lips, taking the tiniest sip. Lime, tequila and something sweetly floral dance along my tongue, chased by the tangy aftertaste of orange.

My eyes widen. "Holy fuck."

His fingers twist through strands of my hair, and he gasps. "She said the f-word again."

Hyperaware of his hand behind me, I take a larger drink. "This is so good, Julian. Why have you been hiding this from us?"

"If I remember correctly, I told you about this drink in February and you weren't interested in straying from the tried and true."

Julian has never touched me like this, playing with my hair, almost absently, like he's not aware he's doing it. *Is* he aware? Does he somehow sense my piquing interest?

Raven glances at us. Her gaze dips to his fingers tangled in my hair. Julian straightens and withdraws his hand. Pretending nothing happened, Raven returns to the conversation, but after a few moments, she throws us a curious look.

I feign ignorance and face Julian. "If I'd known what I was missing, I would've been asking for this every night."

I replay my words and hear the double entendre. Heat flickers over my face.

He suppresses a smile. "Would you? Every night?"

"Ha, ha." I set my cold glass against the fire of my cheek.

But he's not done. A devious humor lightens the deep brown in his eyes. "Would you say please?"

"Shut up, Julian."

"Yes, please." Kai toasts me. "Do shut up."

Alesha giggles, nudging him with her bare toe. "And you thought you hated it when they were fighting all the time."

Kai winces. "I know. This is so much worse."

Dr. LaShay is a scatterbrained ditz. I don't know how she graduated high school, let alone medical school. Dr. Echols insists that LaShay was top of her class, but LaShay is also sixty-eight years old, so I doubt he found records of her class rank.

Proof or it didn't happen. That's what I say.

She's a private attending with a bustling OB practice and delivers all her babies at St. Vincent. Her greatest love is to use the residents for her grunt work.

"Where's the resident?" she squawks.

I pop up from my place at the dictation desk. "That's me."

She looks at me like she's never seen me before, though we've worked together dozens of times. Her short white bob is so starched with hairspray it doesn't move when she cocks her head. "What year are you?"

"Uh—second."

"What's your name?"

"Grace Rose, ma'am."

She looks me up and down. "Fine. I need help with my next C-section and Dr. Echols is busy."

"Yes, of course. I'll be there."

"Be ready in ten."

I reseat myself and go back to work, but a small chuckle to my left draws my eye. A man sits at the computer next to mine. He's young, handsome and his blue eyes shine through silver-rimmed glasses.

Cute.

I guess I have a thing for glasses.

His badge declares him a fellow resident, but I'm not sure what specialty.

"Something funny?" I raise an eyebrow.

He nods his head toward LaShay, now squawking at one of the nurses. "She seems like a trip."

I glance at LaShay. "Oh. Yeah. It's—whatever."

At least she lets me operate, unlike Levine...

"I'm Trevor." He holds a hand out for me to shake.

Warm hands. Not pretty, though. Not like—

"I'm Grace."

"So I heard." He pulls up an MRI report. "Are you taking care of the patient in twenty-three?"

I nod.

"She has an unstable Lisfranc injury. She'll probably need surgery."

Lisfranc? Isn't that a foot thing?

"Oh. You're ortho." I sigh. "Shit." The woman is thirty-eight weeks pregnant.

He laughs. "Indeed. I'll talk to my attending. You talk to yours. We'll make a plan."

"Yeah, all right."

He signs out of his computer and spins toward me. "Why don't you give me your cell? It'll be easier to coordinate that way."

I blink. "It will? How?"

His lips roll inward as he tries and fails to hide a smile. He leans toward me. "I'm just trying to get your number."

"Oh. Oh!" I ignore the flare of warmth across my cheeks and stutter out my number. Wait. Did I want him to have my number? Why am I so awkward? It's like as soon as a stranger speaks to me, I lose all sense of myself and become a bottle of butterflies.

But it's too late now. The dude has my number.

I scrutinize his face for any signs of preconceived notions. Has he heard the rumors about me? Does he believe them?

A squawk startles me. "Where'd that Grace girl go?"

I leap to my feet to face Dr. LaShay. "Right here."

She looks at me again like we've never met. "No. You're Dr. Rose."

I struggle to keep the smile on my face. "Yes. Sapphire Grace Rose."

"Oh. Well, come on. Dr. Echols is still busy."

Waving a goodbye to Trevor, I follow LaShay to the OR. She may be crazy, but the woman lets me perform the whole surgery, barely touching an instrument herself. Small wins, right?

Afterward, I grin at the waiting text.

> **Trevor:** It was nice to meet you Sapphire Grace Rose. Maybe next time you'll be able to tell I'm flirting with you.

> **Me:** haha

> **Me:** Maybe so

Do I want him to flirt with me, though? This new flirtation with Julian is all tingles and excitement. It's natural. Easy. Flirting with someone else will still be as awkward as it always is.

But maybe…

Back at my apartment, I FaceTime with Mom and Dad before I grab my laptop and flashcards and head to Julian's like we planned. My knock on his door is answered at once, but only wide enough to show his face.

"Oh hey. What's up?"

I laugh at the sliver of him I can see and display my flashcards. "Didn't we have plans to study tonight?"

"Oh—um—" He glances into his apartment, hesitating.

My shoulders fall. "Did I misremember?"

"Yeah." He lowers his voice, words rushed. "Look. Maybe we can do it tomorrow. Would you mind?"

"No, that's fine. Sorry I bothered you." I glance at his hand white-knuckling the doorframe, suspicions forming. "Do—is there someone else in there?"

"Um—" he says at the same time I flush and say, "Sorry, that was rude. It's not my business."

"No, that's not—"

A female voice interrupts him. "Julian, is someone here?"

Julian's eyes flutter shut, and he lets out a slow breath. His hand goes slack on the door right before it's jerked open by a girl.

Silky dark hair. Knockout body. She's taller than me and my gaze falls to my feet as an overwhelming flood of embarrassment and jealousy threatens to drown me.

Wait. Jealousy?

No. That can't be right.

It's Saturday night. It only makes sense he'd be dating. Of course he brings girls to his apartment. *Of course* he doesn't want to spend his free nights studying with the dorky girl downstairs.

I'm so stupid.

Before I can stop it, my subconscious swipes right over the image of him snuggling a baby, and my entire soul droops.

Your eggs are dying, my ovaries remind me, and throw crying emojis all over my mind.

Ridiculous. I'm only twenty-seven. I don't even really want him! He's just…pretty. Or something.

"Who's this, BB?" The girl's tone makes no sense. Instead of suspicion, she's full of…triumph?

Julian sighs. "Can you just not do the thing that you're about to do right now?"

"Whatever could you mean?" The girl's hand clamps on my wrist and drags me inside the apartment.

I trip over the threshold, gripping my laptop and flashcards to my chest. My eyes meet Julian's, then this stranger's and a click takes place in my mind. The depthless eyes staring at me from this beautiful woman's face are familiar.

She sticks her hand out. "I'm Tori Santini."

Santini.

Joy fills to the brim, and an inexplicable fondness for this woman wakes inside me. "Oh." I grasp her hand, masking my relief behind a bright smile. "Grace. I'm Grace Rose."

Her eyes light up the same way her brother's do and she switches her gaze to Julian. "This is Red Dress?"

I drop her hand. "You know about my dress?"

"Mmm." She narrows her eyes at Julian. "I think you've been keeping secrets."

Julian scowls. "We work together. We study together. That's it."

Oh. Well, that's one way to put it…

We're friends too, Julian.

And why did he tell her about my dress? Ugh. I wish I didn't know that confusing crumb of information. Something's sparking in my chest.

"Then why were you trying to hide her?" Tori flings herself on Julian's couch.

"*This.* This is why, Tor." He turns to me. "I'm sorry. My sisters are nosy and she's the worst of them. I forgot you were coming because she arrived *unannounced.*" He shoots a pointed glare at Tori.

She shrugs. "You know I don't plan ahead, BB. Besides, if I warned you, then I wouldn't get the pleasure of witnessing things like this." She pats the couch beside her. "You can still study. Don't mind me."

My uncertain gaze meets Julian's.

He rubs a hand over his face. "We'll study another time, okay? It's better this way. Trust me."

My head bobs as I fight a nagging sense of disappointment.

He must see it though, because he dips his head, examining me closely. "What is it?"

The heat in my cheeks stirs again. Why must it always do that? "Oh, it's just, I—I made you new flashcards."

His lips twitch, and he raises a hand to cover his mouth. Humor gleams in his eyes.

"What?" I squeeze my laptop to my chest, hugging tight.

"You. You're just so—"

"Cute?" Tori laser-focuses on Julian. "Adorable? Sweet?"

Julian's in full-on predator-staring-contest mode with me. The darkness sparkles. "Dorky."

Chagrin courses through me in the form of a full-body blush, though I'm not sure what else I was expecting him to say in front of his sister. So why am I sweating? Why is he still staring? Why has my heartbeat decided to drop to my uterus?

How does this man wake every impulse I'd buried six feet under a gravestone etched with the words *Ice Queen*?

My libido is rising up like a starving zombie, and I need to figure out how to master it *soon.*

Hmm. I bet Julian could master it…

Ack! No!

My voice turns scratchy. "I think we've established we're both dorks, but okay. I'll go. You should visit with your sister. The flashcards can wait."

"You really don't have to go," Tori says as I head to the door. "In fact, I insist you stay."

"It's fine. I'm tired, anyway. Long shift."

"No, please stay." Tori leaps up and grabs my arm. "We'll watch Netflix. I'll make Unicorn Blood. Everyone loves that, right?"

Unicorn Blood? A smile threatens, but I bite my lip.

Tori throws her hands up in victory. "Yes! She stays." She grabs my laptop and flashcards, setting them on the table by the door, then takes my hands and leads me to the couch. Julian is subjected to the same manhandling. He's placed directly beside me.

"Tori." Julian's voice holds a hint of threat.

"You're welcome," she says in a singsong voice and disappears into the kitchen.

I stare after her. "I think she thinks I'm into you."

"No." He sighs. "She thinks *I'm* into *you*."

"Oh." I should have worn shorts. The leggings were a bad choice for the constant heat flaring in my skin. "Should I tell her we're sworn enemies?"

He snorts. "Don't bother. She'll just try harder. You really don't have to stay if you don't want to. She'll be insufferable with the matchmaking all night."

A small lock of hair has flung itself over his forehead, and I can't resist the urge to push it back. My fingers thread through his hair before landing in my lap. "I don't mind it if you don't. Would you like me to stay?"

This man wields eye contact like a weapon. He can steal oxygen from my lungs with a single glance. "Yeah," he murmurs. "I'd like you to stay."

The smile that grows on my face is like quicksand—I sink into the joy, transfixed. "Why does she call you BB?"

Faint color washes over the bridge of his nose. "Oh. Um. It's—nothing."

Captivated by his stare, his nonanswer barely registers. This close, the amber hiding in the depths of his eyes flirts with my sanity. He leans in. Draws a breath.

"BB, where are the oranges?" Tori shouts from the kitchen.

His eyes fall shut and he pulls away. "I hate you, Victoria."

I giggle.

Tori pokes her head around the corner, grinning. "I'm going to tell Mom you used the *H* word."

Julian

OCTOBER, YEAR 2

"Are you in love with her?"

I glare at Tori across the restaurant table, the bevy of juices for our mimosas between us. Brunch has been her favorite meal since I turned twenty-one and we could both legally get trashed on champagne at eleven in the morning. Since she leaves tomorrow, she demanded we brunch.

She also demanded Grace be invited, but sometimes I get my way.

Our table by the window at this busy gastropub is packed full of food and alcohol. Halloween decorations hang from the ceiling. Spiders, witches and ghosts spin above us in the circulated air.

I flick a straw wrapper at her. "Will you please stop asking me that?"

"I would if you'd answer it."

"I have answered it." I take a swig of what is essentially champagne with a drop of pineapple juice. "Multiple times."

She rolls her eyes. "Not truthfully."

"If you think you know, then why do you keep asking?"

"Because I want you to admit it." She leans her elbows on the table. "I've seen the way you look at her. That puppy longing. You didn't even look at Carlee like that, and you brought her home to meet Mom."

I lift a finger. "*Carlee* withheld sex until she met Mom."

Tori's mouth drops open, then she descends into mocking laughter. "You fell for that?"

"Sex is a powerful motivator, Tor."

"Hence the puppy longing for Grace and her flashcards," she says with a wide grin.

"That's not longing. It's annoyance."

Tori snorts. "Yeah. Annoyance that she hasn't let you in her undies."

My breath expels in one long sigh. "Have you noticed that I never harass you about your love life?"

She waves a hand, dismissing me. "That's because I don't have one. She's wonderful, BB. Mom would love her."

I know. "Can we talk about something else?"

"But, Julian—"

"She's not interested, Victoria." My voice sharpens, rises in volume, and a few patrons at the table beside us shoot curious glances our way.

Victoria scrutinizes me. "Are you blind?"

"No—"

She rolls her eyes. "You're a man, so the answer to that question is one-hundred percent yes. Just trust me. She's into you."

I take in her brown eyes, her set mouth, and search for the joke. "You're lying."

Her tone softens. "Why would I lie about something like that?"

That…can't be true, can it? I think over the last couple months—the interlaced fingers by the pool, the brush of her hand in an elevator, that quickly hidden flash of disappointment the moment she realized I had another girl in my apartment. The first was my doing, and the second was an accident I embellished just to embarrass her. That last I chalked up to simple displeasure that I chose a date over studying—something Grace herself would never do.

Except lately, when she looks into my eyes, I'm seeing something deeper. I've ignored it. Attributed it to familiarity or budding friendship.

But maybe…

Electricity wakes inside me, a current connected to a tenuous thread of hope. It adulterates my chemistry, immersing it in nonsensical endorphins. My face scrunches as I try to stop it, but it's no use. The hope exists now, along with the potential for disappointment.

"Julian?"

I match Tori's gaze, jaw clenched. "I don't want to talk about this anymore."

Eyes shuttered, she nods. "More mimosa?"

The night of Asher's annual Halloween party, Grace swings her apartment door open, grinning. A red-and-purple-corset dress with skirts that brush the floor covers her body, and a purple cloak hangs from her shoulders. In addition to the devil-red lipstick, dark makeup coats her eyes and a beauty mark dots her chin.

"Are you…a wench?" I ask.

Her shoulders fall. "I'm Sarah Sanderson."

I rack my brain. "Am I supposed to know who that is?"

She sighs. "Were you abused as a child? How do you not know *Hocus Pocus*?"

"Oh. Right. The witches. Yeah, I remember that."

Satisfied, she grabs her phone and shoves it into her dress beside her breast. That can't be comfortable...

She eyes my outfit. "What are you?"

I hate dressing up, but Asher insisted that no costume meant no entry.

And costume means costume, Santini. No showing up in street clothes and insisting you're Regular Joe.

Hip cocked, Grace inspects me, so I begrudgingly put on the mask and raise my hood.

Her face lights up. "Kylo Ren?"

I grunt.

"The scion of darkness himself?"

"Can we go?"

She latches onto my arm. "Take a picture with me."

"What? No." I back away, still attached to her.

"Please, Julian? I must chronicle my meeting of Ben Solo."

I try to free my arm from her grasp, but she tugs, so I spin and she launches onto my back, taking selfies while I struggle to remove my mask.

She's giggling next to my ear, arms around my shoulders, and the length of her exquisite body is pressed into my back.

Maybe Tori was right...

Is this a signal?

I give up the struggle. "You got your picture, okay? Do you need a piggyback to my truck?"

Still laughing, she returns the phone to her corset, slides off me and locks her apartment, sliding the key beside her breast as well. What else does she keep in there? Are there hidden storage containers in dresses I'm not aware of?

"Thanks for DD'ing," she says once we're on our way.

I offered on impulse, thinking solely of the drive to and

from Asher's, knowing I'd have her to myself. If I'm going to pursue this, I should probably work up the courage to make a real move at some point, though. This is sort of a sissy way to go about things. A little pathetic.

The fear of rejection is high-key terrifying—having to work with her for two more years, wanting her while she's all awkward about it. No thanks.

"Sure," I say, glancing at her profile. "You excited?"

Devil-red lips curve into a bright smile. "Oh yeah. Asher has promised me this will be a good time."

My stomach decides right that moment to cramp painfully. What else has Asher promised her? It's been months since he declared his interest, and nothing. Well, I *think* nothing. Maybe they're in a secret relationship and blissfully in love. Maybe he's in her bed every night, waiting for her to finish studying with me so he can make her moan. Or maybe he already tried, and she turned him down. That thought cheers me.

We can't help but argue over the music for the rest of the ride, and she skips off to find the girls as soon as we arrive. I lose track of her when Maxwell and I fall deep into a game of poker with a few others. The party is massive. Residents from all specialties filter through the house, as do most of our attendings and some nurses.

Once the poker game fizzles, I dive into the drunken fray. Raven and Alesha are dressed as the other Sanderson sisters, and close to midnight, all three of them take to the karaoke machine set up in the living room. They sway to "You Don't Own Me" by Lesley Gore, their skirts brushing the floor.

Afterward, Asher hops onstage with them, and they sing "Come Little Children" which is much darker and has far more verses than I thought. I refill my glass with soda as they sing. Grace's voice is melodic, almost haunting.

Sticky liquid spills onto my hand when my cup overflows. I curse and snatch a paper towel to clean the mess. When I lift my gaze once more, Grace leans in to share a mic with Asher, smiling while they sing together.

Ugh.

A twisting pain beneath my ribs has me eyeing the rows of liquor. A drink would be nice to take the edge off. Instead, I head outside. Several of us congregate around the firepit, chatting. It takes everything in me to strangle my groan when Rebecca sidles up to my side. She's a chief resident now, so her free time is abundant, and she still drops hints about her interest on the reg.

I'd heard she found herself a boyfriend, but if the gleam in her eye is any indication, she's free tonight.

She smiles. "Hey, Julian."

"Hey, Becca. Having fun?"

"Eh." She grimaces. "I'm DD, so…"

I chuckle and shake my cup of Coke. "Heard that."

"You, too?" She holds her hands toward the fire. "Sucks."

Shrugging, I reach toward the fire myself. Heat licks over my skin in comforting waves. "Could always Uber, I guess."

She tilts her head back and forth, considering. "Nah."

The drunken laughs and whoops around us draw my attention to the side.

"Can I ask you a question?" Rebecca asks. The fire gilds her face, gold light glistening over her eyelashes and blond hair. Her lips are turned down into a frown. "Was it—was it me?"

Oh.

Okay.

So we're doing this, then.

I don't pretend to misunderstand, though I wish I did. Despite the flames, prickly cold wraps around my neck and torso. Lying tastes like vinegar, but hurting her isn't an option either, so I settle on, "You can't control attraction, Becca."

"And you aren't attracted to me?"

My slight hesitation makes her grimace.

"Never mind." She shakes her head. "I don't want to know. I don't know why I even asked that."

"Becca, you're great—"

"Seriously, Julian." Her voice grows pointed. "I don't want to know."

I hold a hand up in submission. She brushes off her arms and walks away without a backward glance. I should probably feel bad, but instead, a wave of relief washes over me. That episode is finally closed. Thank you, universe.

A bench seat at the far corner of the deck calls my name. Out in the yard, some inebriated fools light old fireworks and screech in delight. Sitting stone-cold sober in the corner, I find them a tad obnoxious, but prepare to be entertained nonetheless.

Asher falls next to me, intoxicated and smiling. "Santini!"

"Hey, Asher."

"Good party, right?" His words are slurred.

"The best."

He laughs and claps me on the shoulder.

"Are you—" I eye him closely, taking in the fake mustache and glasses "—dressed as Dr. Chen?"

His eyes crinkle in merriment. "It's great, right?"

I glance at his white coat, pointing at the embroidered name there. "You even stole his white coat."

Asher waves a hand. "Meh. He'll never know it went missing." His head lolls to the side, a dopey smile on his face.

"You need some water, buddy?"

"Nah. I'm fine." He rests his head on the side of the house. "Just need a minute."

The scent of burnt wood mixes with the chilly October night, and I relax into it, breathing deep.

"It's a good night, isn't it?" he murmurs.

I take a moment to study the lines of his face, tapping my finger against my leg. "You look...happy."

His eyes open. "Yeah, I—"

A fraught feminine voice from around the corner cuts him off. "Wait. No."

My ears home in on that voice. Those words. Grace's voice. Grace's *dissent*. My body tightens.

Asher glances toward the corner of the house, then at me. "Was that—"

"Come on, Grace." Whose voice is that?

Her slurred voice thins. "I'm sorry. Will you stop, please?"

"Oh come on. I've seen the way you look at me. I've heard what you like."

Asher and I stand, making our way toward the stairs that lead to the side of the house.

Grace's voice becomes strained. "What? I'm so sorry. I don't want—no. Trevor, stop. I—"

Her words are smothered, and my entire life distills to two primitive desires—kill him and save her.

The cold air barely touches me as I fly around the corner, finding her pinned to the wooden fence by his body. His hands are splayed over her waist. She turns her head away as he tries to kiss her.

My hands grip his arms before I register my own intrusion. I rip him away and she stumbles to the side, tripping over her purple cloak. Asher catches her.

"Get off me!" Trevor yells and takes a swing at me, but he's drunk. Dodging is as easy as a quick duck beneath his unco-ordinated fist.

I assume he'll stop then, but he doesn't, and I'm forced to react. Pain explodes in my knuckles when my fist connects with his jaw. He hits the ground, cursing my name.

"What the fuck, Santini?" Trevor presses a hand to his face.

I point at Grace without looking at her. "Did you hear her saying no?"

Trevor looks up, confusion glazing his eyes. "I—what?"

"You just assaulted her." I turn to Grace, now shivering in Asher's arms. "Are you okay?"

She has a hand over her mouth, eyes wide, but she nods. Asher slowly releases her. The happily drunk man from a few minutes before disappears. His edges go sharp, and he approaches Trevor without hurry. The same dark anger that fills my chest glitters in his eyes.

Asher steps on Trevor's hand. "Get the fuck out of my house and don't *ever* come back."

My aching fist clenches again as Trevor stands and cradles his hand, stumbling backward. "I—I didn't mean—I'm sorry."

Kill him. Slowly.

"Stay the fuck away from her," I say. "I'll kill you if you come near her again."

He flees toward the gate, pulling his phone from his pocket. Once he's gone, I turn to Asher, who nods, then to Grace.

She's wide-eyed, her face a pale smudge in the darkness.

Asher takes one step toward her. "Are you okay?"

Instead of answering, she throws herself at me, ringing her arms around my neck so tight I almost choke. "Thank you."

Her lips brush my neck as she speaks and every hair on my body lifts.

I meet Asher's gaze around Grace's hair. He's dumbstruck, his mouth parted as he stares at Grace in my arms.

"No one has ever not listened." Her voice is a raspy whisper. "When I said no, I mean. And I pushed, and he—he wouldn't stop—and—"

I touch her lower ribs tentatively, waiting to see if she'll flinch before I slide my hands around her. She doesn't protest, so my grip tightens to match hers. Her scent envelops me, threads through me, interlaced with heat and something a little painful. My attraction to her fragrance has grown thorns, prickly ones meant to grab on and never let go. Extracting that scent will leave scars, I'm sure of it.

Asher brushes past us, his face crumpled.

I wince. "Asher—"

He ignores me.

Grace hasn't moved from my arms.

"Why were you apologizing to him?" I murmur in her ear.

She nuzzles closer. "I felt bad. You know...that I didn't want him."

"Grace. You never need to feel bad for not wanting to be kissed."

Her grip loosens and she lifts her head to meet my eyes. "I didn't say I didn't want to be kissed. I said I didn't want *him*."

Wait.

Does—Does that mean—

Sparkling lights turn my blood incandescent and shimmer with heat. Each pulse spreads dazzling illumination like she's crawling into my veins and lighting them on fire. Darkness keeps her expression hidden, but the glittering reflections in her eyes dance as she takes in my face.

Her voice softens, a whispered song in the shadows. "Julian."

"Yeah?"

She smiles. Her hands retract to rest on my shoulders. "I was kinda hoping I'd end up in your arms tonight."

Skrt.

What?

Did she admit that out loud? And how deep in my arms does she want to be? Because I'm dying to find out what she tastes like.

Her red lips are right there, waiting. Except—

"You're drunk."

"I'm not drunk." She tips to the side. "I'm falling."

"Whoa." I steady her by the arms.

With a hand pressed to her head and a dramatic wince, Grace's booted feet slip on the wet leaf-strewn ground. "I think I need to go home, Julian."

"Yeah." I rub her arms a few times. "Let's say goodbye, okay? Can you walk?"

"No." But she traipses away in a decently straight line.

I trail after her. "How much did you have to drink?"

"All of it, Julian. All the drinks."

She celebrates with a clumsy little jig when she makes it up the stairs to the back porch, each step a loud thunk on the wooden planks. Most everyone is crowded around the firepit now.

"Where'd you two sneak off to?" Raven asks.

"To have sex around the corner, *obviously*," Grace slurs and waves vaguely toward the dark area beside the house. "Isn't that what everyone thinks?"

"Nope!" I yell, drawing far too much attention. She doesn't need that rumor added to the mill. "Nope. No, no, no. That didn't happen. Nope."

From the shadows behind Raven, Asher scowls and disappears inside.

Drunk Grace glares at me. "It was a *joke*. God! Could you proclaim your disgust any louder?"

Disgust? *Disgust*?

Chuckles follow her words, but most people turn back to their own conversations.

How on earth does she think that?

But right this second, maybe it's better if that's what she thinks. I can get a huffy, irritated Grace home with little fuss. I've got more than enough practice with that. It will be far more difficult to cart off a wistful, inebriated Grace who wants me to kiss her.

I shouldn't kiss her.

Not while she's drunk and I'm painfully sober.

So I give her my bland smile. "I could probably shout my disgust, if you'd like."

Alesha, Maxwell and Raven huddle closer to us, eavesdropping. The fire gleaming in Grace's eyes is fascinating. She's plotting how to fly me to the deepest circle of hell and make it back in time for shots.

"I will destroy you," she says in a low purr, and I can't help it. A fantasy rips through my mind—of her climbing on top of me, forcing me to remain still while she rides me like her own personal vibrator.

I think she's already destroyed me.

"Good luck," I say. "You ready to go home?"

Alesha laughs and pulls Grace into a hug, whispering in her ear.

Maxwell bumps my shoulder as I shake his hand, a knowing glint in his eyes. "You finally getting lucky tonight, bruh?"

"She's drunk, Max."

Maxwell shoots a pointed look at Grace, who's witch-cackling at something Alesha said. "Okay, maybe you're right. Sucks for you."

"Story of my life."

I wrestle her into my truck, making sure her seat belt is buckled tight. Halfway home, Grace's head lolls toward me. "You're not really disgusted by me, are you?"

"No," I say at once, glancing her way. "You're beautiful."

Her pleased smile hits me right in the chest, and she proceeds to do one of the best things a woman can—she accepts the compliment. No apologies. No humble disagreement. No questions designed to pull more praise from me. She meets my eyes and slurs out a warm, "Thank you. That's really nice to hear."

I pat her hand.

"How come you offered to DD?" she asks.

"So you could have fun."

"We could have shared an Uber."

My thumb kicks a steady tap on the steering wheel. "It's—it's just better if I'm not drunk around you."

She sits straighter, but still slurs her answer. "That's an intriguing statement I'd like explained further."

I spare a surreptitious glance at her pretty face. "I tell too much truth when I'm drunk."

"Hmm." Her inebriated smile is both worrisome and charming. She is *hammered.* "Something happened tonight I wanted to remember, but now I can't remember what it was."

I laugh. "Was it the part when you jumped into my arms?"

An adorable crease forms between her eyebrows. "When the hell did I jump in your arms?"

We're at a stoplight, so I stare at her. "Seriously?"

She blinks somewhere around a million times in four seconds. "What are we talking about?"

"Should I be worried about your hippocampus, Grace?"

Pleasure ignites her smile and her eyes glow. Her voice turns throaty. "You called me Grace."

Holy shit.

She has *never* looked at me like this. Like she somehow wants to wrap me in a gentle hug *and* fuck me hard.

I'm struck dumb and all the blood leaves my brain to pool below. *I would spell your name over your clit with my tongue if you'd keep looking at me like that.*

A horn honks behind us and I jump. The green light flares over her ecstatic face. I remind myself where I am, what I'm doing, and don't dare look at her again until we're safely home.

In the complex's parking lot, she sways as she walks, her purple cloak sweeping the damp ground. Cold air laces around us, scented of woodsmoke and rain. The place is busier than normal, people in costumes heading to and from parties.

At her landing, she turns, leaving me a step beneath her. "Thank you, Kylo Ren. The First Order lives another day."

The glimmer of humor in her hazel eyes makes me chuckle. "It's Ben to you."

She giggles. "You know, I'm finally running out of bad guys for you."

I take the last step, crowding into her space. "Maybe you've just realized I'm not the bad guy." I give in to the perpetual urge and let the soft waves of her hair sift through my fingers. Bending closer, I breathe in the soul-destroying fragrance of her skin. "I want to kiss you."

Her smile stretches, glows. "It's about time."

Huh? "Have you been waiting for me?"

She gives a slow nod, still smiling. "I think about it way too much."

I stare at her tempting mouth and the desire to close the distance nearly mauls my restraint. "Would you even remember it?"

She shrugs.

I can't help the frustrated groan that crawls up my throat. "I really want you to remember it."

Her tiny hum resonates in her chest, like a purr. "Then you should probably wait."

A couple emerges from a nearby apartment and we move to let them down the stairs, ducking into a dark corner.

"If I wait, you won't want it." My fingers slide deep into her hair. "When you're sober, you despise me."

That's not true, but I want her to say it. Admit it.

Tell me how you feel.

"You think so?" She touches my chest. "Then I guess you'll have to work harder for it."

Cocking my head, I meet her challenging stare. "You want me to work for it, Grace? I will if you can admit right now that you don't hate me."

A wickedness gleams on her face as she leans toward me, instilling a fresh shot of blood below. "If Sober Grace hated you, Julian, then Drunk Grace—" she takes hold of my hand, lifting it to eye level as she weaves each of our fingers together "—wouldn't want this gifted hand under her dress."

My fingers clench on hers.

She doesn't mean that, does she? Am I not just the nerdy boy upstairs who studies with her sometimes?

And she wants my hands under her dress.

She wants my hands on her body.

She's drunk.

What the hell kind of torture is this? How drunk is she really?

Drunk enough, obviously.

I doubt Sober Grace would ever have the courage to say these things to me, but suddenly, I'm craving it, longing for it—her clearheaded words, declaring she wants me.

God, I want to fuck her against the wall behind her. Just hike that dress to her waist and wrap her legs around me. Dirty and gritty and hot. I release her hand instead. "You're going to regret saying that in the morning."

With a secretive smile, she stretches to her tiptoes and devil-red lips press a kiss to the corner of my mouth. "Good night, Julian."

Her scent lingers as she draws away, curling around pleasure centers in my brain. My heart stops because there's no blood left for it, and my world laser-focuses on the woman walking away from me. I want to go after her. I want to run away.

I want her.

It's been stalking me. For months, the fascination has shortened its leash, grown tighter about my neck. I've told myself she's annoying, judgmental and so high strung she probably wouldn't climax even with my best moves, but it's all bullshit. Lies I tell myself because she's climbed her way onto some pedestal in my head. One I'll never rise to. It lingers above my reach, untouchable.

She's too good for me, but she still wants my hands on her body, and one day soon, I'll convince her to admit it.

She wants me to work for it? I'll work for it.

Cold showers are the devil's favorite torment, but I refuse to jack off to Drunk Grace, and that's exactly where my mind will go, so I settle for lukewarm. I torture my toothbrush with excessive toothpaste and violent brushing, pausing when I catch my reflection in the mirror.

Devil-red lips have survived my shower, tattooed across my cheek, a brand for all to see. I pull out my phone and snap a selfie, then hide that picture in a locked album because someday, I'll want proof that Grace Rose dropped her guard enough to touch her lips to my body.

Grace

NOVEMBER YEAR 2

Head pounding, I wish death on the delivery person rapping on my door. I'd told them to leave the food on the mat. Piles of blankets tumble to the floor as I stagger to my feet and yank the door open.

Julian's head lifts, the no-smile firmly in place, and he's put together as always. His hair is expertly styled, and his idiotic glasses that are *not* attractive perch on his nose. I fantasize about pulling on the strings of his black hoodie.

Not to bring him closer. No. To strangle him.

The door catches my weight when I sag against it. "I thought you were DoorDash."

"Sorry to disappoint."

Waiting for him to explain this intrusion into my hangover, I raise my eyebrows at him. "Is there something you want?"

A crooked smile enhances his stupid face, like a half-second glow up.

Heat rushes to my cheeks. "What?"

He studies me a moment, his head tilting. "You—you don't remember, do you?"

My spine snaps straight as a fresh wave of nerves tingles over every surface. "What? Why would you say that? What did I do?" Oh god. What if I said something embarrassing? What if I *did* something?

This is why you don't join in when people are doing shots, Grace!

His smile does confusing things to my stomach. It either wants to empty its contents onto his shoes or fly away with a cloud's worth of butterflies.

"I told you I'd come check on you today. You clearly forgot."

"Oh." I open the door to let him in, relief flooding like cool water through my veins. "Thanks for driving me home last night. Or—I assume you're the one who drove me home."

He drags the scent of fall leaves, cold air and Julian inside with him. "It was no problem." His bruised knuckles take my full attention when he scratches his forehead.

"What happened to your hand?" I grab it, running my thumb over the swollen joints.

A faint laugh reverberates in his throat. "You don't even remember that part?"

Vague recollections of cold air and the sensation of being trapped bubble up to the surface of my consciousness. "What the hell happened last night?"

"Wow. You shouldn't drink if this is the kind of amnesia you get."

I tug him to the kitchen. "I don't usually drink that much. I succumbed to peer pressure. Tell me what happened."

"Trevor Tworek doesn't know how to listen. He tried to kiss you, and you kept saying no, but he did it anyway."

My mouth falls open. What? And I don't remember that?

See? You could've been hurt.

With a cold tingle of shame in my chest, I open the freezer and grab the only gel pack I own—red lips from the medical spa that injects my Botox. "So you punched him?"

"He tried to hit me first, so I retaliated, but I'm glad I did. Guys who don't hear the word *no* deserve to be punched. I can't believe you own a devil-red mouth-shaped ice pack."

I try to retrieve the lost memories from the black wall of last night, but nothing surfaces. Trevor's flirt-texting has kept me giggling for weeks now. I thought if he ever made a move, I might be receptive.

Well…maybe.

He's funny, but he's never made me want things. Not like Julian. Unfortunately.

Did Trevor actually force himself on me?

What the hell?

And Julian punched him. Protected me at my most vulnerable. A flutter of heart-eye emojis skitter through my brain, but I shut them down hard. Now is not the time, not when I'm all nauseated and my brain is too big for my head. I press the gel pack to Julian's hand.

He sucks in a breath. "Shit! That's cold."

I hold tight when he tries to pull away, swatting his forearm. "Hang on. I need more information. What exactly happened?"

His neck cracks and he looks to the side. "I heard you saying no. Went to see what was going on. He had you pinned against a fence outside, trying to kiss you."

"Was he—hurting me?"

Julian's expression turns incredulous as his attention shoots to my face. "Uh… Not *yet*."

My next words fall out in a rush. "It's just—we'd been talking a lot recently, so—I'd hoped maybe you misinterpreted—"

His gaze sharpens. "You aren't into him, are you? Because after last night—"

"No!" I shake my head. "No. I'm not into him. Especially not if he did that." I let out a heavy sigh. "I just hoped—I was wrong about him, I guess."

Figures Trevor would wind up being a dick. He probably believes the most recent talk about me—that I snuck a med student up to the deserted eighth floor of the hospital to *teach* him some things. So dumb. I don't even go to the eighth floor. It's dark and creepy and obviously haunted.

Are all men the same?

I hold the dark gaze of the one standing in front of me.

No. This one's different, isn't he?

Julian's eyes do that predatory thing, and wild flags of color stain his cheeks. Sharp as a scalpel, his voice slices me. "The guy's an asshole. Remember that if he tries to talk to you again."

"I know." Uncertainty crackles in my chest, along with a quiet warning bell. "Julian?"

His mouth tightens.

I step a tad closer to him. "Are you angry?"

"I—" He schools his features and drops his attention to our hands between us, the gel pack gathering condensation. "Yes. Not at you. At him. Think about what could've happened. He could've—you wouldn't even remember it."

"I know. I never drink that much." Shame weakens my voice. "The night just got away from me."

His face softens. "You felt safe with your friends. Makes sense."

A tiny smile breaks through my awkwardness. "Right. Um— thank you."

The edge of his mouth curls, easing the tightness in my chest. "You already thanked me."

I imagine myself calling him Lucifer and adding a thanks as an afterthought. "Was I rude about it?"

Those veiled eyes freeze me in place, searching deep inside me. What is he looking for? What is he *finding*? He tilts his head. "No. Drunk Sapphire actually likes me."

Laughter bursts from me. "Did she tell you that? She's a classless ho."

He shrugs. "Sober Sapphire will catch up to reality eventually. Our drunk personas rarely lie."

My stomach drops. Oh god. Did I tell him I think he's pretty? I will never live that down. "What else did I say?"

A slow smile spreads over his face.

"No." My heartbeat accelerates. "What did I say, Julian?"

He bites his lower lip, but it does nothing to hide the grin.

I cover my eyes with my free hand. "Did I say anything embarrassing?"

"You told me I have talented hands."

My stomach drops. If I said that, then what other secrets did my drunk ass spill? The noise that erupts from my nose is the least attractive thing I've ever done, and he laughs.

"You also told me you'll destroy me."

"Oh." I nod and pull him by the hand toward the couch. "So a typical day for you and me, then?" I collapse on the comfiest spot.

He sits more gracefully, still holding the ice pack against his hand. "I wouldn't call it typical."

"What would you call it?"

He smiles. "Educational."

My eyes narrow. "There's stuff you're not telling me, isn't there?"

"Yep." His black gaze meets mine, the no-smile confusing my insides. "Don't worry. You'll figure it out soon enough."

Don't think about it, Grace.

"Well, let me repay you. I ordered enough takeout for about

six people. Please help me douse the alcohol with grease and binge Netflix."

He settles back into the couch beside me, far closer than needed on this huge sectional with only two people. I don't mind. If it was socially acceptable for friends to cuddle, I'd curl into that man and revel in his scent.

"We're watching *Twilight*. All five movies. Hope that's okay."

He frowns. "I don't even get to choose the movie?"

I feign deep offense. "I am *hungover*, Julian."

"You did that to yourself."

Poking out my bottom lip, I shoot him puppy-dog eyes. "Pwease?"

He sighs. "Only if I'm allowed to make fun of it, and you don't ever compare me to the Volturi."

I blink for several seconds as I process that he knows the word *Volturi*. "Have you *watched Twilight*?"

"I have never seen these movies, no."

"Then…you've read—"

"Shut up. I have four older sisters. Also, I kept hoping Bella would come to her senses and tell them both to fuck off."

The giggles cannot be contained. I spend the next several hours eating noodles and heatedly arguing that *Twilight* is a love story, not a horror that glamorizes domestic abuse, suicide and pedophilia.

He ignores the gel pack. That's the only reason I hold it there until it's warmed. The only reason I continue to touch him once the pack falls away. The only reason my fingers slide between his, my thumb brushing the largest scrape on his first knuckle. When he doesn't pull away, I lean into him, and my head finds its way to his shoulder, my eyes falling shut.

A sense of safety emits from him, drawing me in. He *saved* me.

Whatever magic pheromone dust coats his skin snakes

through my nervous system, and I grow luxuriously warm. Drowsy. I fight the urge not to bury my nose in his neck.

So maybe it is socially appropriate for friends to cuddle.

Or maybe...

We're not friends.

At didactics the next week, a bleary-eyed Alesha sits next to me with a new travel mug sporting a sparkly unicorn with curly letters that read Back the Fuck Up, Sprinkle Tits. Today Is Not the Day. I Will Shank You With My Horn.

"Nights got you down?" I ask. My own sleepiness weighs on my eyes.

She nods. "Up all night. You?"

"Mmm-hmm."

The only good part about nights at Vincent is that Julian is on days instead of someone awful like Ling Ferris-Smith, our chief. Of course that also means I barely see him, and our study sessions have once again come to an abrupt halt.

"Thank god we only have to stay here an hour." My yawn distorts the last word.

Asher pulls a chair out next to me.

I scoot to make room. "Good morning!"

His tight smile is unusual. "Morning, Grace." His tone is neutral, hovering on cold, and I'm confused. Is he okay?

I peer closer at him. "Something wrong?"

He pauses while pulling his laptop from his bag to stare at me and lowers his voice. "Why didn't you just tell me you were into Santini?"

A rush of cold sweeps through me. "What?"

"At Halloween—"

"I don't remember Halloween," I hiss. "Julian said Trevor kissed me."

Asher's expression clears. "Yeah. Santini almost knocked the guy out, and I kicked him out of my house."

I touch his hand. "Thank you."

"And then you threw yourself at Julian and told everyone you had sex with him."

"*What?*" Glancing around, I'm relieved to find everyone else engrossed in their own conversations, including Julian at the end of the table.

Alesha rolls her eyes. "That's not what happened." She goes on to explain the real story, the joke I made, and my insides unclench in relief.

"Whatever." Asher flips open his laptop. "You should have just told me."

"Told you *what?*"

"That you're hot for Santini."

"I'm not—"

Alesha squeezes my hand and gives her head a subtle shake. She pulls out her phone. Mine buzzes.

Alesha: You know you are. Just let him be mad. He'll get over it.

Why does Asher even care? I stare at him a moment, then glance at his hairy legs. "Wait. Are you wearing cut-off scrubs?"

Asher's face tightens. "My legs get hot sometimes."

"But—" I point at his feet "—you paired them with cowboy boots."

His gaze lands on me, and his tone finally morphs into its usual good humor. "I will not be shamed for the cowboy boots."

My laughter dies off when Dr. Chen seats himself for morning announcements. He mentions that the yearly interviews to select new residents are coming up in a few weeks. Unlike previous years, which were performed only by attendings, all residents are expected to participate, even those on nights. I groan inwardly, exchanging sad faces with Alesha.

"Do you think they assume we turn into robots who don't

have feelings or need sleep when we become residents?" Alesha murmurs.

I tally the time in my head. "That's forty-two straight hours. How are we supposed to do that?"

She shrugs. "Meth?"

After the first hour of didactics, night residents are allowed to leave, so Alesha and I hightail it to our cars. After pecking her on the cheek, I peel out of the parking lot and jam to T. Swift the whole way home.

That night, Julian is especially tired at checkout.

Huddled together in our tiny call room, I nudge his knee with my own. "What's wrong?"

He shrugs. "Narayan. Nothing is ever good enough for her." He rubs his face. "Also, my med student is an idiot who checked the wrong hole after she asked me to practice cervical exams, so the fallout from that was really fun to deal with."

I burst into giggles. "The wrong hole?"

"Yes," he says with great emphasis. "And I have this multiple-personalities patient who keeps coming to triage for the same complaints because her personalities don't communicate with one another. I've had to give labor precautions to the woman six different times today."

"That poor girl!"

A tiny smile brightens his face. "Honestly? I wouldn't mind seeing her again. It's easy work."

I laugh. This boy is the best.

"Then listen to this one. One patient today insisted she had a mutation called Demaglobin that would make her baby come out a different race."

"No!"

His smile grows. "Conveniently discussed in front of her boyfriend, who's the same race as her."

I flick his knee. "Sounds like you had an eventful day."

"Mmm. I did deliver a very sweet patient today. Room nineteen. You'll love her. But I pulled a Grace and wound up with bloody scrubs after."

"Ha, ha." I smile as he stands. "Have a good night."

He nudges my chin with his knuckle, a quick affectionate gesture that sets my blood on fire. "Night, Grace. Call if you need help."

He does that every night. The same sweet little brush of skin that makes his face linger in my mind all night long. He smirks like he knows exactly what he's doing before stepping out. The heat takes several minutes to fade after he leaves, and I blink at the bare wall before me.

So.

Okay.

I admit it.

It isn't a fantasy. It isn't a passing fancy.

I am *so* hot for Julian Santini.

And I think he knows it.

Three weeks later, nights have obliterated my spirit. My circadian rhythm is so confused that even when I have the opportunity to sleep, I lack the ability. Every night is filled with midnight Oreos and 2:00 a.m. quesadillas. In quiet moments, I curl up in the call-room bed and binge *The Handmaid's Tale*—not an ideal show for work on L&D.

My morning and evening sign-outs with Julian are the bright spots in my day, and I wish they were longer. Having opposite schedules has only proven that I crave his presence like a drug.

I miss him.

Does he miss me?

Our sign-out on interview day takes place in the residency clinic. I hand him the list, and we review the patients before he's swept off to Dr. DeBakey's interview room.

I'm placed in Dr. Chen's room with Lexie, a third-year. A glance at our schedule shows we have twelve interviews today.

After suffering Dr. Echols's temper all night, my quad venti Starbucks is doing nothing to hide the puffy dark circles under my eyes or quell my yawns.

Lexie gives my shoulder a gentle shake. "You gonna make it?"

"I'm in the astral plane right now. My soul is sleeping."

She chuckles. "It'll all be over soon."

I glance at my phone. Sixteen hours to go...

Dr. Chen sits at his desk, and Lexie and I pull up chairs beside him. Between interviewees, we scarf the candy he hides in his desk drawer while he looks on fondly.

The first three candidates smear together in my mind. They're all women. All wearing black power suits. All answer "flying" when asked what superpower they'd want.

Who the hell would want to fly? Think before you speak, people. It's cold. There are bugs. People could see up your dress. No thanks.

I'll take teleportation. No more dealing with traffic. No TSA. I could visit Bora Bora at a moment's notice. And best of all, I could sleep in until the last second.

The fourth candidate is male, and his answer of "invisibility" has me shrinking in my chair. A male gynecologist who wants to be invisible. What a skeeze.

The fifth candidate is a tall man with a cocky smile, who clearly thinks he's getting a spot.

Lexie throws him off his game when she smiles. "So if you were an STD, which one would you be?"

His face blanks, but he regrows his smile. "HIV."

All three of us stare at him.

"HIV?" I lift my hand in a confused gesture. "Why?"

He shrugs. "Because it's basically curable now."

Lexie shoots him a flat stare. "As opposed to chlamydia, which is *actually* curable."

The sixth candidate is a small intense woman. Chen combats her intensity with rapid-fire medical knowledge questions which she answers without a hint of hesitation.

Finally, he asks, "What's the most common STD?"

She smirks and crosses her arms. "Pregnancy."

Lexie snorts. "You are awesome. Can we give her a spot right now?"

When the seventh candidate enters, trembling, Lexie and I exchange furtive glances.

"Hello." Dr. Chen smiles and waves at the chair before his desk. "Have a seat."

She perches in her chair, and stares, wide-eyed.

We introduce ourselves, then ask for basic information— her name and hometown, med school, favorite classes. She gives clipped one-word answers, and Dr. Chen is at a loss. He glances toward me.

I power-on my megawatt smile. "If you could have any superpower, what would you choose?"

Her hands fidget in her lap. "Superpower?"

"Um—" I glance at Lexie. "Yeah, like teleportation, or mind-reading, or whatever."

"I don't know what you mean."

"You don't—" My shoulders fall. How could I be clearer than that?

Dr. Chen takes over. "Can you describe a vaginal delivery for me?"

The girl freezes, and a sudden rush of tears comes to her eyes. "Uh—"

Oh, this poor girl...

Even I wasn't this bad at interviewing.

"Okay, so maybe just demonstrate how you would do a delivery." He takes the TCU Horned Frog plush from his desk and holds it in front of the girl's face. "Here we go. Where will you place your hands?"

The girl raises her hands, palms out, like the Horned Frog

might attack. She sniffs. A tear falls. Lexie and I side-eye each other.

Dr. Chen pauses. "And...what are your hands doing?"

Her gaze darts to her raised hands, then back to Chen.

He nods in encouragement. "What are your hands protecting?"

The perineum.

"The clitoris!"

Chen clears his throat. "Okay. But what are you trying to protect in the delivery?"

The perineum.

The girl's tears pour. "The clitoris?"

A tiny uncomfortable laugh emerges from Chen. "Yes. Okay. But what are your hands protecting?" He motions how we protect the perineum during a vaginal delivery.

Say anything but "clitoris."

Cheeks wet, eyes desperate, the girl whimpers. "The clitoris!"

Out of the corner of my eye, Lexie snaps a subtle picture of the girl and the Horned Frog, and I lose it. I shouldn't condone it. Shouldn't feed into it. It's terrible. Unkind. But it's medicine. Can't take the heat? Kitchen's not for you.

I'm far too tired to put a wrench in the malignant cog of medicine today. Instead, laughter bubbles from deep inside, and no matter how I try to suppress it, it breaks the surface. A snort rises first, followed by a series of unattractive chuffs as I press a hand over my mouth.

Chen turns to me, understanding in his eyes. "You may be excused, Dr. Rose. Get some sleep."

Ah. He has a heart! Who knew?

"Thank you, sir," I gasp around my laughs. I am so unprofessional. So mean. So tired.

I *laughed* at her, and I'm too tired to even care.

Is this what medicine has done to me? Has it made me callous?

Ugh.

In my car, my phone buzzes, and I pull it out. Lexie has group texted all the residents with the picture of the girl with her face scribbled out. She's captioned it, "PROTECT THE CLITORIS!"

I don't care that I'm an asshole. I'm still laughing when I fall into my bed.

Julian

NOVEMBER, YEAR 2

St. Vincent is the busiest L&D in the region, and for reasons no one can adequately explain, only one resident covers each shift with a single OB hospitalist attending. Half the year, an intern is also assigned, but there's enough work for at least three upper-levels. Covering it by myself as a second-year is like drowning beneath a tsunami while a horde of people on silver surfboards complain about my inability to swim.

Errors often occur—not only mine—and prior to this month, I had vastly underestimated the hospitalists' ability to make me feel guilty for their mistakes.

Grace has been an ideal night resident the entirety of the month. When I arrive each morning, she's bright-eyed and smiling with the patient list in hand, color-coded from her rainbow pens. Sometimes, she even has black coffee waiting for me, so I've taken to bringing her a chocolate donut every morning just to make her smile.

Her sign-out is pristine—far better than mine in the evening. I'm pretty sure she spends the first hour of every shift combing the charts to revise all my mistakes. I read my notes twice before I sign, yet errors persist.

The glory of electronic medical records is that they all have shortcuts for charting—dot phrases and saved templates. Dr. Narayan, the most unfriendly hospitalist to ever grace these sacred halls—and perhaps the worst human on the planet—has removed my "template privileges" in an effort to improve my charting. It forces me to write all my notes from scratch, taking triple the time it normally would.

Grace's notes are flawless, and she rounds on at least half the list each morning, including all the discharges. It significantly lightens my workload, and if I wasn't halfway gone for her already, this would have tipped the scales.

She's my savior.

Four weeks since Halloween. She still has no clue Drunk Grace admitted she wants me. Sober Grace is as reticent as always, but her smiles have grown dreamy and she blushes when I touch her. This has become the longest game of foreplay in history.

I'm desperate for her to let her guard down. I want her to confess her desire, unclouded and sober. And she will.

Once she fully trusts me.

I'm patient. The waiting will pay off. Soon.

Right?

I really hope I'm not kidding myself.

Heading to the hospital before dawn on the last day of November, I smile to myself. Traffic lights reflect through beads of rainwater, red and green fractured around my truck, painting the black leather in Christmas colors. The chilly walk to the back elevator that lands me in the postpartum unit barely pulls my attention from the anticipation of seeing her.

Next month, we'll be on different services—her on L&D days at TUMC, me on GYN surgery. These patient checkouts will be a thing of the past.

I slip into our closet-sized call room, expecting she'll be ready with coffee and a freshly printed patient list. Instead, the room is dark. The overhead multicolor Christmas lights we leave up year-round glow in the dim space, rainbows bouncing off the white walls. The list is indeed printed, sitting beneath the ASCOM on the little fridge we use as a nightstand. Grace is curled up on our twin bed, fast asleep atop the covers.

I nearly trip over one of her shoes as the magnet inside her draws me closer. The rainbow lights dye her in patches, blue across her cheek, pink over her lips, green and yellow in her hair.

Her slow, even breaths disturb the rebel strands that lay across her cheek. My hand moves without direction from me, and my pinky pushes those hairs away from her face, sliding down her temple and jaw. She stirs, and an arousing moan resonates in her throat.

"Julian?" Eyes closed, she slurs my name in a sleepy voice, like she knows me by touch alone.

"Mmm-hmm." I drop to my knees, closer to her level.

Her eyes flutter open. Reflected rainbow lights wink at me in the darkness.

"There's my girl. Rough night?"

That languid smile jumpstarts my pulse. My heart thuds once, then speeds my blood through my veins as I picture crawling into the bed with her.

She blinks, still smiling, then lucidity hits and her body tenses. "Oh my god. I didn't round. Shit. I can't believe I fell asleep."

I withdraw my hand as she sits up, swinging her legs over the edge of the bed and rubbing the sleep from her eyes.

"It's okay. It's technically my job to round on everyone."

She grabs her phone and scowls. "I set my alarm for 4:30 p.m. instead of a.m." She takes the list and yawns.

"You—you wake up at 4:30 to help me round?"

She glances at me and does a double take. Colored lights smear across her skin and hair as she leans toward me, quickly sweeping back the hair that always lays over my forehead. "I just… They're hard on you for stupid reasons, and I'm usually awake anyway, and—" she sighs and looks at her lap, her voice shrinking "—I want your days to be good, Julian."

My breath stalls. It's such a simple statement.

I want your days to be good.

But that isn't what it means. At least not to me.

I want you to be happy.

I'll sacrifice my own comfort for you.

Her light-filled eyes lift to meet mine.

I'm not coming back from this. It's happening in real time, a pistol held to my heart, poised to change everything. Her finger's on the trigger, and staring into her eyes, I'm unsure whether she'll pull it or lay the weapon down and show me mercy.

I'll let her do either one, won't I? Tendrils of frost curl around my veins as the truth unfurls inside me. I'll let her destroy me, and I'll do it with a smile.

I'm hers now.

What if she never agrees to be mine?

"Grace—"

The ASCOM blares and we both jump. I answer, barely listening as a nurse gives a quick report on a patient in triage. I can't look away from Grace even though she's diligently studying the paper before her, avoiding my gaze.

"I'll be right there."

"Thanks, Dr. Santini. Today's your last day, right? We should celebrate."

"Uh-huh, sure." I hang up.

Grace hands me the list, but I'm still fixated on her face, the constellation of freckles over her nose, the one on her lip. Checkout is useless. I miss her entire report until she says, "This last girl is the one you need to worry about."

My attention finally lands on the patient information. The woman is in the ICU. Unusual for OB-GYN.

"She came in through the ER a few hours ago in septic shock from a miscarriage. Positive pregnancy test and bleeding, but the abdominal ultrasound still shows a bunch of crap in her uterus. She wasn't stable enough to take to the OR right away, and I couldn't even do an exam because she wasn't lucid from the fever. One hundred and six! Can you believe that? As soon as she's stable, you'll be taking her for a D&C to get it out."

"Damn."

"I know. The hard part is she speaks some dialect of Burmese or Tibetan or something. We don't have a translator for it. I *think* she said her last period was six weeks ago."

"Jesus. What a shit show."

She rubs her eyes, forehead crinkled. "I really wanted to have her tucked in before you got here, but she was crashing in the ED. Barely conscious. They've got her on drips and antibiotics. It shouldn't be long now."

"It's really okay, Grace." I give her a grin as she cuts her focus to me. "You don't always have to do all the work."

A brittle smile lights her face. "Maybe I like to. It's the last day of the month. I'll...miss you."

There it is. She's so close.

"I'm still here," I say. "Anytime you want me."

"I—really?"

I can't resist brushing my thumb along the corner of her

smile. "Really. Say it, and I'll be there. Whatever you need. Surely you know that by now."

Her gaze warms as it roams over my eyes, nose, then lingers at my mouth.

Say it. Please just say it.

"Thank you, Julian," she says instead.

"You're welcome, *Sapphire*."

She hides her smile and swings her backpack onto her shoulder. Pausing, she opens her mouth, but nothing comes out.

My hopes climb a steep mountain. "Yes?"

"Nothing. Thanks for a good month." She slips from the room and the hope takes a dive off a cliff.

The girl is cagey AF. What happened to make her this skittish? Maybe what I'm interpreting as interest on her part is really just excessive kindness. Maybe this is her letting me down easy.

Guess I'm going to have to man up and actually ask.

I have to reread the list to orient myself, then head to triage. The blonde nurse at the desk sits straight when I approach. Pulling her name from the dregs of my memory, I smile. "Hey, Taylor."

"Yours is in room two."

"What's her story again?"

"Thirty-two weeks. Claims she's a virgin, but thinks she has chlamydia."

I blink. So many contradictions there...

She only laughs.

The patient is a short redhead with bright blue eyes. They gaze at me with unblinking intensity while I introduce myself.

"What can I help you with today?" I ask.

"I was hurting and had this yellow stuff comin' out my twat, so I took a home test for STDs. Said I have chlamydia."

I draw a breath, but she holds up a finger.

"Doesn't make sense. I never had sex."

My eyes narrow and my pen drifts to point at her very pregnant stomach.

She follows the pen's direction and stares at her belly for two seconds before jumping in surprise, like she's forgotten a human grows there.

Blue owl eyes return to me. "I didn't have sex, but I think I know how I got pregnant."

"Did you have a sperm donor?"

"No."

I scratch my head. "Then where'd the sperm come from?"

"From a cup." She has no inflection to her voice. No tonal changes. She's an owl-eyed robot, and a little voice in my mind whispers, *You're being punked.*

"How did it get in the cup?"

Her owl eyes drop to my pants. "Don't you have one? You don't know how they work?"

I tilt my head and beg the universe to keep me from laughing. "Fair enough. How did it get in your vagina?"

"I poured it in."

The image of a red Solo cup filled with cold semen fills my mind, nauseating this early in the morning. My mouth opens, but nothing comes out.

Her blue eyes go impossibly wide. "Wait. Is that how I got chlamydia?"

And that's about how my morning progresses until Dr. Scarlett calls to tell me the patient in the ICU has stabilized and they're moving her to pre-op.

A quarter hour later, I slide a latte toward Scarlett where she's waiting in the OR attending lounge. "Any luck on a translator?"

She pops the lid and glances inside. I know all the hospitalists' coffee orders by heart, so hers is perfectly made, but she still doesn't thank me as she takes a sip.

She shakes her head. "Now they're thinking it might be

Khmer. The reverend from her church showed up, but his translation of her story doesn't make much sense."

I suppress the pang of annoyance that she didn't call me for the interview with the reverend. "What did he say?"

"That her last period was four days ago and she only started feeling sick this morning. Did you look at the ultrasound images?"

I nod.

"What'd you think?"

"Honestly? It looked like a huge gray mess in there."

She chuckles. "I thought so, too."

It's another forty-five minutes before we're gowned and gloved alongside our trusty scrub tech, Livia, in the OR. I sit on the stool, adjust the lights and place a speculum. What I see makes no sense. A shiny white cord protrudes from the woman's dilated cervix. It looks like a—

Livia gasps. "Is that—?"

I grasp it with a clamp and pull, dragging out a term-sized placenta which lands with a splat into a blue basin, its rancid odor drifting up under our masks. I hold up the umbilical cord—cleanly cut in half.

All three of us stare at it in silence.

"Did—" Dr. Scarlett pokes at the placenta in the bucket. "Did she say there was a baby? She said she was miscarrying!"

But did she? The language barrier...

Livia turns away. "Oh my god."

Images fillet my mind. A baby cut away from its mother, kidnapped, sold into slavery, trafficked away for nefarious purposes. Or worse, killed for being unwanted. Abandoned. Cold and alone.

The images won't stop, each worse than the last. Because I'm staring at only *half* the pregnancy.

A ragged breath drags through my lungs. "Where's the baby?"

Grace

NOVEMBER, YEAR 2

My mind swims through the muck of my subconscious as a thump jostles it awake. Nights this month have worn me down. The fluttery anxiety at seeing Julian every shift change keeps me frazzled and on edge. Now that I've admitted to myself that I like him, I don't know how to act around him.

The last time I felt this way...

Yeah.

It hadn't ended well.

If I could, I'd shove this heat and longing for Julian aside, force its brightness into shadow. Instead, it only grows stronger. Each lingering glance, every small touch, they glow in my skin like sunlight.

The persistent urge to touch him. The constant awareness of him. Well, my sleeplessness isn't only work-related.

Say it, and I'll be there. Whatever you need.

Did he really say that this morning? Did he mean it?

The pounding on my door finally jolts me awake.

"Grace!"

I sit up, blinking at the darkness beyond the window. My phone tells me it's 6:45 p.m.

"Grace, are you home?"

"Julian?" I call. ·

"Yeah." A silence passes, and a final thump rattles the door. "Can I talk to you?"

I hop out of bed and dart into the bathroom. "Hold on. I was asleep!"

He's silent, so I pee and brush my teeth at the same time, then lament my bedhead and pj's. At least they're the cute set— black shorts and tank with little gold stars.

With a swipe of the deadbolt, the door swings inward, pulling in a gust of cold air that snakes around my bare legs, raising goose bumps. Julian stands at the threshold, hands braced on either side, head bowed. He's still in his Vincent scrubs, without even a jacket to protect him from the elements, and when he lifts his eyes, I'm struck by the hurt lurking in their depths.

"What's wrong?"

He swallows. "Can I come in?"

I allow him clearance. He moves to the middle of the living room, staring at the floating shelves above the couch, full of unlit candles.

"Julian?" I touch his elbow.

"Remember that patient from the ICU this morning?"

"Yeah. What's wrong?"

"The language barrier… We were wrong about the miscarriage." That dead tone to his voice laces shards of ice through my veins. "She had a home birth. The baby was delivered, but whoever delivered her didn't deliver the placenta."

Oh, that's why her ultrasound looked so weird. Duh.

"She delivered the baby *four days ago*, Grace. Perfectly healthy baby girl."

My mouth drops. "She had a placenta inside her the whole time?"

His head dips. "We got it out. Smelled awful. Got her to the ICU. She started bleeding. Took her back to the OR. Bled out five liters before we took her uterus. But she was bleeding from everywhere by that point."

Oh no. I see where this is going, and a deep ache wakes in my chest. He came here for comfort, didn't he? Something bad happened, and he came straight to me. As he continues speaking, my arms slide around his neck, and I compulsively inch closer to him. I want to hold him, squeeze him until that hollowness disappears from his eyes. His stiff hands settle on my waist, and his gaze meets mine, utterly lost.

"She coded on the table," he whispers. "We tried to bring her back for an hour. Scarlett called time of death at 5:02."

"She *died*?" I can't believe what he's saying. The woman was sick when I left, but stabilizing, and now she's dead. Humans are so fragile. It's terrifying.

Who left a placenta in her for four days? That person is a murderer!

"She died," he says, voice flat. "The dad brought the baby before she started bleeding. A perfect baby girl."

His eyes slide shut when he finishes speaking.

"Oh, sweetie." I move closer. "I'm so sorry."

He hums deep in his chest.

"The baby's healthy, right, Julian?"

He dips his head, resting his forehead on mine. "Yeah."

"At least there's that. A healthy baby." I nudge his nose with mine.

"Without a mom." He pulls tight on my waist and his breath hitches. "I never told you why I chose OB-GYN, did I?"

I shake my head.

"My dad died when I was two, so it was always just Mom and my sisters. We're all really close. When I was fifteen, she almost died when her gynecologist wouldn't listen to her. Nearly bled to death before they took her uterus. And I was *fifteen*. I would have had fifteen years with her. That baby had four days. What if I'd just interviewed the patient more, Grace? Really listened to her. Would I have caught something that could've changed this?"

"She didn't speak English, Julian. I tried the language line, and they had no one with her dialect."

"I know." He sighs. "It's just—today was a terrible day."

"I'm so sorry." I'm flush against him now, trying to soothe him, the heat of his body pressed to mine from chest to knee.

"It was a terrible day, and after it all happened, I kept thinking that if I could make it home, make it here, to you, everything would feel just a little bit lighter."

My skin synchronizes to his heartbeat as I slide my arms more snugly around his neck. "Lighter?" I put a playful lilt in my tone. "Aren't I the bane of your existence?"

"No." His nose slides along the length of mine, and my eyes flutter closed. "I should have told you a long time ago. You're a prison I don't want to escape. You're like drowning in paradise."

Whoa. Really?

He's so close, the graze of his lips as he speaks sends shivers across my skin, diffusing liquid heat beneath.

I stand at the edge of the unknown, and my voice grows breathy. "That sounds…painful."

Voice deep, almost slurred, he says, "Nothing hurts when I'm with you."

Does he really think that? After all these months of vague flirtation, he finally reveals *these* are the thoughts that prowl in his mind?

These aren't the words of a man who thinks I might be fun

to bang. These are the words of a man who cares, who wants *me*, not just my body.

His hands tangle in the back of my shirt, clenching the fabric. "Grace—"

The faint brush of his lips near mine rouses the heat simmering for him into a full boil. Patience snaps, and I graze my mouth over his, soft and warm and waiting. His body tenses against mine before one hot gifted hand cups my jaw, thumb beneath my chin, and he kisses me.

A flood of pleasure breaks through all thoughts of restraint, and I tighten my hold on his neck, rising to my tiptoes to get closer.

Magic sparks between us, and streams of twinkling stars illuminate my insides. His tongue touches mine, teasing, and I'm lost. I cling to him so tight that my toes barely touch the floor. Sliding into my hair, that hand of his massages the tiny muscles of my neck, eliciting a weird humming from my chest.

A dark chuckle answers, and he deepens the kiss, bringing us so close together that the clothes between us are an unbearable nuisance.

"God, Grace." His lips slide over my cheek, teeth catching my ear. "I've wanted to do this for so long."

"Yeah?"

"Mmm-hmm." He sucks on my neck, a sensation that spirals between my legs. I squeeze my thighs together and squirm against him.

His lips find mine once more, urgent, faster. His hand drops to my ass, squeezing us together, and the hardness of him presses into my lower belly, impossible to ignore.

OMG.

He wants me.

This charming, intelligent, kind man *wants* me.

I could tell him to take me to the bedroom, and he'd do it.

He'd lay me down, and if this kiss is any indication, he'd probably give me the best sex of my life.

And I'd probably be the worst of his.

It's like fucking an ice queen.

My fingers spasm at the memory, and I pull my lips from his, pressing slower, soothing kisses over his jaw, letting my mouth sink against his throat. A deep hum rumbles there, but he takes the hint and loosens his grip on me. I slide until my feet are flat on the floor and I'm staring into impossibly dark eyes, a flushed face, a hungry expression.

I rest my palms on his chest, separating our bodies by a crucial few inches. "This probably isn't a good idea."

He makes a face like he disagrees, all pinched eyebrows and twisted mouth.

"I'm—" I drop my gaze to his chest. "We aren't—"

"What? We aren't what?" His voice is rough and dark.

"*I'm* not—" I rub my nose, ignoring my body's insistence that I want him, that it doesn't matter if I'm bad at it because he won't care. He'll use those talented hands to teach me about pleasure I've only read about.

But what if he *does* care?

That familiar anxiety thrusts a hand in my chest and twists, tightening all my nerves to maximum tension.

"Ready," I say. "I'm not ready."

He dips his head, like he's trying to see past my mask of calm. "Do I—should I apologize?"

My eyebrows pull together. "You did nothing wrong."

"Then why do you look like you're about to freak out?"

"I'm—I'm not." I reach out, then drop my hands again. "That was unexpected."

He tilts his head, dark gaze traveling over my pajama-clad body before he takes my wrist and tugs gently. "Was it?"

I think back on the last few months, to all the fantasy kisses

I'd invented for us. Staring into his shadowy eyes, spellbound, I whisper, "No."

His hand at my wrist skates along my arm until his knuckle lands on my jaw, and he slides sparkly pleasure across it. He lifts my chin. "No, it wasn't. And I kind of want to do it again."

Breathless, I nod, and his soft lips are on mine again, slow and agonizing. He tastes like that cinnamon gum he favors with the barest hint of black coffee, a heady mixture that has me hunting for more.

On my toes again, I ache to be closer. A raging fire turns my blood to molten gold, hot and lavish and glittering. Our bodies find a natural rhythm, my hands in his soft hair, his splayed across my back.

I break the kiss to nip his jaw and neck, and he digs into the muscles of my back, then dips lower. The tips of his fingers sneak beneath the elastic of my pajama shorts. His skin tastes like salt and Julian, and my mouth finds his pulse, sucking while he murmurs encouragement in my ear.

A growl rumbles in his chest, and he steals my mouth again, harder, hands roaming, skirting along intimate places, but not touching.

He's staking a claim. I sense it in the way he touches me— no push for more, but no hesitancy, either. It ransacks all my desires. He's pillaging my body for his own. A frickin' pirate in the open ocean, chasing the horizon.

We're writhing. Bound together. Aching. A storm gathering electricity.

My skin is on fire.

I want him.

I need him.

I need release.

His mouth is on mine. My leg wraps around him. His hand sinks into my hair. Mine drops to the waist of his scrub pants, fingers curling around the band.

Panting, he drops his forehead to my shoulder. "I have to stop."

No, don't stop.

My pounding heart clangs against my ribs, and I suck in breaths trying to calm it. Is there no oxygen in this room?

His nose brushes my neck. "Unless you're offering more."

Ice queen.

It's a splash of cold water that chills my throbbing insides. It shouldn't be there, still haunting me, but it won't stop preying on my insecurities. "I—"

"You're not ready."

"Not—not yet."

A graze of his lips beneath my ear rekindles my nervous system. Tingles chase themselves over my skin.

"I'm patient," he whispers.

I retract my fingers from his waistband.

"But don't think I won't chase you."

Backing away, I meet his gaze, the darkness alight with desire. "Yeah?"

The no-smile comes to life, and he stares at my mouth. "I'll chase until you tell me to stop. Present me with a challenge and I shall rise." The hand in my hair slides out, then holds it back so he can study my neck. He brushes the pad of his thumb over it. "Oops."

I turn toward the mirror on the wall to find a darkening patch of skin where his mouth had been. I cover it with my hand, and return my attention to his satisfied expression, eyes wide.

He marked me. Like a marauder.

This be mine.

Hoist the colors.

"Thanks for the pep talk." He brushes a kiss over my lips and steps away. "I have a cold shower to get to."

DECEMBER, YEAR 2

The story of the four-day placenta becomes instant residency legend. Julian recounts the case in didactics later that week. By then, he's bottled up his external grief, but in private, he's still shook.

About a week after the incident, we meet to study at my apartment, creeping closer and closer to each other on my couch as the night progresses.

He caves after an hour and pulls me into his lap, pressing a kiss to my temple.

"Are you feeling better about last week?" I flatten my palm against his chest and nibble on my lip as I study his face, searching for the hurt I know is still in there.

He shrugs. "I don't think I'll ever feel better about that. But I'll get over it. Someday." His lips move to my neck, and my breath hitches. Pleasure illuminates and sparkles over me before he pulls away to meet my eyes. His desire is written all over his face, open and hungry. I peck a quick kiss on his mouth and scoot off his lap.

Distance. I need distance.

His half smile snags my heart. The life-giving organ skips a beat, then trips over the next several. These ectopic beats disturb me. He's buried an electrode in my chest. My own personal defibrillator.

"Not ready?" He lifts an eyebrow.

I shiver, heat blazing across my cheeks, and pull my lip between my teeth.

He reaches toward the coffee table where we've left our study materials, dark eyes roaming my face. "Could I seduce you with flashcards?" His long fingers curl around the stack of cards.

A wave of heat crashes and settles low in my stomach, but I cover it with a laugh. "How on earth did you manage to make that sexy?"

He lowers his voice, the half smile growing into a full smile. "Because studying gets you hot."

I smack his shoulder.

He laughs and sobers. "All right. Teach me about cervical cancer staging."

Dr. Chen hovers over my shoulder in the doctor's OR lounge where I chart at the computer. We had two C-sections today, and I'm glowing. I made no wrong moves, and I finished in a reasonable amount of time. The smile on my face cannot be quelled.

"You did good today, Dr. Rose."

Chen must be an awful snorer because his CPAP lines have survived the entire morning, leaving indentations over his full cheeks. Glasses still fogged from surgery, he gazes through the mist with kind brown eyes. His salt-and-pepper mustache twitches with a smile.

My throat tightens. "Really?"

"I can tell you're practicing. Good work."

A flare spikes my blood, a torrential flood of exhilaration. Julian did this. His help brought me to this moment.

Chen sits beside me and pulls out his phone. "Would you like to see my pictures from Greece? We were there two weeks, you know. Mrs. Chen would kill me if I didn't show off the pictures."

I smile and settle in to view the photos. He has dragged his trip to Santorini into every one of my conversations with him of late, but I'll look at a million pictures of his Greek meals if he'll shower me with praise like that.

Afterward, he stands and squeezes my shoulder. "Dr. Rose."

"Uh. Yes?"

"Do the right thing."

I laugh as he leaves. Do the Right Thing is Chen's motto, his parting words to all residents at some point or another. Once he's gone, I whip out my phone.

> **Me:** Good day today!

> **Mama:** That's great. I love you, honey.

I open the Pit It or Quit It stream.

> **Me:** Chen just told me I did a good job

> **Me:** First time ever 😆

> **Alesha:** Bout time he recognizes your greatness

> **Raven:** That's amazing, Grace!

Beaming at my phone, my heart jumps to my throat when a hand lands on my shoulder. My head spins toward it, but my heart rate doesn't slow at the long fingers curled around my arm.

"Congratulations," Julian whispers beside my ear and kisses my neck.

"Julian!" I swat him away. "Someone will see."

He chuckles and falls into the chair next to me. Our situationship isn't defined, per se, but we're definitely a thing. Dreading the rumors that will spread when we go public, I asked him to keep us on the DL for now. He agreed, but if his increasingly possessive caresses in private are any indication, I'm certain he'd rather I let him ravish me in the dictation room.

The ends of his dark hair curl like duck tails around the blue surgeon's cap and his glasses strike me right in the stomach. He logs onto the computer, eyes scanning the screen.

I glance behind us. The dictation room is empty, so I graze my knuckle down the line of his jaw. "You didn't shave."

The no-smile appears. "Someone kept me up late, but not

in the good way." He swings his gaze to me. "All she wanted to do was study."

My soft laugh stirs the air between us. "Sounds like a sensible girl."

He shrugs. "Yeah. She's worth the wait."

I check once more to make sure we're alone, then grab his face and press a long kiss to his lips. When we separate, I allow myself three seconds of staring into his eyes before returning to my computer, and he does the same.

Maxwell enters the dictation room, taking the place beside Julian. "Good work, Santini."

Julian nods. "Thanks."

Maxwell nods toward me. "How's L&D?"

"It's fine, Dr. DeBakey."

Julian snorts and scrunches his face, mouthing *Dr. DeBakey.* I smack his shoulder.

Feet stretched out in front of him, fingers laced over his stomach, Maxwell looks between us. "You two still pretending you hate each other?"

I straighten and face my computer, sticking my nose in the air. "He's evil incarnate."

Julian nods. "And she breathes misery with every breath."

We match glances from the corner of our eyes, suppressing smiles.

Maxwell sighs and stands. "Y'all weird."

Julian

DECEMBER, YEAR 2

I can't concentrate.

Nothing new, right? Nope. I am *beyond* distracted.

Grace has invaded my life. Every thought, every idea…they filter through her first.

Focused on the laptop before her, her fingers fly over the keys while Ling Ferris-Smith lectures at didactics. The screen of her computer glows in her eyes, and she chews on the inside of her lip, then reaches for the Starbucks cup beside her.

"Dr. Santini?"

I jerk my head to the side, meeting Ling's stare.

She raises her eyebrows. "Can you name the causes of abnormal uterine bleeding?"

Grace's flashcard appears in my head, and I recite the causes from memory. Hey, look at that. Is all the sex-free studying paying off?

Ling's mouth tightens. She nods and continues her lecture.

I return to Grace, who's now smiling triumphantly at me. I'm magnetized to her. If the lights disappeared and plunged us into blackness, I'd still find her. She'd glow, a glittering star illuminating the dark.

CREOGs are next month, the yearly assessment exams for OB-GYN residents nationwide. I'm meant to study. To concentrate.

Instead, I'm haunted by the imprint of her in my mind.

My watch buzzes.

Grace♥: Pay attention, Dr. Santini

I cock my head and stare at her. Her skin dyes an exquisite shade of pink. The vibration at my wrist pulls my attention down.

Grace♥: You're being very obvious, Julian.

I pick up my phone to reply.

Me: I want you.

Her face goes crimson, and she slams her computer shut. She presses her palm over her mouth, pretending to pay attention to the lecture. The hungry predator deep inside me growls in rapture.

She won't go public. Won't let others know about us. I try not to think about that, to worry that she's somehow ashamed of me, but the thoughts are there anyway. Is she keeping me a secret because I'm the embarrassing fling she'll look back on and cringe? The dumb guy she settled for when nothing else was available, who couldn't even afford the good letters?

Flirting with her like this—in plain view of all our colleagues—satisfies the purely male portion of my brain that wants to claim her as mine.

Such a primitive desire, but I can't help it.

I want her the way I want oxygen, and I'm desperately trying to maintain her boundaries until she's ready—if she's ever ready. I guess growing up in an overly affectionate household with four sisters who never stopped telling me how much they love me turned me into an incredibly needy man.

But I just like words of affirmation! Come at me.

So here are my rules:

1) No pressure allowed.
2) Follow her cues.
3) Don't ask for more.

The lecture ends, and Ling begins the usual program announcements. I pay less attention to them than I did the lecture.

Until she says, "We have a scheduling issue we need to talk about."

All eyes turn to Ling, and silence falls.

The schedule.

The scourge.

The bane of our existence.

As the scheduling chief, Ling owns the unfortunate task of assigning residents to each service line—L&D, surgery, weekend call, etc. She chooses what we do each month and which hospital we cover on the weekends. It's a piteous, thankless job.

We all hate her for it.

She makes us do the shit we don't want to do.

All services must be covered, and all residents *should* receive equal call. *Should* is a loose term, though. Hierarchy plays a large role in the schedule. As the most newly licensed physicians, the five of us second-years have it worst.

Ling's unfriendly face stares around the room. "One of the second-years has decided to take an extended leave this year."

Beside me, Raven shrinks in her seat. By law, she's allowed twelve weeks maternity leave. It's unpaid, but it's law. When she broached the subject with Dr. Levine, he told her residents only take four weeks. She argued and was shut down.

She elevated the argument to GME. They confirmed twelve weeks is indeed allowed for parental leave.

Levine laughed at that, and spat, "You're going to regret this."

Now, all stares bore into Raven as Ling continues. "One month of L&D shifts, six weekend calls and a month of oncology need to be covered. Does anyone have an idea how we can manage this?"

My jaw clenches. "You could rearrange the schedule."

Ling's cold stare lands on me. "I've reworked this schedule four times. I'm not messing with it again."

"Maybe you could use the float person the way they're meant to be used." Kai shoots Ling a death glare. "For *coverage*."

As she's the float person for one of those months, Ling's eye twitches. "I have an idea." Her tone is flat. "Since it's a second-year who's taking off, maybe the second-years should cover the slack."

The five of us exchange glances.

Alesha glares at Ling. "*That's* your solution? There are fourteen available residents, and you're going to split the work amongst four of us?"

Ling blinks twice at Alesha, then turns to Raven. "Since your fellow second-years will be covering for you, it would behoove you to ingratiate yourself to them now." She stands. "I'll be sending the revised schedule out in the next few days."

Group Therapy that week is expectedly heated. We've gathered at Grace's apartment, crammed together on her sectional. Linkin Park plays through her sound bar.

Linkin Park is Grace's I'm-angry music.

Unicorn Blood in hand, Kai growls. "I've had pathologic fantasies about drowning that bitch. I'm serious."

Alesha eyes him. "You need a therapist."

"Psh. Don't pretend you weren't sharpening your scalpel."

Alesha takes a sip and shrugs one shoulder.

"I'm really sorry, you guys." Raven sniffs, worrying the tissue in her hand.

Of all the unjust things in this situation, Raven's tears make my blood simmer the hottest. Raven is nothing but kind.

"Oh, Raven." Grace hugs her tight. "Please don't cry. It's fine! It's just a few weeks of work."

Raven wipes her face. "But it isn't fair."

My phone buzzes.

Maxwell: Sorry, man. No luck.

I sigh. I'd asked him to talk to Levine and Chen. See if he could do anything.

Me: What did they say?

Maxwell: "We back the chief 100%"

Me: Fuckers

Maxwell: You surprised? The path of least resistance bro. That's their motto.

Kai jumps to his feet, pacing and ranting while steadily draining his glass.

Alesha's gaze follows his path. She leans toward me. "Should we be worried about him?"

I shake my head. "Let him vent. It makes him feel better."

The pager on the table explodes in beeps and all five of us

flinch. Raven's on Mommy Call tonight, meaning she takes all the patient calls overnight.

Mommy Call is a special form of torture. I once spent forty minutes on the phone with an eighteen-year-old who decided 3:00 a.m. was the best time to learn about her contraceptive options.

Raven reaches for the pager, but Kai snaps it up. "Nuh-uhh. You ain't talking to no one with those tears." He yanks out his phone and dials the number, ranting the whole time. As soon as the patient answers, his voice softens to a professional hum. "Hi. Yes. This is Dr. Campisi. I received a page."

Alesha giggles silently beside me. "He is one of my favorite humans."

Grace rocks Raven, who's now crying into her shoulder.

We drink our Unicorn Blood in silence while Kai drones on.

"Mmm-hmm. Yes. Okay. Great. Thanks. Bye." Kai hangs up and roars at his phone. "If I get one more call about the goddamn mucus plug, I'm gonna lose my shit. I mean it. I will smear the walls with my shit."

Alesha snorts. "His anger is like a special form of comedy."

Kai paces again. "I'm gonna write a book. *Mucus Plug Myth: The Kai Campisi Story.* Chapter one. Please stop calling."

Raven gives a watery laugh. "They're first-time moms. Give them a break."

Kai sits on the coffee table in front of Raven. "I'll give them a break when someone gives you a break."

She bursts into tears again and hugs Kai.

The night proceeds similarly from there. I'm the last to leave, lingering in Grace's doorway.

Let me stay.

Her finger slides down the placket of my black Henley. "Long day."

"You should get some sleep," I say. "Those babies won't deliver themselves tomorrow."

She smiles, her gaze riveted to her finger as it trails down my chest. "You busy tomorrow?"

"There are a few cases in the morning. I'll be done by noon."

"You want to come visit me?" A shy glance flashes. "We could eat lunch."

"Why don't I bring you lunch so you don't have to eat TUMC food?"

She beams. "Chipotle?"

I chuckle and kiss her cheek. "Sure, beautiful. See you tomorrow."

As I climb the stairs to L&D, the bag of food in my hand reminds me it's been two weeks since we first kissed, and I need to take Grace on a real date. Takeout at the hospital doesn't count.

Where, though?

Somewhere with margaritas.

If lime was a drug, Grace would be an addict.

In the call room, I set down the bag.

Me: I'm here.

Grace ♥: I'm coming.

I stare at that text. If only...

Me: That's what she said.

Grace ♥: You wish.

Truer words.

She smiles when she enters. The door clicks behind her.

I stand and slide my phone into my pocket. "You busy today?"

She lifts her shoulder. "I don't want to jinx it, if you know what I mean."

Grace abides by the common medical myth—saying you're not busy will make you busy. Chuckling, I pass her the fountain drink I brought. "So superstitious. I got you Mountain Dew."

She glows as she takes it, smiling bright. "We should study while we eat. CREOGs are coming. Alesha works tonight, but she might meet us here."

"Mmm-hmm." I drag her closer and press a kiss to her cheek.

She sets the drink on a small table beside us and rises to her tiptoes. Her soft lips land on mine. Gentle. Chaste.

Unlike her desire to keep me a secret, I haven't taken her hesitation with the sex stuff so personally. Something clearly happened in her past that makes her shrink away from intimacy. Grace's anxiety is a fundamental part of her, one that takes finesse to dissipate. One day, she'll tell me why she's nervous, and earning her trust in the meantime has been an entertaining and rewarding adventure.

As usual, I hold back from the kiss, but her hand caresses my throat, sliding around my neck and into my hair. She pulls me closer.

My sanity is on such a thin thread. Her eagerness is all it takes to snap it.

She hums her desire as I deepen the kiss. My arms encircle her, pull her close, and she's flush against me, but not like that first kiss when she was clad in flimsy, stretchy cotton. Braless. Nothing but warm, soft curves molded to my body.

Now, the starched scrubs scratch as we move. The rainbow pens in her pocket poke my chest. The pager clipped at her waist digs into my hip.

I don't care.

Her tongue touches mine, and I'm gone. My hand slides beneath her shirt, skimming her ribs, and she steps backward. She retreats. A cold disappointment swells before her hands clench onto the fabric of my shirt and drag me with her.

We reach the bed. She pulls me down on top of her. The kiss

has its own motive, running away from me as my body acts on pure instinct. The scent of her skin travels deep into the fabric of my being, weaving throughout.

Her legs part to make room for me. They stretch wide, and we fit together. The scrubs do nothing to hide how much I want her, but she doesn't balk when I drive that point home against her.

The kiss breaks, and we stare at each other. Hazel eyes have gone forest green, and a fever-bright gleam radiates across her skin. Her hands fall away, landing beside her face, and her body undulates against mine.

She doesn't break eye contact, but the dazed, thirsty glint in her gaze burns like white-hot steel through my limbs, making me impossibly hard—a torturous pleasure-pain only tolerable because she craves the friction I can give her. She nips my lip and rocks against me, and her breath catches as her eyes flutter closed.

"I was thinking about you all day," she whispers against my mouth.

"Yeah?" We find a rhythm together. "What were you thinking about?"

"This."

I stare at her face. "Grace, are you...close?"

"I was close before you even touched me, Julian."

Fire catches in my bones at that admission. She was hot before she walked in the room just from thoughts of me.

The smallest pressure has her right at the edge. I would rip apart the fabric between us if it could get her there faster. This pleasure on her face is exquisite. Priceless. I need this image burned into my memory, this proof that I can make her want it. Want me.

I move faster, and she stifles a strangled cry, then whispers my name.

My lips find hers again in a messy kiss. Wet. Hot.

A rattle behind me sinks into the cacophony of desire. "Grace—Oh my god!"

We both freeze and twist toward Alesha as she looks everywhere but at us, pink hair flying around her face.

"Oh my god." She retreats enough that the door closes, but her muted voice filters through. "Stop dry humping my friend at work, you perv."

Grace turns to ice beneath me. Her wide eyes stare at me. "Shit. We're at work! What are we doing?"

No, no, no. Don't panic.

I brush her still-flushed cheek. "Um. I think you were about to come."

She smacks my shoulder, but the frazzled tension melts from her body. "I was not!"

"I *really* think you were."

On the other side of the door, Alesha clears her throat. "I can hear you."

I roll off Grace and wince at the pressure below. *Fuuuuck.* "Go away, Alesha."

Grace's uncertain hand touches my shoulder. "I'm sorry. Do you need—"

I curl onto my side. "I just need a minute."

"Can I come in now?" Alesha calls.

Grace stands, then wobbles on unsteady legs a moment before she reaches the door. Alesha slips into the crack Grace provides.

I glare at her.

Cockblocker.

She glares right back. "I expected better from you."

"Why? Because I've always been so good at controlling myself around her?"

She rolls her eyes and turns to Grace. "What were you thinking? What if I'd been Chen?"

Grace stares at the floor and shuffles her feet. "Oh. Um. I—"

The pressure finally eases off, and I sit up. "Don't lecture her. This really isn't your business."

"No. You're right. It's not." Alesha's shoulders droop. Her voice lowers. "Aren't there already enough rumors floating around, though?"

I compel myself not to growl. *Don't mention the rumors right now!* God, Grace is already a hunkering ball of nerves. Did we need to remind her of her insecurities?

I stand and take Grace's elbows. She looks into my face, lip clamped between her teeth.

"You did nothing wrong."

She nods and forces a smile.

A notch forms between Alesha's brows as she stares at Grace, and her mouth tightens. "Girl, you don't need to feel guilty. It's just...maybe your apartment is a better place for this sort of *activity*."

The tiny smile on Grace's face eases the tightening knot in my chest. She narrows her eyes at Alesha. "Why don't you seem surprised?"

Alesha laughs outright. "Grace, I've known this was coming since our first Group Therapy. I take it this wasn't the first time?"

Grace turns bright red.

Alesha settles into the rolling chair at the desk. "That's what I thought. Now, you guys eat that delicious food, and we'll pretend I never saw what I saw."

Grace glances at me. "Uh—"

"One question, though." Alesha holds up a finger. "Are you guys *dating*, or are you just...you know..." She forms a circle with one hand and slides her index finger in and out a few times.

Grace's mouth drops open. "Ew! Alesha!"

Unapologetic, Alesha raises her eyebrows.

Grace sputters.

Her innocence is torturously adorable, and laughter has overtaken me, but I scowl at Alesha. "Not that it's any of your business, but we aren't fucking."

Grace smacks my arm. "Julian!"

Wincing, I rub my shoulder. "What? We're not. *But* we could be dating." I give her the smile that always flusters her. "Tonight?"

Her glowing cheeks go brighter. "Really? Tonight?"

I lift an eyebrow. "Unless you have plans with your other boyfriend."

Her grin is infectious, and she shakes her head. "No. He's busy tonight. I'm free."

I'm locked into her again, unable to look away. "Good. It's a date."

"Aww!" Alesha jumps up. "You guys are so cute."

Grace

DECEMBER, YEAR 2

Dating Julian is far more fun than clashing with him all the time, though it still involves frequent disputes. Julian's love language is winning our teasing arguments. The satisfied smile on his face every time I concede defeat is an addictive shot of dopamine.

I'm falling, yet floating. Flying high in the sky and sinking beneath an ocean of hectic heat. Somewhere in the space between Julian and me, someone is throwing sutures that connect my heart to him—a row of vertical mattresses in permanent silk, ever tightening.

I never wanted to feel this way again, but here I am.

In love.

I don't believe in love, do I?

Is there a difference between *in love* and *love?*

He squeezes dates in small crevices of our packed schedules—restaurants, parks, Christmas light extravaganzas. I try to make him study, but I nearly always wind up beneath him on one of our couches, debating whether I'm ready to let him strip me bare and do whatever he wants to me.

I'm not ready.

I'll never be ready.

Maybe I'm broken.

At Christmas, three thousand miles separate us as I fly home to my family and he travels to his, but I receive near constant texts from both him and Tori apprising me of their activities.

The most recent picture is Julian at a beachside bar, pointing his thumb at a sign behind him that reads As For Me and My House, We Will Serve Margaritas. Salt 24:7. He captions the picture, "Found this. Made me think of you."

"What are you smiling about over there, angel baby?" Mom asks.

"Julian. He's so cute."

Mom snuggles next to me on the couch, peeking at the picture while she munches on a stalk of celery. My parents are on a cleanse in which they eat only green foods, though my dad keeps cheating with green Skittles.

Mom gasps. "Oh. He *is* cute."

I grin down at the picture. From my peripheral vision, Mom's stare pulls heat to the surface of my skin.

A soft smile plays at her mouth. "Is he good to you?"

I nod. "He's—he's wonderful."

"Just be careful, baby. After last time—"

Ice water threatens to break through my levees, and I stop her. "I know, Mom. I don't want to talk about Matt."

It's like a slap to the face, this reminder that I'm lacking the portion of my brain that knows how to make good judgments when it comes to men. Julian's good *now*, but what happens when—

Mom sighs. "Come on. Let's go make sugar cookies."

Laughing, I follow her into the kitchen. "I thought you were on a cleanse."

She waves her hand. "I'll put green food coloring in it."

Alone in my room later, I twist the tube of my Inappropriate Red lipstick and meet the eyes of my reflection in the mirror. With a small smile, I redden my lips before stripping off my shirt and red bra and lay facedown at the edge of my bed. Being sure to hide all the scandalous parts, I snap a selfie with the bra dangling by its strap from my fingertip. I hit Send before I overthink it.

> **Me:** Found this. Made me think of you.

Three dots appear and disappear three times before his text comes through.

> **Julian:** How'd you know I wear red bras

> **Me:** Wild guess

> **Julian:** You are so hot Grace

My body flushes, heat collecting in intimate places.

> **Julian:** Do you know what I would do to you if you'd let me?

"Oh my god." Electricity comes to life in my skin. "What do I even say to that?"

Tell him to describe it.

What? No!

This horny hag in my mind is a bitch.

Me: You're making me blush, Julian

Me: Please don't send a dick pic

Julian: haha

Julian: No. I know what my girl likes.

He sends a picture of my flashcards, and I collapse onto the bed in laughter.

JANUARY, YEAR 2

The cold January evening should deter me from a short dress, but I'm impractical and want Julian to see my legs. It has long sleeves, and I'll be indoors the whole night anyway. Who cares?

I book it upstairs and butterflies with barbed wings become trapped in my nerves, struggling to free themselves. This month, Julian is on nights at Vincent and I'm on days at TUMC, so we've barely seen each other since the new year started.

I was hoping for alone time, but Alesha insisted on Group Therapy, so I told Julian I'd come early. The door swings open seconds after my knock, and he gifts me the no-smile, the darkness of his eyes twinkling. Stars in the black of night.

Drawn toward him, my attention latches on and doesn't let go. The door closes behind me, and he takes hold of my chin, lifting it up.

"Hi, there," he says before brushing a light kiss over my lips, stirring my pulse.

"Hi." Stupid breathy voice.

He takes my hand and pulls me into the kitchen. The accoutrements of Unicorn Blood litter his countertops.

"That's a lot of limes," I say.

He smiles. "We drink a lot."

I chuckle as he grabs a lime, slicing it in half. Fingering the bottle of Patrón Silver, I tap my sparkly gold nails against the glass. "Have you ever thought of using a citrus vodka with it?"

He lifts an eyebrow at me. "What?"

"I mean—"

"Experiment on your own time, Rose." He grins.

My playful, feigned outrage has him laughing. I hop on the counter beside his workstation.

He spares a quick glance at my legs, and satisfaction ripples through me. "There's no improving upon perfection," he says.

I hide my smile while he returns to the cutting board. His strong long-fingered hand grasps the knife and slices through another lime. He drops one half in the squeezer and fills a measuring cup with the juice, then does the same with the other. The moves are practiced and quick. Efficient.

The man is so good with his hands. An immature teenager fanning herself inside my head tells me to slap him on the shoulder and giggle.

I'm such a terrible flirt. How on earth did I manage to snare him?

I clear a thick sensation from my throat. "Where'd you learn to make this?"

He slices another lime. "My ex. She was…difficult. But she made great drinks."

I pick at the hem of my dress and lie to myself that I don't *care* whether Julian has been with other women. "When did you break up?"

He sets the knife down and his dark eyes lift to meet mine. "Before I moved here. She wasn't interested in long distance."

My heart trips. "Were you interested in long distance? With her?"

"Nope."

The jealous creature within rejoices.

I dig my fingernail into the skin of my knee over and over, forming crescents. "What time are they supposed to be here?"

Out of my peripheral vision, Julian shrugs. "Kai said around eight."

The clock on his oven reads 7:23 p.m. Thirty-seven minutes alone. Why aren't we making out?

He rinses his hands and leans against the stove as he dries them, considering me with a tilted head. "Can I ask you a question?"

"Sure."

He runs his teeth over his lower lip. "I know there's been interest. Is there a reason you never dated anyone here before me?"

An uncomfortable thread of ice slithers through my veins. I'm not ready for this conversation. I'll never be ready for it. Does he really need to know?

"Well, the rumors make it hard for me to trust anyone," I say, hedging. "Like Trevor. I thought—"

He winces. "Yeah. Okay. That makes sense."

"But," I add, "I haven't been on a date since second year of medical school."

He crosses his arms. "Why not?"

My attention drifts to the cabinets above his head. "That's when my last boyfriend broke up with me."

"What?" He lets out a small laugh. "Why on earth would he do that?"

The bewilderment on his face is disarming, and my insides cheer at the idea that Julian Santini can't imagine breaking up with me. The truth falls from my mouth before I can stop it. "He said I was cold."

His eyes narrow. "Cold?"

Agitation compels me to explain more than I need to, and words pour from my mouth. Terrible words. Despicable words. Words I can never take back. "I mean…he said I was like…distant. Um. Wait. That's not—he just meant—like…unresponsive." *Oh god. Stop talking.* "Like…because of how I get nervous. And sometimes… I worry about being good at—"

Julian's expression hardens. He's staring, frozen, jaw sharp.

I can't stop filling the awkward silence. "I didn't want to seem uninterested. I told him I wanted—like, guidance, or something. I was willing to learn. But I get nervous I'll do something wrong and it was hard for me to—you know, like, *get there*, sometimes. Then he got…weird. Spiteful. Oh my god. Why am I still talking?"

It's like fucking an ice queen.

I flinch. God, Julian's never going to touch me now. I cover my face with my hands.

I can't believe I just told Julian Santini that I'm bad in bed.

"Can you forget I said that?" I ask behind my hands.

"No."

Of course not. He's always been difficult that way, my Julian.

A painful silence passes before he draws an audible breath. "Is that why you—"

"It's not a big deal. That was a long time ago. He—he doesn't—like—*matter*, or anything. I don't even care." I peek out from behind my hands to find a new tension in the lines beside his mouth.

"Clearly you do."

"That's not—Julian—"

"You're not cold." His voice is deeper and a new intensity burns in his dark eyes.

My hands fall away. "What?"

He pushes off the stove. "You—" he points at my chest "—are not cold."

"You don't know—"

His laugh cuts me off. "I've had you in my arms, Grace."

"That doesn't mean anything."

"It doesn't?" A wicked smile dawns over his face. "Do you need me to prove it?"

Yes.

He moves until he's standing before me. Those long fingers

perch on the granite on either side of my hips. A pulse stirs in my lower abdomen.

"H-How would you prove it?" I ask.

His gifted hands land on my bare knees, a featherlight touch that forks lightning through my nervous system, sweet and drugging like spiked honey. "I can think of dozens of ways I'd like to, but I need you to say yes first."

My breath vanishes. Just…disappears. And my heartbeat slams against the surface of my skin, nearly painful in the thinnest areas—my wrists and temples, my throat, between my legs.

His dark eyes grow feverish, unblinking, and his fingers connect directly to pleasure centers in my brain. Every light brush shivers down my legs. His skin caresses mine, right at the hem of my dress, back and forth.

I'm empty. Wanting. My body clenches on nothing.

Be brave, Grace. Let him touch you.

His fingers skim around my closed knees, down the sides of my calves, and every hair on my body stands at attention. A tiny whimper escapes my throat.

His eyebrow perks. "Is that a yes?"

I give myself three seconds to reconsider, but ultimately surrender to his irresistible smile with a nod. His clever hands slide between my knees and press them wide open.

I let him do it.

I'm spread for him, and instead of awkwardness or anxiety, all I can find inside is a surging desire to open wider, show him more, make him ache like I do.

"Let's start here." He brushes his knuckles on the inside of my thighs, raising my dress. "Warm skin. Nothing cold there." One hand leaves my leg to press a thumb against my lower lip. "You're staring at me like you want this. That's not cold, either."

My lips part, teeth catching his thumb. His gaze drops to my mouth as the tip of my tongue touches his skin, tasting of lime.

His hand slides farther up my leg and I subdue the urge to

scoot closer. "Do you want to hear all the things I've imagined this mouth doing? God, Grace. Look at you." His gaze sweeps down my body, lingering where my dress has ridden up to my hips, exposing my black lace thong. "Who the fuck would think you're cold?"

My breath stutters as his fingers climb higher. Where is the embarrassment? The fear that always accompanies this? The worry that he won't like the sounds I make, the way I look, the time it takes to warm me up?

It isn't there, and the impression of Julian Santini's fingers against my flesh burns through the cells in my body, rewriting their DNA. *This is how it's supposed to be. This is who you want.*

"And here?" he says.

I can't help the moan that gathers in my throat when his fingers brush over the lace. His thumb falls away from my mouth as I lean back without thought, my hands flat on the countertop behind me to give him better access.

"This is not cold." His eyes have gone from fevered to inferno, and he's leaning toward me, one hand bracing his weight, the other drawing teasing circles over the lace. "And any man who can't figure out how to make you moan like that doesn't deserve you. Your body knows how to do this. You just need the right touch."

I stare deep into his eyes, mesmerized. Everything about him is like a drug designed specifically for me. I can't think. Can't breathe. A lick of trepidation slides along my spine at the power he has over me, at the look on his face that says he wants to turn me inside out in the best of ways. I won't be the same after this, will I?

"Do you need me to prove that too, Grace?" he asks.

A wave of pleasure shivers through my spine. "Please."

He slips aside the lace barrier between us at once and slides a finger against my skin.

I tremble at the contact, at the sparks that shower through my abdomen.

It's never been like this, and my control falls to pieces around me. All hesitation disappears, and I reach for him with one hand, fingers yanking at his collar until his lips land on mine. He takes his time with the kiss, devouring me while his fingers dance across my nerves below.

Sighs echo through the kitchen with each of my breaths and my body finds a rhythm against his hand, riding it to find the highest sensation. His other hand slides up my waist until he reaches my breast. Even through my bra, pleasure echoes, spiraling down between my legs.

He teases me with the tip of his tongue, and I chase him, begging for a deeper kiss. I move faster. Harder. Grind against his hand.

"Fuck, Julian." I lose my rhythm after several minutes, and the kiss breaks.

He gives a deep hum as he brushes kisses over my cheek. "Have I ever told you how much I love the way you say my name?"

I pant against him.

He chuckles, changing the tempo of his fingers until embarrassing noises spill from my mouth. "I really do, Grace. You say it like you're planning to lecture me."

The pinnacle is close, but out of reach like usual. I'm desperate for it, whimpering.

"Look at who's getting the lecture now." His teeth nip at my neck. "Such a good little student."

"*Julian.*" I beg him and I don't care, whispering pleas of *Yes* and *Please* and *Faster.*

It draws nigh, the release. Hovers. I'm staring over the edge, unable to fall.

His lips touch my ear. "It's right there, beautiful. Just take it."

He does something that has me biting his shoulder through his shirt to keep from screaming. It shoots down my legs into my toes and blossoms with hot dazzling waves through my entire body. My fingers creep around his neck and clench as I ride his hand. When it passes, he draws out a few more shock waves. I jerk against his fingers before he pulls them away.

My eyes blink open and I find him staring at me with a flushed face.

He grazes his lips against mine. "Not cold."

He starts to move away, but I grab the fabric over his stomach, and slide my hands to the button of his jeans, undoing it before I change my mind.

"Grace, you—"

After one wet lick to my palm, my hand slips around him, thick and hard, and his words dissolve into a curse. I've always felt like an idiot doing this, but when Julian's eyes flutter shut and he bites his lip, a tiny bolt of pride zaps through me. His forehead falls to my shoulder.

I nudge his ear with my nose. "Show me what you like."

His hand closes over mine, guiding. It gives me enough confidence to grip harder, eliciting a smothered groan from him. His hands climb my spread thighs while his breath fans over my throat. He breathes deeper, faster.

Mouth at my throat, the obscenities he mutters vibrate against my pulse. After a while, his fingers clamp on my thighs. "I want to be inside you."

I'm breathless, desperate, reckless. "Okay."

He freezes, then jerks his head to look me in the eye. "What?"

I nod, never losing my rhythm. "I want you."

He blinks twice before an exhale bursts from him. "Thank *god*."

He smothers me with kisses. Tongue tangled with mine, he slides me to the edge of the counter and I wrap my legs around him when a knock pounds at the door. We both startle mid-kiss, staring at each other, wide-eyed.

"Shit!" I whisper.

He backs away so I can slide off the counter. Shit! Shit! Shit!

I wipe my hand over the countertop. Dry. But still, where is his kitchen cleaner? I turn to ask him about it. The two fingers he'd used to get me off are in his mouth, like he's sneaking cookie dough straight from the bowl.

Heat flares like a sunburst through my whole body.

"Definitely not cold," he murmurs before washing his hands.

The door opens. "Yo, Julian. You in here?" Kai asks.

"In here." Julian's voice is magically unaffected, but he shifts his refastened pants with a pained expression.

Meanwhile, my legs are Jell-O and my skin prickles with awareness. I almost had sex with Julian in his kitchen. I let him finger-bang me to the best climax I've ever experienced.

Vicious horny hag beams. *If he can do that with two fingers, what could he do with his tongue? His dick?*

It's been almost four years since I've had a man inside me, and now all I want is to order Kai home and let Julian learn every inch of my body.

Kai sets a bottle of St. Germain in front of me and makes a scrunched face. "You look weird."

"Hmm?" I shake myself. "Just tired."

Julian halves another lime without looking at either of us. He pulls his breaths in a little deeper than before but is otherwise relaxed. Kai glances at me, eyebrow raised.

Get it together, Grace.

The door opens again. Raven calls a greeting. "I brought the oranges."

Julian reaches out as she rounds the corner to the kitchen. She hands him the plastic bag. His gaze finally meets mine and his knowing eyes sparkle as one corner of his mouth lifts. Butterflies tickle my insides.

"You want to peel these?" he asks.

I'm frozen, staring at his face. Kiss-swollen lips. Fever-bright eyes.

He jiggles the bag. "You gonna take it?"

Warmth blooms across my neck. *It's right there, beautiful. Just take it.*

I clear my throat as Raven settles on a stool. Reaching for the bag, I abruptly remember where my hand has been when Julian stares at it. He clears his throat and sets the bag on the counter while I wash my hands.

Beside me, his practiced movements grow clumsy, but he says nothing.

Swollen stomach brushing the granite, Raven reaches for a lime wedge to suck on. "Alesha's running late."

I pull an orange from the bag and grab a sharp knife. "How are you feeling, Raven?"

"I'm all right." She pokes her belly. "I'm running out of room in there."

"I bought you some ginger ale," Julian says. "It's in the fridge."

Beaming, she slides off the stool. "Thanks!"

Kai mixes the liquor. "Two to one to one, right, Santini?"

"Yeah."

Pouring the shots into the shaker, Kai chuckles. "No wonder these always fuck us up."

Drinks made, the four of us move into Julian's living room. Raven settles into the lounge chair while Kai snags a seat on the floor. Julian and I take the sofa.

When Alesha knocks and lets herself in, Kai points at the kitchen. "We left yours in there."

She does a little jig as she grabs her drink, then shoves me over to take a seat, forcing me closer to Julian. His hand brushes my bare leg as he scoots. Our eyes lock for a fraction of an instant, and I tear my gaze away, tingling from head to toe.

"Why were you late?" Kai asks.

Alesha shrugs, looking away. "Oh. Traffic. You know. The usual."

We settle into our familiar camaraderie as the night passes, but nursing a single drink for the evening leaves me sober and strung out when the evening draws to a close. I can't believe I almost screwed Julian in his kitchen. What was I thinking?

It's like fucking an ice queen.

Julian's voice whispers through my thoughts. *Not cold.*

Oh god. I still have no faith that I can please him with any competence. That was instinct, a culmination of heat and hormones. He liked it well enough if the look on his face was any indication, but what if I can't do it again?

My phone buzzes, startling me out of my thoughts. The screen flashes a text from Julian.

Julian: Get out of your head, Grace.

I glance at him, but he's paying attention to the conversation around us. No, *participating*. Maybe what we'd done hadn't blown his mind like it had mine.

Of course not. He didn't come.

Ugh. I'm going to have to remedy that situation soon. What if I freeze? What if he hates it?

Julian: Seriously, Grace. Chill out.

How am I supposed to chill out when my mind spins in a dozen directions, all ways I could screw this up?

Raven lets out a huge yawn and pats her stomach. "I'm ready for bed. I'll see you all next week."

Kai helps her out of the chair. She waves goodbye.

Alesha smiles at the closed door. "She's such a cute preggo."

"Two kids under five during residency." Kai shudders. "No thanks."

Everyone but me laughs.

"Gracey?"

I startle and meet Kai's gaze. It darts to Julian, then back
to me.

He lifts an eyebrow. "You okay? You've been really quiet."

"What?" I force a smile. "Of course. Just tired."

None too convinced, Kai stands to fill both our glasses. My
phone buzzes.

> **Julian:** Do you need help relaxing?
>
> **Julian:** I could go down on you right now.
>
> **Julian:** Do you want to give our friends a show, Grace?
>
> **Julian:** Is that what you want?

Fire tears through my system. He still doesn't look at me.
He's arguing with Alesha about the best way to manipulate Dr.
Scarlett into sneaking us into the attending lounge for free ice
cream. My skin tingles with awareness. He's mere inches away.

Kai sets my drink in front of me, and I reach forward to grab
it. When I lean back, Julian's closer than before. Close enough
that my every movement brushes his body and my skin becomes an oversensitive magnet, aligned to him.

His texting goes ignored by the others. Julian is always texting someone, either his sisters or Maxwell or us. No one pays
it any attention, but my screen comes to life once more.

> **Julian:** Do you think I could make you scream?
>
> **Julian:** Or do you always bite when you come?
>
> **Julian:** I could probably get used to that.
>
> **Julian:** If you let me.
>
> **Julian:** Will you let me, Grace?

My body thinks we're working out. It's the only explanation for this sweat and galloping heart rate.

"'Lesha, you want to share an Uber?" Kai asks. "Mine's here."

"Huh? Oh sure." Alesha stands.

I follow suit, ignoring the subtle brush of fingers down the back of my thigh. Julian tracks behind me like a predator.

"Night, Julian." Kai gives him an overlong stare I don't understand, but then drops his attention to me. "Have a good night, Gracey." He pecks me on the cheek.

Alesha grabs her purse and opens the door, looking at me. "You leaving, too?"

A light tug at the fabric over the small of my back keeps me from escaping.

"Oh, I need to grab my stuff from the kitchen. You go on."

Alesha nods and wishes us good-night. Door closed, the tug on my dress grows more insistent. I take an obedient step backward, the scent of his skin enwreathing me.

Except for the two fingers pinching my dress, he doesn't touch me, but his breath caresses my face as he whispers in my ear.

"Is the answer still yes?"

The words *ice queen* and *not cold* argue in the back of my mind, but as his nose slides along my ear, I give in to him.

I love this man. Even if I'm terrible, he won't humiliate me for it.

I hope.

"Yes."

Julian

JANUARY, YEAR 2

I'm lost.

Dropping to my knees, I glide my hands up her smooth thighs. I thought her scent was intoxicating, but the slide of her skin against mine is an addiction I won't ever overcome. I'll want this for life.

Cold?

How could anyone have this woman in their arms and call her cold? Her uncertainty is not cold. Her desire to please is not cold.

She's a flustered ball of nerves with performance anxiety, but I've spent the last few months learning how to calm the storms. The bruise on my shoulder where she sank her teeth to stifle her cries is proof I've finally broken inside.

I'm on my knees before her as she sits at the edge of my bed in nothing but a lace bra and thong, subtly encouraging me. I kiss her knee, moving slow in case she wants to stop me.

Please don't stop me.

Her hands thread through my hair, manicured fingernails scratching along my neck until she reaches the collar of my shirt and drags it up. She tosses it to the floor, and I return to her thighs, palms sliding past her hips, waist, ribs. I pull her to the very edge of the bed and her legs part around me. I'm struck by the longing on her face. Her lower lip is caught between her teeth, and her hazel eyes are dark and hungry.

My fingers skate around her ribs to the clasp of her bra, undoing it so the garment falls loose, and she throws it beside my shirt. She doesn't cover herself. Instead, she grabs my face, lips crashing down on mine. Luxurious, decadent kisses shove my thoughts over a cliff into dark dirty places.

My hands magnetize to her body, roaming, squeezing, pulling her closer, and she responds in kind. Those delicate fingers drift over my throat and chest, then descend lower to undo my pants, relieving the near painful pressure.

I have to get her off. If I let her touch me now, I won't last. My fingers hook around the flimsy lace hiding her from me, and she moves to let me slide it down her legs. I toss it across the room.

We lock eyes.

"Still worried you're cold?" I ask.

She nibbles on her lip. "I'm worried *you'll* think I'm cold."

How? In her arms, I've never been less cold. The world could end. The seas could drown us. We could plunge into a nuclear winter, and descend to unending darkness, and I'd still feel her heat.

"You're hot as the fucking Sahara, Grace." I push on her stomach so she lays back. "I'll never think you're cold." I nip her upper thigh, coaxing a moan. "God, I love you."

She has no chance to respond, her words stolen by my tongue and the gasp of air that collects in her lungs. The rest of the evening is a hazy mess of warm skin, messy kisses and learning new ways to torture her with pleasure.

Like I expected, the first time is a quick glide of wish fulfillment, but the next two, I manage to make her bite and purr and squeeze me closer like my weight on top of her is a blessing she doesn't want stolen.

It's nearly three in the morning before reality creeps into my dreamy paradise.

I told her I love her.

I hadn't even admitted that to myself. I've never said that to *anyone*.

She dozes in my arms, her fingers tangled in mine, and I blink at the dark ceiling.

She—

She never said it back.

FEBRUARY, YEAR 2

The next few weeks blur into a muddle of laughter and sex, sleepless nights and shifts at the hospital. We spend every spare moment together.

I'm love sick and she—

Still hasn't said it.

I told myself I wouldn't pressure her. I'd follow her cues. I wouldn't ask for more than she was willing to give. But it's so fucking hard. Guarded and cautious, she's been one step behind me in the Feelings Game since we met.

My subconscious warned me against this. It knew she had the power to break me. It tried for months to keep me safe in the shallows.

Be careful with this one, Julian. She's the real thing.

I ignored the hell out of it and dove right into the deep end.

How do I ask if she's swimming beside me without seeming desperate? Without applying pressure?

How did I become the clingy one?

In early February, the printout of my CREOG score crinkles in my sweaty hands.

"Your score dropped significantly from last year, Dr. Santini."

Sitting in the chair at his desk, I stare at Dr. Chen in silence. The open blinds of his corner office frame the hospital behind him. His TCU Horned Frog plush sits beside the gold nameplate on his desk. Behind them, a scattered pile of papers and a large bag of candy take up most of the free space.

Chen offers me a mini Snickers. "Did something happen?"

"No. Well, yes. I mean, no. Nothing happened."

She still hasn't said it.

Behind his glasses, Chen's eyes narrow.

I rub my eyes beneath my own glasses. "I've just been distracted."

"Focus is important, Dr. Santini. If you don't test well on this, you may not pass your board exam."

"This score doesn't even matter right now. I have two years before boards."

Dr. Chen's black gaze penetrates deep. "It goes faster than you think."

Sighing, I nod. "Yes, sir."

He hands me a Reese's cup. "Do the right thing, Dr. Santini. You can go."

Outside his office, I snap a picture of my score, then shred the evidence and send the picture to Maxwell.

> **Maxwell:** You're off your game, bro.

> **Me:** It's just a test.

> **Maxwell:** BrOB-GYN hang out tonight. You in?

> **Me:** Nah. Hanging with Grace.

I'm in my car headed home for the day before Maxwell answers.

> **Maxwell:** You think maybe you're spending too much time with her?

> **Me:** No such thing.

The last four weeks with Grace have been blissful despite my shitty second-year schedule. A few of our friends have discovered us, but we're still keeping it private. We hide in our apartments and date in places we likely won't be seen.

Sometimes we don't leave the bed.

It's paradise, but I'm smothered beneath its crushing weight—preoccupied and distracted to the point of bombing national assessment exams. My mind flitters from one thought to another, always straying back to her.

I'm dangerously in love with her.

I've never experienced this...this breathlessness. This obsession. This all-consuming need to be closer. When she's not there, my skin remembers her. If I'm alone in my bed at night, I can taste her.

I want to breathe her into me, and a primitive desire has woken inside me. It tells me to claim her. Possess her. Absolutely destroy her for anyone else.

It's barbaric. Chaotic.

I'm a physician. I understand human physiology. I know the chemical changes that occur when a human falls in love—the early rush of dopamine, the euphoria, the blindness to consequences.

This high will fade eventually. The unhealthy fixation will ease, but Grace will still exist inside me, her fist curled tight about my heart.

Her laugh. Her kindness. Her incessant need to study. How easy she is to rile up. The shy smile any time she catches me staring. The sound she makes when she comes. That tender question in her eyes the first time she wrapped those red lips around me, silently begging for approval.

She owns me.

And she still hasn't said it back.

She waits in my apartment when I arrive home, books and printed PowerPoints spread over my coffee table. Highlighter in hand, she scans the page before her, brows furrowed in concentration.

A female singer trills through my sound bar.

Is that Dua Lipa?

No.

Lana Del Rey.

Wait...

They sound nothing alike.

"Who is this?" I ask.

She doesn't look up from her book. "Halsey."

Ah. Wrong on all accounts.

I kiss the top of her head. "Why are you already studying again?"

She greets me with a quick kiss when I sit beside her. It misses my cheek and lands at the corner of my eye. "My CREOG score didn't improve as much as I wanted."

"Oh no. We need fresh flashcards stat."

She nods. "I know. I already started—" She turns to me and narrows her eyes. "You're teasing me, aren't you?"

I nudge her cheek with my nose. "What gave it away?"

That scent beneath her ear is intoxicating. A strategic chemical adulterant created only for me. It pierces through my body's defenses and spreads a buzzing electricity. I turn her head to catch her lips with mine.

A hitch in her breath gives me clearance to take more. The

kiss escalates and I maneuver her on top of me. Straddling my lap, she presses all those soft curves against me.

This is so much better than studying.

She stiffens. "Oh! I forgot to ask. How did you do?"

Nope. Don't need that bucket of cold water right now. I grip her legs and stand.

She giggles, wrapping her legs tight around me. "Julian! Where are you taking me?"

To fuck you until I can't remember my own name, much less my CREOG score.

"To bed."

Afterward, she wilts against me, hot and sweaty. "You are so good at that."

My fingers thread through her hair. "You make it easy." *Because I love you.*

She yawns. "I'm glad we're doing this, Julian."

"What? Fucking or dating?" *Say it.*

Her soft laugh tickles the hair on my chest. "Both."

A small silence stretches before I decide to stab myself in my own heart. "Why?"

She lifts her head to look in my eyes. A little notch appears between her eyebrows. "Why what?"

"Why are you glad we're doing this?"

A tiny smile appears on her pretty lips, the freckle drawing my attention. "Because I'm happy. Aren't you?"

Studying her face, I find no recalcitrance, no secrets. I nod and pull her closer. She snuggles into my side.

After several minutes, her breathing slows. I hold her as she sleeps, ignoring the sensation that I'm standing on the firing line, that every beat of my heart is numbered.

What the hell have I done? I can't undo this. I can't unlove her. I can't escape it.

Why hasn't she said it back?

What are you hiding, Grace?

★ ★ ★

I swing open the door to the GME office a week later, and Alesha jerks to a halt on the other side. Her deer-in-the-headlights expression gives me pause.

She presses a hand to her chest. "Wh-What are you doing here?"

I hold open the door, taking in her new teal hair and street clothes. "I'm picking up a reimbursement check. What are you doing?"

"Oh." Her shoulders relax. "Same."

My gaze drops to her empty hands. She has no purse. No pockets. No check. "You are?"

"Yeah. It—um—it wasn't ready."

I laugh, skeptical. Definitely not a reimbursement check. Is she in trouble? Did she cross her work-hour limit or get some sort of complaint from staff? Whatever it is, she clearly doesn't want me to know, so I don't press.

"Okay," I say. "We'll pretend I believe you." I move aside so she can pass. "Go ahead."

She glances at her phone, then shrugs. "It's almost five. I'm off for the day. I'll come with you."

We head into the office, and I turn toward the registrar's desk.

"Haven't talked to you much lately." She tosses out a knowing smile, her previous unease gone.

"Busy."

"Whatever could be keeping you so busy, Juju?"

I ignore her and give the woman at the registrar's desk my name. She files through a stack of envelopes and hands me my check. Each resident receives a yearly stipend for books, conferences and educational equipment. Each resident also buys books on Amazon, prints the receipt, then cancels the order to cash in the reimbursement check from GME.

Is this considered fraud?

If it is, I don't care. I made less than minimum wage last year, and they yell at me when I try to take the hospital's disgusting complimentary food home for dinner to save money.

Alesha and I pass Steven Langston as we head toward the door. I suppress my glare while Alesha nods a reserved greeting.

"Don't you hate that guy?" I ask.

She waves her hand in a dismissive gesture. "He has a thankless job."

"He's the COO of the hospital. His thanks is his pretty salary."

She chuckles. "I heard about your CREOG score."

I stare at her a moment before we enter the stairwell that leads to the main lobby. "How do you always know everything?"

"This stuff gets around. You just don't pay attention to all the gossip." She points at me. "You're lucky they're talking about this and not about you boning Grace. I know y'all still trying to keep that hush-hush."

I tilt my head. "That's true. She's keeping me her dirty little secret."

The front doors of the hospital whoosh open and let us into the cold February air.

"Do you wonder why?" she asks.

Yes. "I have a couple theories."

In the lot, we head to the farthest corner where residents are allowed to park.

Alesha hooks her arm around my elbow. "Care to enlighten me?"

"I think it's the rumors." I sneak a glance at her face, curious how she'll react. "I think she's afraid to let anyone know because the rumor mill will go crazy again."

Alesha's expression pinches. "You really think so? I don't think they bother her that much."

I lift my shoulder. Grace has spent the last eighteen months laughing it off and rolling her eyes, but I still remember the tears and anger the day I met her—the day she learned what people were saying about her. But I also know Grace, and she'd rather shred every flashcard she's ever made than let anyone see how much it upsets her. So I don't argue with Alesha. Arguing means divulging things Grace might not want revealed.

"Would it bother you?" Alesha asks in my silence. "If you were public and people talked about her sleeping with other people?"

We reach my truck. Alesha's Prius is four spots down, but she perches on my bumper.

I drop my messenger bag to the ground. "I have a naive hope that her being in a relationship will tone down the gossip. But yes, it would bother me. It's always annoyed me that she has to deal with this. Doesn't it bug you?"

Pressing her lips together, Alesha stares at the ground by my feet. "She's always told me she doesn't care."

"Trust me. She cares."

She studies me. "This isn't a fling for you, is it?"

I snort and bend to pick up my bag, blowing her off.

"Julian."

Her serious tone stills my movements, but I don't look her in the eye.

"You love her?" she asks.

Something lodges in my throat and I can't speak. Instead, I tighten the strap of my bag unnecessarily and glance at the sky.

"Never mind." She sighs. "It was a stupid question."

It *is* a stupid question. Of course I love her. The real question is—

"Does she love you?" Alesha asks.

My attention cuts to her, taking in the solemn steadiness of her gaze. "I don't know."

The tiniest flicker of movement at Alesha's mouth hints at a frown. "I think she does."

Nervous energy has me grabbing a stick of gum, popping it

in my mouth. The cinnamon does nothing to curtail the rising taste of acid in my mouth. "Why do you think that?"

Alesha stands and grips my shoulder. "I see the way she looks at you. The way she's looked at you for the last year. That girl is in love with you, Juju. She's just scared to tell you."

"Nah." I kiss her on the cheek and adopt a mocking tone. "She's just letting me down easy."

She rolls her eyes as she walks away. "Whatever."

Halfway home, a text interrupts the music through my Bluetooth: "Message from Grace. I'm not feeling well tonight, J. Why don't you hang out with your boys?"

I call her at once.

"Hey, sweetie," she sings into the phone.

I smile. "You don't sound sick. You trying to play hooky from me?"

She laughs. "Alesha changed out my IUD earlier. My uterus is in revolt. I'm heading straight to my heating pad and a *Bridgerton* marathon."

Ah. Reason number four million why I'm glad I'm a man.

"Poor Sapphire. I'm sorry."

"Eh. Worth it for no periods or Santini babies."

Santini babies? My chest constricts as an entire potential future with her spreads out in a split second. I subdue it by sheer force of will.

I am way too deep in this.

My hollow laugh echoes in the speaker. "Leave your door unlocked and I'll come say bye before I leave. Tuck you in."

"All right. Bye, sweetie."

"Santini!" a chorus calls when I enter Asher's backyard that night.

The firepit's already well underway, and most of the men have drinks in hand. I toast my beer as I join them, taking a seat next to Maxwell.

He nudges my arm. "Thought you were busy, bruh."

"Changed my mind."

"Good." Maxwell smiles. "It's good to get away once in a while."

It's not *getting away*, like she's some sort of prison I'll have to return to once visiting hours are over. She practically kicked me out to do this. I'd rather be with her. But as I settle into the familiar atmosphere, a sense of comradeship I've forgotten steals over me. Why don't I ever come to these things anymore?

A conversation to my right draws my attention. Third-years Liam Heaney and Greg Kelly argue over which of the women in the program they'd bang, and in which order. Ranked—of course—by the size of their tits.

Oh yeah. This is why.

Hard to be raised by sisters, then stumble into the real world only to realize this is the way men talk about them. When we were in college, I remember Tori overheard some guys objectifying her at a party. She drunkenly—and facetiously—demanded they drop trou so she could decide which of them she wanted based on the size and look of their dicks. Their outrage was hilarious, but the fallout wasn't. Tori was branded a whore. The men got off without another mention.

"God, I fucking hate Lexie, but her tits—" Greg says, doing the whole chef's kiss thing. "I'd do her first if I could tape her mouth shut."

Liam laughs, but Asher shoots Greg a disgusted look. "Bro. What the fuck? That's called rape."

Greg rolls his eyes. "That's not what I meant."

"Okay, yeah. I'm sure Lexie would agree." Asher stands and walks away, leaving Greg to glare after him.

Huh. At least they're not *all* assholes. I sort of wish I wasn't starting to like Asher, though. Does he still want Grace? I can't really tell.

Ignoring the scene, Max shakes my arm, bringing my attention to him. "I'm glad you're getting this out of your system."

Getting...what? I glance at him. "Huh?"

"This thing." He motions toward me. "You know. With—" He mouths, *Grace.*

Inspecting his dark eyes, I try to decipher his meaning. "This...thing?"

"Yeah." He leans his elbows on his knees and sips his whiskey. "I mean, she's been in your head since the beginning."

"What?"

"You remember why you started this, right? All those strongly worded papers you wrote about women's health. Maternal mortality rates. Wanting to change the landscape of OB-GYN."

Where is this going? Of course I remember the papers. I'll never forget what happened to the women in my life.

Maxwell shrugs and stares at the fire instead of me. "You forgot it all when a pretty girl batted her eyes at you."

My stomach tightens, and I set my bottle on the ground between us. "I didn't forget—"

"You're slippin', bro. Your CREOG score. You don't think that has to do with her?"

Of course it does. "I've always been a bad test-taker. All she ever wants to do is study."

It's not her fault I can't concentrate on anything but her.

He snorts. "Yeah. I'm sure."

"Maxwell, you need to back off. You don't know what you're talking about."

He sighs. "All right. Maybe I'm wrong. I'm sorry. Okay?"

I say nothing. Is he right? I'm haunted by her, but it will pass. Won't it?

Maxwell meets my eyes. "It's not my business. I just... Be careful, man. What they say about her—"

Anger slices through my doubt. "Stop. That's all bullshit, and you know it."

Maxwell shakes his head, almost like he pities me, and every organ in my body turns to stone.

"Tell me you don't believe it," I say.

With a deep sigh, Maxwell turns back to his drink. "No. I don't. Not really. She's too straitlaced to do the shit they say. She just... She's in your head, and I don't know if you're in hers."

That lands about as gently as a boulder in my chest. "Why would you say that?"

Has he heard something? Did she say something? Am I Grace's Rebecca, reading into things because I'm so desperate for her to be interested? Should I start sending her cat memes?

I hate this needy, insecure person I've become.

"I don't know, man," Maxwell says. "You can tell when people are into each other, and I just don't see it with her. She's—I don't know. Unfeeling."

Unfeeling?

That's the last word I'd associate with Grace. Grace feels. Sure, she hides behind safer expressions of emotion, but the feelings are there below the surface. I can see them in her eyes. She just never fucking tells me what those feelings are.

Maxwell's dark gaze slides my way. "You remember your first day, when she showed up to L&D all fuming about her senior resident with zero perception of the hierarchy? Like she was owed something. She was just...entitled. Then at Christmas, you drove her to the party to be nice, and when I asked her about it, she pushed you away like being associated with you was embarrassing. Hell, the day we met her, she blamed us for something we didn't do. It's like Grace only cares about what's happening to *her*, how *she's* perceived, what *she* feels, and nothing else matters." Maxwell takes a sip of his beverage. "Just be careful, is all I'm saying."

I think about what he's saying, but then I think about other things. Grace making me flashcards. Grace sending me a picture of a coffee mug praising DOs after she sensed my insecurities. Grace offering me comfort when my patient died. Grace waking up early to help me round. *I want your days to be good.*

She isn't unfeeling at all. She's sweet and thoughtful and kind. But she's also hesitant to let people see her—the real her—especially when she started this new life amid a pile of nasty rumors. She's paranoid about her reputation, and she's wildly selective in who receives her affection, almost like she's...afraid.

There's a reason for it all.

Something happened to her, didn't it? I've suspected it for months. I even asked her about it that night at my apartment. My memory flickers over the stuttered story of her past relationship, the one I'm sure has far more detail than she gave me.

So now I'm left with two possibilities. Either she doesn't love me—a terrible option I'm not willing to explore—or this thing in her past is keeping her from admitting it.

Do I fall back on my trusty rules and follow her cues, or do I apply a bit of pressure?

I don't know what to do.

"I need to go home," I say.

Maxwell winces. "Nah, bro. Don't leave. I'm not trying to make you mad—"

"I'm not mad," I say. "I just—I need to go home."

His reply is lost on me as I make my way to my truck, then stare at my steering wheel for several moments before turning the engine.

Back at the apartment complex, I find myself heading toward Grace's apartment instead of my own bed, like she's my north star. My home.

"Come in!" she calls at my knock.

I push open the door. "You just let strangers into your apartment?"

"I know your knock, Julian." Her voice comes from the bedroom.

My smile is instantaneous. There's that prissy tone.

She's curled up in bed, surrounded by pillows, hair in a damp braid down her chest. *Bridgerton* plays on the small TV over her dresser.

She pauses the show. "I thought you were going to hang with the guys."

I lift my shoulders. "I wanted to hang with you more. Can I sleep here?"

Her huge grin eases the knot in my stomach. "Come cuddle me in my time of need."

Laughing, I strip to my boxers and crawl into bed beside her.

Under cover of darkness later that night, she snuggles deep in my arms. "Thanks for being here, Julian." Her voice is dreamy, half asleep.

I squeeze her closer, turning my face into her neck. "I love you."

The following silence turns jagged, cuts deep. It leaves wounds, filleted open, bleeding.

Why won't you say it back?

Grace

MARCH, YEAR 2

Love.

An interesting concept from the outside.

On the inside, it's like standing in a diamond while sunlight shines through. Facets of light reflect in every corner. Dazzling rainbows sparkle over each surface.

All is warm and bright and endless.

I don't trust it.

Diamonds are beautiful, but hard. They can break under pressure.

They can be faked.

Julian wouldn't do that, though.

You've thought that before.

Two months have passed since he claimed he loves me, yet

I can't silence the voice in my head. It reminds me of the last man who declared himself in love with me.

He lied.

Love doesn't leave scars.

It doesn't humiliate.

It's not conditional.

That man's "love" broke me, and I wish I'd healed. I wish I could forget him. I wish I could trust myself and this gut instinct that says Julian isn't lying.

But I don't. It all feels too good to be true.

I roll over in bed and kiss Julian's shoulder. He's deeply asleep, one hand laying on his chest, the other curled around my wrist. Even in sleep, he finds ways to touch me. The silver March moonlight lines his face. His jaw and nose cut sharp edges through the dark, but sprinkles of moon dust settle on his cheeks and eyelids, highlighting his eyelashes. He's silver-lined.

I love you.

In my mind, the words are easy. In my mouth, they disappear.

I'm selfish not to tell him. He opened himself to me. I should give him the same courtesy. This adoration deep in the marrow of my bones is unmistakable. I love him, but if I say the words, it's real. If I say them, I relinquish all power.

I need to trust him, and I can't figure out how.

Tears spring to my eyes. Trusting someone with the most vulnerable part of myself nearly destroyed me once. How do I find the capacity to risk it again? How do people fall in love over and over again? How do they heal their broken and betrayed hearts? How do they erase pathologic beliefs buried in their minds?

My finger drifts down Julian's chest, over his hand to his stomach. He stirs with a deep scratchy rumble in his throat. It's hours before either of us need to wake, but I roused from a nightmare not long ago, and this man is human perfection.

I can't say it, but I can show him how I feel.

Pressing my naked body against him, I kiss his chest, then

his neck. He grunts again when my lips brush across his throat, over his pulse, the turn of his jaw. The rumble in his chest vibrates against me.

My teeth close around his earlobe. "I want you." *I love you.* "Yeah?"

"Mmm-hmm." *Because I love you.* "Is that something you can help me with?"

His hand slides to grasp mine, linking our fingers, and he tugs me on top of him. "Like this?"

"However you'll give it."

Take me.

Own me.

Please.

The remaining space between us vanishes as we meet in an urgent kiss. He tightens beneath me. Every muscle wakes and clenches, and his arms become iron bands around me.

My insides melt into liquid heat. His hands slide down my sides and cup my thighs. He pulls and I obey, spreading my legs around him.

Magic sparkles between us, both of us struggling to get closer, taste more. He strokes and caresses everywhere he can reach with the ultrafine, barely there touches he's learned turn me on the most. In his arms, I'm a live wire and he's my ground.

Our connection is breathtaking—it always is—and I'm whispering his name with the little air I have. He hums his agreement, and grasps my hips, thumbs digging into the little divots beside the bone. I sit straight and let him guide the rhythm.

He knows this part of my body far better than I ever have. His hands are gifted at so many things, but this...this is my favorite.

One hand drifts over my chest while the other slips between us and ensnares me with pleasure. Heat unfurls. I brace myself on his chest. The moonlight glints in his eyes. They're fixed on me as I ride him.

It doesn't take long.

It never takes long.

He fractures me every time—a task I'd previously believed impossible.

Ecstasy dawns. Golden light breaks over my horizon, then scatters inside my body like a lens flare. Sunstars sparkle deep in my belly, and I barely have a moment to breathe before he flips me to my back and starts all over again.

I whisper his name into his skin, hoping he can hear the love and devotion, the reverence, the tenderness and affection.

Afterward, when he's asleep and I'm nestled in his arms once more, the brave, head-over-heels woman in my subconscious lurches forward.

"I love you," I whisper.

He doesn't stir.

Maternal Fetal Medicine is a subspecialty of obstetrics that deals with high-risk pregnancies. Everything from diabetes to congenital anomalies are followed in the MFM clinic. It should be fascinating. Instead, I spend my days standing in a dark ultrasound room, watching a tech scan babies. I then sit in the consultation room with the patient while the attending explains said ultrasound.

Shadowing at its finest.

Two MFMs lord over this clinic, Dr. John and Dr. Hoffman. Constantly vying for my attention, the divas complain if I spend too much time with one or the other.

John is a large man with little personality. He's bipolar in his attitude toward me, either mildly jovial or flat-out nasty. He has an unhealthy obsession with pointing out the baby's nasal bone on ultrasound.

"See this baby's nasal bone? Such a beautiful nasal bone."

Every. Single. Time.

The quartet of harpies who serve as ultrasound techs naturally hate me as I am apparently a deterrent to all women who work in health care. Their saccharine smiles never touch their eyes when they look at me. Sweet to the patient's face, the claws always emerge in the privacy of their computer room.

Mandy is the worst of them. "My arm hurts after that scan. The bitch needs to lose a few pounds. Couldn't get a good picture of the baby's profile because her fat rolls were in the way."

I lean on the door since no chair has ever been offered to me. "God forbid you don't get a shot of that nasal bone."

I mean it as a joke—some commiserating camaraderie—but she turns her mouselike face in my direction and screws it into something resembling a sneer. "Weren't you asked not to speak to us? You're distracting me."

I sigh and turn away. On March 1st, my first day in the office, John asked me not to speak with any of them during the day, so as *not to distract them from their duties.*

Sit down and shut up. That's what MFM is about.

I follow Mandy to her next ultrasound. She adopts her usual falsetto voice to hide her malevolence from the patient. Reviewing my mental flashcards allays the annoying niggle in my brain every time she insists on calling the tibia and fibula the "tibia and fibia" while taking pictures of the baby's legs.

Afterward, I head to Hoffman's office to review the images before his consultation with the patient. Unlike John, Hoffman has too much personality and talks through his nose. Gossip is his favorite food, and he drools at the juiciest morsels. Today, his primary complaint is that he can no longer afford to buy the saltwater fish tank he's been eyeing because recent storm damage has forced him to re-stucco his house.

Hoffman is the king of first-world problems.

He spins in his chair toward me when I enter, nasal voice on high power. "You know, I've got some beef to pick with you."

That's not the expression, you nitwit.

I perch on the sofa beside his desk, back straight. "Yes?"

"I'm a little ticked off you didn't tell me you're dating, Sapphire." He crosses his arms. "I told you about my affair with my attending when I was a resident."

He'd volunteered that information against my will, actually, but my stomach drops. "What?"

"I had to hear it from another resident."

"Who?"

He waves a hand. "It slips my mind."

Uh-huh. Sure.

"She said you're dating a couple who are both radiology residents. Said you were caught in one of the call rooms."

My mind goes still, followed swiftly by my body. Radiology? A *couple*?

He grins and readjusts the glasses on his nose—glasses I'm in fact *not* attracted to. "Now that I know you're into thrupples, I have a lot more stories to tell you."

"I'm not." I clear my raspy voice. "I'm not into thrupples."

He snorts. "That's not what I heard, and let me tell you, she was *very* explicit—"

"Stop." My tone is honed to a sharp edge.

He jerks his head. "What?"

"None of these rumors are true. They've never been true."

His demeanor closes off. His eyes shutter, and he flings his arm toward the door. "Fine. Go get me a Starbucks, will you?"

I hold out my hand for money to pay for his ridiculous drink—tall decaf Americano with one inch of nonfat foam.

He sneers at my hand. "Don't you have money left on your meal card?"

Because we're poor, each resident receives $150 on a meal card to pay for the myriad meals we have to eat when working at Vincent. Hoffman's drink is $5 and he wants at least one per day. Three weeks into my month at MFM, and he still has yet to pay for a drink.

Half my money for food has gone to his Starbucks habit, but tears build behind my eyes and I don't have the energy to argue with him. I flee his office and head to the sky bridge that leads to the cafeteria.

Another rumor.

Why does this keep happening?

I hear rumors all the time. Not just about me. Talk of residents dating who aren't. People cheating when they haven't. Interns screwing up when they never did.

Where do the rumors start? How do they grow?

My reputation is in such tatters that my name is dragged into any speculation about sex in the hospital. Witnesses immediately assume I'm involved.

Weird noise in the surgery call room? Probably Sapphire Rose blowing a plastics fellow.

Provocative laughter in a stairwell? Definitely Sapphire Rose leading a pediatrics resident to his downfall.

I'm sure those radiology residents were caught alone, then someone joked, "I'm surprised Sapphire Rose wasn't with them" and off flew the newest rumor.

I wipe my face.

Oh god.

What if Julian hears it?

I yank my phone from my white coat pocket.

Me: It isn't true.

Julian: I know.

I stare at his answer. My chest hollows.

Me: you already heard?

Julian: it doesn't matter grace

Me: what exactly did you hear?

The three dots appear, then disappear.

> **Me:** what did you hear julian

> **Julian:** grace

> **Julian:** it doesn't matter

> **Julian:** it isn't true, right?

Ice freezes my fingers as I stare at that question, and my steps slow to a stop. Texts lack tone. He could be stating that it doesn't matter because it's not true, or he could be genuinely asking if it's true.

My gaze lifts to the floor-to-ceiling sky bridge windows, looking over a parking lot.

Does he really think I'd—

The screen flashes with his contact photo when he calls me. I sniffle and hold the phone to my ear. "Hello?"

His tone is gentle. "Gracey, listen. It isn't even true, so why does it matter? It's never mattered."

Oh thank god. He didn't believe it. Of course he didn't believe it! What was I thinking?

"What did you hear?" I ask.

He's silent for several seconds. "Grace—"

My voice sharpens. "What did you hear, Julian?"

His sigh shreds through the speaker. "Maxwell heard you went down to the radiology reading room the other day and someone caught you with two fifth-year residents."

I lean against the window. "Doing what?"

"What do you think, Grace? Do you really want the details?"

"Yes." *No.*

"Well, I'm not giving them to you. I told him it wasn't true."

I surrender to the tears. "Hoffman asked me about it."

Darkness overtakes his voice. "What?"

"The rumors will get to the attendings, then to my future

employers. Medicine is a small world, Julian. This could ruin my life."

"We'll deal with it." He pauses. "What if—what if we showed our relationship publicly? People would—"

I scoff. "The rumors would go nuts. Don't drag yourself down into my mud."

A long silence follows. A blue sedan circles the parking lot beneath me.

Lot's full, buddy. I can see it from here.

"Maybe I want to be in the mud with you," Julian murmurs.

At those words, a tiny bit of the ice inside me melts. He's so sweet. So loving.

But it isn't enough. People would talk about what we do together. Where we do it. They'd probably ask him how I like it. Then rumors would spread that I cheated. They'd pity him for staying with me. They'd laugh at him behind his back.

He thinks he wants to roll in the mud with me, but eventually bitterness would grow. Resentment.

This will be the thing that drives him away. With Matt, our lack of sexual chemistry—and his narcissistic tendencies—ruined us, but Julian...he'll decide I'm not worth the hassle of having to scrub my shitty reputation, of constantly defending our relationship.

I swallow. "Let's talk about it tonight."

"All right, Grace. Don't cry about this, okay? Don't catastrophize. It's not worth it."

Nodding even though he can't see me, my voice shrinks to a bare rasp. "Bye, Julian."

"Bye, Sapphire."

That name pulls a laugh from me, and I hang up.

When I return with his Starbucks, Hoffman is cold and complains they put too much foam in it. I fantasize about pushing him out the window of his sixth-story corner office.

Mandy has descended past the level of Nasty and arrived at

Satan. She turns on the fake falsetto and hands me a note from John. "Really nice you can take a coffee break in the middle of the day. Dr. John asked me to give you this. He needs records from your clinic EMR for this patient."

I glance at the note to find a patient name and birthday. "Did he say wh—"

"I believe I asked you not to speak to me."

Would her blood even be red if I stabbed my pink pen into her throat?

I march away without saying anything else.

In a corner of the copy room sits a janky computer on its last breath. This is the computer I'm allowed to use. I power it on and rack my memory on how to remotely access our clinic EMR. It's such a complicated process that I've only done it one other time.

On the first login screen, I type my name and password. I'm redirected to another login screen. Security aside, I hate multifactor authentication. Without my laptop and its keychain of saved passwords, I can't remember which login this screen needs. I try a few. No luck.

A waking bear growls in my chest, hungry for blood.

I have to call IT.

My fingers drum on the desk. Not even my mental flash-cards can mask my hatred for this situation. My blood acidifies and heats to boiling.

By the time the IT help desk person answers, I'm ready for a massacre.

The problem: there's an invisible space after my username.

"The username is SGROSE space?"

"Yes. Space after the E."

My fingers on my phone turn to claws. "How was I supposed to see it?"

"I'm not sure."

I disconnect before I totally lose my cool. The records on the patient print without issue. I set them on John's desk.

He feigns surprise. "I didn't realize you still worked here. Haven't seen you all day."

"Here I am. Oh, but here's my best part." I point to my nose. "Don't I have such a beautiful nasal bone?"

His bewilderment takes the form of a slack jaw and clouded eyes. "What?"

"I started my period and bled everywhere. I have to go."

His face whitens. "Yes, of course."

I don't spare him another glance before flying out the door.

I'm halfway home when my phone rings, and Dr. Chen's name takes over my car's display. A ball of lead settles low in my stomach as I click the green button. Am I in trouble?

"Hello?"

"Hello, Dr. Rose?"

"Yes, it's me."

He coughs away from the phone. "I—um—we need to have a conversation."

A pause follows while I try to make sense of that. "All right."

"Can you come to my office now? Please tell your attending I've excused you from duties."

Acid builds in my throat, but I swallow it away. "Yes. I'm on my way. What is this regarding?"

"It's—ah—it's better if we speak in person."

Oh god. This can't be good. Did I make some egregious mistake? Am I being sued?

The drive to the office is a blur, but the TCU Horned Frog smiles at me as I sit in the chair across from his desk. Dr. Chen hands me a Milky Way. It's soon crushed in my sweaty fist.

"Dr. Rose, how are you?"

"I—um—what's this about, Dr. Chen?"

"Right." He glances at his computer screen and clicks his

mouse a few times. "I was approached today by a director from another program, who had raised some concerns regarding your—um—professionalism."

"My professionalism?" The weight in my stomach expands to encompass my diaphragm, my ribs. I can't suck in a breath.

I'm not being sued.

I'm being slut-shamed.

Dr. Chen hands me a Baby Ruth. "Speculation has been made that perhaps you're seeking unprofessional ways to complete your training."

"I don't." My voice shakes. "I'm not. I don't do any of these things they say about me."

"I know. Trust me, I know. You're a great doctor, and you work hard. I think it's important that you hear this from me. Steps are being taken to squash these rumors, but as I'm sure you know, they're—"

"Impossible to stop."

He sighs and rubs his eyes under his glasses. "You're an ideal resident, Grace. I can't remember the last time I had a resident so engaged in didactics. And your surgical skills are improving tremendously. I can see you making a great chief one day. You should be proud of what you've accomplished."

"And yet I'm not known as a good resident. When people say my name, they don't think *good resident*. They think *slut*."

"I—" His eyes meet mine, true remorse shining in their depths. "I'm sorry, Grace."

The dream I once had, the one of myself finally reaching some pinnacle of self-actualization, of shedding my anxiety and becoming someone to be respected, falls to the floor and shatters.

I'll never be that woman, will I?

I will always just be this.

Sapphire Rose. Anxious. Distrustful. Cold.

Unable to speak, I dip my chin in a jerky nod. Eventually, I swallow the tears that want to break free. "We could've had this conversation over the phone. Why'd you want me to come in?"

"Steve Langston has gotten involved. He's planning to meet with each program director individually."

My heart no longer beats a normal rhythm. I've developed a pathologic tachycardia. "Why? Isn't that only going to make things worse?"

"He said it's gone on long enough. He wants to discuss the role of gossip and the damage it can do, and what we can do to end it. I just wanted you to know that we're doing what we can to stop this."

It won't work. It will only draw more attention to me, but it's pointless to mention that. Nothing will stop a man with a bad idea and good intentions.

"Th-thanks."

A tear slips past its barrier.

His voice softens. "You can go now, Grace. Take the day if you need it."

The bottle of IPA I pull from my fridge is zipped into its coozie and halfway gone before I remove my shoes. My white coat is heaped in a pile beside my coat rack. I fling my dress clothes across my unmade bed and don leggings with a med school T-shirt of Julian's he left on my dresser.

Ravenclaw fuzzy socks perfect my outfit.

I pace my apartment.

A single rumor has spiraled into insanity. How have I become the poster child for sexual promiscuity?

Why do you care?

Because it isn't true!

The people who matter know that.

Julian wants us to date in public. At some point, I thought we could do it, but now...

It will taint us. We won't survive it. These rumors won't stop because I'm dating him. They'll gain traction, go haywire.

You'll have to go public eventually. You going to marry him in secret?

Why would he ever want to marry me?

He said he loves you.

Did he mean it, though? I can't trust my own judgment. I've been so wrong before. I'm so sick of love.

He's never lied to you.

Tears have stained my face. I down the rest of my beer and pop the cap of another.

I hate everything about this day, and it's going to get worse, isn't it?

Julian's coming, and I'll have to tell him the truth.

I can't drag him down into my mud, and I won't risk falling, then hit the ground when he decides he doesn't want to be with the hospital slut.

Julian doesn't love me.

He can't.

Who would?

His familiar knock precedes him cracking the front door. "Grace?"

I pause in my harried pacing of the living room. "I'm in here."

He enters with a soft smile and kisses my cheek. "Hey."

"Hey." I stare into those dark eyes. So loving. So beloved. "How was your day?"

"Well, I should have been in surgery, but I was covering L&D instead, so…it sucked."

A hollow laugh is my answer.

He leads me to the couch and slips the half-empty beer from my hand. "I'm glad Raven had a healthy baby, but covering for her the next three months will be pretty shitty."

Scowling, I curl into my throw pillows while he sips my beer and sets it on the table. I'd forgotten about our increased workload over the next twelve weeks. This is just...the worst day ever.

His hand threads through my hair and gently massages. "Did your day get better?"

I let out a bitter chuckle, then reach for the bottle. Sitting up to take a drink separates us. His hand falls away. The hints of amber in his eyes when he looks at me strike deep into my chest.

He's so open. So caring. So kind.

He deserves better than me.

The pain hits me like a sledgehammer. It freezes my veins, then slams into my chest. Shards of ice scatter over everything.

I'm cold. Broken. Emotionally unavailable.

I come with a crap ton of baggage in the form of rumors, anxiety and mistrust.

I am darkness and he is light.

I can't even tell him that I love him. I'm too broken to say the fucking words.

Everything inside me goes numb. "We can't go public."

He nods like he expected that comment, then leans forward to rest his elbows on his knees. "Why not?"

I set my bottle on the table but say nothing. My throat aches.

He studies my face. A spark appears in the black of his eyes. "Are you ashamed of me, Grace?"

"What? No." I reach for him, but he leans away.

His head tilts. "Then why?"

"We *can't* go public—"

"Because people will think you're slumming it with the stupid little DO?" He raises an eyebrow.

"What? No. That's not—no one thinks of you like that. No one who matters."

His expression tightens. "Do you hear yourself? No one who matters thinks these rumors about you are true, either."

Tears burn behind my eyes. "It's not about me. It's about

how it will affect you. People will make fun of you for being with me, Julian."

"I don't care—"

"You *will*. The girls will pity you. The guys will tease you. They'll talk about me. About *us*."

He lets out a sharp sigh, staring at the floor between his feet. "Maybe at first, but it will die down. It always does. And I—I just don't care."

"I do." I touch his forearm. His muscles bunch beneath my fingers, so I pull away.

"You think things will get worse," he says, "but I think things will get better. I mean…people just don't talk about guys the way they talk about girls. I hate to say that, but it's true. This isn't going to affect me like you think it will."

Maybe he's right. It doesn't lessen my fear, though. How will I survive if I let him all the way in and he leaves me? If not because of the rumors, then because of any one of the hundreds of ways I'm lacking? I never planned on falling in love like this, and Julian…he deserves better than my petrified love and tarnished reputation.

"I care what people think of you," I say, "and I don't want what we had to be stained by this."

His head whips around. The darkness in his eyes sharpens to honed ebony. "What we *had*?"

My voice drops to a whisper. "You deserve better than this, Julian."

"No." His body is frozen, every muscle tight. "Don't do this."

"I don't think us being together is good for you." My voice tightens, grows cold and clinical in a way I can't stop. "Between the rumors, and my trust issues…and—and I heard you got the worst CREOG score in the program, Julian. You didn't even tell me! I'm distracting you from training."

"Fucking Maxwell," he mutters under his breath, rubbing his face.

"Julian—"

"Screw my CREOG score, Grace." He stands and paces across the living room. "Now you're claiming you don't trust me?"

"I'm trying to do the right thing for you."

He pauses to stare at me. "By breaking me in pieces?"

I exhale. Tears fight their way to the surface. That's not what I'm doing. I'm protecting him. He just doesn't see it yet.

Those dark eyes see straight through me. "The idea of not being with me—that does nothing to you?"

Giving him up will hurt. It will slice ribbons into me I'm sure will never heal. But a day will come when his infatuation with me will dim, and he'll realize I'm an anxious mess with intimacy issues, and I can't give him what he truly needs.

He'll leave.

That will hurt so much worse.

I'm scared. Scared of how much I love him. Scared of what he could do to me. Scared he's too good for me. Scared the rumors will follow me the rest of my life. Scared that I'll never be the competent, respected doctor I always dreamed I'd be.

Then tell him that.

I open my mouth, but all that comes out is, "Julian—"

"Do you remember how I feel about you?" He crosses his arms, but his fingers tap a fluttery rhythm against his biceps.

"How you *think* you feel." A tear slips down my cheek. My gaze falls to my lap so that broken look on his face doesn't cut so deep.

"Now you're telling me what I feel?" His voice scrapes over rough edges and valleys. "I *love* you. I want *you*. Why can't that be enough? Why don't you believe me?"

A tiny sob catches in my throat. "I just—I can't be what you need. Being with me will hurt you."

"More than you're hurting me right now?"

I flinch.

"Oh, you don't like hearing that? Did you think I'd be relieved that you're breaking my heart? You act like you're setting me free."

"Julian—"

He paces again. "Would you prefer I pretend I'm happy about it? That losing you won't rip pieces out of me? I'm way too far gone, and not nearly a good enough actor to manage that."

I wrap my arms around myself and try to hold in the flood. "You told me you don't want to be involved in scandals. Do you remember that? It was one of the first things you said to me. You'll be happier unattached to me."

His steps slow. The bewildered horror on his face guts me. "Happier? Do you know me at all?"

"Julian—"

"Do you love me? I need to know the answer to that. The truth."

His face smears behind my tears. I love him so much in that moment that my heart cracks and crumbles, an aching pain I'll never be rid of. My voice stutters over the word, but I manage to give him the truth. "Yes."

The flash of relief on his face disappears behind a forced calm. His eyes grow bright and dewy. "Then *why?*"

"For you." My breath hitches and I rise to my feet. "For me. For both of us. God, Julian. You think you love me, but you don't even know the mess that I really am. Things from my past have just—I don't know. You are such a good man, and I'm…broken. I've *been* broken. I can't trust. I don't have faith in love." I approach him, moving to stand close enough to touch, though neither of us reach out. "Even if you think these rumors won't touch you, once you see who I really am, you'll leave."

The darkness sparks again. "I *do* know you, Grace. I'm not perfect, either. Why are you so convinced that I'm not all in on this? What have I done that makes you think I won't keep loving you even when it's hard?"

"That's not—"

"What do I do? What do you want me to do? I'm here, offering to prove it. How do I prove it?"

Don't let me do this to us.

No words form.

He lets out a breath. "Wow. Seriously? Nothing to say?"

My arms cross, and I bite my cheek to hinder the tears.

"This is the way it ends?" He rakes his fingers through his hair. "When you wouldn't tell me you love me, I thought I must have been a fling for you. Just a little bit of fun or something. I never thought you'd finally admit you love me, then tell me you don't trust me in the same breath."

The lump in my throat will no longer allow me to swallow.

"Just so you know, I *do* know you. I love *you*. What you're doing right now isn't you. This is fear talking, and I don't know what happened to make you so scared, but I would *never* hurt you like this. You're letting this thing from your past control your life. It's taking things from you that don't belong to it. I would have helped you heal, Grace. All you had to do was ask. But sure, break us if you want. Just don't think for one second that you're doing it for me. I don't want this, and you're right. I *don't* deserve this."

"Please," I say on a sob. "I'm not trying to hurt you. I'm trying to protect you."

His dark eyes flash as they meet mine. "That's some solid logic. Protecting me by shattering me? Why don't you go ahead and cut me with all the broken glass left behind while you're at it?"

I have no words.

His jaw clenches. "I can't do this." The door slams as he leaves, and I fall to the sofa, curling in on myself to cry.

This is the right thing.

I'm a wreck of a human with insecurities piled so high I can't see the top. Julian deserves someone whole. Someone confident. Someone untainted by rumors.

Someone who believes in love.

I'm a coward.

An idiot.

And now I'm alone.

Julian

MARCH, YEAR 2

My heart isn't broken.

It's gone.

Disappeared.

She fucking stole it.

Am I even human anymore?

I make it through the rest of the week and my weekend twenty-four at Vincent without remembering much. All the patients survived, so I don't care about anything else. At shift change, I sign out the patients to Alesha in our tiny call room, then gather my things.

"What did you do to her?"

I freeze in the middle of shoving things into my bag. "What?"

"What did you do to her, Julian?" Alesha glares at me. "She's crying every day."

I shake my head. "Not now, Alesha."

"Yes, *now*, Julian. She's my best friend, and—"

"Just stop. You don't know what you're talking about." I go back to packing my bag.

Alesha stands and raises her voice. "I won't stop! You broke her heart, Julian."

I whirl on her. "*I* broke *her* heart?"

"Yes! Why would you—"

I abandon my bag on the bed to stand tall, staring down at her. "Did you stop to think for one tiny second that maybe hers wasn't the heart that was broken?"

Alesha jerks back, eyes wide.

"I didn't choose this. I would *never* choose this. I would choose her all day, every day for the rest of time." I sit at the edge of the bed, dropping my head in my hands. "She—she didn't want me."

Cracks form in Alesha's cold facade. "Julian—"

"I tried to stop her." I stare at the floor. "She broke us anyway."

Alesha is silent, but the bed dips beside me. Her arms settle around my shoulders and her purple hair falls over my scrubs as she leans in.

"Do you know why?" Alesha asks.

My entire body droops. "That latest rumor—she found out and she just lost it. Started talking like being with her will hurt me. She said she can't trust me. That I don't even know her. She said if I really knew her, I'd leave."

"Shit." Alesha squeezes tighter. "I'm sorry, Juju."

"I need to go, Alesha." I pat her arm. "Need some sleep."

She releases me.

"Have a good shift."

At first, I convince myself Grace will realize her mistake and apologize, but two weeks pass without so much as a glance from her, and my hope dims. How did I fall so hard for a girl who would do this? When did I become this pathetic?

"Get your head in the game, Santini!" Maxwell barks after a poorly tied pedicle on my side of the uterus bleeds.

"Fuck." I shake my head and go about fixing it.

Once the bleeding is under control, Maxwell pauses to stare at me. "Take a breath and get it out of your system. We have a job to do."

"I know. I'm here. I'm in it."

After surgery, I sit in the men's locker room rubbing my face when his hulking form clunks onto the bench beside me.

He thumps my shoulder. "She fuck you up?"

"Yeah."

Maxwell lets out a long breath. "Come have dinner with me and Cat tonight. It'll get your mind off it."

"Yeah, okay," I say, even though any social interaction sounds like nothing but work.

A long silence follows as I stare at the green tile floor, trying to remember how normal people converse.

"Did I ever tell you Cat left me once?" he asks.

I turn toward him and shake my head.

"Yeah. During second year, actually." He chuckles. "It's a shit year, isn't it?"

I let out a single bitter snort as my answer. I haven't had a day off since Raven had her baby. At least work is a distraction from the train wreck Grace unleashed on my life.

Maxwell shrugs. "Under all that stress, I was probably a dick to her. She couldn't take it anymore. Left for a couple months and moved in with her mom. I was a wreck."

"Yeah?"

He nods. "We got married that fall, so it all worked out in the end."

I return my gaze to the floor. "Good for you, man."

Maxwell pats me once on the shoulder. "You'll be okay."

That evening, after dinner with Maxwell and his admittedly lovely wife, I drive home under a deluge of rain, thankful its presence will likely keep Grace from straying outside. We've had no less than five awkward run-ins on the stairs. My search for a new apartment is well underway.

Changed into dry shorts, I fall onto my couch and ignore Netflix to scroll through Insta—which inevitably leads to a rabbit hole of pictures of Grace. After a few minutes, the family chat lights up.

Tori: You feeling any better, BB?

Me: I'm fine

Me: You don't have to keep checking on me

Me: She's just a girl

Bethany: Am i gonna have to cut a bitch

Sabrina: we will fuck her up BB

Me: I

Me: Am

Me: Fine

Lauren: I think this is real you guys

Tori: BB do you need us? I'm there in a heartbeat.

Me: Please don't come here. I'm not a child.

At didactics Thursday morning, I try my hardest to ignore Grace. While Kai took the space beside me, Alesha sits alone at a corner of the conference table, typing furiously. Raven is still on maternity leave. She sends daily pictures of her new son. Baby Derrick is unbearably cute—enough to give me a boost each time I receive one.

Didactics is the only time I'm forced to see Grace—a blessing and a curse.

She's beautiful.

There's no sign of sleeplessness. No tightness to her smile or shuttering of her eyes.

She's fine while I'm wondering if my insides have been put through a food processor and replaced in the wrong order.

The only upside is all her forcing me to study has finally paid off—I know most of the answers when I'm pimped.

My distraction and concentration issues from earlier this year have returned to their normal borderline ADHD status. Maybe her presence in my life *was* bad for me.

I consider that for three full seconds before I laugh inwardly.

Nope. She's the only reason I know as much as I do. Grace was the sun and now I'm cold and shivering in the dark.

Pathetic.

Between lectures, the room bustles. Asher sits across from me, huge smile in place.

"What?" I ask him when he meets my eyes.

He shakes his head. "Just wait for it."

"You okay?" Kai whispers next to me.

I stare at him and say nothing.

He turns away. "You don't have to talk about it."

I nod, swallow and return to the notes on my laptop—a document I started at Grace's insistence.

"But you can," Kai murmurs. "If you want to."

My typing slows, and on a new line I write, *If I talk, it's real. Not ready for real yet.*

"Fair enough, man." He drums his fingers on the table. "Maybe we could go out tonight."

I give a half-hearted shrug. "Maybe, but I don't think it'll work."

"Then take out one of the nurses. Half of them are already in love with you."

The idea has merit, but a self-hating imp in my mind makes me hesitate. What if she changes her mind?

I. Am. So. Pathetic.

I shake my head. "Not ready for that, either."

The next lecture is given by Dr. Chen, who sweeps in and takes a seat at the head of the table. His CPAP lines are crisp across his cheeks, but he's in fine spirits. He wraps up his talk on complex vulvar pathology with a labeled diagram of a normal vulva.

Grace's hand shoots in the air before Chen's last word has left his lips. Her usual twenty questions follow. I stare blindly at the screen before me and play Silversun Pickups on my Air-Pods to drown out her voice.

"Any other questions?" Chen asks when she's finished.

"I have a question." Kai eyes the diagram with a skeptical brow. "Is there something wrong with straight men? 'Cause like—" he gestures toward the screen in a circular motion "—I'm looking at this, and all I can think is, this is not that hard to figure out."

Asher snorts.

"Uh—" Dr. Chen's mouth twitches.

"No, seriously." Kai points at the screen. "This is like an instruction manual. Am I missing something?" He turns to me. "It's not that difficult, is it?"

I give him a hard stare.

He relents and lowers his voice. "Oh. Right. Sorry." He flips his laptop closed. "Imma stick to dicks anyway so it doesn't matter."

Lexie bangs her hands on the table and adopts a mock-serious tone. "The most important part is that you PROTECT THE CLITORIS!"

The room fills with snickers, and a chuckling Chen stands to make his exit. I do a double take. The back of his white coat is covered in unrolled condoms.

Asher bursts into laughter. Several others follow suit.

Chen turns, narrowed eyes aimed at Asher. "What?"

The tears in Asher's eyes as he laughs shine bright, his face red.

"Oh my gawd." Kai snorts. "Dr. Chen, what did you do to your coat?"

Chen looks down at his coat, then pats his back. A resigned smile tugs at his mouth when he looks at Asher. "I suppose this is your doing, Dr. Foley?"

Asher is soundless in his laughter. Everyone else cracks up. Everyone but me.

Chen takes off his coat and holds it out for all to see, dozens of condoms sutured into it. "I don't know how I didn't notice when I put it on."

Asher splutters, but manages to get some words out. "Me, either."

"You sewed all those in?" I ask.

Eyes gleaming, Asher nods. "What else did you think I was gonna do with all those condoms on my fridge?"

I chuckle, unsure how this douche managed to pull a laugh from my shattered, depressed mood.

Thanks, Asher. You're good for something, after all.

The levity is short-lived. When the amusement dies down and Chen leaves, Asher turns toward Grace. He whispers something *way* too close to her ear, and she smiles at him. I fantasize about stabbing a scalpel into his chest.

Kai leans closer. "She looks fine, but she's messed up, too."

A shot of adrenaline wakes my pulse.

Yeah? If it hurts, why did she do it?

My body disobeys my mind and swivels toward her, gaze landing squarely on those hazel eyes. The connection between us yanks. She turns in my direction.

The chatter around us falls away. Asher's words near her ear go unheeded as her lips part, and she mouths my name.

Fuck this.

I don't care if I'll be punished for jetting early. I swipe up my things and thrust them into my bag, leaving the room without a word. I'm at the middle landing in the back stairway when the door opens and she calls my name.

I face her. The signs of strain finally shine at me—the sharpness of her cheekbones, the circles beneath her eyes.

She holds her hand up. "Wait."

"Why?"

She says nothing. The silence sucks away all the air between us, and this is the first time I see it...

She's cold.

Unfeeling.

Cruel.

I take three steps up while she takes three steps down—still standing on her pedestal.

Why did I put her up there? I would have given her everything.

"Are you—" She swallows. "Are you okay?"

A pinch of wrath stirs into the icy misery inside me. "You're kidding, right?"

"Julian—"

"I have a knife in my throat. I can't fucking breathe. Why are you here? To twist it?"

She presses her lips into a flat line.

"Nothing to say?" I stretch my arms to either side. "Do you like standing up there, watching me drown?"

She takes two steps toward me. "I don't want this."

"Changing your mind, then?"

She looks devastated, tears sparkling, then shakes her head.

"Then go." I hate how hollow my voice rings. "If you're not willing to put a little faith in me—"

"The risk-reward ratio here isn't—"

"I'm not a risk," I snap.

"Can you swear that you'll stay no matter what?" She drops her gaze, eyes shining like she already knows my answer. "Can you promise me forever?"

Forever.

Pictures spread over my mind, memories that don't exist. Grace meeting my mother. Watching her walk toward me in a white dress. Endless days of laughter and arguing, nights of pleasure and passion.

I want it. This future she won't give me. I want it more than anything.

Taking one step up, I stare deep into her eyes. "What if I could? I love you, and I want you forever."

She shakes her head. "You *don't*. Haven't you figured out there's no such thing as forever?"

Ouch. Wow. I lay it on the line, and *that's* her response?

Does she really think that? Does she think if I put a ring on her finger, I wouldn't honor that promise? How could I not have realized before now how little she trusts me?

She's too scared to put any faith in me.

"You're a coward," I say.

Swallowing, she nods. "I know."

I shrug my messenger bag higher on my shoulder. "You'll regret this."

"I know."

"Then why are you doing it?"

She closes the remaining distance between us and stands on the stair above mine, putting us close to eye-level. "Because I just—I can't. And you deserve better."

A cold spike lodges behind my ribs and my blood stirs. Fury strikes like lightning. She's going to try to play the martyr? After ripping my heart out and taking a pickax to it?

"So selfless, aren't you? You think you know everything." My voice is serrated. I hope it shreds through her like paper. "Tearing me apart and convincing yourself it's for me. Does my blood on your hands make you feel good, Grace?"

She sniffles.

I stare her down. She doesn't balk despite the tears. She's ensnared in my fire, and I throw out my next words in a selfish desire to hurt her. "You think I deserve someone better? Fine. Let's see if I can find her."

It's only after I leave that the self-hatred punctures my anger.

I'm not this person. This bitter, angry, heartbroken man. Regret soaks in, spurring the desire to apologize.

My pain doesn't give me the right to hurt her back, does it?

I don't know what's right anymore.

I don't know anything.

"Motherfu—" My heart throws a tantrum when I step through the door and become aware of the second presence in my apartment.

"Hey, BB."

"Goddamn it, Tor. You scared the shit out of me."

She unfolds herself from the couch. "You really should find a better hiding place for your spare key."

"What the hell are you doing here?" I throw my wallet and keys on the table by the door.

She tosses out her devious smile. "It's April. Snowbirds are gone. Season's over, and I had vacation time to spare. Plus, my baby's hurting."

"I'm only eighteen months younger than you, Victoria. You act like you're my mother."

She drops her mouth open in faux outrage. "How dare you. I take personal offense to that. I am *way* better than our mother."

"Why are you here, Vicky?"

She grins and offers a plastic bag from the coffee table. "I come bearing gifts from everyone."

A tender warmth spreads through my chest. "Please tell me there are Norman Love truffles in there."

Her grin widens to rival the Cheshire cat. "Tahitian Caramel."

"God, I love you."

"I know." She juts her cheek out to be kissed.

After I change and settle on the couch next to her, she pats my knee.

"Tell me what happened, BB."

I shrug and grab the box of chocolates she brought, taking out a truffle. "What's to tell? She didn't want me."

Tori's brown eyes follow my movements as I throw the box on the coffee table. "You're still in love with her, Julian?"

"It's not a big deal."

"Julian." The quiet tone of her voice gives me pause.

I turn toward her, and she lifts an arched brow.

Victoria is a feminine version of me. We have the same dark hair and eyes, the same curves in our faces, so reading her expression is like staring in a mirror. Right now, she hurts.

"What?" I ask.

"What can I do?"

I laugh. "Can you make her change her mind?"

"Do you want me to?"

I relish the vision of Victoria putting Grace in her place for a few moments before shaking my head. "I just need time. I'll get over her."

"You sure?"

No. I'm not sure.

Because what if I don't? What if I never find the feeling I had with her ever again?

My bitter laugh is uncontrollable. "It's that, or drown myself in the bathtub, so…"

"Ha. Ha." She purses her lips. "Do you work this weekend?"

I lift my eyebrows. "Miraculously, no. First weekend off in three weeks."

Her evil smile spreads. "I'm taking you out tomorrow night."

This is a mistake.

I'm so drunk.

Fucking Victoria. She's a bad influence. Or maybe she's the best influence. Hard to tell at the moment.

"Julian!"

The world keeps spinning when I whirl toward my name and stumble two steps on the dance floor.

The girl with me giggles and reaches for me. Our hands meet. She winds up against my body. We sway to live country music, her lips against mine.

"Julian, I just won $82." Kai's arm is clamped around Tori's as he approaches.

I blink, then smile because this is the best news since someone invented sex. "That's awesome!"

"I told Dr. Chen!" He holds out his phone to show me the message to Chen.

I'm too blurry to focus on it, but I plummet into uncontrollable laughter. "What did he say?"

"He told me to get my charts done. I may have gotten his privileges suspended for not finishing my discharge summaries." He shrugs. "Whoops."

Tori laughs. "Your friend has a way with the slots."

The girl I've forgotten about latches onto me, her mouth finding the sensitive place beneath my ear. I stare into her face. Right.

Kai convinced me to invite Ariel the Mermaid to our foray past the Oklahoma border, and the magical casino here. Still trying to figure out why I thought that was a good idea.

Maxwell materializes beside them. His wife is drunker than me and attached to his arm, giggling.

"How much did you have to drink, bro?" Maxwell asks.

I try to remember, but the night is already half destroyed by alcohol. "Twelve?"

"Jesus." Maxwell takes my arm, guiding both me and his wife to the benches at the side of the dance floor while the band on the stage takes a quick break.

A scantily clad waitress asks if we need anything.

"Shots!" I yell before Victoria slaps my hand and asks for water.

I glare at her. "I thought this is what you wanted."

She rolls her eyes. "I wanted you loosened up, not dead."

Ariel the Mermaid falls into my lap. "Hey, baby." She sucks hard on my neck. Well, that's...not pleasant—

"Julian." Kai widens his eyes.

"What?"

"Oh, let him have fun." Tori waves her hand.

"You willing to let him get herpes?"

Ariel moves to my mouth, and now we're making out in front of my friends and sister, but I don't care.

For once, there's no pain. Everything is numb and this girl kisses nothing like Grace.

Grace is all slow and shy and sweet. This girl is trying to suffocate me.

A chuckle emerges somewhere to my left and Victoria says, "Don't worry. He's way too drunk to do anything serious."

Little does she know. The last time I fucked Grace, I was so hammered thanks to her love of Unicorn Blood that I barely remember it, and she still came twice.

I stare at the girl in my lap. Blue eyes. Round face. Could I get it up for her right now?

Maybe.

Honestly?

Probably not.

The raucous laughter to my right draws my attention. Kai is doubled over, and Maxwell has his face hidden in his hands. Still in my lap, Ariel glares at me.

Tori lifts an eyebrow at me. "You realize you said all that out loud, right?"

I shrug and roll my eyes. Everyone here is well aware I have no filter when I'm drunk. This is why I never drink like this.

Why is Ariel here again? I slide her to the seat beside me, tired of her bony ass digging into my legs.

"Who is Grace?" she demands.

Kai leans toward her, smile in place. "Dr. Rose."

"What?" Ariel the Mermaid laughs. "You slept with her, too? I heard she'll screw anything with a pulse."

I really don't like this girl. Kai frowns, exchanging a glance with Maxwell.

Tori clears her throat. "I don't think—"

Ariel giggles. "She's a total bitch to the nurses. Are you glad you got rid of her?"

I meet her sea blue eyes. "No. But you're really fuckin' rude, so now I'm kind of wishing I could get rid of you."

The smile drops off her face.

Cat bursts into laughter. "Drunk Julian is my *favorite* Julian."

"Same here, girl!" I raise my hand and she gives me a high five.

"Why don't you take me upstairs?" Ariel whispers in my ear. "I'll remind you why you brought me here."

"I'm sharing a room with my sister. You want me to fuck you in front of her?"

Her cheeks turn a fantastic shade of red.

"Jesus, Julian." Tori slaps my shoulder. "You're worse than I remember."

"Can we *please* get some water?" Maxwell asks the sexy waitress.

"Sure thing, handsome."

The cover band returns onstage, striking up a Carrie Underwood song. Cat and Ariel go wild and head for the dance floor. Maxwell shoves a glass of water in my hand. "Drink it all."

I chug it and wipe my mouth. "Now what?"

Tori slides next to me. "You feel better yet?"

A hollow laugh bursts from me. "How do you come back from dead, Vicky?"

She rolls her eyes. "Don't be dramatic, Julian."

"Stop." I meet her gaze, voice razor-edged. "I know you mean well, bringing me here and taking my phone and trying to distract me, but you've never been where I am. There's no amount of alcohol that can make this better."

She sighs. "Then I don't know what to do for you."

My voice drops. "I'm submerged, Tori, and there's no air anywhere. I'm a grown man. Just let me be."

After a long moment, she nods, eyes shimmering, and kisses my temple. "Do what you have to, BB."

She hands me my phone, which she confiscated at the beginning of the night.

"I'm not going to text her," I say.

"Well, now the choice is yours."

The next morning, my eyes open to a brain-shearing light, and pain explodes through my entire nervous system, but for the first time in weeks, a lightness settles about me. Maybe I *will* survive this.

The feeling persists until I look at my phone to find an unopened text from Grace. Apparently, I *did* text her last night.

> **Me:** I miss you grace

> **Grace:** I miss you too Julian.

APRIL, YEAR 2

By mid-April, I'm accustomed to life without Grace—sort of. Not happy, but surviving. Tori stays until she's convinced I'm on the mend, and I breathe a sigh of relief at her departure.

I love my sister, but for the last seventeen days, my every move has been scrutinized and likely reported to my entire family. I'm not exactly sad to see her go.

Crashing onto my sofa, I can't find the energy to reach for the remote. Instead, I stare at the ceiling. Patterns emerge from the popcorn texture—a mountain range beside a river, a lobster with eight legs, and...a perfectly shaped uterus?

How have I never noticed that before?

My phone buzzes on my chest.

Kai: Did you hear?

Me: Hear what?

Kai: Alesha ELOPED

I stare at my screen. That has to be a typo. Alesha isn't dating. I hit the call button.

"Dude." Kai's voice is jubilant. "This is crazy."

"What the hell are you talking about?"

"Dr. Chen was at their wedding! He showed me the picture. Been dating in secret for *three years*."

I rub my forehead. "Whose wedding? What are you talking about?"

"Alesha married Steven Langston."

For five full seconds, I can only blink. Steven Langston is the director of GME. Steven Langston is a douche.

"She—what?"

"Julian. *Alesha* is the girl who was screwing someone from GME."

Coldness unfurls deep in my gut.

"This whole time!" Kai adds in my silence.

All those rumors. All Grace's problems. Her insecurity. Her pain. The source was *Alesha*?

"Julian?"

"Alesha screwed someone to get into the program, then married him?"

Kai laughs. "No. Apparently they were dating before, and Langston stepped back from resident selection our year to remain unbiased."

A silence follows. Kai clears his throat.

"And yet there were still rumors," I say. "But not about Alesha."

The buoyancy disappears from Kai's voice. "Yeah, true."

We fall into silence again.

My hand covers my eyes. "Alesha knew she was the source of that original story this whole time and never said anything."

"I—" Kai clears his throat. "Yeah, I guess so."

"Why would she let that happen to Grace?" My voice sharpens despite an attempt to remain neutral. She could have set the record straight from the very beginning. She could have stopped it.

"Uh. I don't know," Kai says. "Maybe she was protecting him. Langston. Maybe he would have gotten in trouble if people found out."

I drop my hand, and my gaze strays at once to the uterus on the ceiling. She protected her boyfriend and threw her best friend to the wolves? "This is fucked up."

Kai grunts. "It kind of is."

My throat is thick. "I have to go."

"Yeah." Kai sighs. "Listen, man. I'm sorry."

"You're not the one who should be sorry."

When I hang up, I relive the last two years with new eyes. Alesha had defended Grace from the beginning, had never believed the rumors. I'd thought it was some girl-code thing, but no. She'd known it was all fake and let the rumors spread, anyway. Over and over she watched Grace stumble and fall, stuck in muck that didn't belong to her.

Grace's reputation is in tatters because of Alesha. I lost the love of my life because of her.

Alesha let us crumble for a rumor she could have quashed with the truth.

I open my private message with her.

Me: wtaf

She doesn't answer.

Grace

MARCH, YEAR 2

The right thing is never easy.

We were *so close* to something good and it all went to hell.

Protecting Julian is the right thing, but it's shredded me. I'm cut deep. Bleeding. My world is shattered, and I'm walking barefoot over the jagged remains.

The high of him was so wondrous, it shouldn't surprise me that the crash is an untamed inferno of sorrow and torment.

No escape.

Life without Julian Santini is my own personal perdition.

I really did love him, didn't I? Still do, I guess. I tried so hard not to fall for him, but the pervasive magic in his blood has called to me since the moment I met him. Even now, my attention drifts to him when he's near.

He ignores me, and I can't blame him for it. He's in self-preservation mode.

I'm the person who broke his heart. Why would he spare me a glance?

I need out.

The weekend after our fight in the stairwell, I book a Saturday flight home and spend four hours in the air reliving every moment with him.

Can you promise me forever?

What if I could?

Would he? If I told him I wanted forever, would he give it to me? Could I trust it?

Matt promised forever, too...

But Julian is nothing like Matt!

My stifled tears turn into ugly sobs when I reach my mom's arms. She rocks me on the airport sidewalk until the officer yells at us to move. On the forty-five-minute drive home, I spill everything. She listens without any interruption except to hand me tissues and whisper, "Oh, honey."

"So that's it. I broke up with him."

She nods and glances in the rearview mirror before changing lanes. "I take it neither of you are happy about that decision?"

I shake my head. "But it's the right thing."

"Okay," she says, remaining neutral. "If you're sure."

I narrow my tear-filled eyes at her. "What does that mean?"

"It's just—are you sure you're not using this as an excuse to beg off before he has the chance to hurt you?"

I turn away to stare at the car beside us. "Maybe. I love him, but I don't want to go through that again. I don't want to be hurt again."

"But that's what love is, honey." She glances at me. "Giving someone a weapon to hurt you and trusting they won't use it."

My fingers curl into my sweatpants. Sparkle-silver nails mangle the fabric. "It's the trust part I have a problem with."

Mom nods. "*Do* you trust him?"

A ragged breath expels through my nose. "Yes. No? I don't know. I think I do, but I'm so scared. I've been wrong before. Really wrong."

A short silence passes before Mom fills it. "Did you tell him what happened with Matt?"

"Of course not." My voice goes diamond hard. "That isn't something I ever want to discuss again."

Her eyebrows pinch. "Oh, baby. If you ever want to be in a meaningful relationship, you're going to have to share what happened to you."

"Yeah." My fingers twist hard into the fabric. "Maybe."

At home, Dad has all my favorite movies in his streaming queue and a plate of chocolate chip cookies on the table. The tears return as I fall into his safe arms.

He sighs. "Today, I focus on making my baby feel better. Tomorrow, I figure out how to kick this guy's ass."

I giggle-sob into his chest. "He didn't do anything. It was all my fault."

"Meh. Still feel like I need to kick his ass."

In my childhood bed later that night, stomach full of cookies, I battle a raging case of insomnia. Scrolling through my phone, I force myself not to look at pictures of Julian, and instead open my messages to the one person who may still be awake.

> **Me:** Well

> **Me:** I made it safe to Cali

> **Kai:** yayyyyyy hows the fam

> **Me:** wonderful as always

I wait for him to answer, but nothing comes through.

> **Me:** I can't sleep

Kai sends a picture of himself holding a casino slot ticket worth $82.

Kai: me either!

I zoom in, smiling at Kai's tipsy grin, but my heart clenches as the background grabs my attention. A blurry version of Julian stands with a girl in his arms. Her mouth is fastened to his neck.

He...he has another girl? Already?

Because I'm a masochist, I press and hold the live photo and a three-second loop plays. The girl backs away enough that I recognize her as that malicious nurse from Vincent. Julian smiles at her, and the photo freezes.

A spiky piece of barbed wire slips between my ribs and constricts my heart. It's pain I deserve, but I wince and silently sob into my pillow.

About an hour later, I'm drifting in twilight sleep when my phone buzzes in my hand.

Julian: I miss you grace

My entire body hollows out and I'm a human-shaped shell. Why would he be kissing other girls if he misses me?

Because he's trying to forget.

The tears return, and my thumbs move before I can rethink it.

Grace: I miss you too Julian.

When I arrive home Sunday afternoon, I throw my bag on the floor and fall face-first onto my bed. Being home with Mom and Dad healed some of the ache in my soul, but I'm still only half-living. I groan into my coverlet as I visualize the godforsaken schedule and how I'm slated to work the next twenty-six days in a row.

With a sigh, I push to my elbows and check my email—something I've avoided all weekend. My gaze catches on a message from Dr. Chen.

> Dr. Rose,
> This message is to inform you of the specifics regarding the meeting held by Steven Langston with the department heads this past Friday.
>
> As you are aware, the negative impact of gossip in the workplace is far-reaching, and in an effort to quell the repercussions to both you and others who have been the victims of unfounded rumors, we have decided to assign a task force. This task force will make efforts to subdue the toxic culture which has developed, and create resident education programs to address the elements which are contributing to it. We would welcome you as part of this task force if you are interested, but if not, I do understand.
>
> I hope this information serves to alleviate some of your stress. While we cannot take the current rumors away, we can at least try to improve ourselves moving forward.
>
> Warmly,
> Dr. Chen

I stare at the email until my eyes water, reading it over and over again, uncertain how to feel.

On one hand, a sense of justice envelops me. Here in my hand is absolute proof that the damage done to me is real, that these rumors about me are more than just idle gossip, that they have hurt more than just my feelings.

On the other, it can't heal the scars that are already torn into my soul.

But at least it's something—not something I ever want to be a part of, that's for sure. Why should I spend effort trying to fix what someone else broke? But maybe it will be enough to stem the river of gossip against me. Maybe I won't have to keep paddling upstream.

Someone pounds at my front door and I jolt. "Who is it?"

Instead of answering, the knocker pounds again.

Jeez. It's either an angry neighbor or Kai. No one else is so aggressive. I push myself off the bed and head into the living room. The door swings open wide.

The girl on the other side freezes my blood.

"Hey, Grace." Tori Santini shoots me a fake, placid smile identical to Julian's. "Can we talk?"

She doesn't wait for me to open the door. Instead, she shoves her way in. I remain frozen as she slams the door and flops onto my sectional. With her silky hair pulled into a topknot, her black spike earrings serve as a warning. Her exploratory glare makes my hackles rise.

She looks so much like her brother.

"What are you doing here, Tori?"

"Oh. I came to visit my brother." The fake smile reappears. "He's sleeping, so I thought me and you could catch up. Girl talk."

I cross my arms. "Sleeping off his fun night with some other girl?"

Fire blazes from Tori's dark eyes, far more obvious than it ever is in her brother's. "You don't get to be mad about the way he heals what *you* broke."

"This is none of your business." The barbed wire constricts in my chest again, and tears rise to the surface.

Tori sits up. "You're right. It isn't my business. But *he* is my business."

I collapse onto the opposite side of the sectional. "You here to give me a warning?"

"No."

"Then what?" I reach for the box of tissues. What does it matter if she sees me cry? I probably won't ever see her again after this.

"You might not agree, but Julian is great. He's in pain because of you and that pisses me off. I'd love to wring your neck, but I won't. I just wanted to say my piece."

"Fine." I motion for her to continue. "Say it."

"My brother is a both-feet-first kind of person. I'm certain he told you how he feels, so let me highlight the gravity of that. When that boy loves, it's fierce. I've never heard him talk about a breakup the way he's talked about this one."

My heart speeds, but I keep my expression neutral.

Tori stands, face sharpening into unadulterated fury. "That's how I know this is the real deal for him. If you ever decide you want him, he'll come back. I'm telling you right now that if you do that, you better be real fucking sure he's what you want. If you break him again, I will cut you into pieces so small they won't even know it's human until they test the DNA."

I blink.

Tori smiles the fake smile once more, eyes cold. "We good?"

"Yeah. We're good."

"Bye, Gracey." She slams the door.

Instead of the GYN surgery month I was originally assigned for April, I'm covering most of Raven's L&D shifts. As I step into the resident lounge at TUMC for lunch, a familiar figure standing near the drink station makes me grin. "Hey, Asher."

He looks up, usual smile in place. "Hey, Gracey-poo."

"What are you doing here?"

He grabs a coffee cup and slides it under the automatic machine. "Just finished a hyst with Levine."

I eye the brew that comes from the machine. "You trust that stuff?"

He lifts a shoulder. "Better than nothing."

"I disagree." I pointedly snatch a foam cup and fill it with Mountain Dew.

He chuckles.

After I load a plate with a meager banana and dollop of mashed potatoes—the only part of the complimentary lunch offering that appears edible—I take a seat beside him. We're early so the room is nearly empty.

"How have you been, Asher? I feel like I've barely seen you lately."

He sips his coffee. "You've been a little preoccupied, I think." He smiles when I shoot a curious glance his way. "I've been fine."

"Good." I take a bite of potatoes and grimace. Ugh. That's awful.

Laughing, he leans forward onto the table. "Yeah. I avoid the food here when possible."

"I heard you signed a contract near Houston. Private practice?"

He bobs his head. "Yep."

"Aw." I smile. "I'm so happy for you. I'll miss you, though."

He tilts his head. "Will you?"

I pause in peeling the banana to stare at him. "Of course. Why wouldn't I?"

He studies my face. His brown eyes have a ring of green at the outer rim. How have I never noticed that?

He gives his head a slow shake. "You have no idea, do you?"

Um. Huh? "No idea about what?"

The embittered laugh that follows my question raises the hairs on my neck.

"It's nothing." He sighs and drinks his coffee. "I thought there might have been something between us. Clearly, I was wrong."

My mind stumbles over that piece of information. "Wait. What?"

He waves a dismissive hand. "Just wishful thinking on my part."

The door opens to let in a horde of family medicine residents.

I lean closer to him. "Asher, I thought you were teasing me. I had no idea you were serious."

"Doesn't matter, does it?" He sends me a shrewd stare. "You were into someone else."

No longer hungry, I stare at my uneaten food. "I guess."

"Hey. No hard feelings. I'm off to Houston in a few months, anyway."

I try to smile. He does the same.

"Still friends?" I ask.

"Always, Gracey-kins."

The door opens again, and Dr. Levine wanders in. He nods at Asher and grabs some food before heading our way. "I guess you guys heard the news?"

He settles into his food while Asher and I trade glances. Asher sets his cup on the table. "Heard what?" he asks.

"Alesha married Steve Langston last Sunday," Levine says, chuckling. "Crazy, right?"

My body stills.

Asher laughs. "What? You punking us?"

Levine shakes his head. "Saw the pictures myself."

"That—" I let out an awkward laugh. "That can't be right."

Levine takes a bite of food. "Guess they've been together a while. Since before she was an intern. She's the one who had a relationship with someone in GME."

A flash of heat precedes an entire ocean of ice water spilling over my body. Asher's stare pierces me, but I'm frozen. Not even my chest will move to let in air.

Levine laughs and matches my gaze. "And to think I thought it was you this whole time."

He shrugs. He just...shrugs. Like none of it matters.

"Grace, you okay?" Asher touches my shoulder.

I nod and force my breathing to a normal rate. My shaking hands drop beneath the table, and I stuff them under my legs.

Alesha?

It was Alesha?

Asher faces Levine. "So, Alesha was given a spot because she was in a relationship with him?"

Levine turns from his food. "Oh. No. Langston wasn't involved in resident selection that year. He stepped back. I didn't think anything of it at the time. Now it makes sense, though." He takes a bite of potatoes. "Alesha got in fair and square."

So did I.

No apology is forthcoming. No remorse lines his face. He doesn't care. Or maybe he doesn't know enough to care. What I've gone through and how it affected me—it doesn't matter to him. It affects him in no way. The slut-shaming and side-eyes I received are just a part of the culture. Business as usual. This man and all the ones like him are a part of the insidious underpinnings of medicine. The good old boys' club.

It's this moment that flips a switch in my mind, and I decide to join Chen's task force. This is wrong. What happened to me is just...it's wrong. If I can stop it from happening to even one more person, it will be time well served.

People tell me I put too much stock in the rumors. And sure, maybe I care too much about what other people say. Maybe I should let it all roll off my shoulders. But it's been so hard when I know I'm innocent.

Like Matt, I allowed the rumors to take more from me than they deserved, but Alesha... Alesha had the power to stop it. She could have explained how they started in the first place, but she did nothing. She placed her transgressions on my name and walked away.

Since the fallout with Julian, my heart is like delicate spun glass, shattered. I've been painstakingly gluing the pieces back together, but this has knocked it off the edge. Smashed on the floor, it's unrecognizable. Irreparable.

I thought I was broken before, but this is the true breaking point. This is proof that I continually place my trust in the wrong people.

Alesha is my best friend, and she screwed me.

"Why don't you go home?" Asher says, touching my elbow. "I'll cover the rest of your shift."

My movements are leaden as I turn toward him.

He offers a comforting smile. "Go on, Grace. Take the afternoon. You need it."

I can't say anything, so I squeeze his shoulder in thanks and leave the room.

Four days later, Alesha still hasn't responded to my texts or calls, and I've had time to stew. When she didn't appear in didactics on Thursday, I checked the schedule. She has the week off for vacation—something I'm certain wasn't on the schedule the last time I checked it.

I've never been so pissed. Twenty-two months she's had the key to stopping all these rumors. Why didn't she? To protect herself?

I want to hear the truth from her mouth. Maybe she'll have an excuse that makes sense, one that can set me on the path to forgiveness. Small chance, of course, but this anger is festering deep in my gut. Unhealthy. I need to talk to her.

Except she won't answer her goddamn phone.

My twenty-four at TUMC that weekend is blissfully slow. I spend the majority of my time sleeping, rewatching *The Office* and answering pages.

Normally, a page details a phone number, a patient name and a brief reason for the page. The one I stare at now has me scratching my head. It gives me the phone number and patient name, but then says, *WARNING. SHE'S A LITTLE ANGRY.*

Hmm. Well, this should be interesting...

For the next twenty-five minutes, I serve as a bystander for some woman's rant against an OB who works in a different city. She ends her tirade by asking whether our clinic is taking new patients.

"Yes, ma'am," I say.

"Great. What's your name? You sound like you could probably help me."

A judge in my mind who craves justice blurts out a lie. "Alesha Lipton, ma'am. I'd be happy to take care of you. Be sure to ask for me when you call on Monday."

"Will do. Just don't screw it up like the last doctor."

"I won't, ma'am."

She disconnects, and I shoot a sinister grin at nothing in particular.

A while later, I check out the few patients on the floor to Greg Kelly, hand him the pager and abandon the hospital. The parking lot is half-empty, so Alesha's familiar shape sitting on the bumper of my Camry is visible from a long distance.

My gut twists, and I briefly consider turning around, but she hops off my car and beckons to me.

"Please, Grace!" she shouts.

Shrugging my backpack on tighter, I march in her direction, then stand in front of her and cross my arms. "Congrats, Dr. Langston."

She winces. "I didn't take his name."

"How feminist of you," I say, dripping with disdain.

"Grace, I can explain."

In one fell swoop, my energy drains and I'm utterly exhausted. My shoulders slump under the weight of everything that's happened, and I want to crawl in my back seat and sleep for the rest of time.

"You got married." I head to my car. "What's to explain?"

"Grace—"

I slip into the driver's seat and cut her off with the sharp slam of my door. She ducks into the back seat before I can reverse out of my spot.

My head falls to the headrest. "Fine. Explain."

She meets my eyes through the rearview mirror. "Right before third year of med school, Steve came to talk to our class about the residency programs here. Afterward, I went to ask him questions, and we hit it off. I kept him at a distance at first. He's fifteen years older than me, and it seemed weird, but the more I got to know him, the less that difference mattered."

I shut my eyes. "I'm really glad you found someone, Alesha. I am. I just—"

"Let me apologize. I want you to know where I was coming from, even if you don't agree with my choices."

I roll my eyes.

"By the time I realized I wanted to actually date him, I was well into third year. I knew I wanted to match OB and in order to be close to him, I'd have to match here."

"There are other OB residencies in this city, Alesha."

She clicks her tongue. "This is the best one, and you know it."

I say nothing.

Alesha's voice softens. "So we agreed that he'd step back from The Match our year. I interviewed, and Steve found out I matched here at the same time I did. We celebrated so hard that night."

I scoff.

"I know. I'm sorry. I didn't know that word got out about us until you mentioned that everyone thought it was you, that you'd bought your spot with sex. I mean…it doesn't even make sense, really. The program directors have final say over the rank list. You'd have to have screwed Dr. Chen."

"Ew!" I turn to shoot her a disgusted face.

"I know! But I couldn't come out and say it was me, Grace. Our relationship wasn't exactly allowed, but... I loved him. I loved him so much, and I just couldn't live without him. There's no direct rules against us being together, but there's vague wording in his contract about it. He could have been brought in front of the board of executives. It was his career..."

"It was *my* career." My voice is barbed, and she flinches. "You let everyone think I did those things! One rumor spiraled into *dozens* of slanderous stories."

"I didn't know! I swear, Grace. I didn't know how upset you were by it. In the beginning, I'd always defended you, so I think people stopped talking trash around me. You always blew it off like you didn't care, and I guess—I guess I wanted to believe it didn't bother you. I'm your best friend, I should've—"

"You are *not* my best friend. A friend wouldn't do this to me." I spear a glare through the mirror.

Alesha's shoulders slump. "Okay. That's fair. But I had no idea how much it was all hurting you until you pushed Julian away because of it. You love that boy! You have for almost two years. Why did you do that, Grace? You two belong together."

"It wasn't just about the rumors." I stare blindly out the windshield.

"He would weather any of those rumors with you, Grace. He'd do anything for you. I would have too, if you'd have just talked to me, I could've—"

"What was I supposed to say? Hey, Alesha, did you hear the latest rumor about how I screwed an intern on an OR table? Yeah, pretty funny, huh? It kind of makes my soul want to curl up and die. Maybe you should have used a smidgeon of empathy and put yourself in my shoes. How would you feel if those things were said about you?"

"I know. I—I read it all wrong." She stumbles over the words, tears thick in her tone. "I'm so sorry."

My own empathy strikes. It goes against my nature to witness tears and not provide comfort. I stand strong, but my voice shrinks. "And I don't know why you're lecturing me about telling the truth when you've been keeping this secret for two years. There is no *sorry* for this, Alesha. You broke my heart. You broke my trust. I—I don't know how to move past this."

She leans back so her reflection in the mirror disappears. A shaky breath fills the silence before she continues. "Once Julian told me you broke up with him, I knew I couldn't watch it anymore. Steve was in the middle of dealing with some ridiculous talk that you'd done something with an attending to get you a pass on a rotation. He knew none of it was true, and when I told him it was enough and asked him to fix it, he agreed. He set up those meetings and we agreed to marry so we could go public. It's all—" she lets out a tired sigh "—so stupid, honestly. Anyone who knows you knows you wouldn't do that."

A derisive snort escapes my nose. "Thanks."

"I wanted to protect both you and Steve, so I discussed it with him and we decided to marry. We'd planned to do it, anyway. His contract is very clear that married couples aren't subject to those no-relationship rules. We made the decision two weeks ago and we married last weekend."

A poisonous wrath stirs in my gut. "Congratulations."

Her voice peps up. "No, don't you see? This way, everyone will know it was me, and the rumors about you will fizzle."

"How do you know they'll fizzle, Alesha? Preconceived notions don't vanish overnight."

She climbs into the front passenger seat and faces me. Tear tracks stain her face. "Yeah, there will probably still be a little talk, but I've discussed this with Steve. He's going to speak with all the program directors, set the record straight."

I scoff. "It's like you're blind to reality. The rumors spawn on each other. There's no stopping them. I'm a running joke, and *you* did that to me. This is your fault."

"I'm trying to make it right." Her gaze drops to her lap. "I'll do whatever to fix this. I'll listen if you want to scream at me, or if you want to tell me how it all made you really feel. Whatever you need."

If she'd asked me to confide in her a week ago, I might have done it, but she never asked.

Because she didn't want to know.

I can't help but assume that her failure to ask was entirely selfish in nature. She didn't want the guilt of knowing her actions hurt me.

But maybe I'm judging too harshly. I rub my eyes. Several silent moments pass until the wave of exhaustion rears its head again. "I need to think, Alesha. This is a lot."

"All right." She pats a quick rhythm on her knees, then faces me, eyes dewy. "I—we got back from our honeymoon this morning. I wanted to talk to you as soon as you got off. I do love you, Grace. If I'd known what you were going through—"

"It's fine."

"You gotta talk to me more. Open up, okay?"

No thanks, hypocrite.

She takes my hand, and the giant marquis diamond on her finger becomes apparent.

I lean forward to study it. "This is beautiful."

"You could have one, too."

I spin my head toward her, brow lifted.

"*Please.*" She scoffs playfully and wipes some moisture from her face. "You think that dork wouldn't give you the world if you asked for it?"

Tears spring to my eyes and I shake my head. "He wouldn't. I broke us."

She squeezes my hand. "Broken things can be fixed, Grace. Look at us. I'm going to fix this. I promise."

Strong doubts rise to the surface. I'm not sure what she could do to fix it, or even if fixing it would be enough. I swallow down my tears. "I need time."

Pulling away, she exhales a sharp puff of air. "That's fair. Let me know when you're ready." She opens the door but pauses when I say her name. "Yeah?"

"Thanks for trying to fix it. But... I don't know if it will be enough."

Her mouth twists. "You're my girl. No matter what, remember that."

After she leaves, I stare blindly through the window and relive the conversation. Alesha's naive hope that the rumors will fizzle is foolish, right? It won't all magically stop because she married a higher-up.

But does any of that matter, in the end?

You two belong together.

Does she really believe that? Alesha may have gone about it the wrong way, but when she found her love, she jumped for it. Made sacrifices for it. Does she think I should do the same?

It's something Julian would do for me.

The thought strikes like lightning.

He'd do it for me.

Julian would *absolutely* do that for me. I'm certain of it. Does that mean—*do* I trust him? Did I somehow learn to trust when I wasn't watching? Somewhere on the narrow path between his unfailing constancy and my inability to resist him, did I set down my defenses and hand him my heart for safekeeping?

What have I done that makes you think I won't keep loving you even when it's hard?

Nothing. He did nothing. All he ever did was love me.

Gaze frozen on my steering wheel, I think about Julian. About his raspy voice whispering he loves me in the dark of night. His capable hands teaching me how to use laparoscopic instruments. His patience with my gnawing anxiety. His kiss and his no-smile and his perpetual kindness.

He is nothing like Matt. He is Matt's antithesis.

If I believe that, then why am I still trying to convince myself I can't trust him? It will always be true that I'm a mess of a human, but maybe I can learn to believe him when he says he loves me how I am, flaws and all.

I need to tell him what happened to me.

Because I belong to him, don't I? He's a part of me. I'm a part of him. Even the parts I don't necessarily like. Once he knows, he can make an informed decision. He can accept me, or he can take the out I gave him. He'll have the whole picture.

Matt doesn't fit between us, and the rumors don't have a place there, either. The ice queen? She'll go to her grave before I let her squeeze into the space separating us again.

I love you, and I want you forever.

Oh my god. He said that, and I let him walk away.

What the hell have I done?

Julian

APRIL, YEAR 2

Alesha takes an entire week to respond to me. She'd apparently been on a honeymoon in Cancún.

Lucky her.

The last weekend in April is the only one I don't work this month, and Alesha begs to take me to brunch. Her explanation is expected but fails to relieve the gnawing anger low in my gut.

She messes with the crumbs on her plate, cutting them into smaller and smaller pieces with her butter knife. "If she'd ever told me how much it bugged her the way people talked…"

I scowl. "She internalizes everything. How have you not figured that out by now?"

She shrugs.

"Maybe you should have asked her. You should have used

a little logic. No one likes to be gossiped about, and everyone will put a brave face forward to deal with it. Why would you think Grace is any different?"

"She *said*—"

I lift a hand to stop her. "No. Don't lie to me. This is on you. You didn't know because you didn't want to know. Because it was easier for you that way."

The server comes to clear our plates. When he leaves, Alesha takes a deep breath, eyes bright. "I'm having to face some difficult truths about myself lately."

My hard stare is unwavering. "Please forgive me for the zero fucks I give."

Her face scrunches and her voice breaks. "I hate that I hurt her."

I finish the weird cucumber-lemonade cocktail the server recommended, unsure what to say. I hate that she did that too, but I've probably heaped it on enough.

By the end of the morning, I've all but forgiven her, even though I'll never forget. I'm far too mushy and have no ability to hold grudges. Grace would call me a softie and smile.

God, I miss her. And that's Alesha's fault. Alesha and some mysterious villain from Grace's past.

I should stay mad. I should be furious. I'm too numb to manage it.

Before we part ways in the parking lot, Alesha hugs me. "I'm going to talk to her today."

"Good luck with that."

A melancholy laugh answers me, and she reaches into her giant purse, jingling her keys.

I turn toward my truck but hesitate. "Hey, Alesha."

Her eyes are still wet from tears.

"Apologies are well and good," I say, "but we're not really okay, you and me."

Her eyebrows lift.

"I lost the girl I love because of you. This—this will take me a minute."

Her full lips pinch and she gives a stiff nod. "I understand."

I leave her in the parking lot and head home.

The BrOB-GYN hangout that night is a welcome distraction. Maxwell brings a ridiculously expensive bottle of Glenlivet that impresses even Dr. Levine. Most everyone is out on the deck smoking cigars, but I linger inside after refilling my glass. The empty cookie jar atop the fridge kindles a smile.

When Asher enters with three empty glasses, he pauses. "'Sup?"

"Nothing." I point at the jar. "Just thinking about the condom prank."

He chuckles. "His face was priceless."

We exchange places so he can refill the glasses and I wander into the connected living room. While he works, I study the rainbow art above his sofa.

I'm not a gynecologist. I'm a vagician.

"Where'd you really get this, Asher?"

He glances at the poster, a subtle smirk lifting one edge of his mouth. Hands busy with the bottle, he tilts his head. "A patient gave it to me."

I laugh. "What? Really?"

"Yeah." He leans against the kitchen counter, gaze matching mine. "It's kind of a weird story. At the end of first year, I had this patient who came to me with severe pain with sex."

My eyebrows lift.

"She was in tears, man. Wanted so badly to have a baby, but her pain was… I couldn't even touch her. I did so much research on it. We tried everything. Topical creams. Physical therapy. Vaginal Valium. She saw pain specialists and tried vaginal lasers. She even went as far as seeing a fertility specialist, thinking if she could just be inseminated, it would be easier."

"Jesus." I glance at the poster again.

"Yeah. Her husband was supportive, but it was all just so—sad." He shakes his head. "So, we got a little unethical. She bought a bottle of Botox from some local medical spa and brought it to me. Begged me to try it."

I laugh. "You did it?"

He nods. "I injected it every three months for almost a year. That shit works, man. When she got pregnant, she gave me that." He nods at the poster. "She had her baby, and all the pain sort of resolved. I haven't seen her for a while now."

I stare at the poster again, my view of him entirely reshaped. That poster isn't swagger. It's pride. I'm not certain where the line between the two lies, but it's distinct.

When I turn back to him, his scrutinizing gaze is fastened on me.

He crosses his arms. "What do you think about all this stuff with Alesha?"

A muscle in my jaw twitches. "Honestly? I think keeping it a secret and letting Grace drown under all those rumors was a really shitty thing for her to do."

A humorless laugh bursts from Asher. "Yeah. Do you ever think about how terrible it must be to be a woman? Rumors like that never spread about men."

Surprised, I step a little closer. "I've got four sisters. I think about it all the time. Did you know Alesha thinks now that she's public with Langston, the rumors will just...go away?"

Asher's skeptical face says everything. "I always kind of thought Grace wasn't interested in dating because of those rumors."

"She wasn't," I say.

His head tilts. "I kept trying anyway—until it became obvious it wasn't that she didn't want to *date*. She just didn't want to date *me*." He gives me a pointed stare. "But I guess I should be glad. Dating her looks like it hurts."

I avert my gaze and take a sip of the smooth liquor. "How do you figure?"

Ice clinks against glass as he goes back to work. "Because you got hurt."

My chuckle is bitter and tastes of fine whiskey. "I guess we weren't as secretive as we thought, huh?"

"Nah, man. The second you guys stopped fighting in didactics, we all knew you'd fucked it out of your systems."

"Well." I swallow against a knot in my throat. "It wasn't the dating that hurt. It's the *not* dating that hurts."

"What happened?" His voice has gone thready, like he doesn't want to know, but can't help himself.

I glance at him from the corner of my eye. "When an insecure woman decides she's not good enough for you, there's no convincing her otherwise. Can't force her to be with me. What else could I do?"

He doesn't look at me. His gaze is fixed to the glasses as he grins. "I guess you keep trying til you find the Botox."

The next day, my drooping eyes win against a documentary on recalled medical devices. I'm not sure how long I've been asleep when a soft knock raps on my front door. I blink at the uterus on the ceiling, confused. The stranger raps again, a little louder.

I rub my eyes and take a sip of water. The documentary is going strong, so I snap the TV off before I head to the door. It swings open in silence, and my stomach drops.

Grace stands at the threshold, unsmiling. Her wavy hair hangs limp, T-shirt and leggings rumpled. Hazel eyes meet mine and blink once. "Can I talk to you?"

The mangled organ in my chest lurches out a single throbbing beat. "Why?"

She looks down and pulls her lip between her teeth. "Just— please?"

I stare at the top of her head, at the slump to her shoulders, and the hopeful, self-destructive part of my brain urges me to hear her out. My feet move away from the door, allowing her entry, and her presence invades my space once more. Her scent fans out and clings to all the places it had dissipated.

Ugh. I'll have to extract her all over again.

The door clicks closed, and I lean against it while she perches on my coffee table.

Silence.

She says nothing. I hardly breathe. Looking at her hurts, so I stare at the door to my bedroom and wait.

I squeeze my eyes shut against her sniffle. Her tears are knives in my flesh. I want to comfort her, but I also want to scream. She did this to us.

"I want to tell you a story," she whispers.

My gaze slices to her.

Two tears drip down her face and she wipes them away before meeting my eyes. "I—I'm not sure where to start."

"The beginning is usually a good place."

A harsh laugh falls from her mouth. "The beginning. All right. Let's start at the beginning." She reaches behind her to grab a tissue from its box. "It started in med school. I was all bright and shiny, ready to tackle my dreams." Another watery laugh. "I met him on the first day."

My fingers go numb. *Him?*

"Matt was...wonderful. So charming. Handsome. He had the best smile. It wasn't a week into classes before he'd taken me out, and we were studying together, spending our time together. Falling in love."

A muscle in my cheek won't stop twitching. Why is she telling me this? Is she trying to tell me she's still in love with him? I don't want to hear this.

"It was blissful. My grades soared. I'd never been so happy."

Stop torturing me. "Grace—"

"Just let me finish, Julian. Please?"

My hands clench, but I nod and move to the sofa.

She turns to face me, her skin pale and waxen. "I took the physical part slow. I've always been a little...nervous about that stuff. In high school, people had certain misperceptions. Teenage boys are jackasses, and I have big lips and big boobs and my name is Sapphire Rose. You can imagine how it was. They thought I'd be easy. Wild. Down for a good time, you know? And I was expected to be experienced. To know what men like and want to give it to them. When I lost my virginity, it hurt a little bit, and he just laughed and told me to take it all and shut up. Like it was...porn, or something. Like I was a porn star."

A knot twists hard in my stomach. No. That happened to her? I'm too frozen to reach out. Tension builds in my muscles—potential energy poised to spring.

She shakes her head and stares at her lap. "When I finally gave myself to Matt, it wasn't very good. I was too on edge, so I couldn't climax and he kind of took it as an insult." She sighs. "Things got weird after that. He kept trying different things, but the more he tried, the more pressure I felt, and I just couldn't—"

My throat tightens. I reach for her. She lets me take her hand, her small fingers curling around mine.

She swallows. "He—um—started wanting things I wasn't comfortable with. Sexual things. And I—I was scared to lose him. I thought I loved him. There came this sense of threat, like if I didn't do these things, he'd leave. Like...*let me ram you in the back door, Sapphire, or I'll walk* or *if I'm not so deep in your throat that you're vomiting, then why are we even doing this?*"

I blink. What the *actual* fuck?

"So I did it all," she says. "He didn't ask. Consent was... questionable. But I was afraid if I told him I didn't like the kink, that I didn't want to be tied up and hit and left hurting, he'd take away all the happiness I thought we had." Her breath hitches. "I was so stupid."

A sick cold settles in my chest. "Are you—Grace, are you trying to say I hurt you like this?"

She raises her head, keen gaze meeting mine. "*No.* No, Julian. You are wonderful. You were always wonderful."

The relief is palpable. "Grace—"

"Just let me finish." Her fingers claw onto my hand. "It went on for months. I hated myself, but somehow, I still thought I loved him. I convinced myself I loved him. That I was doing it for love. We were already second-years by that time and the workload was lighter. He started wanting to hang with his friends a lot. He got distant. Then one day, we were in his apartment and had sex, and it was totally normal. I thought that maybe he'd decided to give up on all the weird stuff. I was so happy." She looks away. "But then he said, *I can't do this anymore, Grace. It's like fucking an ice queen.*"

Cold.

This was the man who called her cold.

I'm immobilized and have no idea what to say. My heart turns electric, pumping more fury than blood through my body. It's pain with a slow sharp edge. Hatred with a frigid, calculating vendetta.

I'd hurt him. If I could, I'd hurt him.

"He was still inside me when he said it," she says. "He was *inside me* when he broke up with me."

I pull on her hand.

She scoots closer to me but remains on the table. "It gets worse. I found out he'd actually been seeing other women for a while. He'd spent months sexually coercing me into...hateful things, calling me names, *hurting* me, and he'd been screwing other women on the side, like a total cliché." She blows out a slow breath. "*But*, I thought I loved this man, right? I wanted to keep him. He promised me forever. We'd looked at rings.

I thought I wanted a lifetime with him. So I begged him to stay. I *begged* him, Julian, and when he wouldn't take me back, something broke in my mind."

A cruel artist paints pictures of what she's saying all over my mind and I can imagine exactly what happened to this sweet, delicate girl when some monster tormented her mind and body, then fucking blamed her for it.

Don't ask, Julian. You already know.

And yet—

"What do you mean?"

She sniffles and wipes her tears again. "All that abuse, all those things I'd done for him—things I look back on now and cringe for how it made me feel—I didn't want them to be in vain. When he left, I broke down. I was still functioning, still going to class, but my mind wasn't there. I was...empty."

I want to do more than hurt him. I've never known wrath this cold. He tried to destroy her. *My* Grace.

But this isn't about me, so I try to push that away. I lift her hand to cup it in both of mine, kissing her fingers. "It's not your fault—"

"I did a lot of weird stuff in those months, alienated a lot of people. The few people who knew the truth judged me and not him. They told me I should drop out, that I should be embarrassed for not knowing better. It all destroyed me, and I lost my ability to trust. Not just men, but myself. I never wanted anyone to have that kind of power over me again. I never wanted that vulnerability. It was better to be alone than risk being treated that way ever again."

Understanding dawns and everything clicks. "Gracey—"

"Then I got here and I thought I could start fresh. Put it all behind me, you know? But—"

"But the rumor."

Fucking Alesha.

She sighs. "Yeah. It opened the door to all the speculation

about me. People gave me weird looks, treated me differently. It brought it all back. Matt broke me to pieces, and I'm not sure I was even in love with him. It was nothing compared to how I feel about you, but I couldn't let myself trust that I wouldn't be completely wrong about someone again."

I take her face in my hands. "I would never do that."

Tear-filled hazel eyes sparkle as she studies my face. "The last man who promised me things left me even after I debased myself for him. I was so scared that you—" She shakes her head. "I should've trusted you. You—you were always there, from the very beginning. You ran into the street, handed me a cocktail napkin to dry my tears even though you didn't know me. You took me at my word that it wasn't true, then defended me, and remained loyal even when you didn't like me. You took time to help me with surgery when my own attendings wouldn't bother with me. You never pressured. Nothing was ever hard with you. It was easy, and I fell in love. God, I've been in love with you forever, Julian. Way before you could have known it. Way before I knew it."

I pull her into a hug.

She relaxes against me like she always has, her arms around my shoulders. "It scared me. I made so many mistakes with Matt, and I was scared I was making them again, that I'd wind up hurt *again*. I was a coward, and that wasn't fair to you. Because you aren't him. You'll never be him. He was poison and you are paradise."

A tingle wakes in the part of my chest I thought had died, but I still don't know what to say. She isn't telling me she wants me back. She's explaining why she left.

She pulls away to grab another tissue. Liquid eyes lift toward mine. "A baby died the other day."

My heart catches. "What?"

"Yeah. The mom was in a car wreck. She was bleeding. We did what we could, but the baby died." Tears pour down her face and she squeezes her eyes shut. "The mom is in the ICU now, but I—it was so awful. I wanted—I *missed* you. I wanted to fall in your arms, and I couldn't because I pushed you away. I hurt us both because I'm a fucking coward."

I feign a gasp. "She said the f-word."

Her teary laugh is a warm breeze across my skin.

I brush away another tear as it falls. "Grace, I'm so sorry about…all that. If I'd known—"

"You did everything right." She grips my shoulders. "I'm the one who did it all wrong. I wanted you to know all of it. The full truth."

A lump forms in my throat. "Yeah. Thanks—um—for trusting me with that. That can't have been easy to relive."

She smiles through her tears. "I love you."

My head tilts. "I—"

She presses her finger to my mouth. "No, don't say anything. I love you and I'm sorry I couldn't trust you. I still have trust issues, Julian. I still struggle with severe anxiety and I worry about what other people think about me. I'm so far from perfect, but I think—I think we belong together. I want you to think about it and after you've processed everything, if you think you might still want me, even though I am, like, *seriously* flawed, Julian, I'd really like to make this work."

My voice drops to a whisper. "Grace—"

"I can promise you forever." She presses a kiss to my cheek. "Forever is what I want. If that's what you want too, you know how to find me."

Extracting her warmth from my grip, she stands. I say her name as she rushes to the door.

She glances back before the door shuts. "Just take some time to think about it."

Five full seconds pass. Eight erratic heartbeats.

What the fuck is there to think about? The woman of my dreams just sat before me and promised me everything I've ever thought to want. Before Grace, I didn't know what desire was—not only physical, but emotional, too. I thought I did, but I was just a child playing pretend, seeing a single star and thinking it was the galaxy.

Wanting her is part of every breath, buried deep in the most primitive areas of my brainstem, impossible to live without. Deprivation is lethal.

Seriously flawed? The only thing about her that's seriously flawed is her belief she's not good enough.

I stand and run to the door. She's already halfway down the stairs when I nearly fall over the railing. "Grace!"

Sunlight strikes her long hair as she turns toward me at the landing. It flashes over the brown, highlighting her, a golden lodestone drawing me closer.

She frowns. "That's not thinking about it."

I make my way toward her. "I don't need to think about it."

"Yes, you do."

At the top of the stairs, I pause. "Do you need me to pretend like there's a choice?"

"Julian—"

"There's no choice here." I descend the stairs slowly. "I could fake like I really need to think about this. I could make you plead for me to come back. But what's the point? I'm all in. I'm so deep I can't see you treading the surface. If you say you're ready to dive under, then come get me. I'm swimming blind in the darkness. Come light the way."

I reach the landing.

She stands with her arms crossed, bottom lip between her teeth. "You're sure?"

I nearly laugh. "Are *you* sure?"

Her arms drop to her sides, and she nods.

Thank god.

Her body against mine is familiar, but it's also like a fantasy come to life—something I thought I'd never have again. My fingers sink into her soft hair, and one arm wraps around her back, anchoring her to me.

The taste of her relieves a pressure I didn't know had built inside me. The air around us crackles. Or maybe I'm delirious. The kiss is probably too hard, but I can't ease up. Everywhere we touch sizzles and she matches each move I make, giving as good as she gets.

"God, I missed you," she whispers when I give up on kissing and crush her in my arms.

If I had more shame, I'd try to quell my satisfied smile. As it is, I'm practically laughing.

No. I *am* laughing.

She turns her face toward me in the tiny amount of space I've allowed her. "Are you—Julian, are you laughing?"

"I feel like I won the lottery."

She giggles. "Aw, that's sweet."

"Mmm-hmm. And now I want you." I pick her up and steer toward my apartment. "In bed. For a long time."

She submits to my manhandling, glancing at my face. Hers goes bright red. "How long?"

"Forever."

A wicked grin lights up her face.

Fuck, she's hot.

Blood drains from important areas to shoot downward and I'm suddenly dizzy. "Yeah, you're not leaving my bedroom today."

"That's fair." She nips my jaw. "Let me show you how much I love you."

Grace

DECEMBER, YEAR 4

Dr. Chen's Holiday Extravaganza as a fourth-year resident will be a true party. We have nowhere to be. No pagers. The lower levels are on call. None of us work tomorrow.

Needless to say, I've got my red dress on tonight.

When I step out of our bedroom, Julian stands from the couch and groans. "The red dress? You're killin' me, Rose."

I smile. "You don't think I look pretty, Julian?"

His dark eyes flash, and he sweeps a predatory look down my body. "You know where I like that dress best, Grace."

I grab my coat from the closet. "On the floor by our bed?"

"Mmm-hmm." He grabs my waist from behind before I can don the coat, then kisses my neck. "Interested?"

"Nope. We're late."

He releases me with a sigh. "And *that* is why you're killing me."

I turn and tap the tip of his nose with one finger. "I think you'll survive."

While he flips the lights, I spritz one more spray of glitter into my hair, and we step outside. The small house we rent isn't far from Chen's place, and the drive barely gives us enough time to argue over the playlist, but Julian ultimately relents to my demands.

The party jitters have grabbed hold, and I leap out of the truck as soon as he parks, hurrying toward the house. Four years hasn't done much to quell the anxiety that tightens my chest before each social gathering. It's not like these people bite.

Much.

But at least the rumors about me finally died down. The gossip task force Chen created—or Rumor Wranglers as we like to call ourselves—initiated educational exercises for the new resident orientation activities each year. It's helped to set clear expectations that gossip isn't acceptable. It encourages open communication between residents and attendings. It's not perfect, and gossip still exists, but I like to believe we've had a positive impact on the culture of this hospital. I will leave this place better than when I found it.

Turns out, I didn't need Alesha, Julian or even Steven Langston to save me. I just needed to save myself—by becoming the leader of a well-structured and aggressively researched task force, one that warms my overly organized and color-coded heart.

I made those rumors my bitch.

As I reach for Chen's front door, Julian grips my wrist and spins me into his arms. His lips find mine and he kisses me breathless.

"What was that?" I ask when he releases me.

Tone innocent, Julian lifts a shoulder. "A kiss." He reaches for the door.

I snort. Boy is up to something...

"They're here!" Alesha shouts when we enter the packed house. She bulldozes her way through the crowd to hug me.

Her husband isn't far behind. He shakes Julian's hand before kissing my cheek. "You look lovely as always, Dr. Rose."

The guy is nice, I'll give him that, but we aren't close.

Alesha grabs my arm before I can respond. "Drinks!"

Behind me, Julian falls into conversation with Steve. They remain by the door. Alesha drags me to the crowded kitchen, where Kai holds a glass of red wine for me.

I take a sip. "Where's Raven?"

Someone taps my shoulder.

I turn and smile. "Raven!"

She envelops me in a hug. "Last holiday party all together."

Squeezing her tighter, I laugh. "We're almost done!"

We release each other. She hugs Kai, then Alesha. "I'm gonna miss you guys so much."

While Alesha plans to become faculty at TUMC to stay close to Steve, Raven and Kai have chosen jobs farther away—Kai in Colorado and Raven in upstate New York.

Julian and I... Well, we haven't quite decided our futures.

"Should we get a picture of the grads?" Dr. Chen enters our group and holds up his iPhone.

"Yes!" Alesha goes to her tiptoes. "Juju!"

She leads us to a quieter area of the house. Julian joins us and the five of us stand shoulder to shoulder so Steve and Dr. Chen can snap a few photos.

Afterward, Julian kisses my cheek. "Have some fun, Sapphire."

"Don't I always?"

He winks before slipping away to join the annual poker game with Chen and Maxwell.

"Has he decided what he wants?" Alesha asks once he's out of earshot.

Her hair is laced with red and green tonight and she wears a flowy black dress. The two of us never quite recovered from the fallout—an element of trust is irreparably broken—but she's proven her loyalty time and again.

We're friends.

Not best friends.

But friends.

I shake my head. "The contracts are sitting on our kitchen table. He won't tell me which one he wants to sign."

She tips her glass toward me. "California or Florida. Quite the decision."

Kai sticks his head between us. "Don't forget about that private practice in Austin that wants them."

Chuckling, I sip my wine. Julian and I decided to search for jobs together. We have offers near my family and his, but we also interviewed between them just in case. He says he wants to go where I'll be happy. I say I want to go wherever he chooses.

Two months and we've reached no decision. With anyone else, I'd be worried about cold feet, but the man is as doting and romantic as ever. He loves me. I feel it deep in my bones.

"We'll figure it out eventually," I say.

Raven pats my shoulder. "Of course you will. Take your time. It's an important decision."

We meander back toward the crowded kitchen. The younger residents are clustered into groups, chatting and laughing. Interspersed throughout the crowd are others—Levine rosy-cheeked near the sink, Dr. K laughing with his wife, Hoffman complaining about the food, Narayan unsmiling in the corner.

Joy overtakes me, an illogical fondness for everyone in the room, even the ones I don't like.

"You'll miss it, won't you?" Alesha asks.

I nod. "Bittersweet memories."

She hugs me tight. "Been a crazy four years, but it wouldn't have been the same without you."

You either, unfortunately.

Kai leaps on my back so I'm sandwiched between them. "My girls!"

We laugh and reluctantly separate. I head toward a group of second-years to chat. When Julian joins my side in the dining room an hour later, he wears a satisfied smile.

I kiss his cheek. "Did you win?"

"Nope." He pulls me closer and lifts my chin.

"Then what's that smile about?"

His grin grows crooked. "Did you know you're sparkling again?"

I scowl. He's always pestering me about the glitter. "I like sparkles, Julian."

He pecks a quick kiss on my mouth. "I know."

Two second-year women beside us squeal. "Aww!"

Still wrapped in each other's arms, we turn toward them.

"You guys are straight up relationship goals," one says—the woman who called pregnancy the most common STD in her interview.

I let out an awkward laugh.

The other nods. "Please say I can come to your wedding."

Julian snorts. "Sure. Come on." He looks at me. "Did you set a date yet?"

"Um." I wiggle my bare left hand in his face, eyes wide.

"Oh right. Poor Gracey."

I laugh. "Why must you abuse me so?"

His head dips closer and he whispers, "Let's go home, and I'll make it up to you."

A thrill flutters through my stomach as his lips brush my ear. His hand traces my waist before he backs away. I'm distracted while we make our goodbyes, my gaze straying back to Julian again and again. Carefree, he laughs with Kai and shakes Maxwell's hand.

Back in the truck, Julian capitulates to my music demands

again, and a growing intuition wakes in my mind. "What's going on?"

Streetlights flash over his face. "What do you mean?"

I narrow my eyes. "Something's up."

Chuckling, he shakes his head. "Nothing's up."

My Christmas red nails drum on the center console, and I stare at his profile. A suspicious creature lurking inside pokes her head out and squints at him.

What are you up to, Santini?

He takes my hand in his and we ride the rest of the way in silence.

At home, the truck rolls to a stop on our deserted neighborhood street. I slip out and head toward the house while he locks up. My phone buzzes in my bra on my way to the door. I pull it out and chuckle at the classic text from Julian: **Found this. Made me think of you.**

I anticipate an unflattering photo he captured at the party, but Face ID unlocks my phone, and the attached picture pops up. In Julian's wildly sexy hand sits a black velvet box filled with a rose gold princess cut engagement ring.

My heart thumps as my steps slow and I stare, unblinking, at that picture. He took it outdoors during the day, so sunlight strikes the diamond and casts rainbows through the stone.

Skin prickling, I spin in place, expecting to face him, but he's not standing behind me.

He's down on one knee.

Julian Santini gazes up at me, one hand supporting his opposite elbow so his fingers rest over his cheek. A diamond ring is looped around his pinky. The no-smile is firmly in place.

"So." He taps a finger against his cheekbone. "I was at the jewelry store the other day for no particular reason. I passed by a glass case full of sparkly objects, and I thought to myself, hey, I know a girl who really likes sparkly things."

Nerves alight, a tiny laugh escapes me. "Julian—"

He clears his throat meaningfully, the no smile mutating into a real smile. "I'm telling a story, Grace. It's rude to interrupt."

"All right. Fine. Continue." I clasp my hands before me, barely resisting the urge to swipe that ring off his finger and put it on mine. My blood flitters through my veins, tingles spreading.

He's proposing.

This wonderful man wants to marry me.

"Okay. Like I was saying, this girl really likes sparkly objects, and I really like this girl, so I was hoping that if I bought her one that was really, really sparkly, she might want to wear it for me."

I grin. "Sound logic, Dr. Santini."

His eyes flash. "Oh, but there's more to it."

"I thought there might be." I step closer to him.

"See, if she chooses to wear the sparkly thing, then she has to promise she won't take it off." He slips the diamond off his pinky and holds it between his thumb and forefinger, lifting it toward me.

My smile is uncontainable. "Ever? What if she's doing dishes, or gains weight, or is performing surgery?"

He shakes his head, laughing. "*Metaphorically*. See, this is me promising forever. Wearing it is her promise to be mine."

Close enough to touch him, I draw one finger down the sharp line of his jaw. "That seems like a fair trade."

"I love you, Grace."

"I love you too, Julian."

He looks at the diamond in his hand. "Before you, everything was just...quiet. Then you came along and suddenly there was music. Like...a love song. The kind you want to listen to over and over. It's stuck on repeat in my head and synced to your heartbeat."

My breath catches. God, could he be any sweeter?

His dark gaze lifts, starlight sparkling in his eyes. "It's become the rhythm of my life. I'd be completely lost without you, so I'd really like it if you wanted to wear this, Grace."

My voice drops to a whisper as I say the stupidest thing on earth. "Okay."

Okay?

Okay?!

He says you're the rhythm of his life and you say okay?

How dare you?

He takes my hand and hovers the ring over the correct finger. "Marry me?"

I nod. "Of course. Yes. *Always* yes."

That's better.

The ring slides on my finger like it belongs there, and he stands. His lips catch mine as he pulls me flush against his body, and my back arches. Arms wrapped about me, Julian squeezes tight. My hands sink into his soft hair.

His lips trail kisses over my cheek until he reaches my ear. "Can I take off the dress now?"

"Yes, please."

We stumble toward the locked front door, still kissing, and my back slams into the wood. Instead of reaching for the key, his hand finds my bare leg and sneaks beneath my dress, fingers fanning over the edge of the lace beneath. My entire body thrums at his touch. His mouth drops to my neck.

My eyes snap open. I'm female, newly engaged and adore all things sparkly. I *must* seize the opportunity to lift my left hand and study the ring.

Squee!

Perfection.

How does this man know me so well?

"Unlock the door, Grace," he murmurs against my neck. "Unless you want to give the neighbors a show."

"I have one request first."

A questioning rumble escapes his throat His finger hooks around the thin fabric.

"Can you please decide where we're going to live next year? Your sister won't stop texting me."

His fingers pause beneath my dress. "I really don't want to talk about my sister right now."

My hands slide around his torso. "You're driving your mom crazy, Julian."

"Ugh." He backs away to stare down into my face. "Don't— why are you mentioning my mom *now*?"

I giggle. "Pick a place."

"I don't care where we go, Grace. I just want to be with you."

It's like he lit a candle inside my chest, slowly melting the organ into a puddle of heart-eye emojis. "Really?"

"*Yes*. I don't know how many times I have to tell you that. *You* are home. You're all I need. Wherever you are, that's where I want to be."

If someone asked me right this moment, what is happiness? I could answer with an absolute truth: happiness is the man I adore telling me I'm all he needs. How does he not realize I'm getting the better end of this deal?

My lips touch his. "I love you so much." I pull the house key from my bra and unlock the door. My hand grips his, and I drag him inside, heading straight for our bedroom. Halfway, I turn and grasp his belt loops, walking backward. "I'd do any-thing for you. Did you know that? How's it feel to have that kind of power over me?"

His head tilts, gaze predatory. "Feels pretty good, if I'm being honest."

Electricity shoots through my whole body and the horny hag in my mind wakes, reminding me I'm empty and he always feels *so good*. I pause in the doorway to our bedroom. "What will you do with that power?"

He pulls his bottom lip between his teeth, a quirk at the

edge of his mouth promising indecent and wonderful things. "I have a few ideas." His knuckles trail down my cheek. "You want to see?"

★ ★ ★ ★ ★